T0005496

PRAISE FOR JO RICCIONI

"An outstanding fantasy debut, evocative and thought-provoking. Jo Riccioni combines a poet's touch with the skill of a true storyteller, making *The Branded* a compelling read."
— *Juliet Marillier, author of the* Sevenwaters *and* Warrior Bards *series.*

"*The Branded* is a timely and passionate adventure, a story for today's women, for those who refuse to back down. With a vivid setting, and a tough and sassy female lead, Riccioni has tapped into the very pulse of the female empowerment movement."
— *Bronwyn Eley, author of* The Relic Trilogy

"A rich and thought-provoking tale. Riccioni explores a world of distorted matriarchal structure, where fertility is a commodity. I was biting my nails the entire time. A beautifully crafted high fantasy world with a heroine that speaks to my heart and sometimes breaks it."
— *Stacey McEwan, bestselling author of* Ledge

Jo Riccioni

THE BRANDED

ANGRY
ROBOT

ANGRY ROBOT
An imprint of Watkins Media Ltd

Unit 11, Shepperton House
89 Shepperton Road
London N1 3DF
UK

angryrobotbooks.com
twitter.com/angryrobotbooks
It's all about the Brand

An Angry Robot paperback original, 2024

Copyright © Jo Riccioni 2024

Cover by Pantera Press
Set in Meridien

All rights reserved. Jo Riccioni asserts the moral right to be identified as the author of this work. A catalogue record for this book is available from the British Library.

This novel is entirely a work of fiction. Names, characters, places, and incidents are the products of the author's imagination or are used fictitiously. Any resemblance to actual events, locales, organizations or persons, living or dead, is entirely coincidental.

Sales of this book without a front cover may be unauthorized. If this book is coverless, it may have been reported to the publisher as "unsold and destroyed" and neither the author nor the publisher may have received payment for it.

Angry Robot and the Angry Robot icon are registered trademarks of Watkins Media Ltd.

ISBN 978 1 91599 855 2
Ebook ISBN 978 1 91599 856 9

Printed and bound in the United Kingdom by CPI Books.

9 8 7 6 5 4 3 2 1

MIX
Paper | Supporting
responsible forestry
FSC
www.fsc.org
FSC® C171272

For my sisters, Suzanne and Sylvana.

PART ONE:
THE ISFALK
SETTLEMENT

The Call of Fornwood

The snap of a twig sounds as clean and close as a popped knuckle. At first, I think it might be Brim or one of the other Warder guards sent to find me, but then I spot it in the half-light – a snowjack, raised on its haunches at the bole of a spruce. The hare digs in the snow. He's lean from the winter, but then so are most of the villagers in Isfalk Settlement. I line him up and it's like I can feel the race of his pulse in my own veins, smell the earthy lure of roots in my nostrils, the clutch of his hunger wringing my belly. I exhale slowly, steadying the beat of his blood in my head. My bow hums, fletches quivering.

Next time I blink, the snowjack is pinned through its neck to the frosted tree.

The rusty taste that fills my mouth is familiar. Pressing a cuff to my nose, I retrieve my arrow, then squat and hang my head between my knees, letting the blood fall. The bleeds often come after a kill. Maybe it's the Fornwood exacting its price – a little of my blood for the hare's. It seems only fair. The adrenalin thud in my skull slowly eases as the flow ebbs. I don't notice the squeak of snow under boots until the steps are almost upon me. I've nocked an arrow before I see them – two scrawny kids, a boy and a girl, their eyes wide in sunken sockets, as startled as I am. We size each other up, fearful, wary. They're Brands, that's obvious – the sign of the Brume

9

virus is marked clear across their faces. The midnight blue flecks snake up the girl's neck and along her jaw like spattered ink; the boy's are more severe, joined together in a slap across his cheek and around one eye. Other than their brandings, the pair are grey as tundra mists, mangy furs hanging off their thin frames. Slum kids from the Settlement, and starving by the look of them. They'd have to be, to risk venturing so deep into the forest, far from the protection of Isfalk's Warder patrols, especially before true day. I lower my bow.

"Don't come any closer," the girl warns.

"It's alright. I'm clean. You won't catch anything from me."

"Why's your nose bleeding then?"

I swipe at a nostril. "I'm not sick," I say, but she's unconvinced, pulling the boy back by the arm. He's smaller than her, a little brother perhaps, more susceptible to diseases. Our Brands have a good chance of surviving common colds and cradle coughs but, despite the Settlement's remoteness, they're fearful of the poxes and fevers outsiders might bring from the rest of the blighted Continent.

"Relax," I tell the girl. "I'm no outlander. I'm from the Settlement too." It's not a lie, but it's not the whole truth either. She glances in the direction of Isfalk and then to the hare at my feet. I can see her weighing up her options, wanting to get her brother to safety, but knowing that fortifications and Warder patrols are pointless if she can't feed them both. Perhaps she's not the kid I took her for after all. She might be closer to my age, but it's hard to tell with Brands, especially those from the slums. Constant illnesses as children and the lack of decent food makes them small, sickly adults.

"You're trapping deep in the Fornwood." I look at the empty snare in her hand. "Slim pickings in The Fold?"

The girl relaxes a little, loosening her grip on the boy's arm. Only another Isfalki would call the scrubby forest and heath around the Settlement *The Fold* or know it's been over-hunted these past three winters. "You're from the village?" she asks.

I nod, pulling my hood closer as I bend over the hare. It'll be easier if they think I'm another Brand. But the boy tugs away from his sister's grasp and I can already feel him studying me. He cants his head to take in my height, my movements, the flush of my cheeks as I busy myself dressing the snowjack.

"You're big for a villager," he says with childish frankness. And he's partly right: I would be tall, healthy-looking, if I lived in the outer settlement, but inside the citadel, among the privileged and well-fed, I'm on the small side for a seventeen year-old. His gaze travels over my face and neck, my hands – the places where Brands carry their markings, and I know what's coming next.

"If you're from the village, where are your brandings?" he asks. When I don't answer, he looks at his sister, then at me again. His eyes widen and a slow grin begins to light his face. "You don't have any, do you?" He's quick, canny, despite his hunger. "You're from the citadel." His voice is wheezy but he can't disguise his excitement at being this close to one of the Settlement's precious immune – as near to nobility as he's likely to get. "You're a Pure, aren't you?"

His sister isn't so easily convinced. She cranes to see more of my face and neck inside my hood, as if she wants proof of my unblemished skin underneath, evidence of my untainted blood, resistant to disease. "If she's a Pure, where are her Warder guards?" she says, scanning the trees. She might be from the slums, but she knows citadel rules as well as any Isfalki: Pure women are too precious to be allowed outside the Settlement without the protection of bodyguards. Her attention falls to the bow in my hands. "What's she playing at?"

"Hey," I snap, holding up the snowjack. "I wasn't playing." The edge of authority in my voice makes the girl flinch. She lowers her gaze as if she's suddenly found herself in front of the Isfalk Council itself. I clean my knife with snow and try to ignore the stab of guilt in my stomach. She has a point. In a way, I am playing: I don't need to hunt. There are servants in the citadel tasked solely with preparing my meals, fetching and carrying for me. Yet here I am, alone in the Fornwood, gutting a hare. Old habits are hard to kick, I guess.

"I'm sorry, Mor," the girl offers with gruff respect. The title almost makes me wince. None of its meanings has ever sat easily with me: Pure blood, Holy Mother's chosen, hope of the Settlement. She might see my status as the ultimate privilege, but to me it feels more like her snare caught around my neck.

I catch the boy peering at me again, trying to make sense of how someone so entitled could be wandering the wilderness in grubby hunting suedes, dirt and blood under her fingernails.

"I know who she is," he whispers to his sister, his small chest swelling with pride, as if he's solved a riddle. "She's one of the Flamehairs – them wild ones the citadel took in." Maybe he's spotted Osha and me behind the altar during Morday Mass or else watching the Warder Trials from the Pure stands. It isn't hard to notice a pair of redheads in a sea of white-haired Isfalki. When I don't deny it, the boy can't tame his grin. "Nara Fornwood." He says my name with naive delight. "They tell stories about you in the taverns."

"Really?" I'm more interested in finishing my work on the hare than hearing him repeat ale-fuelled fancies about my origins. My sister and I can be cast as orphaned princesses or Fornwood witches, depending on the mood of the teller, or so our maid, Frida, tells us. Isolated as they are from the rest of the Continent, the Isfalki love to gossip about the few outlanders they let enter their walls, particularly when those outsiders happen to be Pures.

The boy is about to continue, but a wracking cough robs his words and leaves him gasping for breath. His sister rubs between his shoulders, trying to calm him.

"You should get him out of the cold," I tell her, but I'm already thinking he'll be lucky to see next spring. "Here." I toss the snowjack across the space between us. I would have left it in The Fold for some villager to find in their traps anyway. "Take it."

But the girl doesn't pick up the game. She only stares at me, her face pale and brittle as the hoary trees, and I wonder who will break focus first. It should be her – my position, my rank– demands it, but it isn't. My gaze falters to the branding across her neck and jaw, spattered like inky droplets I might wipe away with my cuff. Except I can't. Her lot was cast at her birth, the message of her weak blood written on her skin. She swallows, then bends quickly to snatch up the hare before hurrying her brother through the snow. There's no backwards glance, no smile of thanks, and the small satisfaction I usually feel at giving away my kill rings suddenly hollow.

The Moon Pools

From the bluff of Heitval Ridge, I squint out across the treetops of the Fornwood to the Settlement. From this height, the ancient keep of the citadel squats grizzled and scarred, like an old guard dog chained before the great threshold of the tundra. I can make out Warders on the inner battlements extinguishing their torches one by one and nearer, along the outer fortifications of the village, the lazy change of mounted guards tells me it's been a quiet night in The Fold – no sightings of Wastelander convoys or raiding parties, no random Brands seeking refuge from the diseased south.

The icebound River Ungar arcs around the Isfalk colony like a question mark, the furthest most Isfalki are willing to venture from the Settlement's protection. To the north, the whistling extremities of the permafrost are hardly inviting; the barren Edfjäll lava fields in the east even less so; and to the west, after the Fornwood, is nothing but ocean, frozen for eight moons of the year. Or so I'm told.

It's the south and its human menace that the Isfalki fear the most: pockets of Solitaries scattered through miles of forest, random gangs of Wastelanders scavenging the long-abandoned settlements of the vast plains, and Reis nomads said to live far beyond the Storm Sands at the furthest reaches of the Continent. To the Isfalki, all southerners represent disease, lawlessness and barbarism – a threat to the delicate balance of Settlement order.

I watch the colony wake for the day: thin lines of smoke struggling skyward, the ever-hopeful fires of survivors built in the ancient hearths of what my teachers tell me was once a thriving outpost of the Continent's timber and fur trade. Once, centuries ago. Before the Great Malady.

Somewhere in the hovels of the Branded slums, under one of those columns of smoke, I imagine the girl from the Fornwood waiting impatiently for the hare to cook, her brother's face ashen in the firelight, save for the angry slap of the Brume. In the citadel, high above them, my sister Osha will have woken to a steaming breakfast tray, our dormitory maid, Frida, helping her to dress for morning prayers. My own stomach grinds with guilt or hunger, but before I can tell which, a dull clanging breaks my thoughts. The bell of the Mor school calling its Pure girls to chapel. Poxes! There's no way I'll make it back in time now. Arriving halfway through matins will only make Father Uluf realise I've been missing. I may as well stay out until the tutorial bell. It won't be the first time I've dodged morning prayers, or meridiems. Or vespers, for that matter. Osha will cover for me. She always does.

Turning away from the Settlement, I cross the ridge, clambering down the boulders and basins of the frozen waterfall on the other side. Further into the ravine, between the trees, steam billows and the tinge of sulphur grows strong. The terraced troughs of the Moon Pools appear and disappear below, pale blue as birds' eggs clustered in the snow. Mor come to this place to bathe after our monthly bleeding. The thermal waters are the strict reserve of Pure women because Isfalki believe the sulphur increases fertility. But visits for ritual cleansing always involve a full Warder protection unit. Now the pools are deserted and peaceful, and I'm imagining the luxury of bathing alone – the tingle of my numb hands and feet in the hot water – when the sound of movements nearby makes me stop. I pick up the faint clap of leather, the ring of metal among the snow-muted trees, and when I hold my breath I can sense the labour of someone else's. I start to run, drifts breaching the cuffs of my boots as I scramble, almost throwing myself down the final descent to the springs. Quickly, I shrug out of my hunting coat and drop it with my bow and quiver on the rocks between two pools.

When he bursts through the clearing, I'm ready and waiting, crouched in the frosted scrub. He scans the mists for a second, seeing my suedes and looking for me in the waters. That's when I strike, launching at him from behind, kicking out his knee and wrapping an arm around his throat. He stumbles, tries to reach for the scruff of my neck to haul me over his shoulder, but it's his signature move and I'm expecting it. I grab his wrist, hook a foot across his shin and shove. He goes down, clean as a felled tree.

"Holy Mother!" Brim pants. "What was that for?"

"For sneaking up on me." I offer him a hand but he ignores it, brushing off his leathers and spitting snow from his mouth. If he's impressed, he's not going to let me know.

"I was good, huh? Pre-emptive, prepared, focused." I count off the combat lessons he's taught me but he only exhales, long and hard. "What, you won't even praise your own pupil?" I squat beside him. "It's not my fault I can read your moves like a book."

Brim is quiet as he gets to his feet, eyeing my bow on the rocks. There's no point lying to him. He can guess where I've been.

"These solitary jaunts into the Fornwood, Nara, they have to stop." He runs a hand over the back of his neck where his blond hair is shorn to stubble. A muscle in his jaw clenches, his brows a heavy line. He's angrier than I expected. "I could have been anyone tracking you."

"But you weren't, Brim, so relax. You know I'd only ever let myself get caught by you." He isn't amused. Lately, he hasn't been playing to my banter like he used to. "You were never such a stickler for the rules when we were children." I remember all the times we'd sneak past the Warder guards and out of the citadel hand-in-hand, making the Fornwood our playground, fearless of bears and wolves, or Wasteland raiders. Perhaps we were unafraid because the greatest dread of childhood had already happened to both of us: the loss of our parents. We were orphans together, egging each other on, making a competition of our recklessness.

"We're not children anymore," Brim says. "We have responsibilities, duties. You'll put both our necks on the line with the Council if you keep on like this."

"Well, I didn't ask you to follow me."

"Nara," he breathes, rubbing at his neck again as he always does when I frustrate him. "I'm a Warder. It's my job to follow you. Just because I taught you a few combat skills, doesn't mean I can completely ignore Council law."

A few combat skills? I cross my arms. "Go on, then. Call your dogs. Do your duty and round me up, *Captain*." I'm being unfair and I know it. I should be congratulating him on his promotion, not playing with his loyalties. He could have ordered men from his unit to fetch me, washing his hands of me and adding to my already tattered reputation in the citadel. But he didn't. He came himself because, more than a soldier or a protector, Brim's my closest friend. Has been since the day Osha and I walked into the Settlement ten years ago. Still, ever since his promotion to captain, he's been like a herding dog, snapping at my heels, bringing me back to the letter of Isfalki law again and again.

I dip my fingers in the steaming water, then straighten to undo my tunic.

"What are you doing?" He sighs, running a hand over his scalp and turning away, more embarrassed than angry now.

"What's it look like? If this is to be my last day in the Fornwood without a full Warder escort, I'm going to enjoy it."

I crouch to untie a boot. "You coming in? Or are you going to get your Council rule book out?"

Brim starts to pace on the other side of the pool. "Haven't I always done whatever you've asked, Nara? Played truant, taught you to ride and fight when you knew no one else would. And now I'm somehow a stickler for the rules?"

"Hey, it wasn't always me leading you astray! You were eager enough for my hunting lessons when we were training for your Warder test." That was two years ago now. We used to head to the forest or the tundra so I could show him how to read scat and spoor, how to disguise his scent, to nock and draw in complete silence – all the subtle ways of a Fornwood Solitary that my Amma taught me when I was a child. Before the Settlement and its walls. Before all the rules and expectations. "You seemed to think the forest was safe enough for me when you wanted it to be."

"Well, I was younger then… irresponsible. I shouldn't have agreed to that." He looks sheepish, but it doesn't distract him for long. "You must've heard the reports? Reconnaissance units have counted three more ransacked cabins burning on the western edge of the Fornwood in the past month alone. Wasters aren't waiting for spring anymore. And you know as well as I do they're not journeying all this way in the middle of winter to loot Fornwood Solitaries." He gives me a pointed look. The ultimate prize for any Wasteland raider is Pure women, I know as much. Only Pure mothers pass their immunity to the Brume on to their offspring. Only Pure mothers have bigger, healthier children. It's what Isfalk Settlement has become known for – a burgeoning population of breeders, Mor capable of producing immune sons who can become stronger warriors. Waster convoys might breach the southern expanse of the Fornwood to raid for furs and meat, medicines or Old World loot in Solitary camps, but it's a different kind of treasure that entices them as far north as Isfalk. Human traffic.

"The Fornwood's never been safe for Pure women, but

least of all now." Brim gazes through the frigid expanse of the forest, as if imagining the lawless Continent beyond. "Of all people, *you* should know the dangers of being alone out here." His gibe has the desired effect. Images from my childhood flash before me: Amma, face down in the snow; our cabin ablaze; my sister's hand gripping mine as we hide in the hollow tree, listening to the ring of curved steel, the roar and crack of burning wood.

"Listen, Nara." Brim touches my arm, bringing me into the present. "Mor like you have been given a gift. You can't ignore it. Your immunity is the future strength of this settlement, perhaps the future of the whole Continent." He says the words with reverence, but to me they're nothing more than the rhetoric of the Isfalk Council or the sanctimonious preaching of Father Uluf. "Your blood is a chance for Isfalk to rise from the ashes, to return to the prosperity of the Old World–"

"Oh, give it rest, Brim!" I shrug off his touch. "You sound like Elixion Fjäll." When we were children, Brim used to do a wicked impersonation of the nasal-voiced Councillor that made my belly ache with laughter. But now that Fjäll Mikkelson has risen to Elixion – Head of the Elix Council – Brim doesn't even smile at the memory.

"Whether you like it or not, Nara, you need to grow up," Brim snaps. "You and Osha have barely a few months left at the Mor school. You should be thinking about making a good match, getting ready for your Pairing ceremony, your duties as a mother, not running about the Fornwood like a wildling."

I turn my back on him, but inside I'm smarting as if he's slapped me, my heart pounding. He's never been so outspoken about my future before, never preached the doctrines of the Council and the Church so wholeheartedly. But what did I expect? He's only repeating his Warder pledge, taking it all the more seriously now he's a captain and must be an example to his men. He's obliged to protect the Settlement at all times, Brands and Pure alike, but particularly Mor whose bloodlines are the key to Isfalk's strength. Still, his disregard for our friendship hurts more than I want to admit.

"So, this *good match*," I say, scorn thick in my voice, "do you mean good for me or good for the Settlement?"

"Both." When I look at him I see he truly believes it. "Is it really such a hardship to be treated like royalty, Nara? To be waited on hand and foot, given the best of everything, the adoration and hope of the people–"

"In return for being penned in and fattened up like a breeding sow? Birthing every year until I drop?"

His face falls. "The other Mor don't seem to see it that way. It's not a punishment. They feel honoured to be the key to the Settlement's future." He runs his eyes over me and something softens in him. "Look, I've always known you're not the typical Mor princess. I mean, you'd rather track a snowjack through these woods in hunting suedes than spend the afternoon grooming for an appearance at Morday Mass. And you can hold your own with a sword or staves... even fists." He touches the bridge of his nose – the lump from a left-hook I gave him weeks ago still hasn't gone down. "In fact, I'm pretty sure you could have bested half of last year's Warder recruits." I stop unlacing my undershirt and look at him. Brim's compliments are rare and I let his words seduce me. "But the fact is," he continues, "you don't have to. You will never have to."

I kick off my last boot. It tumbles across the rock platform. "And what if I *want* to?"

"Want to what?"

"I don't know... become a Warder." My tone is far more nonchalant than I feel.

He frowns at me for a second, then lets out a bark of laughter, as if he's in the mess hall, catching the punchline of a joke from one of his men. I watch him silently and when he doesn't stop, I reef off my undershirt and step naked into the steaming water.

That shuts him up.

He angles away, awkwardly. We used to skinny dip here when we were children, disregarding all the rules; it's nothing he hasn't seen before. But I guess what he said is true: we're not children any more.

I sink below the surface, the water bubbling under my chin, admiring his captain's furs, the fit of black leather over his thighs, the trim of his cuffs and boots stitched in Warder red.

"What?" He's self-conscious, still pink-cheeked, even though I'm the one naked in the pool.

"Your uniform," I say.

"What about it?"

"You *chose* it. You delayed taking the seat under your uncle on the Settlement Council because you wanted a life of action, not citadel politics and scheming and gossip. And yet you're laughing at me for wanting the same."

He shifts to a squat, letting his arms hang over his knees, trying to read my expression. I think he might concede my point, but then he says, "You can't be serious, Nara. You'd voluntarily swap a life of indulgence and ease, half the citadel pandering to your every whim, for what? Guard duty on the outer gate in a blizzard? Policing brawls between drunk Brands in the village taverns? How about a Waster arrow in your back during a scouting mission? Why would you want to make that trade?"

"You did."

He stands and sighs up at the brightening sky as if it might shed light on my contrariness.

"Even if you managed to pass the tests, you seriously think the Council would let a Pure woman become a Warder?"

"There's no law that says I can't."

"There doesn't need to be! No Mor's stupid enough to want to try."

"I must be very stupid then."

He frowns and shakes his head in disbelief.

"Look," I say, trying a more rational tack, "isn't Father Uluf always harping on about the strength and valour of Pure women in his Morday sermons? How they took up arms to defend sick and infirm Brands in the early days of the Settlement?"

"That was over a century ago! The Isfalk Pures were barely a handful of families then. Under attack, the colony needed every strong fighter they could get."

"And don't we still?"

He looks pained, torn between being Brim, my childhood friend, and Brim, the Warder Captain. "Things are different now," he says, the Warder in him winning out. "The Settlement isn't the tiny colony it once was, and we all have our duties and roles to play." He studies me carefully. "If you're planning on doing something crazy, Nara, drop it now."

"Why? Are you worried you'll get laughed out of the mess if they find out you trained me to fight?"

"Please, I do have a little integrity!" He throws me a disappointed look. "I'm more worried you won't survive the Warder tests. Some of the strongest candidates I know have taken serious injuries in the combat assessment. And for a Pure you're not exactly–" He stops abruptly, glances away again, flushing.

"Not what?"

"You know what I mean."

I raise my eyebrows at him, but I can guess what he was going to say. He used to tease me about it all the time when we were children.

"Not very big?" I answer for him. "I think *scrawny* was the word you used to taunt me with." I can see from the way he looks at me through the shifting steam that it's not necessarily the description he'd choose now, but I am still pretty short for a Mor. "Anyway, I've got my strengths – speed, accuracy... brutal stubbornness." Usually he'd laugh at that, but he grants me no joy today.

"And how do you plan to manage hand-to-hand combat against men two heads taller than you?"

I give him a crooked smile. "Didn't I just show you how?"

At that he toes the snow testily and grips his fist over the hilt of his sword. "I'm telling you, Nara. Drop this. You're an orphan. You have no family behind you. If you get offside with the Council, they won't think twice about shipping you out to Torvag."

Torvag. He's scraping the barrel if he's threatening me with that. Our sister settlement to the south-west, on the frozen seaboard, is supposed to be another growing hub of Isfalki strength, according to the Council. In reality, everyone knows it's little more than a penal colony for the dregs of Isfalk society – disgraced Pures, court-marshalled Warders or misbehaving Mor. "Well, then, at least I'll finally get beyond the Walls and see some of the Continent."

Brim's face hardens. "Can't you take anything seriously, Nara? Face it, there's no place for Pure women in the Warder guard and the Council will tell you as much."

His conviction makes my lungs feel as though he's kicked the air out of them. But I won't let him see it. "The Council tells us we can't do a lot of things, Brim, but haven't we done them anyway?" I swim closer to the edge of the pool, propping my chin on my hands. "The Council says I shouldn't be outside the citadel alone, but here I am." I look up at him coyly through the steam. "The Council says you shouldn't swim in pools reserved for Mor cleansing rituals, and yet here you are."

"Well, I'm not swim–"

Before he can finish, I've reached for the scabbard of his sword and pulled, threatening to yank him in.

"Don't you dare, Nara, I swear–" he says, correcting his balance. But instead of stepping away he slides his eyes over my wet hair and shoulders, making a heat rise in me far warmer than the thermal water. When we were children, I wouldn't have thought twice about pulling him in, but things feel so different now.

I release the sword and swim to the other side of the pool. "Get in or don't. Makes no difference to me."

He rubs a palm over the top of his head, agonising. "One last time, alright? I mean it."

Brim starts to undress, slinging his furs across the rocks, shucking his tunic off so his back muscles torque in that way I've always admired. We soak at opposite ends of the pool, smirking at each other through the billowing mists, waiting to see who will be first to look away. His blue eyes are softened, as if he's given in to the warmth of the water, the shared memories, the vague sadness that something once innocent and carefree is already lost to us.

"Nara..." There's no exasperation now when he says my name, only a kind of longing.

"Don't," I tell him.

"I wish things could be different—"

"Don't. Don't say it." When I stop him, his expression changes from wistful into something raw. I know what he wants to say, but I can't bear to hear it.

"If I was only a Warder captain, if I didn't have the blood I have, you know what I'd ask."

He moves closer to take my hand under the water and I let him lift my palm to his lips for the briefest moment before I pull away and sink to the warm depths, ending a conversation that can't go anywhere. Brim may have chosen a military career, but he's still a descendant of one of the Founding Four – the very first families who formed the Settlement more than a hundred years ago. Eventually, he'll have to relinquish his Warder career and take up his seat on the Elix Council, just as his uncle did before him. His Pairing remains a political matter, a strategic move in the great game of Pure alliances on which the citadel is founded. The Elixion has a brood of Mor daughters that Brim might pick. An orphan Fornwood Solitary with no Isfalki bloodline is hardly a match for Brim Oskarsson.

I hold my breath under the water and try not to feel the ghost of Brim's lips on my palm. Instead, I think of all the times we used to sneak here to swim at dawn or dusk, the caution we threw to the wind, how brave we were when everything was simpler. Part of me wants to stay here forever, suspended in that warm easy place of childish memories, but another part makes me push up in a sudden panic to the surface, the life force in me stronger than anything else, like my Amma always said it was. I wring out my hair, wishing my frustration and anger could run off me as easily as the water.

Brim is looking up to the sky at a sudden chatter of birds. A flock of sicklewings swoops through the mists and up into the pale morning, fluid as ink in water. "If only we were that free," he says, propping his head against the rocks. I stay quiet. I know that flight formation. It's evasive, masking: some bird of prey is close. My Amma taught me to read such signs almost before I could walk. Brim might see freedom, but I see life and death in the balance. Anyone with Fornwood blood knows as much.

Moments later I hear it: the faint tinkle of a talon bell. Released for a morning hunt, the ghosthawk traces a lazy circle above us, then plummets. Mother Iness's tiercel has found its mark.

Sisters

By the time I've changed out of my hunting suedes and into my smock, the chapel bell has rung again. I slip out of the dormitories and run through the cloisters, ignoring the wet snow that splatters my hose as I cross the quad. I might make the first lesson of the day. Just. Mor schoolgirls tread the same routes between the Chapel of First Mother, the instruction rooms and the refectory, over and over again, churning the courtyard to slush, but at night the pathways freeze, making the ice underneath a perfect trap to catch students running late. Students like me.

"You there!" a voice commands across the open space. "Mor Nara!" I halt mid-jog, skidding and almost landing on my arse for my pains. Father Uluf emerges from the shadow of the chapel, my sister at his elbow. Osha's shoulders sink when she sees me, clearly relieved that I've returned safely. But as I cross the quad towards them, she gives me the death stare. I know that look well enough to keep my mouth shut.

"You've recovered from your moon cramps, I see," Father Uluf says. He's one of the oldest priests in Isfalk, but he still leads all the services in the Mor school chapel and most of the important ones in the Roundhouse Church. He's known for the vitriol of his sermons and his uncanny ability to make the lesson awkwardly relevant to the private affairs of citadel families. His bald pate and the cowl about his stooped neck always make me think of the carrion-vuls that hover on the outskirts of the Branded village, searching for rotten morsels among the dung. Uluf has a similar eye for scandal and vice.

I glance at Osha and place a hand to my belly, groaning a little. "I'm not quite recovered, Father. But I didn't want to miss any more of my lessons."

"Very conscientious." The priest offers me a slippery smile. "Although, it is worrying that you seem to have your courses several times a month." Osha bites her lips, looking away. Uluf doesn't miss a beat. He scans me from head to toe and I lower my skirts, attempting to cover my splattered stockings. Too late. "And do try not to run. It's unseemly for a Mor your age. There are eyes upon you now, remember?" He glances to the raised arcades and upper windows of the central keep where eligible males from the Pure ranks might peer down on us in the school grounds. *Surveying the wares,* I often complain to Osha. "Good Pairings rest on good reputations," Uluf says, quoting one of the Mor school's favourite dictums, "and it's especially true for you two, given your disadvantages in the Pairing negotiations."

He means our adoption into the Settlement and unknown parentage, despite our Pure blood. Osha and I both know where this is going; we've heard it so many times before. My sister studies the slushy pathway, but I hold Uluf's gaze, unflinching. I might lose sleep at night yearning to know a single detail of my parents' faces – my father's smile, the colour of my mother's eyes – but I won't let Uluf or anyone else shame me for not knowing their bloodline.

"Of course, some Elix will overlook your sister's murky heritage because of her bearing and temperament, her... inner light, let's call it." Uluf smiles at Osha and my stomach turns at his yellowed teeth. "But you," he says, running critical eyes over me again, "with your smaller hips and less womanly frame, and all these debilitating moon cramps." He lowers his voice to a whisper. "You know what the rumour mill in the citadel is like. We don't want potential suitors thinking you have a blighted womb, do we?"

It's a veiled threat. That rumour would certainly come from Uluf himself. He suspects where I've been, what I've been up to, and he's pulling me into line, just as Brim did. The only difference is that the priest is enjoying it.

"Come now, that scowl won't do you any favours," he tells me. "No young man of any influence in the citadel is going to choose a Mor with such a sulk on her face. Look to your sister's example. See how alluring she is... how placable." Osha's cheeks flush pink. "She understands the true purpose of a privileged place at this school, don't you, my child?" Uluf raises his eyebrows expectantly. He loves prompting us for the school creed, as if we don't already recite it three times a day in chapel.

"*Through Pairing and Progeny to Purpose,*" Osha replies blandly.

"Not to mention *power.*" Uluf winks conspiratorially. He thinks he's being candid and worldly, adding that to the school's motto. And, in a way, it's the truth of the matter. Mor our age pray almost constantly to the Holy Mother, first for an alliance with an influential family and then for babies, one a year, ideally. Pairing and progeny boost the ranks of the Pure, making Isfalk stronger, but they are also a Mor's path to greater respect and influence in the citadel. After all, even Uluf has to answer to a woman. Mother Iness is the oldest and most prolific matriarch of the Settlement's Founding Four families. Rumoured to have delivered eighteen children, fifteen surviving, she's related by blood or Pairing to every man of influence in Isfalk. Everyone knows it's really her voice behind both Church and Council.

I struggle to arrange my expression into something more *alluring* and *placable*, hoping to put an end to the interview, but Uluf's eyes flit from my sister to me again. "Really, if it wasn't for the mirror of your faces I'd find it hard to believe the two of you were born of the same womb."

His comment pains Osha, I can tell, but it's hardly the first time we've heard it said. She's at least a head taller than me, her figure fuller, her manners and bearing gentler than mine. We may share some of the same facial features and hair colour but sometimes when I look at her it's like seeing the summer version of myself – brighter, more generous, less lean and rangy. I loathe Uluf for pointing it out, not because of any insult to me, but for making Osha feel guilty about her beauty.

"Well, I shouldn't keep you from your studies any longer," he says at last. "What is the lesson today?"

"We're preparing for a safe childbed, Father," Osha replies. "Learning the correct orisons to First Mother." And all the while she holds my gaze as if willing my mouth to stay shut. "Excellent. Such important prayers, with motherhood around the corner." Uluf steps aside and my sister slips her arm through mine, almost dragging me towards the schoolroom.

"So true, Father," I say over my shoulder, my voice bright and innocent. "Where would Isfalk be without prayers?"

Uluf raises an eyebrow and scans my face suspiciously as he pulls up his cowl, but he says no more, shuffling into the shadow of the cloisters.

"Hell's poxes, Nara!" Osha rounds on me as soon as he's out of earshot. "You couldn't resist the last word, could you? Isn't it enough that I have to lie for you and he sees straight through it?"

"I guess you've used the moon cramps excuse a little too often this month, huh?"

"What do you expect when you put me on the spot without warning? It's one thing to sneak out hunting for a couple of hours, but to be gone the entire night and half the morning without telling me! I was worried sick. I had to ask Brim to go looking for you."

I take her hand in mine, but she won't squeeze back – not yet anyway.

"And don't give me that sorry pout. I'm not falling for it."

"What was the price of the old vul's silence this time?" I ask, nodding towards the rooms in the chapel where Uluf holds court.

"I poulticed his chilblains."

I wince, imagining the priest's gnarled feet. Osha would have handled them willingly enough, though – not out of any love for Uluf, but from sheer curiosity about the condition. Our Amma might have taught me to track and hunt, but it was my sister who inherited her true gifts: Fornwood herb-lore and the curative arts.

Unfortunately, the rest of the Settlement doesn't benefit much from Osha's talents. Old World apotheka and the healing arts are all but forbidden in Isfalk. The Pure rarely get sick, and even minor ailments aren't spoken about for fear citadel society would see the afflicted as having "weak blood" like the Branded. Breaks and strains, toothaches, boils and battle-wounds are all treated by Uluf's priests with a mixture of what Osha calls *excision and exorcism* – brutal surgery on the one hand and fervent prayer to First Mother on the other. Her own healing skills have become little more than an academic pursuit she's forced to study in secret.

"The hypocrisy of that man," I say. "Preaching that medicines are sinful, then bribing you to treat his aches and pains in private!"

Osha's used to my outrage on her behalf. She only shakes her head in exasperation, tucking into place a strand of hair that has escaped my messy bun. Her own neat braid circles her brow like a chaplet, bright as burnished bronze in the snow-lit quad. "I take it as a compliment," she says. "If Father Uluf seeks the witchcraft of my medicines at the risk of his mortal soul, then it's praise indeed for my skills." She's always better at swallowing the inequities of the Settlement than I am. I think she got my share of patience and equanimity when we were born.

"I'm sorry you had to lie for me, O, really I am. But that two-faced altar rat! The way he carries on. *Disease is the manifestation of evil, and weakness the wages of sin,*" I drawl, mimicking Uluf's sermon voice. "*Behold the brands of iniquity upon the Fallen, the sickness that is their punishment–*"

"Shhh, Nara. He might hear you!" But when I see her biting down a smile, I ham up the impersonation even more. "*Apotheka is nothing but the idle magicking of Fornwood spae-wives.*" I waggle a finger at Osha. "*The work of witches, I say! Heretics wishing to meddle with the Natural Order of Pure pre-eminence as ordained by First Mother... Now close the door, young Mor, and put that compress on my inflamed feet.*"

"You're a terrible actress," Osha says, but the sound of her laugh warms me inside.

"Brim's impression of Uluf is better... well, it used to be, before he became a captain. But, see, I made you giggle at least."

Osha looks guilty. "You know, Uluf has Bone Fire in his knees... and crippling constipation."

"That explains why he's so hypocritical, then. He's literally full of shit."

"Oh hush!" Osha drags me further from the chapel. "The Pure might live twice as long as the Branded, but we'll still have to face old age too, one day. It isn't easy for Uluf."

"I guess not, especially since he's spent his whole life preaching that infirmity and weakness are the wages of sin." My sister gives me a disappointed frown. "Mother's tits, O, you're such a bleeding heart. Uluf's a self-righteous bastard who deserves what's coming to him."

"Maybe." Osha's expression turns thoughtful. After a moment she says, "*No creature deserves pain when Nature gives us the ease of it.*" They're Amma's words, her creed, whether teaching me to hunt or Osha to heal. Having my sister remind me of them feels like yet another reprimand in a long line of them this morning. I can handle a scolding from others, but not from her, not when she reminds me of our grandmother, of who we were before the Settlement. Mor may be expected to seek First Mother's guidance three times a day in the school chapel but my anchor, my compass, is Osha. She's the only person who, with a single look, can make me strive to be... better. To be more than my petty instincts. Just as Amma used to.

"Oh, cheer up, Narkat," she says, when she sees me brooding. "We've already missed half the class and it'll be lunch soon." She knuckles me in the waist.

I still feel sulky, but I nudge her with my hip in return. She always gets the better of me with that pet name. *Narkat.* Amma gave it to me when Osha and I were children. She said I was like the small fleet-lynxes that prowl the Fornwood because I had sharp eyes and an even sharper bite. Narkat sometimes steal into The Fold to hunt livestock more than twice their size, singling them out before a lightning strike to the jugular. The Isfalki call them Snar Grim – the Scourge of the Snows – but in the Solitary dialect, the word *narkat* means something small and wild and fierce. Osha only ever calls me it in private now – we'd be teased mercilessly at school if anyone heard us using the slang of wildlings. But to me, that name in my sister's mouth tells me I'm forgiven.

"What? Yes... Quiet now!" Mother Gerda says when we enter the schoolroom, as if we've disturbed her nap. "Ah... the Fornwood Flamehairs. So, you've decided to grace us with your presence." The other girls in our year turn and snigger. Osha offers an apology – something about Father Uluf needing us. "Well, sit down, sit down." Gerda flicks a lazy hand towards the rear of the room, straightening the burlet and veil that sit crookedly over her grey hair.

"Mother." Osha and I bob our respect, taking the vacant seats. We don't address our schoolteachers as Mor since they're past their fertile years. Widows whose children are fully grown, or women from families of lesser standing must earn their keep in the citadel as the tutors of future generations of breeders. Generally, I don't mind Mother Gerda's lessons. Her terminal apathy suits me well enough. Like her, I usually catch up on sleep during the class.

Today, under the vaulted window at the front of the room, a small group of girls are demonstrating a prayer circle. Within their ring, a heavily pregnant woman reclines on a pallet of furs, evidently for the purposes of the lesson. I don't remember her name, but I recognise her face as someone two years above us. Now strategically Paired, it seems she's a blooming paragon of a fruitful Mor, hand-picked by the school to help with demonstrations and inspire the soon-to-graduate. She lies prettily on the pallet, her hands in their soft suede gloves resting on her distended belly, her legs crossed at the ankles under a fur-trimmed kirtle of rare Old World damask – a display of Founding Four wealth if ever I saw one. She looks as far from the throes of childbirth as is humanly possible. The girls around her are flushed and busy-eyed, taking in her sophistication, the jewellery and hair that indicate her Mikkelson status, clearly stirred less by thoughts of pregnancy than by imagining their own social mobility once shot of the strictures of the Mor school. At Mother Gerda's nod, though, they resume the song of their prayers, while she settles into her chair at the fire.

Osha takes out her quill and copybook.

"Seriously?" I whisper. "You think *this* worthy of notes?"

"Please," my sister mutters, rolling her eyes briefly at the performance in the schoolroom. Osha was delivering babies when we were still children ourselves. Fornwood Solitaries would trek miles through the forests looking for our grandmother when their time drew near. Osha wouldn't have been much past seven years old when Amma started teaching her how to birth them, and soon after how to stop inner bleeding, how to treat milk fever and the yellow blush, even how to bring back a blue-born whose fate would usually have been a shallow crib under the snow. They were Branded babies, of course, and some didn't live for very long, but that only made Osha all the more determined to understand why.

I watch her now, quietly turning the pages of her book, where she's hidden loose papers between the end leaves. They're covered in her scrawl, a messy frenetic script, which always fascinates me for it's the exact opposite of her neat and graceful appearance.

"How many candles did you burn through this time?" I ask, my voice masked by the chorus filling the room.

She shrugs, stifles a yawn. I wasn't there to make her go to bed. She would have stayed up all night, as I did.

"Don't look at me like that," she answers. "The Fornwood might call to you, but Fenderhilde calls to me."

"Fenderhilde? Which one is he again?"

She shifts in her seat, glances at the students seated ahead, making sure no one's listening. "The Old World apothek I told you about." Her fingers rest over the blotchy copy. Obviously, they're her notes from his journal – the manuscript she discovered only last month. I want to appear interested but, in truth, I don't know how Osha can stand to spend all night burrowing through the citadel's long-abandoned archives. Whenever I go down there to fetch her to sleep, the maze of narrow windowless vaults gives me heart palpitations and the shakes. Even the musty smell of the shelves makes me restless for the clean air of the Fornwood.

"I know there's more down there that I haven't found yet. I just need the time to look," she whispers.

"Well, good luck with that." From what I've seen it's mainly mildewed manuscripts of ledgers and inventories, rat-eaten scrolls of trade routes and endless bills of carriage from when Isfalk was the northern trading hub of the Old World, centuries ago. In the two years since she discovered the archives, Osha has only found three treasures, as she calls them. The first

is a tome called *Anathomia and Physik*, thick and heavy as a
doorstep; the second, an illuminated almanac of herbs in a
language she can't decipher; and the most recent, the tiny
scrawled chronicle of this apothek – Fenderhilde. She spends
half her free time poring over the manuscripts and the other
half working through the forgotten crypts of records, looking
for more that might have been discarded under the detritus of
times past. I doubt she'll find much. Most manuals of apotheka
and healing were probably destroyed by the priests long ago.

I watch her now, dipping her quill, glancing up at the
chanting girls occasionally, the picture of Mor conscientious-
ness, should Mother Gerda turn her attention on us. She's
smarter than me, playing to citadel expectations so much
better than I ever manage.

"What does Fenderhilde say?" I ask.

Osha shakes her head. "Not much I don't already know,
but–" She stops suddenly. The orisons have fallen away as a
new group of girls stand to replace the others in the circle.
Mistress Gerda nods, warming her legs at the fire, eyes closed
as the incantation starts up again.

"But then I found this," Osha continues, and I can hear the
excitement even in her whisper. "Here." She runs a finger over a
line of writing. I'm hardly able to decipher her midnight scrawl,
but I can make out a reference to the Brume. This is the gold
Osha searches for night after night. Not recipes for poultices and
tisanes that might be useful to treat the minor discomforts of
an old priest. My sister wants to understand the Great Malady
itself, *why* it decimated the Continent over a century ago, *how* it
branded the majority of survivors while such a small minority –
us privileged Pures – remained untouched.

"Fenderhilde describes early manifestations," she says. I
squint, slowly making sense of the lines:

*The Brume is the Potentate of Maladyes, like to some cunning
tyrante who brandes his subjects with the lash, thereby to show his
henchemen where to do his slaughter.*

I try to look enlightened, but obviously fail for she sighs. "It's not the Brume that kills people, but its henchmen – the common ailments to which it leaves the Branded vulnerable. Fenderhilde says the apothek's true calling is to protect against the Great Malady itself because doing so will safeguard against those other diseases."

"But you already knew that."

"Yes, but he goes on to postulate the idea of shielding the Branded in infancy, protecting them from the Great Tyrant before he marks them for a life of contagions and poxes."

"Shielding them how?"

She shifts in her seat again and scowls at her notes. "Here, I part ways with Apothek Fenderhilde."

"Surprise, surprise." My sister parts ways with much of *Anathomia and Physik* as well, apparently.

"They're Old World texts," she often tells me, tired and frustrated, when I fetch her from the crypts. "They're written by academics who've clearly never put aside the quill to actually touch a sick human."

"So, what was Fenderhilde's shield?" I ask.

"He suggests the Branded drink the blood of the Pure to give their offspring immunity."

"Ewww." I squirm away from her notes. "Yeah, perhaps you need to keep researching."

"Perhaps you need to stop whispering, Mor Nara!" Mother Gerda's voice shrills across the room. I flick my eyes to the front where a new circle is waiting for Osha and me to join them. "Let's see if you and your sister have been paying attention, shall we?"

Osha and I rise and shuffle forwards, joining hands with the other Mor around the pregnant woman. I mumble my way through the orisons, watching my sister's lips as a prompt for the words. But all the while she sings, Osha is focused on the sight of the woman's swollen belly, the way she's started to shift from her relaxed position, restless. She draws her knees up under her kirtle, her breath snatching as she rubs at a spot under her sternum. My sister lets go of my hand, breaking the prayer circle and hovering her palm above the woman's stomach, asking wordlessly if she can touch. The Mor hesitates. Those with child are attended and delivered only by the priests and other mothers, usually the most senior and experienced Mor in the Settlement. There's little reason she should let a mere schoolgirl lay hands on her. But it doesn't surprise me when the woman nods. My sister has this effect on others – drawing them in with a quiet self-possession, a confidence even those who've never met her seem to trust.

Osha places her hand gently over the aching spot, and I watch as her face takes on a look so familiar from childhood, that same expression she'd get when Amma let her treat patients in our cabin: eyes glazed, head cocked, nostrils flaring faintly, as if she's smelling and listening as much as touching. The other girls in our circle keep up the orison but their eyes flit worriedly between my sister and Mother Gerda, as if expecting a reprimand. The old teacher only chokes on a snore by the fire.

"Don't worry," Osha says in a soft voice. "Your baby is well. It's only a little heartburn." When she moves her hand a fraction, I notice the woman's body ease, her breath coming steady now, fingers unclenching. "You have another scorenight yet, by my reckoning. Try to eat less allium."

The woman gazes at my sister, her mouth ajar, her expression a mix of confusion and admiration, but she slowly nods her assent.

Osha rejoins her hand with mine and her face is bright as morning on new snow. It's been a long time since I've seen it that way. I raise an eyebrow at her, shaking my head a little at the utter waste of her talents locked up in this school, this citadel. But Osha ignores me, singing the orisons again in her limpid voice, her fingers warm and comforting in mine.

* * *

"I brought you something from the Fornwood," I tell Osha when she enters our room at the end of the school day. We share a private chamber in the Mor dormitories, a privilege of being in our final year, and she closes the door behind her, keeping our conversation from passing gossips in the passageways. I pull my grubby hunting satchel from its hiding place under the bed.

"What is it?"

"Can't you guess?"

"I don't know… a dead snowjack?" Osha's voice is tired as she unrolls her damp stockings and tries to get warm by the fire. She's been across the quad and down to the kitchens, seeking out our maid Frida about something or other.

"Come on, O." I grin. "I know you can do better than that." I hold out my fist, keeping the contents closed tightly inside. She lifts her nose towards it and sniffs.

"Paper lichen?… No, wait… skeggan moss."

Even as a child, Osha could sniff out herbs from only a pinch of their powdered leaves. I drop a cloud of the silvery moss into her palm and I'm gratified when her face lights up. She can make a concentrate from its brew that helps bring down fevers.

"Your nose truly is occult, you know. You sure you're not a witch?"

She tuts, rubbing the moss between her fingers to savour its scent. "Don't lump my work alongside the flim-flam of spae-wives. Amma didn't teach me to peddle random panacea and potations to exploit the desperation of the Branded."

"Not just the Branded. I've heard there's a witch in the southern glades who targets Councillors desperate for a male heir… and Mor wanting to catch the attention of a particular suitor." I let out a scoff. "You reckon I should pay her a visit?"

"It's no joke, Nara!" Osha snaps. "Not for the Branded, anyway. Every time they leave the Walls in search of those hawkers they risk bringing back more than nonsense cure-alls."

"Hey!" I say, surprised at her outburst. "I'm on your side, remember?" I nod at the skeggan in her hand and she sighs in apology. Usually, I'm the prickly one, rankling and restless to her rational and measured.

"What is it, O? Tell me."

She hovers at the fire, fiddling at the thong of the pendant at her neck. "Frida told me a strawberry pox is running through toddlers in the village."

"Oh." Now I understand her touchiness. "That's a bad one, isn't it?"

She nods. "It can be fatal in weaker Brand children. Apparently, it was spread by a smithy who visited a spae-wife in the south." Osha paces out her frustration. "It's hardly the Brand's fault. His newborn son looked unlikely to survive the night, so he went to the witch asking for a potion to *cleanse* the babe's blood. Frida said he was hoping to turn him Pure." My sister struggles to keep the scorn from her voice. "That spae-wife gave him far more than a bottle of nettle water. Two children have already died of the pox he's carried to the village, and they're only the ones Frida knows about."

To stop her pacing, I draw her to the window and make her sit in the casement beside me. She always finds it hard to hear of death among the Branded, as if it's a personal failure. "These outbreaks are nothing new, O. They're an unfortunate fact of life in the village. You know that better than anyone." She pulls her hands impatiently from mine and I try a more sensitive tack. "Look, at least up here in the north, Isfalki Brands have a civilised life. They're secluded from the worst of the Continent's diseases... and they're protected from Wasters by our Warder army. But we're never going to completely stop fevers and contagions from being introduced. You're doing as much as you can."

"Am I?" She works at the leather thong with restless fingers. "I want to do what I'm good at, Nara. I want to help the sick. I'm tired of having to treat people by proxy and in secret, making Frida administer my medicines under cover of night like a criminal. I want to be able to examine the Branded out in the open without the risk of being shipped off to Torvag as a blasphemer and subversive."

"I know, O. I know." I turn to look through the window, out across the battlements and the snow-blanketed Fold, towards the wild expanse of the Fornwood. I open my satchel and show her the rest of its contents. It's the only way I can think to cheer her up.

"Mother's love, Nara! Where did you find this much skeggan?" She pulls out clouds and clouds of the moss stuffed inside. Her face is full of delight at first but drops as she begins to understand. There's only one place either of us knows where skeggan grows prolifically. A place where it blows in the trees like the hair of the mist sirens the Brands tell tales about on wintry nights, ever fearful of the forest. "So that's why you were gone so long," she says. "You went home."

The word makes my gut twist. *Home* doesn't exist anymore. Amma's cabin, our vegetable beds, the animal stall – all gone. The place deep in the western Fornwood where we spent the first eight years of our lives is now nothing more than ashes under the snow.

"Why didn't you tell me you were going?"

I shrug. "You'd have said it was too dangerous. And then you'd have worried even more when I ignored you and went anyway."

She doesn't bother arguing; she knows I'm right. Besides, I can sense her curiosity getting the better of the scolding she wants to give me.

"Was there anything left? Did you see–" Her voice hitches. I shake my head, sparing her the pain of asking.

She's silent – her turn to stare through the casement towards the line of the forest. Amma used to say the green of spring bracken was in Osha's eyes, but they seem more grey now, as if Settlement life has dulled them. I watch her absently worrying the pendant around her neck, her gaze catching on a Warder reconnaissance unit crossing The Fold. Perhaps she's remembering the silhouettes of other mounted men, lit by flames, our grandmother's silver hair like a path through the blood, the curve of those strange Reis swords, slicing as cleanly as a sickle to wheat. We don't speak of our memories of that night anymore. There's never been much point. I already know from the fevered breathing of her sleep, the damp tangle of her morning hair, that Osha's nightmares are the same as mine.

I still her fingers on the pendant and draw my own from beneath my smock. The small, filigreed medallions of spiralling glyphs are identical, even if we as twins are not. "Hey," I whisper, bringing her attention to me. "You and me, sis, remember?" I touch my pendant to hers, our foreheads together, and I feel her warmth, her special energy, the way it comforts me. And I know it calms her too. I can sense it. The necklaces are the only things we had with us when we fled the Fornwood. The only things we have of our parents, of our past.

Run for the Walls and don't look back. Ask for Oskarsson, do you hear? Only Oskarsson. And show him these. My Amma's voice rings clear in my head whenever I comfort Osha like this. *You're the strong one. Look after her. You'll be safe as long as you stay together.* And we have been safe, here in the citadel. Well fed and privileged, too. For a price. The price of our freedom; the price of happiness.

"You know, we don't have to stay," I tell Osha in a low, hurried voice. "We could leave Isfalk, return to the Fornwood." I search her face. "I could hunt and you could treat the sick – I mean properly, not like some crazy spae-wife. You'd build a reputation like Amma did. We don't have to lead this–"

"Stop, Nara! Stop," she snaps. When she finally holds my eye, she says more gently, "Please. Don't start this again. We've been through it before." She slips the necklace back inside her smock, putting the memories, the reminder of who we once were, out of sight. "It's too dangerous out there for Mor like us, you know that." Standing, she turns from the window, then takes my hand, her gentle touch assuaging the firmness of the words I know are coming. "Brim told you about the latest Waster attacks on Solitaries, the looting and pillaging. It would only be a matter of time before our lives are burned down in front of us again. And I won't lose you like I did Amma. We're safe here, and even if you do insist on slipping out to the Fornwood now and again, I have Brim to bring you home to me." She glances to her desk, the messy spread of copybooks, ink and quills both used and uncut. "Anyway, I want to help the sick here, in a community. I don't want Brands to risk leaving the Settlement to come looking for my treatments. I can do better work helping them here in Isfalk."

"So you'll go along with the Pairings, like a good little Mor?" My disappointment turns sour and comes out as scorn. It always does.

"Nara." Osha offers me a sad smile of acceptance.

"It's just, I'm not sure I can bear it like you can, O."

"But, don't you see? If we make half-decent unions, we'll have our freedom. We'll be out from under the eyes of this school, running our own households, with brandservants of our own choosing to help. And as long as we fulfil the public expectations of the Council, in private we'll be left to do as we wish."

"That's easy for you to say. You're beautiful and desired and you'll have any Elix heir eating from the palm of your hand in a matter of months," I tell her, trying not to whine. "You'll be able to spend all day in the archives finding a cure for the Brume while Frida sneaks Brands to you to treat at night." I've already overheard the pair of them planning it. With a powerful husband behind her, it's possible the citadel might turn a blind eye to Osha providing the Branded with basic remedies and treatments. And, given enough time – and enough sons and grandsons – she might even campaign from within the Council for the church to relax its stance on healers. If anyone could do it, Osha could. Unlike me, she has the patience to think in terms of years and decades, not hours and days.

"In the meantime, what kind of cretinous third son will I end up with?" I ask. "I need the Fornwood, at least from time to time. It's like air to me. I can't be trapped within these Walls."

"I know. I know." She presses my knuckles to her lips. "But you're going to be fine, Narkat, believe me. Brim won't be able to bear the idea of someone else Pairing with you and then he'll dig his heels in with his uncle and Fjäll. He loves you. He'll come around, you wait and see."

I smile, not because she's right but because her love for me makes her wrong about Brim's. I know him better than she does. He may have a rebellious streak, but his duty to the citadel ranks ahead of any love for me.

Before I can tell her as much, a knock on the door startles us both. I tuck my pendant inside my smock out of habit, keeping what little I have of our past hidden from public scrutiny. But it's only Frida, bringing in clean laundry.

"Mother's Blessings, Frida," I greet the dormitory maid.

"Mother's Blessings, Mor Nara," she answers. "I'm glad you're better now." She's referring to my imaginary moon cramps. Frida will have covered for me just as much as Osha, but she'll keep up the pretence and mention nothing of my absence. She shakes out the clothes and I notice the flimsy Mass gowns we wear on the few occasions we're officially allowed out of the citadel. She hangs them beside our thickest travelling furs.

"Hell's poxes! Please don't tell me it's Morday Mass? Not tonight." I fall onto my bed in a lethargic slump. Most Mor students look forward to the monthly mass as a chance to leave the confines of the school, to have our importance and privilege on full display for the entire Settlement to admire. But the thought of going out into the cold only to sit on exhibit in the cavernous Roundhouse Church while Father Uluf drones through a full mass to First Mother makes me want to curl up under my bed furs.

I squirm in a feigned cramp.

"Don't even think about it," Osha warns, pulling the covers from me. "Frida and I aren't telling any more lies for you today." I look at the maid. She doesn't smile at my antics as she usually does, her expression preoccupied, eyes heavy. I feel guilty, slowly getting up and unbuttoning my smock. It's usually her job, but she looks exhausted. Besides, I hate the feeling of being dressed by someone else. She holds the gown out to me.

"Sorry you had to cover for me, Frida," I tell her. She shakes her head, uncomfortable with an apology from a Mor. She bends to set down my mass shoes, her long braid falling forward. The branding on her neck is small and delicate, almost pretty, like a curl of loose hair at her nape, hidden enough to allow her this job waiting on Mor schoolgirls, but far too dark for her to become a maid for an Elix Councillor or one of the more influential Pure families. The citadel's elite are fussy about such things. *The worse the branding, the weaker the Brand*, so they say. Servants in Pure households must be strong and healthy, their skin as unmarked as possible even if their blood is tainted underneath. I think of the slum children in the Fornwood this morning – their small frames, the slap of brandings across their faces, blue-black as crow feathers, the boy's bone-rattling cough.

"Osha tells me there's an outbreak of pox in the village," I say.

"Yes, mistress." She tries to concentrate on straightening Osha's dress, but I can see her eyes are distracted.

"You're worried for your boy?"

She blinks then nods quickly, busying herself with the laces at the bodice. Frida's son is cared for by her mother while she serves us in the citadel all day. Osha tells me he's already fought two earlier poxes and three agues in his young life. I stop her hands. "Your Jarl's a fighter, though, isn't he?"

She nods and tries admirably for a brave face.

Osha steps in. "I've already told her, every time he bounces back from one of these childhood maladies it's a good sign. I believe it'll make him hardier to other sicknesses. Here, Frida." From the drawer of her desk Osha retrieves a bottle of milk and a twist of paper. "You need to get this treatment to those mothers whose babes have the strawberry pox," she says. "Mix the powder with the milk into a suspension and tell them to spread it all over the skin. It'll relieve the itching. And tomorrow I can give you skeggan essence to lower their fevers. Nara harvested half the Fornwood, thank the Mother. Make sure to set some aside for yourself, though, in case Jarl needs it."

The maid nods, taking the powder, but hesitating over the milk. The Branded village only retains part of the produce they farm, especially precious dairy in the thick of winter. Warders requisition most of it for the citadel to fatten up pregnant Mor, their babies, and those soon-to-become mothers, like me and my sister.

"I don't know about the milk, Mor Osha. Warders on the gate seem more watchful lately." Brandservants are randomly checked as they leave the citadel for the night, in case they've decided to steal food or valuables from Pure households. But dormitory maids like Frida routinely take bundles of laundry to the washhouse, allowing her to smuggle the contraband medicines Osha makes.

Frida touches the bottle, visibly torn. "If they find out a fec's taken milk from the mouths of Pure girls, I'll be out on the tundra."

Osha stiffens. "Please don't call yourself that, Frida." The maid lowers her eyes, chastened. She's only repeating what Pures commonly call the Branded, but my sister can't bear the slur. "Fec isn't even accurate. Just because you've inherited the Brume markings, doesn't mean you're infectious."

I give Frida a knowing look; we're both familiar with the lecture that's to come.

"There hasn't been an actual Brume outbreak in almost a hundred years and you can't *catch* brandings, you can only be born with them." Osha walks to her desk, rests her fingers pensively on a copybook and I can tell from her glazed eyes that she's back in the archives, poring over manuscripts. "I wish the Branded wouldn't keep leaving The Fold. They put the whole village at risk. Don't they realise contagions run rife beyond the sanctuary of Isfalk's patrols?"

I move to the desk where a tray of food still sits – slices of thick brown bread, cured meat and cheese. My untouched breakfast. I begin to wrap it in the napkin, exchanging a glance with Frida. My sister always focuses on disease and sickness, but I'm beginning to understand there's another reason the Branded might venture beyond The Fold. I saw it this morning in the Fornwood on the faces of those slum children.

"Will you be able to find milk for the suspension in the village, Frida?" Osha asks the maid.

"She won't need to." I remove the bottle from my sister's hand and bundle it with the napkin of food in the smock I've taken off. "She'll take the milk. And she'll take my breakfast as well." I hold out the roll of laundry.

"I can't, Mor Nara," Frida says. "It's not right. I shouldn't be taking from the mouths of Mor."

"We can't even eat all we're given, you know that," I tell her. "And Jarl's a fighter, right? So, let's keep him strong." I press the bundle into her arms. "Use the eastern gate and don't leave until just before vespers bell." It's the least used exit from the citadel and the Warders are lazy. I should know. I've sneaked through posing as a brandservant often enough. "The guards won't even look under your hood, believe me." I wink and she nods, offering me a nervous smile. "It's only breaking the rules if you get caught… So don't get caught."

Morday Mass

The sleds that take us to Morday Mass are lined up in the courtyard of the Warder barracks. We file out of the Mor school, youngest girls first, into the fog of dozens of baying dogs, the shouts of drivers wrangling their teams. Here, the gate in the northern walls of the citadel leads directly onto the ice plains and the dogs whimper and strain at the smell of the open tundra beyond. It seems almost cruel to get their blood up for a ten-minute run. We could go by foot to the Roundhouse Church with a lot less fuss. The south side of the Settlement isn't that far. But Mor students are not expected to lower themselves trudging the serpentine streets of the Branded village, and especially not on Morday Mass when we're put on a pedestal to be admired by the whole of Isfalk. So, we wait our turn as Warders settle the girls ahead of us into sleds, escorting each pair and their driver on horseback towards the moonless black of The Fold.

As we wait for our ride, the first snow of the night begins to fall, catching on our shoulders, the fur trim of our travelling mantles. Osha pulls down her hood, turning her face up to the flakes, trying to catch one on her tongue. Frida has styled her hair into a crown of latticed braids, but the majority of the curls fall loose underneath. They pool in her hood like amber resin in the torchlight as I reach to brush away the flakes that have started to settle. At my touch she startles. "My pendant. I forgot," Osha says. She huddles into me, furtively reaching inside her furs for the leather thong about her neck and slipping it over her head. Our low-cut mass gowns are designed to reveal as much skin as possible and certainly don't conceal the necklaces, so we take them off and tuck them inside our bodices for mass. There's enough speculation about us already without encouraging any more.

That's when I sense someone watching.

Leaning against the driving bow of his sled, one of the dog wranglers has Osha in his sights. His face is partly obscured by the coarse knitted hat pulled low over his forehead, but I can see his eyes drifting over my sister, his lips parted. He's displaying far too much interest for a brandservant, even one assigned to the Warder guards. When he steps into the torchlight, I notice his skin is unusually dark for an Isfalki.

"Seen something you like, Wrangler?" I snap, pulling up Osha's hood.

"Maybe," he says suggestively, and it's loud enough for me to hear above the excitement of his dogs.

"*What* did you say?" I move closer to stare him down. His Warder commanding officer could have him whipped merely for speaking to me, let alone making such a comment, and if he acted on that look he gave Osha, he'd be saying goodbye to his family jewels as well as life in the Settlement. The Council has no tolerance for liaisons between Branded men and Pure women, the offspring of such unions having equal chance of being Branded as Pure. Isfalk doesn't waste Mor fertility on Brands.

"What's going on?" a voice calls above the barking. "Is there a problem here?" Brim strides up to the sled, stepping in so close that the fog of his breath engulfs the wrangler's face. I'm surprised to see the servant's almost the same height and build as Brim – freakish for a Brand, even one fit and strong enough to lackey for the Pure army. The wrangler doesn't answer, but he doesn't flinch either. His size unsettles Brim; I can tell by the way he draws himself up to his full height. "Get this off when a captain's talking to you!" He yanks on the wrangler's hat, releasing a fistful of long hair, black as a raven's wing. It's not cut in the Isfalki fashion, nor braided in the style of most Solitaries, but rather loosely twisted into messy locks and clamped with metal rings. It's clear he's no Wastelander. His skin holds the sun in it – far more sun than the Isfalki or central plains people ever see, even I know that. I glimpse the lick of his branding rising like the blue tongue of a snake from the neck of his furs.

So, this is the Brand who works in the Warder stables. I've heard talk of him in the dormitories. His height and build, skin and hair colour are enough to set tongues wagging all over the Settlement, not least among cloistered schoolgirls titillated by difference. Mother knows, they have little else to excite them and a ride across the snow with a Brand rumoured to have Reis blood will certainly do it. "Nara?" Brim's voice demands my attention. "I asked what the outlander said to you."

I should tell him of the wrangler's insolence. What do I care for a Reis fec? The glint of those curved swords against the flames revisits me, searing my heart. I open my mouth.

"Nothing," Osha says quickly. "He said nothing."

Brim glances at me for confirmation and in my sister's face I see all the taunts and teasing, all the times other girls call us *outlanders* and *wildlings* behind our backs and to our faces, making fun of our hair, our looks, our lack of pedigree.

"We're cold, Brim," I say. "Can we get going?"

The wrangler looks at me, surprised, but I only tug Osha into the sled, settling under the hood and wrapping the furs around us. Brim slaps the hat into the wrangler's chest and keeps it pressed there for a second, his eyes locked on him in warning. "Well, what are you waiting for, fec?" he asks. "You want these Mor to freeze to death?"

"No."

"No *what*?"

The wrangler holds Brim's gaze with an audacity that makes the air between them thick enough to slice. "No, *Elix*," he says pointedly, before stepping onto the footboards behind us.

Elix not *captain*, then? The title lingers in my mind as he urges his dogs into the night, the sled bumping from the packed snow to the fresh powder beyond the Walls. The wrangler ignored the military rank Brim has worked hard for on his own merit, using instead the title that marks him as a member of the ruling elite, the one he's been handed on a silver platter as heir to one of Isfalk's Founding Four. If I know Brim, he'll be smarting at that. But it's a clever taunt, masked in a veneer of respect that would be petty to punish. The wrangler took the measure of Brim with a single word.

"What are you smirking at?" Osha asks as we race across The Fold.

"Nothing."

But I guess I *am* entertained. Reis he might be, and disrespectful he certainly is, but I can't help thinking the wrangler's got some balls for a Brand.

Father Uluf drones through the mass in the Roundhouse Church. His turgid voice incants the liturgy while other priests tend the altar fire, wafting the heady fumes of burning clearfrage leaves over the heads of the congregation. Osha and I sit on the central stage with the other girls who are in their last year at the Mor school, while three of our group take pride of place by the altar, their Pairings to be made at the end of the rite. Stripped of our travelling furs, our mass gowns are designed to reveal our unblemished skin to full advantage, but flushed by the fire, I feel like ripe fruit primed for market. All too soon, it will be Osha and I taking our seats in the front row, no longer on exhibition, but about to be Paired, our unions secured. The thought makes my chest tighten. Brim was right. I might try to ignore the future by sneaking out to the Fornwood, but it's gaining ground on me whether I like it not.

I take a deep breath, greedy for the clean bracing air of the night through the open double doors, but all I can smell is clearfrage smoke as the priests load more of the herb onto the altar fire. My legs jitter with inactivity, my ribs strain against the leather thongs corseting my waist and I dig a finger into my hair. Frida tried to tame the thick frizz into a coronet woven with beads and threads but the tight braid makes my scalp throb. Osha presses her hand over mine, trying to still me. Her face is serene, her chest rising and falling elegantly as she watches the service. Anyone would think she was born to this. I notice more than one Elix heir eyeing her from the front pews around the altar, where the citadel's leading sons sit with their fathers, brothers and uncles. They gossip and ogle us unashamedly, as they're expected to, and I pluck and pull at my gown, feeling like a child caught playing dress-up.

I scan the pews searching for Brim. At formal gatherings like these, he's required to take his place with his uncle among the Elix lords and their heirs, rather than with his Warder unit. When I spot him, I notice a touch of mirth playing about his lips. He's been watching me, no doubt vastly entertained by my discomfort, just as he used to be when we were children, trying to make me laugh through the windows of the Mor school during lessons.

I'm about to pull a face at him when his attention flickers to his uncle and he's serious again. Lars Oskarsson is still squared-jawed, with a head of thick fair hair. A lock of purest silver streaks from his forehead to his crown like the path of a river through cornfields. I know Brim would have the streak too if he ever let his hair grow long enough. The Elix hasn't changed much since the first time I saw him – the day Osha and I walked into the Settlement, two shivering and half-starved eight year-olds speaking his name. *Lars Oskarson* – the name our Amma had drilled into us without ever telling us the who or the why. I look at Brim's profile next to his, proud and serious, donning the face of his birthright, his Elix persona. And then I remember Brim this morning, naked and staring at me across the forbidden water, making heat gather low in my belly. A far cry from the young heir who sits across from me now.

"The spirit of First Mother be upon you," Father Uluf intones, ringing his liturgical bell. "Holy Matriarch, let us breathe the purifying fire of your presence, untainted by the Great Malady, free of the sin of disease that weakens and withers." The priest cups his palms to the flames and draws smoke over the heads of the girls in front of me. "Mother, these Mor are the blessed embodiment of your blood. May their Pairings be fruitful, their offspring plentiful." He raises a benedictory hand to the Mor gallery, where Paired women show off their distended bellies or nurse infants – a blatant reminder of the future ahead of me. "For their children are your children," the priest continues, "The Pure fruit of your womb, who will become Warriors for the weak, Carers to the ailing, Leaders to the lawless and Shepherds to your flock of blighted souls lost in this wilderness of disease."

Father Uluf scans the Branded who are crammed in the standing space of the Roundhouse and spill outside into the snowy night, craning for a view past the lofty heads of the Warder guards who encircle the citadel born. Above the squall of newborns in the gallery, he names each role, indicating the tapestries hanging from the roof above the congregation. They detail four scenes from the founding of the Isfalk colony: Pure men and women defending the Settlement from attack, tending Brands during an outbreak of a pox, seated at Council inside the round chamber of the keep and, finally, in holy vestments administering rites to a mixed congregation of Pures and Brands. I gaze up at the tableaux: Warders, Carers, Councillors, Priests. The roles still exist in name, but their responsibilities have diminished in the century or more since their inception. I look over the pale faces of the Branded crowded beyond the

Pure, thinking about the slum kids I'd met in the Fornwood. I should have done more for them.

Osha nudges my attention back to the service. Mother Iness's sedan is being brought onto the stage. The real business of the Mass is about to begin.

Iness is the oldest woman I've ever seen, perhaps the oldest in the Settlement. Frail as a hatchling, her hair is nothing more than a wisp of thermal mist about her skull, and her skin looks thin as spring ice. The daughter of the Settlement's very first Elixion and the matriarch of the Mikkelson clan, her presence alone ensures silence in the Roundhouse. Hard to believe this tiny, shrivelled woman birthed fifteen children, and spawned an entire dynasty, while the Oskarssons, also a Founding Four clan, have only one surviving male heir: Brim. Even Pure blood can't ensure male progeny. Isfalk rewards fecundity and Mother Iness's shining example gives her the honour of joining the couples about to be Paired.

As if to reinforce her family line, Iness never goes anywhere without her ghosthawk, sigil of the Mikkelson family. The yellow-eyed tiercel perches on the arm of her chair, cocking its wings and letting loose a shrill as the sedan is settled on the stage. The sound makes me think of the woods and the tundra, of a wildness that doesn't belong under roof or behind walls, and I fidget with the lacings of my dress, feeling as trapped as the bird. The crone appeases the ghosthawk with a morsel of food, its golden talon bell tinkling as it shreds the meat.

When Iness raises her gnarled hand, the three young Mor in front of me rise from their seats. Their Pure partners step forward to lead them to the altar. Couple by couple, Iness nicks their palms with the altar knife, folding their fingers into one fist until a drop of blood falls onto the flames.

"Mother, accept these unions and grant them fecundity," Father Uluf recites, "for their Pure blood is the foundation of Isfalk. Through their purity we strive for the strength of the Old World, until you send your Blessed Daughter, Elna, to purify the tainted and heal them of their sin. For such will be her power and her glory. Until She Comes." The priest directs this last prayer to the Branded congregation, some of whom glance at the painted effigy of Elna to one side of the altar and answer with a chorus of *Until She Comes*. A good number stay silent, however, their arms crossed, faces closed as fists.

Mother Iness leans into her sedan with a sigh. "Let's get on with business, Fjäll, for Mother's sake!" she croaks to the Council leader. At the movement, her bird offers up another high-pitched keen, startling the smile from Father Uluf's face and making him scuttle from the stage. I can't help smirking. Iness may be as old as the tapestries above us, but she still has both Fjäll and Uluf tripping over themselves to do her bidding.

"Holy Mother's blessings be upon you and upon these Pairings," the Elixion addresses the audience, racing through the formalities, his thoughts clearly elsewhere. Fjäll has qualities that remind me of Mother Iness's tiercel: merciless eyes and a razor-edged superiority as he scans the gathering, as if he's searching for something and always finding himself disappointed. Rumour in the citadel claims Iness lets her bird off its tether more often than Fjäll. I'm close enough to see the silver fur of his Elix robes trembling under his impatient breath, close enough to catch the nervy twitch of a muscle at the side of his jaw as she keeps watch over him.

"This Morday Mass weighs heavily on the Council for several reasons. Firstly, food stores in the citadel have fallen to unprecedented levels this winter. Levies from the Branded village remain unpaid." He runs his eyes over the heads of the entire gathering, but it's clear his message is not intended for those in the Pure pews. "Warder collectors have been met with resistance in their attempts to call in food tariffs, and it grieves the Council that there are villagers who must be reminded of their obligations… reminded that living in a civilised and ordered community, sheltered and protected from the disease and lawlessness of the rest of the Continent, comes with necessary contributions."

The hall ripples with disquiet. I catch grumbled complaints tossed from the thickest parts of the Branded crowd. Warders stationed around the stage turn to face the villagers crammed in behind them, catching the eyes of their colleagues on duty around the far walls. Near the main double doors, I see three struggling Brands being dragged out, hear the dull thuds and grunts as they're expelled into the night. I've never known a Morday Mass to grow so fractious.

"I will remind you all that the supplies we collect feed our Pure mothers and their children – your future protectors and leaders of Isfalk," Fjäll presses on. "You are effectively stealing from the mouths of First Mother's Chosen." It feels like the whole of the Branded crowd erupts in indignation.

"Hell's poxes, Fjäll!" Mother Iness hisses at the Elixion under her breath. "You're like a bellows to embers, man. Must I put out all the fires you fan?"

The crone struggles to her feet and with a rap of her cane gathers the hall's attention once more. She makes a show of surveying the crowd, her breathing calm, her head nodding slowly as if in sympathy, corralling their attention. When she finally speaks, her voice, usually high and strained with age, has a new depth to it, the tone of someone used to being heeded. "Last year's harvest was poor. Livestock is depleted. The Fold over-hunted." Mother Iness looks directly at the Branded beyond the rows of Warders, voicing the very complaints she seeks to quell. The Elixion's mouth twitches, as if mustering his pride and his patience. "I know you're hungry and summer is still long months away," she continues. "But Wastelander raiding activity on our borders increases every day. In the last month alone Warder scouts reported the remains of no less than three Solitary camps smouldering in the western forests." The hall is completely still and silent now, spellbound by her admission of the truth. "How long, then, before the raiding parties of these barbarians turn their attention to our walls? How long before they return in greater numbers, attacking us

as they did during the seige of Heitval Pass? How long before
our Pure women become their prize, trafficked as bargaining
commodities for their chieftains and liege lords across the
Continent? And how long before you Brands become their
cargo – slaves traded to southern settlements riddled with
disease?" She pauses, letting these images settle in the minds
of the gathering. They know she's telling the truth: Branded
refugees reach our borders from time to time and those who
pass quarantine are soon plied for their stories in the village
taverns. Frida repeats them to us – tales of human trafficking,
of the chaos of the south, its violence, barbarism and disease.
"Our Warder army is already on half-rations," Mother Iness
presses on. "Shall we send them out to defend The Fold with
a quarter of that in their bellies? Is that what you want?"
She casts her rheumy eyes about the faces, her words slow,
measured, forceful. "Is this what you ask of the men who offer
their lives to shield you, who keep order to ensure Isfalk is the
last bastion of civilisation, the hope of the Old World? Men,"
she adds pointedly, "who walk your very streets?" She throws
a shaky arm out to the rows of Warders around the stage,
along the aisles, at the doors. They stand tall at her words, their
leather and fur-clad bulk imposing.

The crowd is quiet as falling snow. Only the crackle of the
altar fire can be heard, and the husky cry of a baby in the Mor
gallery. I feel the compulsive, almost visceral energy of Mother
Iness's influence on the stage and suddenly realise it has
nothing to do with bearing fifteen Pure children or being the
Settlement's oldest matriarch. The woman is a born politician,
a manipulator who can herd the sentiment of a mob in the
same way the wrangler mastered his dogs at the sled, cracking
the whip at the wayward before they got out of hand, keeping
them all yoked and pulling in one direction. But, like his lash,
her rhetoric isn't merely persuasive; it's a controlled threat.
Warder policing has been on clear display at this gathering. No
Brand is stupid enough to want a hungrier and more resentful

version of that in their streets. Mother Iness has been quick to play on such fear and, as she intended, the Branded stay silent, subdued.

"We're in agreement, then," she breaks the quiet. "Citadel food collectors will meet no more resistance in the village. And we can turn to other matters." She lifts her chin for Fjäll to continue, before collapsing heavily into her sedan. He hesitates a moment at her breathlessness. "Mother's love," she pants. "I'm not dead yet, man. Get the disciplinary matters over with. Or must I do that for you, too?"

The Elixion grits his teeth and motions four Warder guards to mount the stage. Each pair drags a Mor by the arms. I hate this part of the mass, the public naming and shaming of lawbreakers and troublemakers – sometimes unruly Brands and Warders, but often misbehaving Mor. It reminds me of Brim's words in the Fornwood – now it could be me up there one day if I'm not careful. Tonight, that message is driven home with double force. It always is whenever I see a girl from school being hauled before the congregation. Beside me, Osha draws a sharp breath.

"Estrid Halvar? Surely not?" Estrid is in the year below us, but her height and grace, her hair like ripe flax and skin pure as fresh milk make her the type of Mor everyone pays attention to, and not only in school.

Such admiration might have made her bossy or arrogant, but Estrid has always seemed the opposite – quiet and self-possessed, the kind of girl who chooses to walk the cloisters alone but soon finds herself surrounded by others, chatting and laughing, despite her lack of a Founding Four lineage to justify the attention. I don't think I've ever heard her say a bad word about anyone, let alone do anything wrong.

I'm horrified to see her here now, slumped before the Council, her face bloated and blotched from earlier tears, her woollen smock grubby from kneeling. She wears a broken expression, as if she's already resigned to her fate. Her hands

hanging loose among the folds of her skirt are the only sign
of any struggle left in her – long pale fingers flaring then
clenching to fists repeatedly, as if trying to rid herself of pins
and needles. I remember those hands. They touched me once.
I'd fallen on the ice in the quad, running late as usual, and split
open my knee. Estrid came across me trying to clean up in the
dormitories. I tried to hide the wound, not wanting a fuss that
might turn into gossip and taunting from the other girls, but
Estrid only smiled and took the washcloth from me without
speaking. She tended the graze, like Osha would have, and her
hands had felt so much like my sister's – gentle but capable,
drawing me in, reassuring me with that spark of something
trustworthy and wholesome – I let her take over. As far as I
can tell, Estrid's never hurt a flea, always played by the rules,
done what was expected of her. So how in Hell's poxes could
she have offended the Council?

"Estrid Halvar," Fjäll begins, his tone practised, dispassionate,
"The Isfalk Council has found you guilty of unnatural liaisons
with a Branded dormitory maid assigned to the Mor school.
Such relations are a heinous insult to First Mother's Natural
Order, and the holy duty of all Mor." He looks towards Osha
and I, towards the girls in our year seated alongside us, and as
a group we instinctively answer the prompt with the school
creed:

"Through Pairing and Progeny to Purpose."

"Such a crime," Fjäll drones on, "is punishable by the
ladder." My breath catches at the severity of the punishment:
the flogging ladder is the most severe penalty in the Settlement,
reserved only for the worst crimes.

A group of Pure youths below me begins to chatter, their
mouths tight with disgust as they assess Estrid. Not so long
ago, I remember them hanging over the arcades, spying on
her crossing the quad with very different looks on their faces.
Now, despite their sophisticated Mass outfits and refined
citadel manners, I can almost sense the racing of their pulses,

an animal excitement among them, like hounds in the Warder stables smelling blood in the air.

"In this particular case," the Elixion continues, "the Council was not unanimous in a sentence, however–" Mother Iness shifts in her sedan, glancing impatiently at Lars Oskarsson. Was it his vote that vetoed the Council? "Taking into account your youth and good record in the Mor school, you will be spared the whip and exiled to the settlement at Torvag instead. Do you accept your fate?"

Estrid is silent. Her mouth trembles. I will the tears not to fall, wanting her to hold on to that inner strength I felt in her, the self-possession and dignity I know she has. For a brief second, her gaze flicks to mine and I hold it, strangely calm.

When she swallows, it's as if I can feel it in my own throat, and as she draws breath, the air is steady, fortifying *my* lungs. The nod she gives the Elixion is dry-eyed, her head held high. And I feel it as a tiny victory, a thrill of pride within me.

Osha's hand clenches mine. She's as shocked as I am at Estrid's fate, but the press of her nails into my skin is also a warning. *This. This is what* you *risk,* her grasp says, *every time you sneak out to the Fornwood.*

I glance at her, eyebrow arched. *This is what* you *risk, too, with your medicines.*

"Annek Mikkelson." The Elixion has moved on to the other woman kneeling before him. She's older than Estrid, the gold threads woven through her dishevelled hair marking her as Paired to the Mikkelson family. The Mikkelsons are one of the Founding Four – Fjäll and Mother Iness's own bloodline. It's rare that a Mikkelson ever takes the stage for sentencing and I notice Fjäll's neck stiffen a little at the task before him. "The Isfalk Council, in consultation with Father Uluf, has found you guilty of neglecting your prayers to Holy Mother, causing the shrivelling of your womb and preventing you from conceiving an heir. Your punishment will be exile to the settlement at Torvag. Do you accept your fate?" Far from resigned, the woman's eyes flash with fury. Her attention jumps from Fjäll to Iness, and finally to an Elix man in the Pure pews, her anger a burning fever in her cheeks. Not only anger, I realise. Hatred.

"*You're* the one who is shrivelled and empty!" she yells down at him. "I prayed! Every matins and vespers, I prayed! You think I don't see how you want me gone, Igor Mikkelson?" She turns to the Mor gallery. "Don't you see? Even a Mikkelson Mor is dispensable. *This* is how they get rid of us... This is how they use us when we don't give them what they want. It's how she *feeds* you." At this Iness quickly motions the Warders. They tighten their grip on the struggling woman, dragging her from the stage just as she releases an arc of spit towards the crone in her sedan. It misses and Iness ignores the incident masterfully, but Fjäll fidgets, the ridge of his throat bobbing with distaste or nervousness, perhaps both.

Another guard hauls someone else to the stage. This time it's a brandservant. Her serving cap is skewed and her hair half covers her face as she kneels. But that delicate curl on the back of her neck – that branding – I'd recognise it anywhere. I hear a muffled cry and realise it's come from Osha.

"Frida Ingerson," Fjäll pronounces, "you have been discovered taking food from the mouths of your Mor charges." The air seizes in my lungs and I feel a wash of cold dread under my skin. "Such a crime is punishable by banishment from Isfalk and its Fold, to a life of survival on the tundra." No, no, no! This is my fault. I forced Frida to do it. "However, given the information you've revealed about a Mor student, the Council has seen fit to commute your sentence."

Information? What information? My mind races ahead of Fjäll's words. Does he mean details of Osha's medicines? They would have discovered her powder on Frida along with the food and questioned her about it. "In light of this, you will not be cast out of Isfalk, but instead removed from your position as brandservant at the Mor school. You will return to life in the village, with permanent loss of all citadel access and advantages."

The Roundhouse seems suddenly distant, the voices on the stage far away. I clutch at my sister's hand in panic. Did Frida just betray Osha to save her own skin?

"Do you accept your fate?"

I'm too busy watching the tears streaming down Frida's face, too busy trying to control my terror as I feel Osha stiffen beside me to notice what's happening. Hands grab my upper arms. I'm lifted by Warder guards towards Fjäll, pushed to a kneeling position beside the maid. I try to stand but they hold me down. Frida clutches my arm and close up I see there's a bright red welt blossoming across her cheek. "Mor Nara, please... please understand," she sobs. "I had to... my boy, my mother... they wouldn't survive on the outside."

But I don't hear the rest. Half of me feels a sudden wash of relief at the realisation it's me and not Osha they want; the other half is already predicting the long list of my infractions: truanting the Mor school, leaving the citadel unaccompanied, enticing a Warder officer to abandon his post and swim illegally in the Moon Pools... so many rules I've broken.

"Nara Fornwood," Fjäll says, "on the testimony of this brandservant, Frida Ingerson, the Council finds you guilty of impersonating a Pure woman in order to lead a life of privilege and status within the citadel." His voice remains aloof but a malicious glimmer of interest is now apparent in his eyes. "We have been led to understand that you carry the mark of sin in the eyes of Holy Mother. We believe you are a Brand."

Written on the Skin

What? My head reels at the Elixion's accusation. *Not a Mor but a Brand?* What in Hell's poxes is Fjäll talking about? Of all my crimes, *that* is not one I was expecting.

"Nara!" Osha says, rising from her seat and grabbing me about the shoulders. "There must be some mistake. This can't be true!" Her voice is breathless and her eyes flare with panic as she appeals to Fjäll. "Elixion?"

In answer, he calls two Warder guards. They lift her up, their knuckles white on her arms, almost carrying her from the stage as she starts to struggle.

"Osha! Where are you taking her?"

"Your sister must be checked thoroughly for brandings at the Mor school," he says. He motions Frida to get up and, despite her tears, the maid obeys, standing over me as the guards hold me down. With shaking hands, she begins to unravel the coronet she braided in my hair, fumbling with the pins. The sound of them falling to the stage rings out in the absolute silence. I feel her fingers, cold and trembling, unwinding the wild kinks of my hair, then parting the thick roots behind my left ear. She shows the Elixion my scalp. To my horror, his only response is to give her the altar knife. A soft noise of despair escapes Frida's throat as she takes it, struggling to steady the blade in her shaking hands. I try to jerk away, but a Warder guard locks my head against his thigh. Frida begins to shave and I wince at the dry chafe of the blade. Long corkscrew twists fall in a pile around my knees and I think of the way Amma would pare apples when I was little, letting me play with the springs of peel. How did I get so far from that laughing child in the Fornwood? How did it happen? How has it come to this?

I'm only vaguely aware that Frida has shaved the left side of my scalp, when Fjäll forces me to stand. He grabs my jaw, angling my head towards the congregation. The murmur that runs through the crowd leaves me in little doubt what they're seeing.

A branding. Hidden under the springy thickness of my hair.

Fjäll allows plenty of time for the scandal to be muttered to the far reaches of the hall, to the villagers spilling outside in the snow. Then he casts me behind him to stand beside Frida.

"It was so faint, so small, mistress," she whimpers. "When I was brushing your hair it was easier to pretend I'd never seen it."

"You've known all along? All these years and never told me?"

She opens her mouth to answer but Fjäll has started up again. I don't hear his words. All I can think of is Osha. Because now, suddenly, everything seems clear. The reason I'm so much smaller than her, why I've always been rangier, less... healthy-looking. You only have to take once glance at my sister to know they're not going to find a single brand on her. We're not the same, she and I. We never have been. And they're going to separate us.

"Do you accept your fate?" Fjäll's terrible monotone breaks my thoughts.

"What?" I flounder.

"Do you accept your exile?"

"To Torvag?"

"Of course not. You will be turned out on the tundra, like any Branded criminal."

Not Torvag, then. Of course not. They don't bother sending Brands there.

That's the irony – they're giving me the freedom I've yearned for beyond the Walls. But I'll never see my sister again. I can't be put out of Isfalk. I have to stay in the Settlement... at least in the village where I can get a glimpse of her at Mass or at festivals or the Warder Trials. Even seeing Osha from a distance would be better than never seeing her at all.

Suddenly, my elbow is pinned in a firm hand. Elix furs brush my side. I look up, thinking it's Brim, only to find it's his uncle. "Fjäll," Lars Oskarsson speaks up, "this is irregular."

"I guessed you'd have something to say about it," Fjäll says, tedium flattening his voice. "How would you like to complicate matters this time, Oskarsson?"

"The sentencing of this case has not been passed by the Council," he states. "The crime was unintentional and does not justify exile." Brim's uncle towers over the Elixion, and his tone is calm, matter of fact.

"Lars," Iness halts him with a sigh. The ghosthawk chatters at the sound of her voice and it feels like the entire hall turns to watch as she hobbles towards him. Nodding, she gives a phlegmy hum as if drawing from some deep well of recollection. "Yes, I remember now. The Flamehairs – you were the one who said we should take them in a couple of years ago."

"Ten years ago, Mother Iness," Oskarsson says.

"Ah. Time flies." She smiles, benign as any grandmother. "Lars, my dear." She shakes her head. "You and your *Branded* causes." But there's no genuine indulgence in her eyes, I can tell.

"She and her sister were checked when they arrived in Isfalk as orphans," he replies, maintaining the pragmatism I can only assume he's practised in Council. "When they were found to be Pure, I sent them to the Mor school under the banner of my house, as any other responsible Elix would. I've hardly seen them since." It's true: after that first charitable act,

Oskarsson felt no obligation to have anything more to do with us. Brim made up for his lack of interest, though, teaching me about Settlement life, becoming my best friend. Becoming much more, in my heart.

Lars Oskarsson holds Mother Iness's eye and I sense the air between them drawing tense as a pulled bow. There's history there, a long-standing battle of wills, if citadel rumours are to be believed. But over what, I have no idea. Brim has never told me the details and Mor school gossip is little interested in political disagreements, concentrating instead on Brim and his impending marriage as the vehicle that will bring the Oskarsson family back in favour with Iness and Fjäll.

The old woman breaks the stand-off now and turns to me. "Come closer, girl." She lifts her cane as if she might hook its handle about my neck like a wayward lamb. "Do you accept this fate?" she asks.

I'm taken aback. Is she asking my opinion? That is definitely irregular too, but I give it anyway. "No, Mother. I've never seen this mark before and I've never been told I had it." I look into the crone's milk-edged eyes. "I... I deserve to stay in the Settlement. Turn me out to the Branded village, but no further."

Iness grunts in surprise. "You speak assertively for one so young." Her brow furrows and her mouth hardens. She gestures for my hand. I step closer, but as I lift my arm towards her something stops me. Her presence this close makes my skin prickle and crawl. I can't explain it. It feels something like the tundra before a summer storm, charged with an edge of danger, but only I can sense it. Instinctively, I snatch away my fingers. She studies my face for a moment with an interest that feels almost surgical. And then she grasps my wrist, her gnarled fingers clamping onto my skin with an unexpected strength.

The moment we touch, the hushed crowd, Brim's uncle, Elixion Fjäll all disappear in an implosion of darkness. A rush of blood pummels my throat and I'm suddenly hot and thirsty.

When my vision returns, I'm no longer in the Roundhouse, but on a high promontory taking in a land so far removed from the Settlement it seems another continent entirely. The sun is only just rising, the wind is dry and dusty in my face, and I'm looking down at a patchwork of tents and gurs, a vast camp sleeping below on an arid plain. I feel a great wash of adrenalin surge within me. A noise tightens in my throat, a shrill of purpose, some strange battle cry... but it's a different scream that rips through my chest – high-pitched, predatory.

A ghosthawk skims up on a thermal from the camp below, its lonely cry shredding the dawn, the tinkle of its talon bell an afterthought on the wind. Iness's tiercel. Instinctively, I home in on the hawk's tripping pulse, until the beat of it begins to slow, merging with my own, becoming one. It circles around me and when I reach my forearm up, the bird settles on it with a satisfying flutter, as if I've been hawking all my life. I stare into its eye, ringed in hard yellow, bright as the sun, making the glassy black centre draw me in like shade on a hot day. But the reflection revealed there isn't my own. It's the face of another woman entirely – tall, silver-haired and white-skinned, unmistakably Isfalki and a Mor. And then I understand: it's a younger version of Iness herself. And I can see she's watching me.

I close my eyes. Fear and misgiving taste salty in my mouth, my skin shivering. When I blink, I find myself in the Roundhouse again, looking at Iness slumped in her chair, her face grey as ashes as she studies me. She looks clammy and frail, as if she's suffered all the fevers of hell itself. But I don't have the strength to wonder what just happened between us. My legs buckle and I sink to my knees, blood gushing from my nose and pouring onto the stage.

There's a clamour of shock and confusion, and then hands are on my shoulders, stopping me from falling further. "Brim?" I call out, but when I look up, it's his uncle.

"Get rid of her," Iness orders, her voice weakened but still commanding. At the questioning looks of Fjäll and Oskarsson, she hesitates, the first time I've ever seen her do so, and she seems to change her mind. "Alright, put her in the Brand village." She flicks an impatient hand. "If that satisfies your bleeding heart, Lars."

"Nara Fornwood..." the Elixion's words float in and out of my consciousness. "Do you accept..."

My fate. I see stars and think I'm losing my grasp of reality again. Except this time the little constellations that blossom in my vision are blue-black brandings in my mind. I touch the shaved side of my scalp. I'm no different from those slum children in the Fornwood, no different from Frida and all the other Brands who've served me for the past decade. My fate was already written when I was born. Written on my skin.

"Stand down!" someone barks. It's Oskarsson, blocking the way of the two guards who've come for me.

"Sir!" one of the Warders acknowledges, and when I look at Brim's uncle, I see the commander he once was before taking up his Elix mantle.

"This girl entered the Settlement under the banner of my household. Her eviction is therefore my responsibility," Oskarsson says. And without waiting for an answer, he takes one of my arms and calls for Brim to take the other. Brim rises from the Council seats, but when he catches my eye, I can see his face burning with shame, and I realise it's not for me but for himself. This scandal will tarnish his reputation, both in the citadel and the Warder mess.

Men in the Pure pews ogle us as we descend the stage and I catch one or two insults tossed at Lars Oskarsson as we navigate the aisle. *Fec lover. Agitator. Fire-Brand.* I don't understand why. All I know is Lars Oskarsson's fist around my arm, holding me up, moves me almost to the verge of tears. When we pass the citadel pews and through the ring of Warders surrounding them, the Branded crowd crammed into the rest of the hall slowly begins to part. Sunken eyes in pale faces scan me, their ranks shuffling closed behind us, until we're standing on the threshold of the Roundhouse's vast double doors. Beyond the weathered portico, it's snowing so heavily I can barely see the Old World market square, empty now and filled only with the curricles and sleds, the yelping dogs waiting to carry the Pure back inside the Walls – Walls I'll never pass through again. This morning my heart might have thrilled at that thought, but only if Osha was beside me, in agreement. Now I can only think of her. *Promise me you'll stay together. Promise me you'll look after her.*

On the Roundhouse steps, I lean into Brim. "Listen," I tell him. "You have to watch Osha for me. I promised Amma we'd always stay together. You have to–"

Brim silences me, eyeing the other Warders self-consciously. But he says under his breath, "You know I will." Oskarsson's grip tightens around my forearm as the guards exert their presence, bearing a sobbing Frida with them.

I look at the Elix's lined face. Close up, I see his eyes are green, weighted and almost regretful, and yet his words when they come are clear and firm, the words of a Councillor performing his duty: "Nara Fornwood, you are found guilty of posing as a Mor when your skin bears the mark of a Brand. You must be cast out of the citadel to live with your kind in the village. May Holy Mother protect you." His hand finds mine between the folds of my dress, squeezing my fingers, a gesture of good luck, before he turns me out towards the night. Stumbling into the crowd of gawking Brands who've filed outside to watch, I feel something in my palm, something small and round and cold as the biting snow.

My flimsy Mass gown leaves me almost naked to the elements, and Frida hurries after me, throwing her wrap about my shoulders. I want to shrug it off, to shout and rage at her, but I can't find the words or the conviction. Instead, I let her lead me dumbly through the night, away from the Roundhouse, but not away from the shame curling inside me.

I have no choice but to follow her. I have nowhere to go, no experience of life in the village, and no idea of what it takes to survive it.

For all her treachery, Frida is the only person this side of the Walls who might care anything about me.

We cross the marketplace and enter a maze of alleyways I think will never end. I feel like I'll be lost in them forever, like the legend of Orhir trying to navigate the diseased ditches of hell. We pass lit windows or doorways, the sounds of coughing or crying from within. Sometimes other Brands loiter in the shadows, and Frida shields me from them as we walk, although whether to hide or protect me, I can't be sure.

Finally, we reach a squat, half-derelict terrace far enough from the square that we're crusted with snow and damp to the bone. Frida unlocks a door in the middle of the row and it swings open on rickety hinges, the rotting wood split and ill-fitting under the ancient lintel. All is quiet within, but the hearth still glows and in its light I see an old woman and a boy fast asleep on pallets.

The maid takes off her sopping smock and apron, and from habit begins unlacing my mass gown. Dazed and overwhelmed I let her, unable to think clearly enough to protest. She drapes me in a blanket and sits me on a stool by the fire, fussing over my comfort, offering me the last heel of bread from the table and bowling up the contents of a stew pot by the fire – dinner that has clearly been saved for her. When I shake my head, my stomach churning at the thought of food, she finally breaks down.

"I know you'll never forgive me," she says, her voice low and desperate, "but please understand. They threatened to turn them out on the tundra with me." She turns a frantic gaze on her sleeping son and mother, her eyes liquid in the blush of the embers. "They'd never survive that life, not my Jarl, not so young and so soon after the last fever." Her tears brim and fall. "I'm sorry, Mor Nara. I'm so sorry."

The boy mouths words in his sleep, his pale hair a mop over his forehead, his small body twitching. "He always kicks off his covers, even when it's freezing." Frida palms her tears brusquely and rises to tuck a blanket over him. "He's worn himself out playing with the boys in the alley," she says, tutting. "I worry he might catch something again, but he fights me on it. *Mama, I'm strong, see?* he says. *The big boys let me play with them now. I won't get sick again, I promise."* She brushes his cheek and I notice his branding there – a blue swash from mouth to ear – punctuated by two or three raised scabs still healing from the earlier pox.

Frida clears her throat, as if swallowing down the tenderness. It's the first time I've truly seen her as a mother... as a daughter... as a grown woman with a life beyond the Mor school dormitories, beyond being my brandservant. Osha and I have loved her, yes, and helped her where we could, but have we ever really *seen* her? How can I condemn this woman for putting me second to her son when I've always yearned for a mother who would love me that way? How can I accuse her when she's only behaving like the kind of daughter I've always wished I could have been? How can I blame her for protecting her family first, when I'd do anything to be with Osha again?

She looks at me with that terrible regret in her eyes. "We'd sell our souls for the ones we love, Frida," I tell her, and she sinks to her knees before my stool, letting her sobs come freely now. I want to join her, to let out all the shock and fear and hopelessness, but I'm still too numb.

"Can you show me?" I ask her, when her tears have ebbed. She hesitates, worrying her lip, but then fetches a broken corner of mirror from above the mantel. When she holds it up for me and I twist my head, I can just make out the tail of the branding in the light of the fire. It's faint, delicate as dust motes at dawn, fine as a scattering of pap seeds on a summer wind. But it's there all the same, written on my skin, never to be brushed away. I lower the mirror and Frida squeezes my shoulder, until she sees I'm shivering with cold. She leads me to the pallet she's made up for me by the hearth and I climb under the covers, thinking of Osha, missing her breathing in the bed beside me. This is the first night in our lives we've ever slept apart.

When all is still and quiet, I open my fist. Inside is the small metal object Lars Oskarsson slipped into my palm on the steps of the Roundhouse Church. The soft flicker of the hearth shows a golden coin embossed with a series of glyphs I can't decipher. But what catches my breath is the pattern the characters form, a design as familiar to me as Osha's face, a shape that has been with us since our births, the question mark of our lives: the symbol on our pendants.

From habit, I reach for the leather thong at my neck to compare the motifs, only to find my skin bare. Frantically, I reach for my mass gown, opening up the bodice and shaking out the sopping skirts, but it's nowhere to be found.

My necklace is gone.

The Wrangler

The day after my eviction, I wait for word from the citadel – a message from Osha, a visit from Brim, even a Warder with a note from Lars Oskarsson explaining the mysterious coin. But nothing comes.

At first, I can't bear to leave Frida's hovel, to see my shame reflected in the eyes of others, but that night, desperate to know my sister's fate, she takes me to another dormitory maid who lives in the village. The girl tells us Osha remains at the Mor school, confirming what I already knew in my heart of hearts: my sister bears no branding; she's Pure. Only I was the imposter, the fraud, the fake.

I try to convince the maid to slip my sister a note, but she won't take the risk, telling me Iness has increased Warders in and around the school. And when I go to the south gate of the citadel to ask the guards if they can get a message to Osha, they only say it's more than their jobs are worth, eventually chasing me off with scoffs and jeers.

The next day, unable to face the stares and whispers of the Branded villagers everywhere I look, I head out to the Moon Pools, waiting for Brim, trusting he'll know to meet me there and bring me word.

But Brim doesn't come, not that day, nor the third or fourth day, either.

Restless and agitated, I kill time at the practice tree in the clearing where he first taught me to swing a sword. He carved a face into the bark of the hoar spruce when we were still children, and its ugly familiarity is suddenly comforting in a world where nothing seems recognisable anymore. It stares at me now – a grim smile with missing teeth and a fat nose that, if real, would have been broken a hundred times over, given the strike marks in the wood.

I take off the furs and loosen the jerkin I made Frida trade for my Mass gown. The pants, some village boy's no doubt, are a little tight in the hips, but the leather will loosen with time and movement. I reach for a quarterstaff from the weapons cache Brim and I keep hidden here, and I begin to swing, soon falling into the rhythm of strikes and footwork, the relief of taking out my anger and frustrations on this childhood whipping boy, who only grimaces mutely from the frosted bark.

Why? Why? Why? my stave rings out, keeping time with the endless round of my thoughts. Why did Amma not tell me Osha and I were different? She must have seen my branding when I was a baby, so why did she let me believe I was Pure like my sister? Is that why she taught me to hunt and not to heal – sending me out into the solitude of the woods and ice plains, keeping me away from sickness when patients came to the cabin? I'd watch her and Osha birthing babies, yes, but she'd always find me game to skin, firewood to chop or herbs to grind when Solitaries came seeking treatments for poxes and agues. Was she worried I'd fall sick? And yet she told me *I* was the strong one. *I* was the one who should protect my sister. Why would she say that when clearly I'm not?

Why? Why? Why? Why did she say so little about our parents? She told us our father was a Brand and our mother was Pure, like her. She let us believe we had the luck to be born Pure too. Except we weren't, were we? Not both of us. Clearly, I'm my father's child. I inherited his Solitary blood, the brandings on his skin. Children like me are the very reason the citadel forbids liaisons between Branded men and Pure women: the offspring of such a union could be compromised, a disappointing waste of Pure potential, the muddying of Pure blood. But why didn't Amma tell me I was marked? Why did she keep it from me? In the citadel, my mother's coupling with a Brand would have been scandalous, punishable by exile for the Mor and death for the man, but she and my grandmother were Solitaries, they lived outside of society. Amma hardly needed to keep my brandings a secret. So why did she?

A thought suddenly creeps into my mind, growing like a lana vine around a healthy sapling, hobbling my heart and stealing my breath. Did Amma keep it secret from both of us? *Did Osha know?* My sister used to brush my hair when we were children, just as Frida did. Did she ever see the mark? *Did Osha keep silent all these years?*

My lungs scream for air, and when it finally comes, I let the stave drop, leaning on the trunk to recover. That's when I catch a movement from the tail of my eye – something stirring in the crystallised underwood. "Brim? Elixion's cock! Finally, you show up!"

But it isn't Brim. A dog bounds from the trees, growling to a crouch two strides away. Its thick coat is the colour of moonlit snow and its eyes are blue as the glacier at Tindur Hof.

"Down, Rakki," a voice grumbles. The dog quietens, dropping to its belly. Stepping through the trees, the wrangler raises his chin towards my maltreated target. "Looks like a one-sided fight to me. I pity your friend."

"He's used to it," I say, still panting.

"I can see. Spend a lot of time waiting for your Elix, do you?"

My mouth falls open at his gall. "And you spend a lot of time minding business that isn't a Brand's concern!" I hear the Mor imperiousness in my bark – a rank, a life I no longer own. He smiles, clearly aware of the irony. Shame rises to my cheeks and I fall silent.

He holds his palm out, as if in truce, but something on it

glints warmly in the cold light of the glade. "See, if I didn't mind your business you wouldn't be getting your jewellery back, would you?"

I edge closer and recognise my pendant in his hand. Surprise softens to relief when I see it again. One small comfort in a sea of loss. "Where did you find this?"

"In my sled. You should be more careful." He dangles the charm from a finger. "It's well wrought," he says, watching my reaction. "You don't often see gold worked so intricately. Not in these parts anyway."

I can't meet his eyes – he could have kept the necklace, traded it for a cask of kornbru or the services of some trull in one of the village taverns. What does he want from me in return?

"It's bronze, not gold," I snap. "And it's nothing but a useless trinket – in case you're thinking of a reward or extortion."

He holds out his arm, nodding for my hand and smugly dropping the pendant into my palm. I slip it round my neck and inside my clothes, the cold metal at my chest like a reprimand for my carelessness.

"No thanks necessary," he says with a grin, knowing full well he wasn't going to get any. "But I know gold when I see it."

"Really?" I say, making clear I find that doubtful.

"What? You assume because I work with dogs I share their sophistication?"

"Not at all." I reach down to scratch his companion about the ears. "I'd never be so insulting to dogs." The hound rises to lick my fingers, wagging his tail.

"Down, Rakki," the wrangler growls at his dog's disloyalty.

"So, you want me to believe that you, a sled driver and stable hand, are also an expert in precious metals?"

"I didn't say I was an expert. But that's Reis filigree on your necklace... in case you're interested."

I think of Oskarsson's coin in my pocket and itch to take it out so I can compare it with my pendant and judge whether either are southern gold as he claims. But there's no way I'm revealing any more about my private affairs for some dog wrangler to blab all over the village.

I study his face carefully. In the daylight his skin is glossy brown as newly opened kasta nuts in autumn, his cheekbones high and strong, dark eyes more complicated than I'd first thought – a paler ring of bronze inside the brown. He's unlike any Isfalki I've ever known. Unlike the few outland brandservants I've met either, or the Solitaries I remember from life before the citadel.

"You're mistaken, Wrangler. My father made the pendant and he was a Fornwood Solitary." Amma told me that much at least. "There's no way it's Reis... even if *you* clearly are."

Snow squeaks as he shifts his boots, reading the distaste, the accusation in my voice and choosing to ignore it. He must have met with enough general prejudice about his origins to have learned to stay quiet about them, just as I did when we got to the Settlement. But my resentment is far more personal. I think of the strange, curved blades, the covered faces of the riders of my nightmares. Reis riders, the men who cut down my Amma, who set fire to our lives, changing the course of them so irreparably. I raise my staff, turning back to the grimacing target and landing a satisfying crack across its face. "You'd better go now," I tell the wrangler.

He retreats a little but he doesn't leave. Instead, he watches me strike and turn, lunge and block, his arms crossed, a mix of fascination and amusement in his expression. Mother's Dugs, I could have had him exiled for the way he's looking at me now. Except... I don't live in the citadel and I'm no longer a Mor. Still, if he thinks he's free to stare however he likes, he can think again.

"Am I amusing you, Wrangler?" I turn and flick the other staff towards him with my own. "Raise that and I'll show you how entertaining I can be."

He laughs outright. "Poxes, woman, where on earth have

you been learning your manners since you left the citadel? Helgah's Tavern?"

"So what if I have? It's no business of yours." I realise my mistake as soon as I've said it. Frida once told me Helgah's is well-known in the village as the haunt of trulls pandering to off-duty Warders with a penchant for drinking and brawling. "Are you saying I've got the manners of a brandwhore?"

"You did just ask to *raise my pole* so you could *entertain* me." He can barely keep a straight face. "Honestly, I'm flattered, but I think I'll pass for now. Your friend looks happy to oblige though." He nods towards my target in the tree. "He seems to know your moves and obviously likes being caned by tough women." How he manages to whistle for his dog with that grin plastered all over his face is beyond me. I'm speechless at his cheek, his familiarity. Almost.

"Just because I was exiled from the citadel doesn't suddenly make me some renter offering her services in a village back alley, you... you... poxy mutt," I spit. Embarrassed by the feebleness of this retort, I compensate with a skilful lunge, bringing the tip of my staff to a clean stop right at his throat.

He barely even blinks.

"*Poxy mutt*? Really, that's the best you can do? Drunk Warders pissing up the side of the kennels have more imagination than that." And almost before I can register it, he's ducked, spun around and pushed me aside. When I gather my wits, he's grinning, the other stave in his hand. I don't give him time to enjoy the triumph. Bracing my feet, I launch a stroke straight to his flank. But he anticipates it, deflecting with a left-handed block so quick and skilful I can't help but admire it.

I circle him, make a sudden feint to his thigh, causing him to lower his defence, then follow through with a swift uppercut. Brim would give me grief for that – the baseness of resorting to fists in stave fight. But I'm no Warder. Never had the chance to be, and I'm not going to pretend I'm one now. The punch sends the wrangler off-balance. I toss away my staff, seize both his shoulders, and bring my knee up to his groin. But he dodges, hooking my raised leg with his arm. Damn, but he's good – faster than Brim, and more agile. He throws me backwards and I lose my balance, falling flat and cracking my head against the packed snow.

"Shit!" he curses. "Shit. Are you okay?" I lie still as death, eyes closed. He thinks it's the end of the fight in me. Just as Brim used to... before he got wise to it. He kneels at my side, feeling my neck for a pulse. And I make my move. Lifting my boot, I aim for his chest, intending to send him sprawling. But he's too quick. He catches my leg and twists, forcing me to flip over. Sitting on my arse, he holds my face in the snow. "If I'd known you liked it dirty, we needn't have messed around with the staves," he says, chuckling.

"Get the fec off me, Wrangler!"

But he takes his time standing up. I roll over, drying my face on my sleeve.

"Don't give me that look," he says. "You started it."

I brush the snow off my leathers and when I meet his eyes again, he's studying me, his gaze faltering on the shaved strip of my scalp.

"Yeah, it's a branding. You want me to come closer so you can get a better look?" I grab the woollen nabhat that came off when he floored me. Frida stayed up knitting it, saying I needed to keep warm, but I think she knew I wanted to cover my shame... and possibly her own. I yank the wool down about my ears.

"You fight well," the wrangler says. "I'll admit it – Pretty Boy taught you a few moves."

"Not enough, obviously."

"No, just not the right ones."

"I see. And I suppose you're going to enlighten me? Shame you couldn't become a Warder. You're arrogant enough."

He rubs his knuckles along his jaw and I notice the small mole on his cheek that twitches as he grins. It's oddly boyish in the cut lines of his face, like it has no right to be there. "I'm no Warder. I'm not even Isfalki, as you well know. But since you asked, your stance is too wide, your swing too ambitious, and you're attempting moves that are too big for you. He's trained you like a man."

"In case you didn't notice, anyone I might need to protect myself from – Wastelanders, Reis, even drunken Warders at Helgah's – they're all *men*."

"And if you fight the way they do, you're bound to lose." His tone is matter-of-fact.

"Well, thanks for the vote of confidence. Brim will be pleased you think so much of his training. You do know he has the best record for hand-to-hand combat in the Warder Trials?"

"Who told you that? Pretty Boy himself, I suppose?" He chuckles again and I scowl at him. "Look, I watch those men training every day. They're preoccupied with upper body strength, the weight and length of their swords, the power they can throw behind an axe or a shield thrust. Speed is rarely their focus. Someone quick and agile like you could run circles around most of them, make them eat snow with a well-aimed kick." He points the toe of his boot to my knee, a strike I've used on Brim before.

I rub at the lump forming on the back of my head. I want to argue but I can't. The stables and kennels are part of the Warder mess and the wrangler would have had more opportunity than me to watch the Warders train. Plus, Brim has always focused on *my* weaknesses, rather than pointing out his own whenever we spar. It makes me curious about the wrangler's approach.

"All I'm saying," he continues, "is that you should play to your strengths. Fight as the person you are, not the man you think you should be... And use your feet."

"So, I'm supposed to take fighting tips from a Brand now? A blow-in from Mother-knows-where?"

He looks at me pointedly. "I'm not the only blow-in with an interest in combat, though, am I?"

I open my mouth but can't find an answer. He doesn't skip a beat. It pains me to confess it, but the truth is he's quick, gutsy and more skilled than any Brand I've ever met.

"Where did you learn to fight like that?"

He hesitates, as if reluctant to answer. "I used to train with my sister... before I came to Isfalk."

"Your *sister*?" Not what I was expecting.

"She's one of the best fighters I know." He pauses, draws a line in the snow with his toe, and studies it absently. Perhaps he's wondering whether to cross it. "Branded or Pure, male, female... where I come from, everyone is allowed to protect themselves. No one has to learn to fight in secret."

"And where is this veritable utopia? You can't possibly mean Reis?" He hears the scorn in my voice, the scepticism and prejudice I've inherited from the Isfalki... from my own childhood memories. And he turns away as if he wishes he hadn't told me, as if he regrets crossing that line in the snow. He makes towards the Settlement, whistling to his dog.

"Hey! Wrangler!" I shout after him. "What's your name?"

But he doesn't turn around. "Narrow your stance," he calls over his shoulder.

A Different Kind of Strength

That night, I hear crying. I get up from my pallet, trying to find where it's coming from, but I'm repelled by a wave of heat: Frida's cottage is ablaze. Except it isn't Frida's cottage. It's our cabin in the Fornwood, flames licking through the shattered windows. I wake with a jolt to find I'm bitterly cold, and when I reach to pull up the covers, my hand lands on the goose-bumped skin of Osha's arm. She's shivering inside the hollow of the greenock trunk, holding her breath, her eyes wide as a trapped snowjack's. *Shhh.* I put a finger to my mouth but make no sound, pulling her into my chest so she can't see the dark shapes of the riders who have chased us through the trees, their faces wound entirely in black scarves, as they always are in my nightmares. Except instead of passing by our hiding hole, this time one of them stops, circles closer, peering through the split in the bark. His brown eye grows bigger and bigger until, with a start, I recognise its almond shape. "We've been looking for you," the wrangler says. "Come on out." I press my sister into the damp spongy wood behind me. He straightens, finds his balance, raises a vast broadsword as if he's about to hew down the remains of the hollow tree.

Osha buries her face in my shoulder, "Narkat!" she cries, but I clench my fists until my nails cut the skin, forcing myself to look.

You're the strong one, see? Amma says. *She needs you. Promise me you'll stay together. You're safer, stronger together.*

I jerk upright at the sound of a sob growled in the dark. "Osha?" I call out instinctively, but the weeping isn't my sister's. It's mine. My Amma's voice is still so clear, so familiar from my dream, I'm shocked to wake and find myself on the pallet before Frida's hearth, the wind whistling through the cracks in the roof and door, cooling the tears on my cheeks. I feel the aching emptiness of Amma's loss all over again. Except now it echoes like a lonely cavern inside me, for there's no Osha dreaming in the bed next to mine.

My hand prickles with pins and needles. I uncurl my fist and find the coin Oskarsson gave me clenched inside. The metal picks up the embers of the fire and glints in the dullness of the cottage, like sunrise over the tundra. I pull my pendant from my neck and compare the two again. They're the same colour gold. *Reis gold*, the wrangler had said. If his words are true, where did my father find the wealth to trade for gold? How could a Fornwood Solitary have afforded to make one such trinket, let alone two? Amma said he had a talent for metal-working and made them at our births, but the wrangler was right, I've never seen detail like it from any smith in Isfalk. The skill and time for such Old World fancies died long ago in the north. And how did Brim's uncle come by a coin bearing those glyphs in exactly the same design? Was that made by my father too? Did Lars Oskarsson know him? It's unlikely an Elix lord would have much to do with a Fornwood Solitary... although, perhaps Oskarsson commissioned him to forge things when he was a commander in the Warder army – weapons or armour... I don't know. I wish Amma was here to ask. I wish I could swap these scraps of useless metal, however fine and pretty, for one more fact about my parents, one less unanswered question. And what I'd give for a single memory of them – the sound of their voices, the colour of their eyes, their smiles.

All Amma ever told us was that our father crossed the

Fornwood seeking her and her daughter for their medicines. His fever was raging by the time my mother found him, close to dead, a few miles from the cabin.

"Mamma cured him, though!" Osha would always cry out in childish satisfaction at this part of the story.

"Of his fever, yes. But she gave him a different kind of sickness... one she couldn't cure." Amma's voice would be wistful, but her eyes ever shrewd. "Your father returned again and again, claiming he needed your mother's healing touch. But he only left in a worse state than when he arrived."

"What was wrong with him? What was the disease?" Osha always wanted to know.

Our grandmother would only spread her hands on top of our heads and say, "You'll learn more about it when you're older."

I'd turn away in frustration at this. "I don't want to learn more about it," I'd sulk. "Not if it makes you weak and gets you killed." For only a month after our mother died giving birth to us, our father was cut down by Wasteland raiders. He'd been smithing at a Solitary camp in the southern Fornwood, trading work for goats whose milk would help keep us alive.

So, I grew up believing love was as dangerous a sickness as any other you were likely to catch in the ailing Continent. And I was right.

Love is what made Frida expose me, to save her boy.

Love is what keeps me here, waiting day after day for word from my sister.

Love is what drives me to the Moon Pools, still believing Brim will come.

I get up from my pallet, dressing quietly, so as not to wake Frida and her family, and push open the feeble door, heading out into the frozen dark. The icy alleyways confuse me, but in the quiet of the early hours, without the distracting stares and whispers of the villagers, I manage to find my way out to the slums, and then to the gate in the western wall. The guards on the outer fortifications let me pass with barely a glance – just another hungry Brand checking their traps in The Fold. But I cross the tundra as quickly as I can, climbing up the ridge to the Moon Pools, desperate to see if Brim will come or if he's left a note for me with our whipping boy in the tree. But my heart sinks when I find there's nothing there, the clearing utterly still and tranquil in the last hour of night. How can Brim have left me hanging like this for so many days? How can Osha? Surely there was some way she might have sent a message to me by now – through a brandservant or a bribed guard? Osha can be very persuasive when she wants to use her charm. I've seen it in action with Father Uluf and our teachers. Something must be wrong. She'd never leave me like this. She'd never want to stay in the citadel without me by her side... would she?

Promise me you'll stay together, you'll look after her.

Amma made me vow it time and again. After everything she knew about me, she still thought I was the strong one, the one who'd keep us safe. But how can we be together now? I need to get to Osha, to convince her that our only option is to leave Isfalk and return to the Fornwood if we ever want to live as sisters again. And I know we can do it. Amma taught us all the skills we need to survive a life in the wilds. We were already doing it long before we got used to our lives as privileged Mor.

I'm pacing beside the Moon Pools, my mind turning circles, when I hear the jangle of metal, the soft squeak of leather through the trees. And I know it's him. Brim calls my name through the steam, panting a little as if he's rushed here. "Thank the Mother, you're safe." He takes me by the shoulders, scanning me from head to toe. "But you're so pale... and you're trembling, look at you! Are you alright?"

"Cock's poxes, Brim! I'm not on my last legs from a few days in the Branded village." I shrug off his hands, making anger distract me from the wash of relief I feel at seeing him, the urgent desire I have to rest my head on his chest and cry. "So, you finally decide to show?"

"I've been twice before, but you were never here."

"And you didn't think to leave a message... or to come find me at Frida's? You didn't think I might have been waiting for you day and night, expecting word... one tiny acknowledgement that you were thinking about me?"

"Nara," he sighs. "I haven't stopped thinking about you. You don't understand what it's been like in the citadel, ever since–" He breaks off, as if he can't bear to mention what happened, to remember the shame of it. "I'm in an incredibly difficult position, can't you see? I'm a Warder captain *and* an Elix heir – I have a reputation to maintain on both counts. And you know very well my uncle already has Mother Iness and the Elixion offside in the Council." He rubs the back of his neck in frustration. "Iness is livid with Uncle Lars over you. She sees you as proof of his weakness – his sympathies towards the Branded. She's claiming the whole scandal has agitated them in already restless times. With all that going on in the citadel, I can hardly be seen walking the streets of the village looking for a–"

"A what? A *fec*? Why don't you say it? That's what I am, after all."

"Nara, please... try to understand."

"I don't want to *understand*. I don't want to hear your excuses, trussed up as citadel politics!" I swipe a hand across my mouth, trying to keep my disappointment under control. "I only want to know if Osha's alright."

"She's fine. She's still in the Mor school with the other–" With the other Pure girls. He knew as well as I did that they'd find no branding on Osha. He casts me a glance from under his pale lashes, as if he's considering all the differences between me and my sister – our heights, our builds, our complexions – evident for all these years and making so much sense now.

"Did she give you a note for me?"

He sighs again. "I heard you tried to bribe the guards at the south gate to get word to her." His cheeks flame. "It's all over the mess."

I imagine the ribbing he's taken from his Warder colleagues because of me, but I couldn't care less about that right now. I hold out my hand expectantly. "So, did she give you a message or not?"

He doesn't answer, only shifting his boots in the snow. "Brim?"

"She said to tell you she's well and to be careful in the village. Make sure you stay away from Brands who are sick."

"*What*?" That can't be all. I know my sister. She'd be desperate to contact me by now. Unless... unless her messages weren't being brought. Unless someone was encouraging her to stay silent.

"Nara," Brim says in exasperation, "I can guess what you're planning, what you'll try to convince her to do. You'll risk both your lives getting her to run away with you to the Fornwood."

"That's for me to decide, not you."

"So, she has no say in it?"

"What do you mean? Of course she has a say in it."

"Osha would do anything for you, Nara. But can't you see how selfish it is for you to ask her to?" He fixes me with that frown, the one he uses when he's rationalising citadel rules and conventions. "The Fornwood is no place for a Mor," he says. "Think about it. It's the reason your grandmother must have sent you to the Settlement in the first place. To keep you both safe, to give you the chance to lead a civilised life, not constantly on the lookout for Wasteland raiders and traffickers. And now you want Osha to give up her security, a life of comfort and ease, all to be with you? If you truly loved her, you wouldn't ask it."

My heart stutters and I swallow something bitter. Trust Brim to voice the guilt I've been pushing to the back of my mind, to name the risks I'm so good at ignoring. I sink to my haunches, cup the thermal water and run a wet hand over my face, hoping to ward off the tears that suddenly threaten. He's right. I know it in my heart of hearts. How can I ask Osha to leave the safety of the citadel? How can I expect her to live hand-to-mouth in the freezing conditions of the forest again, forever looking over her shoulder, always waiting for the night when another flaming torch destroys whatever life we've managed to string together? It *is* selfish of me, especially when Osha has already told me time and again that she doesn't want to go. I promised Amma I'd be the strong one, that I'd always look after my sister. But I never thought it would take a different kind of strength, a different kind of sacrifice to keep her safe – the sacrifice of giving her up.

I gaze at the steaming pool, trying to stay calm when inside I want to rail and rage. "Strange, isn't it?" I say. "Neither of us is allowed to bathe here anymore."

"Really? That's what you're thinking about right now?" He runs worried eyes over me again. "You look pale... tired. Are you sure you're well? You're not sickening with something, are you?"

It's the first time he's ever needed to ask about my health, the first time he's ever seen me as inherently weak, the first time he's treated me as a Brand. I feel like some long-standing family servant he's grown fond of over the years and feels responsible for. It makes me straighten my shoulders, hold my head up. "I'm perfectly fine. I can look after myself."

His expression is full of doubt. "You've been sheltered in the Mor school, kept away from the worst of the outbreaks and fever among the Branded. You need to avoid anyone who's ill as much as you can, do you understand? If you can stay fit and healthy, and keep your head down in the village, maybe when all this has blown over, I can convince the Council to let you take a job in the citadel."

"A job? What do you mean?" But almost as soon as I've said it, I understand. I'm horrified he could even think of it. Doesn't he know me at all? "You'd get me a job as a *brandservant*?"

"It'd be a far better life than scavenging the Fornwood, that's for sure. You don't have a lot of options here, Nara," he says, seeing my reaction.

"I have options. Of course I have options." But really, I don't, not if I want a chance at getting close to Osha, close enough to talk to her, perhaps even a chance at living under the same roof again. I fiddle with the thong of leather at my neck, pondering that possibility. And then I remember.

Reaching into my pocket, I pull out the coin Lars Oskarsson gave me. "Brim, why did your uncle slip me this on the steps of the Roundhouse? What is it?"

Brim examines the coin. "I've no idea," he says, perplexed. "I've never seen this before."

"It matches the design of my pendant, see. And I think it might be Reis gold."

"Reis gold?" He pulls his chin in a little, about to protest, but then thinks better of it. "I guess it could be. Maybe he kept it from his time as a prisoner."

"That's what I thought, too." As children, Brim would regale me with tales of his uncle's past – how Lars Oskarsson, a second son living in the shadow of his Elix brother, had become a Warder captain intent on climbing the ranks of the Pure army by taking on the most dangerous missions. On a reconnaissance trip to the Wasteland Plains, he'd been overcome by Reis raiders and taken for dead by the Settlement. In fact, he'd been convoyed south, as the story goes, held hostage in the deserts of the Storm Sands, before making a daring escape and embarking on the perilous journey home to Isfalk. Meanwhile, his brother had been killed in a riding accident, leaving Lars Oskarsson to take over the Elix title as well as the guardianship of his infant nephew.

I loved the stories Brim told me of his uncle – the distant travels, the dangers, the daring escapes. But Brim had only ever learned them from household brandservants and other Pure boys whose fathers were in the Warder army. Lars never spoke to his nephew of his experiences, and I didn't care whether Brim's accounts were true or simply the exaggerated heroics of a starry-eyed boy. I rarely associated them with the severe man I saw at Mass or striding distractedly down the arcades overlooking the Mor quad on his way to the Council chambers. But now this coin had me feeling as if fact had suddenly burst in on the fable.

"Why would your uncle give this to *me*?"

"I don't know." Brim shrugs. "Perhaps he thought you could trade the gold in the village for food and clothes?"

"But why a *Reis* coin? And one that matches my pendant?"

"I've no idea, Nara." Brim's voice carries the seeds of impatience. He might have been starry-eyed as a boy, but he's grown a lot more practical about his uncle's unconventional behaviour now that it has a bearing on his own reputation in the citadel. "Uncle Lars has always been a conundrum. The talk in the mess is that his time with the Reis was a lot more savage and brutal than I understood as a child and yet he keeps mementos of it, like this one." Brim tosses the coin back to me.

"He has other things from Reis, then?"

"One or two, yes."

"Like what? You've never told me."

"I don't know... there's a dagger hanging in his study and jewelled sand scarves... a braid with hair ornaments in it. Probably the trophies of war that he looted or stole as a soldier," he says nonchalantly. "I used to ask him about them as a boy, but all he ever said is that they help him remember past sorrows, that they're an incentive to create a better, more civilised future as a Councillor here in Isfalk." He scoffs. "Although I don't see how sympathising with Brands and getting Iness offside is helping him do that." His cheeks flush, suddenly realising how this complaint must sound to me... now. "Don't get me wrong, I think my Uncle Lars is a good man. He has integrity and fine intentions... it's just his opinions in Council and his timing, with things so unsettled at the moment..." He lets it go, probably remembering my snarky comment about political excuses. "Like

I said, I'm sure he gave you the coin so you had something to trade in the village. I know he hasn't had much to do with you since you arrived in Isfalk, but he did take you in under the banner of our house and I think he feels responsible. When it's feasible, I know he'll support me in returning you to the citadel. As a brandservant, you'll be protected, well fed, and you'll have a better chance at staying healthy."

As much as I want to fight it, I know he's right... again.

"You want to be closer to Osha, don't you?" he says simply.

I stare through the frosted trees, breathing the sulphuric air of the pools, feeling sick in the stomach. To become a brandservant, though? The thought makes me want to shrivel inside. "Promise me you'll look out for O? I mean, make sure she's not bad-mouthed in the citadel because of me... Make sure she doesn't end up paired with someone cruel or unkind?" I put my hand on his arm to make him look at me. "Promise me, Brim."

He sighs, long and sorrowfully, then suddenly takes me by the shoulders again. "Nara..." he begins, but his mouth can't seem to form any more words. His eyes grow darker, their blue turned to a grey as weighted as the tundra before a storm. He leans down, so close I'm breathing the fog of his breath and he mine. His thumb presses my lip and I think he's going to kiss me. But instead his gaze slides to the side of my scalp. We both know what he's seeing under the thick woollen nabhat.

Brim clears his throat. "I'll watch out for her. I promise." When he turns away from me, I'm glad of it, glad that he won't see my burning cheeks or the suck of my lungs for air like I've run through the Fornwood.

I gather myself together, collect my bow and quiver, and start to walk from the clearing.

"Nara," he calls after me. "It's the right thing, you know. You're doing the right thing."

I don't answer and I don't turn back. Why does the right thing feel like it's crushing my heart?

Outsiders

I distract myself from missing Osha by spending my days in the Fornwood or out on the open tundra, tracking and hunting. Frida doesn't like me leaving the Settlement. At first, she tried to convince me to stay in the house, trying to protect me from fevers and poxes I might catch on the streets, as if she owed it to Osha to shield me from the village. But Frida also knows me too well to believe she could ever keep me indoors for very long. Osha never could.

"If I didn't go hunting, we'd be half-starved by now," I argue, pulling on my suedes as Frida rekindles the fire for the day. "And try telling me Jarl isn't looking better for the meat." She glances at her sleeping boy and I can see in her expression that she knows I'm right. Other brandservants in the citadel have given Frida laundry work, and she rises with me before dawn every day to start her copper boiling. But it would barely keep the three of them in bread, without adding me to the table. One of the few consolations I have is putting meat on the plates of Frida's family, seeing the colour return to Jarl's cheeks, a little vigour in her mother's steps as she cooks and takes care of the boy. "Anyway, you know I have to get out of the village," I say, keeping my voice low so as not to wake the others. "I can't stand the staring and whispering. I thought the gossip was bad enough in the citadel."

"You won't stop Isfalki from talking, Mor Nara," she chuckles. "You're the most excitement they've had since Wastelanders entered the southern Fold four years ago."

"Great," I say, tone deadpan as I lace my boots. At least when I'm out hunting, I feel normal… useful, even. Let tongues wag. I don't care. I straighten the arrows in my quiver and strap the buckle across my chest. The first day of my exile, I retrieved them from their hiding place on the edge of The Fold, and now their weight on my back is like the embrace of an old friend, a familiar comfort when everything else seems strange and foreign.

"Be careful, won't you?" Frida tells me. "Some of the Warder reconnaissance were at Helgah's the other night, saying they saw signs of a Wastelander camp a day south of The Fold."

"I'm always careful," I say impatiently, but it feels good to know that at least she cares, especially when I've heard nothing from Osha or Brim in almost a scorenight. "Anyway, I don't go south. There's better game north on the ice plains if you know where to look."

"The villagers reckon it's too wild and open out there. Aren't you scared of wolves and bears?"

I reach for my bow and when she hands it to me, I smile. It's the first time she's helped me with my gear instead of frowning at me from the fire.

"The most dangerous part is getting past drunk villagers on my way back through the Settlement," I say with a scoff.

"What do you mean?" she asks, straight-faced. I should have known she'd probe beyond the joke.

"Nothing. I've always rubbed people up the wrong way."

"Which people?"

"People who've had a belly full of kornbru," I say, not wanting to make a big deal of it, but she catches my bow, making me look at her.

"Who?"

I shrug. "When I passed the tavern last night, the miller

stepped out and gave me a juicy gob across my boots. That's all."

Frida sets her mouth in a hard line. "If I know Heygor Lysson, that wouldn't have been all."

"Well, apparently, I'm a *fecking reckless bitch who should go back to the scabby Solitaries who whelped me.*"

"He said that? Bloated... greedy... son of a trull!" she spits, making Jarl stir.

"Woah, why don't you tell me what you really think of him, Frida?"

She covers her mouth, worried less about waking her son than cursing in front of me. Old habits are hard to break, but not impossible. I'm learning that too.

"Why does he think you're reckless?"

"He must have seen the game I bag – pine drey, ice mink, that willow-doe yesterday. No one scores that kind of quarry near the Settlement anymore. It doesn't take much to work out I've been beyond The Fold. But I reckon he probably thinks I've been trading with Solitaries rather than actually hunting it myself, because of my Fornwood blood and being a woman. That's why I'm *walking scum who'll put the whole village at risk.*" I pull the nabhat over my shorn scalp, covering the branding, remembering the miller's drunken vehemence, how quickly the village has forgotten my Mor rank. They've accepted me as a Brand far quicker than I've accepted it myself.

"Lysson has always been a selfish swine," Frida says, still outraged on my behalf.

"Can't really blame him for being worried. As far as he's concerned, I could bring all sorts of disease to Isfalk. You've heard Osha complaining about Brands leaving the Settlement plenty of times before."

Frida looks at me for a moment and draws a breath as if trying to reach for the right words. "No offence to Mor Osha, but... well, Brands from the Borg with bread in their bellies, like the miller, have the luxury of that kind of worry." She lets out a humourless laugh. "In the Sink these days, most of us are too busy wondering where the next meal is coming from to worry about the next bout of fever or pox." She runs fingertips over her temple, looking at her boy with soft eyes. "It's no good staying home if you're starving. I'm learning that from you."

I look away, her words heavy in my chest. I didn't expect to be anyone's teacher, least of all for such a hard lesson. Her admiration makes me feel awkward when she's the one who has put a roof over my head, who's already taught me so much about the village. I'm starting to learn that even among the Branded, life isn't an even field to plough. Those who live in the Borg, under the shadow of the citadel walls, work closely with the Pure and reap the benefits of extra food and privileges, while the majority are left to get by as best they can in the slums the locals call the Sink. Frida's a rare exception – she managed to land a citadel job because of her subtle branding, her good, clear skin and strong build. But she's Sink-born and bred, her house in the thick of the slums.

"You should see the children who come to my door, how their faces light up when I have leftover meat to share," Frida continues. "And that's all because of you, Mor Nara."

"I've seen them," I grunt. "Snotty little cherubs." It seems as if half the kids from the Sink are lined up in the alleyway at night, knocking on her door with outstretched hands. "And that's your fault, Frida, not mine. They know you're a soft touch."

"I'm not the only soft touch, though, am I?" Her mouth twists to disguise a smile. She thrusts a heel of bread into my hand and relieves me of my bow. "Sit down and eat before you go." She sets a bowl of cold stew from the day before on the table. I might go out into the freezing darkness before true-day, but she won't let me do it on an empty belly. "I've seen you with the young ones in the alley," she says. "Getting them to hang and dress your game… giving them cuts to take home to their mother's pots."

"So? I'm only paying them for helping me out."

She gives me a spoon. "Seems to me you spend most of your time showing them how to do it rather than being helped."

"Don't have much choice," I say around the stew in my mouth. "Little skelfs tail me all the way home. They pepper me with questions… and your Jarl's one of the most annoying."

She grins outright now, seeing full well the satisfaction I get showing the kids how to fletch arrows, how to string a bow and rig snares – all the things Amma taught me. It distracts me from thinking of Osha.

"Some of those *little skelfs* think you're a Fornwood witch, you know," Frida says, amused.

"Nothing I haven't heard before."

"They say you charm the game because your bag's always so full."

"Frida, you know me. Charm's got nothing to do with it." I swallow a huge mouthful, then lick my spoon, grinning. "I've told them – it's pure skill."

"Well, the less superstitious ones reckon it's because you were trained in secret by that young Warder, Captain Oskarsson."

"What the fec!" I nearly choke on my stew, then lower my voice, trying not to wake the child. "*I* taught Brim every trick he knows with a bow, and I could still out-hunt him blindfolded!"

She chuckles again and I realise she's baiting me. Scraping the bowl clean, I shake my head at her, then push away from the table. "I'll see you tonight." I grab my bow and quiver, and open the door, but nearly break my neck as I trip on the cluttered step outside. A small pile of objects has been laid there overnight, now crusted in frost. Peering down I make out a bunch of dried herbs, a pair of gloves sewn from snowjack fur, a few good fletching feathers, a bottle of what might be kornbru.

"What *is* all this stuff?" I ask Frida, drawing back from the threshold, which looks like it's become a shrine to some woodland god.

She comes to the door to look. "Just gifts. There were some yesterday, too."

"Who from?"

"From people round here… people in the Sink."

"For you?"

"No." She laughs. "For you. They honour you."

"What do you mean, *honour me*?"

"Families in the Sink are grateful for the extra food. They thank First Mother every day for sending you to us–" She breaks off, as if sensing I'm not going to like the explanation. And she's right. The spite of those in the Borg is hard enough to handle without the Sink thinking I'm First Mother's gift to the Branded.

"Frida, if this stuff is meant for me, tell them to stop. I don't want it." There's an edge to my voice, irritation and shame combined.

"It's their way of showing how thankful they are. They look up to you."

"For what? For living a lie? For failing as a Mor?"

"No," she says quietly. "For succeeding as a Brand. For being strong and brave and capable… and still being one of us."

Her words make my guts ache. I don't want to be a Brand. I don't want to be tainted, flawed, even more inferior than I was in the citadel. But, more than that, it's the look I've started to see in her eyes and in the eyes of the slum kids as they take the meat I give them – not just awe and admiration but hope, as if I have all the answers, as if they're desperate for some sign of leadership in me that simply isn't there. That's what sets my teeth on edge. Because it makes me feel even more of a fake than before, living one kind of lie only to be thrust into another, burdened with expectations that I don't know how to live up to.

"I don't want any of this," I snap at Frida as I step over the threshold. "Find out who left these things and give them back. They need them more than we do."

"People can't help being grateful. That extra food is the only good thing to come to some of them in a long time. Don't be angry with them, Mor Nara."

I look down at the sill, trying to muster my patience, to wrangle my feelings. "It's freezing outside, Frida. Shut the door behind me. And please," I pull my nabhat down low around my ears, "Stop calling me *Mor*." I always hated the title: perhaps deep down, I sensed it was a lie. "It's Nara. Just Nara now."

I head onto the ice, pushing further than I've tracked for years. The wind sings like a siren out here, calling me into the purgatory of the permafrost. Most Isfalki are spooked by the ice plains, seeing only barrenness and death, a frigid expanse of nothing. But Amma made me spend many a sunrise hunkered out here, training my eye to the tiny diurnal movements of its inhabitants, teaching me how to read spoor and scat.

It feels like she's with me now, hushing my busy mind, stilling my restlessness, making me find the patience every good hunter needs, even though the air freezes in my nostrils and my fingers feel like they'll hardly be able to draw my bow.

Sure enough, I'm rewarded with a movement: a rosy blur, a hint of breath. I spot my mark. It's a fully grown melrakki, not red or silver like most tundra's foxes, but pure white – all but its pink nose and eyes, the blush of its inner ears. In all my years of hunting, I've never spotted an albino fox, not alive anyway. I saw the pelt of one once, but that was many years ago, a memory I haven't revisited in a long time. On my stomach in the snow, I lie motionless, only my eyes moving as I track the fox. Its gait is delicate, its whiskers twitch, one paw elevated as it stops to scent the air. I'm downwind, but I'll need to be silent, accurate – melrakki are quick, will even mount an attack if they're guarding a den of kits in the forest. I rise to one knee, holding my breath as I always do when I line up. My pulse is loud in my ears, blood pumping with anticipation, but over the top of it I can make out a quicker rhythm – the heartbeat of the fox. I home in on it, imagining it slowing, calming, synchronising with mine, until I'm barely focused on the measured movements of my mark, only the steady lulling cadence of our synchronised hearts. My bow sings of the connection. There's a soft *pock*, the residual shiver of the string, the sad perfection of a hit.

A few minutes later, I'm tugging my arrow from the fox's eye. A clean headshot a double boon, for the pelt will be unpunctured. Frida will be able to trade a skin this rare for at least a month's worth of staples like flour and oats and salt, even if stringy melrakki meat isn't the best addition to the stew pot. Under my hands the fur is so white it blushes pink in the sunrise, and I recall that other albino fox pelt. It was on the shoulders of a spae-wife who'd appeared at the Moon Pools not long after Osha and I had started our courses. We'd begun going there with other Mor when the time came for the monthly cleansing rite, and we'd spotted the witch watching us between the trees. The older girls called her the Blood-wife on account of her hands and nails, stained with what looked like blood, the red stripe daubed across her eyelids and the bridge of her nose.

This pelt is much whiter than the grubby stole the witch wore. Pleased with myself, I set my skinning knife to the fox's sternum and tug it deftly to the tail. The wet innards seethe across the snow like they're still alive and their steam engulfs me with a metallic tang. Suddenly dizzy, I sit down, head between my legs, waiting for the nose bleed to come. But just as it begins to drip, the wind gusts behind me, and there's a beating of wings, a piercing shrill. Spinning, I glimpse a mad ripple of brindled feathers, taloned feet spread wide, aiming straight for my throat. I reel backwards and fall, smacking the air from my lungs. The ghosthawk screams in my face as it claws my furs, its black pupil swallowing me like a hole punched in the ice, shadows moving in the slick depths. They merge and sharpen... and then I'm looking at Amma kneeling in the moonlight as horses skitter, Osha's molten hair, lit by flames, the glint of a curved sword. Another screech shreds the images in two and fear paralyses me as I focus on that hooked beak, waiting for my throat to be ripped out, my lifeblood to gush forth, warm and metallic as the fox's. But death only feels like a frantic beating of wings and a warm heavy weight crushing my chest. When I open my eyes, feathers drift like fat snowflakes, the ghosthawk already wheeling away into the dawn.

The weight on top of me shifts and my lungs suck greedily at the frozen air. A sharp pain sears the base of my throat and across my collarbone. I roll onto my side, dazed and trembling.

"You attract trouble like shit attracts flies, you know that?" The wrangler is panting beside me, his face obscured by his breath.

"You," I manage, and it takes all my strength not to let it turn into a sob. I press a palm to my throat as if to check it's still there. He squats and reaches across to pull open my furs. I knock his hands away.

"Don't flatter yourself," he scoffs, examining the gash the hawk has left behind. He grips my collar with one hand and packs snow over the wound with the other. I wince but the cold feels good against my skin. "It's shallow, but it'll need dressing, so it doesn't get infected. Ground flame bark should do it. There's a tree not far from the pools."

"I know," I say impatiently, batting him away again.

"That's right, you collect it for you sister... or used to."

"Mother's tits! Have you been stalking me, Wrangler?"

He stands, grumbling as he brushes snow from his furs. "No need for thanks. Happy to beat off rogue raptors so you can keep that tongue in your head. Seems it's the sharpest weapon you own..."

I ignore the insult, too curious about what he's doing here. "You happened to be on this remote stretch of glacier at the same time as me, huh?"

He shrugs and gestures to his sled, a good distance across the ice. "Dogs needed exercising."

I shake my head, making it clear I don't buy it, but he pays me no heed, shielding his eyes with his palm and following the flight of the tiercel south in the direction of the Settlement.

"That was Iness's bird, wasn't it?"

He frowns, then nods, and something about the admission makes me feel clammy inside my furs. "It was probably attracted by the fox's blood – easy prey," I say. But he only gives me a dubious look before turning away, saying nothing. "I was off guard, distracted with gutting my kill," I tell him, ashamed I let the hawk surprise me so easily. Why do I feel the need to justify myself to him? "I've only seen an albino melrakki once before."

He examines the creature, its fur rippling in the wind, its dead eyes hard as glacier stones, and I hear him recite something over it, foreign words, quick as a curse, strange as a spell. They make me think of those Reis riders, their covered faces, their strange blades. I want to ask him what he's saying, but he stops when he sees me looking. "The Isfalk think white melrakki are so rare," he says, clearly intending to distract me. "But there's enough of them out here if you know where to look. They're stealthy, that's all, good at blending in, disguising themselves in plain sight… not unlike someone else we both know." He arches an eyebrow and I know he means me. It takes all my effort to swallow my retort. I'm starting to get wise to his baiting and I won't give him the satisfaction this time. I concentrate on dressing the quarry.

"I bagged an albino melrakki once." He can't handle my silence.

"Really?" I say, keeping my voice flat with boredom.

"Gave it to the spae-wife."

"The *spae-wife*?" Knife in hand, I turn to look at him. "You mean the spooky one who sometimes camps near the Moon Pools? The one they call the Blood-wife?"

"Got your attention now."

"You're saying her pelt came from you?"

He nods.

Osha and I must have only been about twelve when we saw the witch at the Moon Pools wearing the white fur. And yet the wrangler looks no more than two or three years older than me. "You tracked an albino melrakki, managed to fell it, then gave it to the Blood-wife, all before you had stubble?" I let out an incredulous laugh.

He folds his arms, indignant.

"Why in Hell's poxes would you do that?"

"Why does anyone give anything to a spae-wife? I wanted something in return," he says simply.

"What did you want?"

He looks up from the fox, his expression suddenly closed, a muscle in his jaw working. I've pried, drawn too close.

Deflecting, he says, "Obviously you know about her and the pelt she wears. Perhaps you've paid her a little visit of your own?"

"Of course I haven't! Mors go to Holy Mother and her priests with their problems, not heathen spae-wives." But I quieten as I remember the vision of the witch in the woods. "I only know about the fur because she turned up one time at the Moon Pools during a cleansing rite," I tell him. "Scared the blessed breath from us with all that white clay caked on her face, and her eyes masked in blood."

I run over the memory, as much for myself as him. "She materialised between the trees like a mist siren and the girls started screaming, thinking she was putting a curse on them so they'd never conceive."

"Ah yes, Uluf likes to feed superstitions like that – keeping you all faithful to Mother's laws... and the citadel's." I look up at him, surprised by that. Against the glare of the permafrost, that brighter ring in his eyes seems searching now, almost as intense as the hawk's. "What happened then?" he asks.

"Well... she kept saying *Where are they? I need to see them.* And she managed to slip through our guards – no idea how she did it. When she got near Osha, I jumped up to shove her away, but one of the Warders finally pulled his finger out of his arse and grabbed hold of her. She looked at us all gathered in the pools and said, calm as a spring morning, *You girls stay together, do you hear? Don't let them separate you. You're stronger together.* The guard gave her a clout and dragged her away in the end."

I begin tying the fox onto my pack. "You reckon it's true what Father Uluf says? That under all the blood paint, her face is entirely covered in brandings?" I stop briefly to picture it. "I guess living alone in the sulphur of the volcanos doesn't help the old bitch either. That'd drive anyone crazy."

The wrangler's quiet, cleaning his hands in the snow, distractedly. And then, as if out of nowhere, that mole in his cheek jumps again and he offers me a grin so contagious I have to fight to hold back my own. I lose.

"What's so funny?" I ask.

"I'm thinking she's not the only crazy bitch in these parts."

"Me? Are you talking about me, Wrangler?"

He casts his eyes around the vast and empty glacier. "Is there anyone else here reckless enough to track game alone on the ice plains? To stalk the Fornwood under the noses of Wastelanders?" He pauses, pins me with a look. "Or lunatic enough to think they can break their sister out of the most fortified citadel in the Continent?"

I drop my grin. "What makes you think I'm going to do that?"

"You seem intent on making the stableboy-halfwit connection."

"And you seem intent on thinking you know me."

"I know you at least as well as Pretty Boy does, Na'quat." How in hell's poxes can he know about that nickname? Osha only ever uses it in private. Did he overhear her in the sled on the way to Mass?

"It's pronounced *Narkat* if you must know. And don't call me that."

"Why? Does it bother you?" He chuckles. "It's a good

comparison – the red hair, the hunting." He curls his fingers and rakes the air, "Those sharp claws."

"Fec off, Wrangler." He's obviously seen fleet-lynx on the plains when he runs his dogs.

"Why, do you prefer Snar Grim? *Scourge of the Snows*? Perhaps the Isfalki name panders more to your pride?"

I refuse to let him see my anger. "Your arrogance is staggering, Wrangler," I say, as calm as I can. "You know nothing about me, whereas *Pretty Boy*, as you insist on calling him, is like a brother. We grew up together."

"A brother, huh? And yet here *I* am beating raptors from your throat, while he... well, where is he exactly? Can't say I've seen him around much of late."

"It's complicated. He's... Son-of-a-trull! I don't need to be explaining our relationship to a fe–" I stop.

"To a fec? You should say to *another* fec, surely?"

"To a fecking Reis! That's what I should say!" I bite out. He's silenced by that. Finally. I want to feel good about shutting him up, but after what he did for me with the hawk, I don't. I only feel confused. "Just stay the hell away from me, Wrangler." I hoist the pack on my shoulder, pull my nabhat down against the snow that has begun to swirl, and make off across the ice.

"Wait!" he calls after me, his voice buffeted by the wind. "Hey!" But I don't turn around. "Please, Nara!" My name in his mouth, the effort it must have taken to say it after what I called him, makes me stop. When he catches up, ice still clumps in his hair, half windswept from its rings, and he has blood smeared on his cheek. I wonder whether it's mine or the fox's. He looks like he almost prowled the tundra himself, half-feral.

"If you're seeking answers, you could do worse than the Blood-wife," he says.

"And what makes you think I want answers?"

"Don't we all?"

I step away, as if to go.

"Your pendant," he says. "Your sister has a matching one, doesn't she? I think the Blood-wife might know something about them."

"Your snooping is downright creepy, Wrangler, do you know that?"

"Look, I'm simply saying she could be worth a try. She's been around a long time – almost as long as Iness." He squints across the open plain. "Besides, outlanders have the advantage of looking in."

I'm surprised by that last part. I look him over again, thinking of his murky past, of my own, of the Blood-wife's. We're all outsiders in our own way, on the periphery, observing but not truly included. I remember again the leathery white face of the witch, her words – *stay together... don't let them separate you... you're stronger together.* They were Amma's words, too, weren't they? And something comes to me then in a rush of realisation, a connection I hadn't made before. I'd always thought the witch was speaking to all of us Mor that day at the pools. But what if her message was for Osha and me alone, the only other *outlanders* in the group. Why would she give us the same message as our grandmother? Did they know each other? Did she know us?

"The Blood-wife hasn't been spotted around these parts for years. What makes you think you can find her now?"

That pretty mole jumps in his cheek as if waiting for the precise moment to draw attention to itself, and I imagine the smile that follows could open many a girl's legs. "Well now, Little Scourge, if you wanted me to take you to her, you only had to ask."

The Blood-Wife

It's midday by the time we reach the edge of the volcanic fields of Edfjäll, but the light still struggles weakly through the sulphurous mists. My throat tightens from the stench, and the dogs hitched to the sled bicker and whine, spooked by the place. Trusting their instincts, I find myself suddenly hoping the Blood-wife is out, trawling the geysers for more mud make-up or foraging ingredients for whatever potions and poisons she concocts. I think of how Osha would take me to task if she knew where I was: *Every time Brands search out those hawkers they risk bringing back more than nonsense cure-alls.* I'm risking more than swallowed pride letting the wrangler bring me here. I could catch something from the witch and end up passing it on to little Jarl. Why am I so impulsive? Why do I always act first and think later?

I stay in the sled, casting my eyes over the Blood-wife's hut. Unfortunately, it shows every sign of being occupied, chimney smoke snaking a blue line through the vapours.

"You getting out or not?" the wrangler says, watching me rub the pendant at my neck as if it's some lucky charm. "Don't tell me the Scourge of the Snows is a tiny bit nervous?"

"Shut the fec up, Wrangler."

He offers me a hand but I knock it away. "If you're worried about catching something, take a look around you." He scans the bleak and empty horizon, not another soul out here as far as the eye can see. "You think she chose to live out here for the social life?"

"I'm not concerned for myself. I'm thinking about Frida's family."

"Well, you should be more worried about what you can catch in the Sink. If you haven't already fallen sick wandering the alleyways of that stinking cesspool of contagion, then you're not going to." He scoffs. "Anyway, Frida's probably put you at risk more times over the years than coming here."

"What do you mean?"

"She's tended you as a maid since you first got to the Settlement, right? So, she's probably exposed you to all sorts of slum fevers and sicknesses in that time. I'd say you're already pretty resilient... especially since your little deception has kept you nicely fed and healthy."

"It wasn't a deception! I had no idea what I was... who I am."

"Then get out of the sled and let's see if we can find out."

"Cock's poxes but you're a pain!"

He grins at me like it's a compliment. "Come on, Scourge, timidity doesn't look good on you."

It doesn't feel good either, but I won't admit he's right. Fear never stopped me before, and I'm not going to let it start now just because I'm a Brand and can add disease to the list of dangers.

I want answers more.

The witch's bothy nestles between two black hills of solidified magma, a deep layer of snow on the squat roof, which I imagine would be bright green with sod in summer. As we approach, I notice a garden out front where the dead tops of cultivated plants poke above the snow drifts. Tiny frosted windows show imprints of bunched herbs hung against the panes and there's the vague smell of something on the boil. The location might be desolate, but the homeliness of the cottage surprises me.

"What? You thought she lived in a cave?" the wrangler says.

From the house I can hear the clank of pots, the sluice of water, someone busy at chores. The noise stops, a window creaks open and a woman's thin voice calls out, "If you're coming in, you'll need to put your shoulder to the door. It's swollen again." She sounds nothing like the ranting witch I remember from the Moon Pools.

The wrangler shoves the door and we're engulfed in a warm infusion of smells: drying herbs and roots, a brew steaming above the fire, something recently ground in a mortar. The spae-wife faces away from us, elbows deep in a bucket. When she turns, I see that she's almost as wrinkled as Iness herself, her grey hair in two long braids, her height shrunken and a little stooped without the bulk of furs, her face without its white clay and red-slashed eyes almost kindly. She crosses the room, unconcerned that blood completely engulfs her arms to the elbows, dripping from her hands and smearing the front of her apron.

I must flinch at the sight for she catches my reaction and scoffs. "It's *dye*. Red bearberry, bush lichen and salt. That's all." Her black eyes glitter with amusement. "The citadel seems to like this colour."

I think of the blood-red doublets of Isfalki Councillors, the red threads stitched into Warder boots and jerkins. Bearberry is rare and only grows around the eastern tundra, making the dye a status symbol among the Pure. I understand now where it comes from, how the spae-wife might trade for supplies during the long winters up here alone. The *Blood-wife*. So, the citadel damns the witch and buys her wares: yet another of the Settlement's hypocrisies.

"Want me to fix that door for you, Frenka?" the wrangler asks the old woman.

"No. Between that door and my bones, I feel the coming of the spring rains, and the snows in autumn. Leave it, Nixim." I dart a look at the wrangler. *Nixim*. So, that's his name. And he knows the witch personally, evidently plays the handyman to her like a grandson. What else has he not told me?

The Blood-wife dries off her arms on her skirts, all the while staring at me with unashamed interest. "I've been waiting for you these six years, girl." She squints at the braid that falls over my right shoulder, what's left of my hair snaking out from my woollen hat. She picks it up – red-stained fingers twisting the plait in the light of an oil lamp hanging above the table – then she raises it to her nose and sniffs, like she's identifying some root or herb. I step back, yanking my hair away and she laughs. "Indignant," the Blood-wife says in a tone of approval, "and touchy. You'll have your hands full with this one, boy." I look at the wrangler. A deep colour spreads across his cheeks that I've not seen before. The crone's dry lips crack into a grin.

"We're here for her, not me, Frenka," the wrangler says impatiently. "Will you read her or not?"

"Will she let herself be read, that's the question. I only lay hands on the willing, you know that."

Their cryptic talk sets me on edge, and I get the growing feeling I'm the riddle. "Hey," I snap, "I don't know what kind of understanding there is between the two of you, but unless you start letting me in on it, I'm out of here." I lay my fists on the rough wood of the table, my face prickling with anger. "What are you not telling me, Wrangler?"

"If you want answers, girl, I must read you," the Blood-wife says simply. "Isn't that why you let him bring you? For answers?"

"I came because... because I'm curious about this–" I pull out my pendant. "He said you might know something about it. That you've been around a long time." But the witch barely looks at the necklace, as if it's somehow irrelevant, as if she's almost disappointed by it. "I want to know... I..." Her gaze as I flounder is unflinching, as if she's peeling away the words, stripping me bare. And then suddenly I find I'm dragging off my hat to reveal my branding, unnerved by my own frankness. I hadn't expected to show her my marks. I'm still uncomfortable revealing them. "I want the truth about my parents," I say finally. And it feels like a confession.

"Sit," the Blood-wife grunts. Taking two horn cups from a shelf, she motions the wrangler to fill them from the pot on the fire. When he returns with the steaming contents, she withdraws a tiny vial from her apron and administers a single tear of liquid into each cup with a dropper. "Drink it." We sit at the table, the lamp casting a ring of light over our hands – mine white and fisted, the witch's gory red. She swallows a mouthful of the tea, but I sniff my cup warily. I can smell some common Isfalki herbs – sleep's bane and heartswort. But there's something else, something smoky, like the heady scent of the Wastelander grog, dramur vit.

"What's in this brew?" I ask.

She pouts, amused, but her voice is sharp as flint. "Answers," she says, draining the cup in one motion despite the tea's heat.

"I'm not drinking this."

She gets up and begins to potter around the kitchen. "Do as you please." She really couldn't care less whether I drink or not, and she seems perfectly well after knocking it back. The wrangler crosses his arms, one foot against the wall, looking bored. After a while, curiosity gets the better of me and I venture a small sip. It tastes like the scent of the autumn woods, and it's warming after our ride across the frozen plains. As its heat reaches my blood, I feel myself melting. I drink some more. The wrangler watches me intently now.

"What? Am I supposed to rant and rave?"

The Blood-wife snorts. "Indignant, touchy *and* impatient." I'm about to shoot a retort when I realise the dim room has grown brighter. Everyday objects – a spoon, the mortar and pestle, the hearth with its spitting embers – have become intricately defined, offering the wonder of newness. My head feels clear and sharp as a spring morning, even though my senses seem to merge into one another: the bright red hands of the Blood-wife becoming the taste of wild berries fresh from the Fornwood, the wrangler's dark skin warm and sweet as roasting kasta nuts, the feathering of a muscle in his jaw like the beating of a night owl coming to roost.

"Give me your hand, child," the Blood-wife says from far away. I feel the force of her drawing me like a magnet, becoming stronger the closer our fingers get, as I had with Mother Iness. The moment our skin touches, the room, the wrangler, the witch herself, all disappear in an implosion of darkness and I'm left with a rush of adrenalin pummelling my throat.

When my vision returns, I'm once again on that high promontory looking over the desert plain – exactly the same view I'd seen with Iness. There's the dry wind in my face, the patchwork of tents and gurs, the sleeping camp spread below in the valley. I listen for the cry of Iness's hawk, but this time it doesn't come. Instead, I hear the jangle of bridles and bits, the nicker of horses, and I realise I'm mounted. When I turn in the saddle, there's a woman wrapped in sand scarves beside me, and beyond her a sea of riders. In the middle distance a throng of foot soldiers watches and waits, above their heads a banner flapping in the wind – a gold circle sewn upon an umber standard, something familiar about the symbol. As the silk unfurls, I recognise the replica of my pendant, the spiral of glyphs Osha and I carry about our necks, the vestiges of our past.

My skin shivers with nerves, but not only my own. They're the nerves of the army at my back, their fear meaty on my breath, the steady rhythm of adrenalin rapping the drum of their courage. Hooves shift, feet brace. Their purpose feels steely, glinting inside me like a drawn blade, and I grasp the hilt of it, imagine bolstering it with my own weight and aiming the thrust. This is *my* army. These are *my* people. And when they raise their weapons and release a volley of war cries, it's the sound of the fire that rages inside me.

Turning to scan the plain, I spot it – the familiar barb of the ghosthawk's silhouette circling high on a thermal above us. Its cry shreds the sky in two and trips my heart, fear gripping me in the throat as if the bird has its talons at my neck again.

"Don't let it get the better of you, girl," a voice sounds in my head, and I realise it's the Blood-wife's. She's here with me in this vision, seeing what I'm seeing. "Close your eyes and listen for the creature's lifeblood. You already know how. Master it." And I do what she says, tilting my head and straining to focus. The hawk's pulse is faint at first but soon becomes a steady lilt in my ears. I latch on, grappling it to the tune of my own blood, until all I can hear is a single beat. The raptor makes a slow spiral against the blue, descending fast towards me. Its speed, its intent, the aim of those spread talons almost makes me lose my nerve, but I grapple control of the rhythm until the bird comes to a flutter upon my arm. Instinctively, I stare into its wet, black pupil as if I've been doing it all my life. And there again is the platinum-haired woman, that younger version of Iness – except this time she isn't watching me. *I'm* watching *her*.

She's on horseback, skirting the edge of vast dunes where a sandstorm is beginning to lift, forcing her to hunch against the lash of it, arms drawn about herself protectively. No, not herself… something else. For when I peer closer, I see her distended belly. She's pregnant. My nerve falters at the sight, and all the certainty I'd felt before, all the courage and purpose I'd drawn from the army at my command seems to scatter, caught up and blown away like sand in the storm of the tiercel's eye.

I come to, my head thrown back, my mouth open, roused by an animal cry. Stars shoot across my vision as I stand too quickly, shocked that the sound has come from me. My chair clatters to the floor. The wrangler is behind me, arms steadying.

"There now, girl," the Blood-wife soothes. "You're alright. The first time's a ride, that's for sure." But her hands are trembling and she's short of breath like me. "Most only get a sniff of the skill at the beginning. It's not many who–" She breaks off, glancing at the wrangler.

"What happened?" I ask.

"Did she see something?" Nixim presses the witch, but she brushes him off with a click of her tongue.

"Sit down," she tells me. "You've had a shock."

"I don't want to sit down!" I pace the small kitchen, shivering. "Tell me what the fec happened."

"Krait's venom is what happened. It's a useful enhancer," the witch says, "but it does have a tendency to make things a little... intense." She reaches towards me and swipes a thumb under my nose. When she draws it away, I see it's smeared with blood.

"You put poison in that tea?"

"Mesmer isn't poisonous in the right quantity. Small amounts induce clarity for those with the skill."

"And it brings visions for those whose ability is strong," the wrangler says pointedly. He squints at the Blood-wife as if she's hiding something. "Frenka? What I sensed in her – is it true?" I've never seen him so serious, so fixated.

"Poxes, let her breathe, boy," the Blood-wife says, eyes evasive. "She's only just found out she has the skill."

"What *skill*? What in Hell's poxes are you both talking about?"

She studies me. "Nixim told me you have an uncanny ability in the hunt?" I shrug impatiently. Her face softens and there's almost pity there. "Did you never wonder, child, why you find game when the bags of other hunters are empty? You don't simply read spoor and scat when you track, do you? You hear the pulse of your prey. You call to it with your own, feeling its need for food or water in your own breast, playing down its fear. You *sway* that animal to your advantage... and you're unaware you're even doing it."

I don't answer, but a knowing warmth creeps up my chest.

Somewhere, deep down, the Blood-wife's words ring true. I feel like a geode, and she's cracked me open, the way I am when I'm alone hunting in the Fornwood suddenly laid bare. I'd suspected others didn't track and stalk like me, but I'd convinced myself it was because they didn't pay attention to their game as accurately or skilfully as I did. That was their problem, not mine.

"So, I'm good at hunting," I say, looking between the witch and the wrangler defensively. "That doesn't make me a freak."

"No one's saying you're a freak, girl," the old woman replies. "But you should know that as a Sway matures, some find they can apply their skill to people as well as animals."

"Wait." I hold up my hands to slow her down. "You can't be serious? First you're telling me I have the ability to control my quarry, and now it's human minds?" I'd feel like laughing if my whole body wasn't still shaking with shock and exhaustion.

"No one can control people's minds, child. Sways can only draw out and heighten emotions that are already seeded there. We prefer to say a Sway channels opinion in a certain direction." She reaches into the pocket of her apron and gives me a handkerchief, indicating my nose. I reach up and touch the blood that's dripping there. "You've had no one to teach you about your ability, so it drains you."

"What do you mean, teach me?"

"There are others with the skill. I like to think of it as Nature's help in the face of sickness and decimation – a mental evolution, if you like." She pauses, giving her words time to settle in. "We Sways are nearly always women and those untouched by the Brume – *Mor*, as the Isfalk like to call them."

And it's then, looking at her, that I suddenly register it: the skin of her face, her neck, now clean of its clay make-up doesn't bear a single branding. "You're a Pure."

"For what it's worth."

"But Father Uluf used to tell us you were riddled with brandings under your face-paint."

"Well, the old vul would say that, wouldn't he?" she grunts.

"That's what I call him! How do you know–"

"Not hard to see the resemblance," she says, with a sly grin. "You're observant to the natural world, girl. Connected to it through your skill. Sways often are."

"But how do you know Father Uluf?"

"Oh, he and I have a long history. We locked horns when I was still at the Mor school."

"*You're* from the citadel?"

"Founding Four, born and bred. I was to make a grand match for the Friskar family – you know how it is. Except... well, I ran away." She winks as if she's recounting some practical joke, like tying Uluf's boots together while he slept, or stealing kornbru from the Mor school cook. "She couldn't fully sway me, you see. Like she can't sway you, I suspect."

"Who?"

The Blood-wife lowers her chin at me expectantly, and the answer comes, sharp as an icy draught through an open door. "Mother Iness? She's one of these... these *Sways* too?"

"Didn't you wonder how she still holds such influence over the Elixion and the Council? How she keeps most Mor content with their blinkered fate? Her sway is exceptionally strong even at her age, I'll give Iness that."

I rub my temples, trying to comprehend it all.

"But you said this skill is rare and only Pure women have it, so how can I be one? I'm a Brand." I turn my head to show her my marks, and she gives them only a cursory glance.

"Who knows?" She shrugs. "I've never met a Sway who was a Brand before. But one thing I've learned living with Nature all these years is that She likes to surprise us now and again."

"But the sister, Frenka," the wrangler interrupts. "I told you she's Pure. This one hunts well, but the other's known to be a healer. She might be a Sway of the highest order if trained."

"Wait, you're saying Osha might have this skill too?"

I flick my gaze from the wrangler to the witch, but she stays silent, only smoothing a hand across the table, collecting dust from the herbs she's been grinding there, an oddly pedestrian action given her revelations. I think about the way Osha heals, how quickly she learned to treat the sick and deliver babies in Amma's cabin, as if it was a sixth sense; the way she relieved Uluf's ailments and the discomfort of that pregnant Mor the last time we were at school together. Something about it all seems to make sense. The wrangler lets out a sigh of frustration at the Blood-wife, and I understand, then, that for him, this isn't about me at all. It's about Osha. If he could have stolen her easily from the Mor school, he would have brought my sister here instead of me. I'm just his second option.

Frenka makes a low hum in her chest. "If your sister has such a talent for healing, she might be a Sway, yes. But I can only be sure by touch." She runs red fingertips over the skin of my hand and I feel the lingering frisson of energy between us. "There's a scale to these things," she tells me. "That's what the boy means by *higher order* Sways. Exerting influence over the instincts of beasts is easier than influencing the human body or its emotions. Some with the skill never progress beyond the simple coercing of Nature's less complex creatures. Others manage to influence the unconscious reactions of the human body, excelling as healers through their touch. But it's only the strongest among us who can channel emotion to sway the will of another person." She gives me a pointed look, as if she doesn't want to acknowledge the vision we shared, the way I'd been tuning into the minds of those soldiers. When I open my mouth to ask her, she squeezes my fingers hard. It's obvious she doesn't want the wrangler to know.

"I've made you aware of what you are. Your skill is primed and might continue to grow if you train it, especially now you're out of the citadel, beyond the shadow of such a powerful Sway as Mother Iness. But there's never any guarantee." She looks at the wrangler as she says the last part.

"Outside the citadel, you think the Pure sister might be even more powerful?" he persists. "That she could even be The One?" He's standing now, leaning towards her across the table.

"What do you mean *The One*?" I snap at him. "What do you want with my sister, Wrangler?"

He ignores me, solicitous only of the witch as she rises stiffly from her chair, helping her find her balance. "Such business doesn't concern me," she says tiredly, turning away from him to the fire. "I deal in possibilities, boy, you know that. I let people see their potential, but I won't strip them of their free will. And I don't read to satisfy the prophecies and fantasies of desperate people." Over her shoulder, she throws him a disappointed look. "Anyone who does is a fool."

She's managed to make him blush again. He folds his arms, trying to mask it with stubbornness. "I'm not a half-wit, Frenka. I know a Sway when I see one. But you won't tell me about her skill. Surely if it's strong in her, then the Pure sister's will be stronger?"

Expecting anger, I'm surprised to see fondness in the old woman's face, her grey eyebrows arched above an indulgent smile. "Whatever I say won't make any difference to you, boy." She hunches over the hearth, chuckling to herself. "You'll still do what you want. That's the way of the young... the way it should be."

The wrangler gives her a hard stare, then turns for the door, slamming it behind him. I hover, uncertain whether to follow.

"Let him go, girl," the Blood-wife says. "He needs to let off some steam, but he'll be back." She prods at the fire and motions me to its warmth. "Best he doesn't know about your mesmer vision. It will only complicate matters."

"You saw what I saw, then?"

She nods. "Some Sways have the gift of reading a person's thoughts with their touch. The venom helps bring clarity to the skill. Usually, we see their past or present – moments of great emotion. But sometimes that can extend to a kind of foresight." She waits for me to digest her words, black eyes still shiny and curious as a bird's in the weathered bark of her face. "Understand this, though, child: what you saw was only a possibility, a version of your future that might come to pass, or might not. It depends on all sorts of variables – the choices you make, whether you train your skill and encourage it to grow. It depends on free will, not fate. Do you understand?"

I nod vaguely even though my mind is reeling. "Why didn't you want the wrangler to know about it?"

"It's a long story." She sighs, a note of sadness overcoming her. "Let's just say, the information he seeks could be dangerous in the hands of the wrong people. He needs to find his own way."

I have no idea what she means by this, but it's clear as she turns her attention to the fire that she's done talking about it. "Go on then, girl, ask your real questions," she says, surprising me once more. "I'm guessing it wasn't burning curiosity about the wrangler that brought you here."

I hesitate. After everything that's happened, I've almost forgotten what my own motivations were for coming.

"I think you might have known my grandmother. She was a Solitary from the western Fornwood, a healer. And a herbalist, like you." The Blood-wife doesn't answer, staring into the flames. "I remember you from the Moon Pools. You told us the same things she used to–"

"I knew of your grandmother, yes. Good reputations travel wide, even if you don't want them to."

"You're saying she didn't want to be known as a healer? Was she a Sway too? Was my mother?"

"Perhaps. I don't know for sure. All I'm saying is that your grandmother was left with two young girls to protect, and one of them Pure. Anyone in this crazed Continent is better off staying quiet about their business."

"Did you ever hear anything about my parents?" I reach again for the pendant at my neck and hold it towards her.

"How my father might have come across Reis gold?" This time she comes closer for a better look at the filigreed glyphs, but her attention soon slides away.

"I live in the present, girl, not the past or the future. It'd be best if you did the same."

"So, you don't know what this symbol means?" From my pocket, I pull out the coin Lars Oskarsson gave me and show her the matching design.

"They're pretty pieces of nothing to me. I told you, I don't trade in prophecies." She bends over and hocks into the fire, examining her expectoration as it sizzles in the embers. "What do *you* think it means?"

"I thought you were supposed to give me the answers."

She chuckles. "You've so rarely been asked what you think, have you? Mor never are. And yet I believe you're made entirely of opinions... and desires. They're what keep your spine straight and your aim true. Am I right?"

Her words surprise me. But I don't reply.

"So?" the Blood-wife prompts. "What do you really want?"

I think of my parents, the constant craving I have to know who they were, to possess a single memory of them, to understand exactly who I am. But perhaps she's right. Perhaps it's a futile desire. What would it change, after all? How would it serve me now? I'd still be a Brand. I'd still be separated from Osha. So, I tell her what I wish for most of all right now. "I want to be with my sister again. I want to be free to live our own lives... lives where we have choices." It comes out all in rush, but her nod encourages me. "I don't want to stand by and watch them bully her into a Pairing *they've* chosen, into a life *they've* mapped out for her... or the life they've forced me into, either." The Blood-wife grunts, a sound of approval, and I add with more bravado than I truly feel, "All of them – the Elix Council, Iness, the Warder army – they can shove the citadel and go to hell!"

The witch presses down a smile. "And what was your question, again?"

I stare at the hearth, breathing hard. Why do I feel like she's given me permission to do something but won't tell me what it is or how to do it? Frustrated and confused, I shake my head and make to leave, but she catches my wrist. "You don't ask me about the boy," she says, "even though he's there under the surface of your skin. An itch you can't scratch. I can sense it."

"The *boy*? Which boy?"

The Blood-wife holds my gaze, unblinking. "Be careful of him. He's a good soul, born of bad. Know that if he betrays you, he will break his own heart doing it."

But before I can ask whether she means Brim or the wrangler, the door opens and he stands in the threshold stamping snow from his boots. He has the melrakki slung across his shoulder. "Payment," he says as he lays the animal on the hearth.

The Blood-wife bends to run her hand through the fur. "The girl brought it down?" she asks.

"Yes," I answer. "Although, I'm quite capable of settling my own debts, thank you, Wrangler."

"Take her, boy," the Blood-wife chuckles, "and watch she doesn't tear you to shreds. That attitude of hers might as well have teeth."

The wrangler makes a show of grimacing and stepping away from me. But when he takes his leave of the old woman, he's solemn again, bowing his head before her.

"Eirafa," he says. I've never heard the term before, but his bearing shows he means the greatest respect by it.

"Child of the Sands," she replies, taking his face between her palms and drawing his forehead down to touch hers. "Remember to look for answers within as well as without," she tells him tapping his chest. She speaks as if resigned to her own impotence, like any crone before a headstrong youth. And yet, she's no more impotent than Iness, I suspect.

With a final glance at me, the Blood-wife turns back to her fire.

A Battle of Wills

"That was a trip!" I shout to the wrangler over the yelping of his dogs. He squats to check the tug lines of the sled, ignoring me. "You didn't think to tell me that you knew her like a grandmother? That you had your own designs in bringing me here?" I cross my arms, staring down at him. "You said I'd get answers, Wrangler. But you were only looking for answers of your own!"

He rises suddenly, rounding on me. "Would it have a made a difference if I'd said I knew her? That she was the closest thing to family on offer for a fourteen-year-old outlander in a place like the Settlement? Are we sharing sob stories now?"

The revelation silences me, a small window into his past. I picture a young kennel boy, the loneliness that drove him to seek comfort from someone like the Blood-wife. But I'm too angry and have too many questions to be distracted.

"What was all that talk of Osha being *The One*. What *One*, for fec's sake?"

He casts a solemn look towards the cottage. "There's a time and place, and it's not now." He brushes past me. "The dogs are getting restless."

"No, you're not going to stonewall me. You said I'd get answers and I want them. After all your deceit, you owe me."

"I owe you nothing. And I haven't deceived you."

"I wouldn't trust you with the guts from my quarry, Wrangler."

"Good to know." He takes up his whip. "Get in the sled."

I stand my ground, even though he looms over me, nostrils flaring, jaw muscle flickering. He's lost that infuriating smirk and is finally taking me seriously. Good.

"I may be nothing more than a Brand these days, but I still have my contacts. I could make life in the Warder barracks very hard for you, Wrangler."

"Could you?" he says, eyes bright with amusement. "You'd have to get back to the Settlement first."

"What?"

"I'm confident you'll manage it. It's only fifteen, maybe twenty miles across the ice – a stroll for such an accomplished tracker as you." And there it is: that poxy mole jumping in his cheek. He knows that distance would be impossible on foot in what's left of the day, and if a storm started, it might cost me a finger or two as well.

"Fine. I'll *make* you tell me. If I'm supposed to be one these Sways, I'll damn-well *sway* you."

He opens his arms wide and barks a laugh towards the white horizon, as if we have an audience. "Be my guest. Show me what you've got, Little Scourge."

His arrogance makes me want to scream, to make him tell me everything, preferably on his knees in the snow. I close my eyes and try to hone my focus, to summon the sensations I feel when I hunt, listening for the sound of his pulse, the fragments of other senses in him. But all I can hear is the chaos of the dogs, jumpy and feral. I try again, this time reaching for his scent like autumn and leather, something to work with. I can sense the draw of his lungs, so close, as if I've laid an ear to his chest, but his pulse eludes me. It's as if he's buried it deep within him where I can't reach... or else this *gift* I'm supposed to possess is as useful as a bucket full of hog-crap.

"I'm waiting," I hear him say and when I open my eyes, he's

bending so our frozen noses almost touch, close enough that the fog of his breath warms my face. His gaze roves over my mouth and I find myself transfixed by the nick of a small scar on his upper lip, the imperfection oddly mesmerising. In this light, the brighter ring of his eyes turns gold as my pendant in the sun.

"Na'quat," he says. His voice is low, intimate, and his thumb brushes my chin.

"Mmm?"

"You leave yourself defenceless. Naked as the day you were born."

I jerk away from him, snatching my breath as if he's lit a torch between us. "You go too far, Wrangler."

"Really? Your face just now seemed to want me to go much further."

I throw myself into the sled and pull up the furs, shivering.

The pack has fallen eerily silent, subdued.

The wrangler steps onto the footboards behind me. "Line out, Rakki!" he calls, but the dogs stay put. "Hike, Rak! Move on!" he shouts again, his whip slicing the air. I can smell the lead's eagerness, can taste his whimpering impatience to be racing across the ice, like a craving for salt in my mouth... but I tamp it down in my chest, settling his excitement, making him stay, making them all stay.

When I turn around, the wrangler is frowning, puzzled, but the smirk on my face must make him realise my game. "Would you like the whip as well, Little Scourge?"

"Don't need it." I still have hold of Rakki's pulse and I let it run wild now. "Get on, Rakki!" I call out. The dog lunges forward instantly, taking the pack with him, their adrenalin a chaos in my chest, the awareness of what I've done leaving me trembling.

"Your will, my hands," the wrangler shouts above their baying.

"Always the last word," I say, even though I know he can't hear me.

And for the whole ride across the frozen plains, I try to ignore the gibe of his voice as he mushes the team, the warmth of his thighs at my back as he steers the sled.

The light is starting to fade by the time I'm alone again, striding into the rimy undergrowth of the Fornwood. Over my shoulder, I see the wrangler's team make their final leg across The Fold. I don't usually set traps this close to the Settlement, but Jarl nagged me to practise the snares I've been teaching him and I didn't want to take the little skelf too far from the patrols. Thinking to check his handiwork, I snake my way through the trees into the forest's snow- muffled quiet, hoping I can surprise him with a reward for his efforts, but as I walk my thoughts soon return to the Blood-wife. Flashes of the vision I'd had run on repeat in my mind, the same images I'd seen with Mother Iness on the stage of the Roundhouse – the desert plain, the army, the ghosthawk. Where did they come from? Where is that place, those people, and why didn't the Blood-wife want to discuss it in front of the wrangler? All I'd hoped for from a visit to the witch was some small detail about my pendant, some clue as to who my parents were... maybe a better understanding of how this branding could be stamped on my skin, hidden all these years, while my twin has none. But instead of answering any of those questions, the witch only raised more. And how come trusting the wrangler feels like following the buzz of a bee, hoping for honey, only to be swarmed by a nest of hornets?

If I'm really one of these Sways the Blood-wife told me of, why is the gift so temperamental? It was useless when I tried to use it against the wrangler. Yet the old woman's hands when she touched me, the way her energy called to mine, felt... well, it felt *right*. It was like she was giving me something, not simply manipulating me. And then there was the way she'd described how I track and hunt. She looked right past the Mor privilege and the marks on my scalp as if she could see who I was on the inside and wasn't threatened by it, as Iness had been.

I think about Amma teaching me how to hunt, how to silently navigate the Fornwood's stillness. But when I concentrate, when I truly focus, I realise the forest isn't quiet or still at all. It never has been for me. Instead, there's a soft medley of hidden pulses and breaths – a colony of sicklewings roosting in branches high above me, the skittering heartbeat of a snowjack sensing my smell, the hungry mewl of a volmus litter in a den nearby. And I know I could tune into any one of these creatures to find them, to understand them, to influence their senses and instincts. I may have failed miserably in reading the wrangler, but I've always been able to do *this*, here in the forest. Did Amma know all along? Did she have the skill herself? I was so young when she taught me to track. In my memory it feels like I was born doing it. Shooting and skinning, field dressing and making snares – I remember her teaching me those things over the years, but whenever we stalked an area of forest or tundra, all I can recall is her smile, her nod of encouragement as I signalled the quarry. *Breathe*, she'd tell me sometimes. *Close your eyes. What can you hear? What can you smell? What can you feel?* Now I come to think of it, I never saw her doing the same herself. Not the way I did.

And what about Osha? If I have this gift, then perhaps the wrangler's right – Osha's bound to have it in spades. She's too good a healer not to. I remember Amma showing her which herbs to harvest for poultices and dressings, techniques for sutures and tourniquets, how to deliver babes. But I believe now there was something else our grandmother didn't teach her, something Osha knew how to do instinctively. Coming home from the Fornwood, I'd sometimes see my sister pressing her small hands to a sick woman or child, Amma quietly watching on. And I'd recognise the expression on Osha's face as she stilled and focused, the way she'd go to that same place I went to when I hunted. That place where all the other senses combined. That place of knowing. Was it our mother who was the Sway, then? Was it her gifts that drew Solitaries to our cabin from far and wide, just as they'd drawn our father? I wish I could know for sure. I wish I could have seen my mother healing. I imagine her now as Osha, long pale palms resting on the belly of the pregnant Mor, head cocked a little to the side, eyes elsewhere, listening, smelling... feeling.

Why did Amma never tell us who we were? What we were? Why did I have to visit some random spae-wife to find out?

Questions chase after one another in my head, and I'm not aware of movement between the trees until I hear voices – a woman and a boy's. I stop in my tracks, shielding myself behind the wide trunk of a greenock. But when the mist of my breath clears, I'm relieved to see it's Frida with Jarl, digging in the snow. They shouldn't be out here alone, but I grin to myself anyway. Jarl might have been sickly but the extra meat is making him grow stronger, restless to be out of the house, like any healthy boy. He probably pestered his mother to let him check his traps, too impatient to wait for me to bring him. "You're looking in the wrong place," I call. Mother and son spin around, startled.

"Holy Mother's milk!" Frida curses, pressing a hand to her chest as she spots me.

"Jarl." I shake my head at him. "The snare we set was over there, by that black pine. But what did I say about taking your eyes off your surroundings? I could have been anyone creeping up on you. We might be close to The Fold here, but this is still the Fornwood." Brim's words echo in my mind as I lecture the boy. Still, Jarl needs to do as I say, not as I do. He nods earnestly, but when he brushes his blond mop from his eyes, he seems worried... sad. So does Frida.

"What is it?" I ask her.

She takes a heavy breath and points to a drift. I can see they've been digging. "I nearly tripped over it. I... I thought it was a log, but then I saw fabric and fur and..."

I look down at their feet. Two blue fingers and a thumb

poke up from the snow. I can already tell before I touch them that they're hard and cold as stone. An image of Osha escaping the Walls and trying to find me comes unbidden to my mind. Panicked, I fall to my knees and begin frantically ploughing away the drift. The body is a girl's, but I soon see her clothes are thin grey rags and mangy furs, the brandings on her neck almost black against her bloodless skin. Panting, I stop digging and brush the snow from her face with my glove. I don't need to see her features to recognise who it is. I remember the marks of the Brume like spattered ink along her jaw, the way she thrust her chin towards me defiantly as she grabbed the snowjack and hurried her brother through the trees – only a few weeks ago. A lifetime ago.

"Jarl," I say, and I hear the crack in my voice. "Go check your snare." The boy hesitates but does as I ask.

Frida kneels beside me. "He's used to it, Mor Nara – seeing death." She shakes her head sadly as she looks at the girl, a resigned expression in her eyes. "We all are. It's part of living in the Sink."

"How long do you think she's been here?"

"By the colour of her skin, several days at least." I think she must be right. I can tell from the depth of the snow.

"Did she get sick?"

"Perhaps," Frida says softly.

I look at the girl's sharp cheekbones, her eye sockets so hollowed I can almost see the lines of her skull beneath. Her thin wrists look so brittle I might have snapped one as unthinkingly as the hoary scrub under my boots.

"Maybe she came out here to look for food and became too weak to carry on?" I say. "There's no sign of Wastelander activity, so it's unlikely she was attacked."

Frida scoffs a little. "It's not Wastelanders girls like this need to be careful of." She opens the shabby furs, crusted with snow. Underneath, the girl's smock is torn and bloody. Frida lifts it, examining her naked body beneath.

"What are you doing?" I ask, horrified.

She gives me a pointed look and lowers the smock again, but I've already caught sight of the bruises and scratches blackening the emaciated skin.

"She didn't starve, did she?"

Frida shakes her head. "But hunger was what got her here in the first place. Young girls in the Sink don't have a lot of choices. They sell what they must to feed themselves. But there'll always be men who don't want to pay. Branded girls go missing all the time."

"You're saying some brute from the village dumped her here?"

"Or some brute from the citadel."

"*What*?"

Frida looks away but I catch her hand.

At my frown she says, "Warders, Mor Nara. Pure lords. Sometimes even Elix Councillors. They come here to do the business so as not to tarnish their reputations. Just because their skin is Pure doesn't mean their minds are." Her nose drips from the cold and she sniffs. "What's a dead slum girl to them, after all? One less mouth taking food from more worthy stomachs in the Settlement."

I take a breath to speak, but no words come out. I knew Warders sometimes visited the village taverns and trull houses to let off steam after days on patrol in freezing temperatures. Brim told me, and I've seen as much with my own eyes since living in the Sink. But I had no idea that Elix liked to escape their responsibilities in that way too. I feel suddenly naïve, blinkered.

Frida begins shovelling snow over the body.

"Wait, what are you doing?" I ask.

"We can't carry her to the Settlement. It's too far. In spring, when the ground thaws, we'll come back and bury her."

I'm shocked at first, watching Frida cover the girl, but then laying her to rest here in the forest starts to feel right. Why take her to the Settlement? Isfalk never gave her the life it promised: protection, safety, a harbour from barbarism and disease. She might as well have tried her luck living wild in the Fornwood or roving the southern plains. Even trafficked as a slave by a Wastelander convoy, she might have at least been fed. I gaze down at her face one last time, her blue eyes fixed unseeing on the canopy above our heads, before helping Frida blanket her body with snow. The injustice of it all catches like a flame inside me, even as I shiver.

"I'll ask around the Sink. She might have had family," Frida says.

"Shit!" I suddenly remember. "Her brother. She had a little brother. I saw them trying to set snares weeks ago. He was young... and sick. Really sick."

The look on Frida's face says it all: he's probably not alive anymore. Why didn't I think to check on them when I was cast out of the citadel?

"I should have found out where they lived. I could have made sure they had food," I tell Frida. "I've been so preoccupied with myself, with my own life."

"It's not your fault."

"Maybe not my fault. But I could have made it my concern, couldn't I?"

"Mor Nara–"

"I could have done *something* about it, if I wasn't still behaving like a precious Mor."

Frida looks at me without answering. Getting to her feet, she brushes the snow from her knees. "I'll ask around the village, try to find out what happened to the boy." But I can tell from her tone she doesn't hold out much hope. She squeezes my arm, the first time she's ever reached out to touch me that way.

"Nara," she says, meaning it as a comfort.

And it does comfort me a little because she didn't call me Mor. And I believe she never will again.

Cylla Leaves

At the next Morday Mass, I don't try for a spot in the Roundhouse with the Branded congregation. Instead, I loiter in the marketplace among the horses and dogs, waiting for the last sleds to arrive from the citadel. I've given up any chance of a good view of the stage inside, hoping instead to get close enough for a few words with Osha as she descends from her sled outside. But all I catch is the fur trim of her travelling mantle, a glimpse of red hair in the dull grey light, before Warders surround her and she's lost to sight. "O." I shout out, but they're already hurrying her up the snowy steps of the great doors, away from the ogling throng. I crumple the note I've written her in my fist and shove it deep into my pocket, kicking at the snow in frustration.

One pack of sled dogs begins to bay as I pass and their lead snaps at my hand. Distracted, I wheel away, sprawling on my arse.

"Oi, watch it!" their driver grumbles. "You're riling my team."

Hearing his tone, the dogs begin jumping and snarling at me. Instinctively, I bare my teeth and growl back, listening for the sound of the lead's pulse, about to cower it with my own. But a fist goes round my arm and I'm yanked to my feet. "Got a live one here," the man calls out. "Not bad… not bad at all," he says, brushing the snow from my backside. He clearly isn't looking at my face in the shadow of my hood. "Might save us a visit to Helgah's tonight." The collar of his furs is in my fist before he can even blink and I'm about to loose a punch, when someone catches my wrist.

"Let's be nice, shall we, Little Scourge?" I whirl around to find the wrangler at my shoulder.

"Holy Mother's holes! Don't you ever stop interfering in my business?"

"Got a mouth on her, too, eh?" the other driver chuckles. His yellow teeth are gappy and goatish when he grins. "A real handful."

"Too much of a handful for you, Sven," the wrangler says, and before I can deflect he's got me in a headlock and is marching me towards a darkened alley on one side of the Roundhouse.

"Get your fecking hands off me, Wrangler!"

"Hey, I found her first!" Sven calls, and then, "Don't be too long about it."

I struggle and twist, hoping to get an elbow free to catch the wrangler in the stomach, but his hold is too good and I can't find any leverage. Eventually he lets me go with a grunt. The alleyway is dim and narrow – just enough room to grab him by the shoulders and put a knee in his groin. I'm sorely tempted. He must sense it for he retreats a little and takes up a defensive stance.

"Are we good yet, Little Scourge?"

"No, we are *not* good... and stop calling me that."

"Calm down. It was either that or leave you in the hands of the charming Sven."

"I could have handled him myself."

"Not without drawing half the Warder guard down on you as well." I stay silent because I know he's right. Morday Mass at the Roundhouse Church isn't the place for a scuffle between Brands. "I presume you were loitering around outside to get a glimpse of your sister?"

"Yeah, well, fat chance of that down here." I glance around the alleyway, my eyes adjusting to the shadows.

He looks up, indicating a series of small ventilation windows under the eaves of the church. Light pools through them, and I notice a row of tanning barrels, almost as tall as me and three times as wide. "Climb up," he nods. "You'll be able to see it all from there."

Is this how he spies on everything? I let him give me a leg up and discover he's right. It's the perfect spot for a view of the Mass, not that I'll admit it to him. The vent I peer through looks down onto the stage itself, so close I can see the thinning patch on the crown of the Elixion's head, the blaze of the altar fire reflected on the Warders' boots, the vine of little leaves loosely twisted through my sister's thick tresses. I've never seen Osha wear decorations in her hair before. Some of the other girls favour beads and silks, but rarely leaves. I study them again. They're evergreen cylla, a climbing plant that never sheds, even in winter. Amma told us it stands for hope and new life – Solitaries have meanings like that for all the plants in the Fornwood. I understand then: it's a sign. Osha knew I'd be watching and meant for me to see it. She's telling me she still has hope – hope for a new life in the Fornwood. She wants to be together again. She wants out of the citadel.

"Your sister looks worried," the wrangler says. He's climbed up beside me, surveying the stage through the narrow opening, his forearm pressed next to mine, face too close. The look I turn on him must be sharper than a skinning knife because he clears his throat. "What? I can't be lacing up my leathers just yet. I need to make Sven buy it."

"It's been longer than three minutes. I think he'll buy it."

"Ouch."

Below us, Father Uluf has signalled the start of the Pairing rite. I spot Brim, his shoulders in his furs impossibly broad from this angle, his hair gold against the Elix silver.

"Why are you blushing?" the wrangler asks.

"Shhh!"

The girls rise now, Mother Iness calling forth the suitors. Osha shifts forward on the stage and I'm suddenly struck by how beautiful she is, the pale glow of her skin, her red hair making the altar flames seem almost dull by comparison. And then she's standing next to Brim and all I can think of is how good they look side-by-side, how perfectly matched in the finery of their Mass clothes, as if they might accomplish anything together. All I can think of is how much I love them both. I don't register what's happening until I hear the words.

"Brim Oskarsson and Osha Fornwood." Mother Iness holds their hands together.

Together.

Everything slows. Time spools out like a thread from a reel.

Osha's eyes flare in shock and she flinches. The crone nicks her palm and joins it with Brim's over the altar fire. He offers my sister a smile. She responds with the smallest nod.

And my heart feels like it's been ripped out and left beating on the open tundra.

"Well, that's an interesting development," the wrangler says. "Not one you were expecting, huh? Although *they* were, it seems." I look again at Osha's and Brim's faces, their expressions composed, in agreement. The wrangler's right: they'd planned this between them. And told me nothing of it.

I can't get enough air. My lungs won't work properly. I try to scramble down from the barrels, but slip. The wrangler grabs my arm before I fall, lowering me to the ground. I sink to my haunches against the wall of the Roundhouse and he stands over me. The look on my face must be a picture because for once he's speechless.

"I didn't... I didn't see it coming. He was supposed to look after her, make sure she was alright, not..." I run a hand over my head, sliding off my nabhat. "She doesn't have a family name behind her... I didn't ever imagine he would ask her." Brim's voice echoes in my head. *Maybe when all this has blown over, I can get you a job in the citadel.* A job in their household? A job serving him and my sister? I remember his eyes when we'd almost kissed, sliding from my lips to my branding. The shaved part of my scalp starts to itch and I want to scratch it, scratch it, scratch it all away.

The wrangler squats down beside me. He draws a flask from the pocket of his leathers and unscrews it. "Here, take a swig," he says. "It'll burn like a bitch, but it'll ease the pain."

"I'm not *in pain*."

"I think you're probably one constant pain, Little Scourge."

For once I don't have the energy to fight him. Instead, I take the bottle and knock it back.

Bare is the Back
of the Sisterless Woman

I wake before first light, my bow and the Fornwood calling. I get up, not because I want to but because it's a habit now. But as I reach for my leather pants, I'm sideswiped by something that feels like one of Brim's right hooks. It takes a moment for the full weight of the hangover to press down on me, a rush of clammy regret following immediately after. Holy fec, what did I do last night? I remember the liquor coursing through my blood, wonderfully numbing at first, and then a bar in some trull house in the Sink, but I don't know how I ended up on my pallet by Frida's hearth in my underclothes, smelling of soap, the furs tucked around me.

Groaning, I rub at my scalp: the stubble is itchy. I freeze mid-scratch. This isn't where my brand is. This is the other side of my head. Jumping up, I grab the copper pitcher from the table, straining to see myself in its burnished curve. The reflection is dim in the firelight but even in my addled state, I can see my entire scalp has been shorn. Nothing remains of my wild hair but a close-cropped stubble. I look like a startled willow-doe, my eyes too big for my head, something fragile about me. Acid burns my empty stomach – anger and the hangover combined. I yank on my hunting jacket and pull the nabhat low over my ears. That fecking wrangler and his sloefire! What in Hell's poxes happened?

I head out to The Fold, hoping I might chance across him exercising his dogs, but the snow is empty, no one to be seen for miles around. I wait for a while, then find myself climbing to Heitval Ridge and descending to the Moon Pools, my mind returning to the Pairing again and again, remembering Osha and Brim's faces as they looked at one another on the Roundhouse altar. As the steam drifts towards me, I catch sight of a figure, squatting to warm his hands in the water. He raises his head, but he doesn't turn around as I approach. "Not so long ago, you'd have taken a chance like this to push me in," Brim says, his voice flat, regretful.

"Not so long ago, you weren't a lying, backstabbing son of a trull."

He sighs as if he expected that. "Nara, listen," he begins. But I won't. I can't. My anger, my hurt, all the unsaid words boil out of me from deep down.

"How *could* you, Brim? After everything you said about your Pairing–"

"Listen–"

"I asked you to look after her, not–"

"But that's precisely why, don't you understand? It's because I love you, because we both love you, that we've done it. You can't stay in the village, sleeping on Frida's hearth, surviving on what you hunt. At some point you're going to get sick. Osha and I agreed–"

"*Osha and I?* It's Osha and I already, is it?" My throat constricts making my voice whine like a child's and I hate myself for it.

"Nara, don't. It's the best way I can make sure both of you are safe. Pairing with Osha means we can take on more Branded servants, once she's with ch–"

"With child!" I spit, appalled that he could even say such a thing in front of me. "And what am I to do then? Bring the pair of you breakfast in bed? Wash your dirty sheets? Play with your children? Did you plan that together too?"

"You were the one who asked me to look after her! This was the only way I could think of to do that *and* have a chance of looking after you too."

"So, Osha is good enough for your precious reputation with the Elix Council, but I wasn't?"

He hesitates at that. "No. If you must know, she wasn't *good enough*. I've laid my whole career, my name, and an alliance with Fjäll and Iness on the line here. We've all made sacrifices, Nara. All of us."

"*Sacrifices*! Oh, my heart bleeds for you, Brim. What a great hardship it must be knowing you have to bed my beautiful sister. How was the wedding night, by the way?"

He shifts, turns away in embarrassment. "She has to go to her cleansing rite at the Moon Pools tonight," he says awkwardly. "We're waiting until after." It's one small relief, I guess: the Pairing won't be official in Isfalk until it's consummated.

"Of course. Following all the citadel rules, like the good Elix you are."

"That's unfair, Nara."

"Is it? I'll tell you what's unfair. You thinking you could take Osha and make decisions about my future without asking me. I might be a Brand now, Brim, but my life is still mine, and I can make my own choices."

"And what choices would they be?" He glares at me through the mist, a muscle in his jaw ticking. "Choosing to shave your head and flaunt yourself in Sink-side taverns? Rousing Brands and getting in enough trouble to be exiled?"

My face burns like he's slapped it. I can't find the words to answer him. It sounds like he's already heard more about last night than I remember.

"It was all over the Warder mess. The unit who broke up the rabble took particular delight in telling me. *That Fornwood Flamehair of yours was sure on fire last night, Brim. You should start drinking at Helgah's – maybe she'll give you a taste for free now she's been kicked out of the citadel."* I open my mouth to object, but he stops me. "I've already heard all about it – how that wrangler threw you over his shoulder before your little show was finished. Really, Nara, is this what you've sunk to? Dancing with renters on tavern tables and pleasuring kennel boys for drinks?" He throws me a look of such disappointed hurt I'd trade any amount of straight-up anger for it.

"That's not what happened. It isn't what you think."

"Isn't it? Clearly, after all these years, you still have no idea what I think."

"And you have no idea what I would and wouldn't do. Although it's apparently fine for you to go drinking with your men at Helgah's and have trulls hanging from you like fresh pelts."

"What are you talking about?"

"Come off it, Brim. I know a lot more than you think about what Warders get up to when they're off duty."

He's shocked and I get a slug of satisfaction from it. "Well, perhaps if you were from a political family trying to be taken seriously as an army captain, then you'd understand. That's how my men bond, how they forget the pressures of risking their lives for the Settlement."

I let out an incredulous laugh. "Really? You poor Warders have to grin and bear terrible things in the line of duty, huh? And Brands are there only to service you... to be tossed aside when you're done?"

"That's not what I said." He frowns at me, puzzled at where this is coming from, I can tell. "Look, this isn't about me, Nara."

"Finally," I yell, throwing up my hands. "You get it!" I bend to snatch up my bow and quiver. "My life isn't about you, Brim. So stop trying to *solve* me." I head towards the forest trail.

"Wait!" he calls, but my injured pride makes me hold my head up, draw a steady breath and continue walking. "If you turn your back on me now, Nara, you're alone. I'm not going to come running any more. You'll be brotherless, do you understand?" It's a low blow – his equivalent of a knee to the balls. The Isfalki proverb is written above the gate to the Warder barracks: *Bare is the Back of the Brotherless Man.* He knows that's exactly what I'm feeling now: vulnerable and painfully alone.

"You forget, Brim," I call over my shoulder. "I'm not an Isfalki. I'm a Fornwood Solitary. We choose to live alone."

It's near dusk by the time I cross The Fold and return to the Settlement. I thought a day with my thoughts in the forest would put things in order, might even make me keep walking into its wilderness, leaving Isfalk and all its ugly rules and restrictions and prejudices behind for good. But thoughts of Osha plague me. The cylla leaves in her hair – hoping for a new life. A life with Brim, was that it? Did she want him for herself all this time? No. I don't believe it. I won't believe it. That's bloody-minded jealousy talking and my jealousy is nowhere near as strong as my love for my sister. Surely she did it to keep me safe? *Stay together. You're stronger together.* Amma made me promise, but I've never considered before that perhaps she made Osha promise too. Either way, I know I can't leave my sister. She's half of me. The better half. She's all I have.

I become aware of dogs baying, a sled catching me up across The Fold. The wrangler draws to halt. "How's the head, Little Scourge?" he asks.

"You going to tell me what the pox happened last night?"

"What didn't happen, might be a better question." He laughs. "But you don't have to thank me. My pleasure."

"You want me to thank you for *this*?" I drag off my hat and show him my hair… or lack of it.

"No, you're to thank me for hauling your sorry skin from Helgah's in one piece." He gets off the sled to check his lines and I notice there's a cut on his eyebrow, three rough sutures in gut thread. He sees me looking. "Yeah, your antics on the bar had an appreciative audience. They didn't enjoy me breaking up the show... Thankfully, you were there to save me," he says, sarcasm thick in his voice.

I clench and unclench my fist: now I know why my knuckles are cut and bruised. Were we seriously in a tavern brawl together and I don't even remember? He's grinning so hard I'm tempted to knock that mole right off his face. "That doesn't explain what happened to my hair."

"Don't you like it as much this morning? You seemed vastly proud of it last night, strutting on top of the tables and displaying your branding for all to see, flipping the finger to the citadel – that was a nice touch, I thought. As was informing everyone that Brands should wear their markings like a badge of honour and all Pures could go pleasure themselves. You got yourself quite the following in the Sink."

Every image he conjures catches like kindling in my memory until my whole body feels alight with shame.

He indicates my scalp. "When you took out your skinning knife and began to shave the other half, I thought I'd better step in and finish the job before you sliced off an ear." His chuckle is low and wicked, and he makes a show of cocking his head to assess the haircut in the light of day. "It's a bit rough, but I think it suits the new you. The crowd certainly went wild for it... until Warder patrols started breaking it up." He drops his amusement. "Had to get you out of there pretty fast."

I look up to the white sky and run a palm over my handiwork. "Shi-it," I breathe.

"Shit, indeed. You certainly like ruffling the feathers of the Council, Little Scourge."

"Oh, come on, one drunken bar brawl's hardly going to interest the Council. I hear there's one in Helgah's nearly every night."

"Not one involving the ex-Mor who just got kicked out of the citadel. Not one where she fires up half the village with anti-citadel sentiments. Feeding Brands in the slums, stirring up discontent in the taverns – you've made sure Iness has you pegged as a fire-Brand."

I'm quiet at that. I think I understand that term now. And what he says makes me nervous. Especially after the vision Iness and I shared on the Roundhouse stage.

"You think she's going to turf me out of Isfalk completely?"

"Are you actually asking my opinion for once?"

I press my lips together, trying to summon my patience.

"Put it this way, if you're planning to spring that sister of yours out of the citadel, I'd get working on it sooner rather than later." And with that he draws something from the pocket of his furs. It's a letter, and it's addressed to me in Osha's handwriting.

"Mother's tits, Wrangler! You're only giving this to me now?"

"You seemed preoccupied with your hair," he says, with a grin.

I rip open the letter and scan it greedily. When I start to blink away the tears that threaten, he says, "Let me guess. She never wanted Pretty Boy for herself. He talked her into it to keep you safe. But it's all been a mistake. How could she ever think you'd settle for being a servant behind Walls when even being a Mor was never enough?"

"You *read* this note?"

"Of course I read it. I need all the facts if I'm going to help you meet her at the Moon Pools and get her clear of the Warder guards."

I grind my teeth. "I don't need your help. And I don't want it."

"Really? So you've got access to horses, supplies, weapons? You're clever enough to cause a distraction among the guards at the same time as grabbing your sister from the pools and making a run for it? And if it all goes arse-up, you're going to take on an entire unit of Warders single-handed? You're good, Little Scourge. But you're not that good."

I turn away, eyes taking in The Fold, the snow almost purple in the last light. I know he's right. But the thought of letting him get involved makes my skin prickle. And after what passed at the Blood-wife's, he clearly has his own agenda for getting Osha out of the citadel, and I didn't trust him even before I knew that. I promised Amma I'd stay with my sister, but I never imagined that would mean getting the help of a fecking Reis-blood.

I can't do it. I open my mouth to tell him where to go, but he interrupts. "Do you have someone else in mind to smuggle an answer back to her, then?"

He knows full well I don't. He has me over a barrel.

Blood in the Snow

Fat lazy flakes are falling at the Moon Pools, forming drifts that dampen the sound of the Fornwood. I spot the Mor party and their Warder guards before I hear them approaching. The trail over Heitval Ridge to the ravine is too steep for sleds or horses, so Mor visiting for their monthly cleansing rite must make the last part of the journey on foot. Warder escorts are always on high alert for signs of raiders, and even more so with Wastelander activity on the rise. But I don't have much choice for getting to Osha: other than the short journey to Morday Mass, this is the only time Pure women are allowed beyond the Walls.

Scanning the party, I count three other girls making the ritual alongside my sister, surrounded by a double detail of guards. That's thirty men to protect four precious Mor. And, as if that isn't enough to make my heart sink, the commanding officer at the rear of the Warder line has a stride I recognise all too well.

Brim.

He suspects me, thinks that I might attempt something – that's why he's put himself on escort duty, guarding Osha personally. Getting anything past Brim is going to be a challenge. I know that better than anyone. But as I shadow the group from a distance, other questions begin to gnaw at me from the inside: if it came to blows, would Brim throw away years of friendship to keep his oath to the citadel? Would I, to keep my promise to

Osha and my grandmother? Would either of us be prepared to
draw our weapons for real this time?

I check behind me, making sure I'm alone. The wrangler
had better be sticking to the plan. He said he'd have horses
waiting for us on the far side of Heitval. This whole gambit
rests on him distracting the guards so Osha and I can run for it,
descending the Ridge and making headway into the western
Fornwood before they can regroup, reach their own mounts
and pursue us. He said he'd cut a deal for the horses in return
for our pendants, but I don't for a minute believe gold is what
he's after. He has some other motivation, I know it. But then,
so do I. If he seriously thinks I need horses to escape in the
Fornwood, he doesn't know Solitaries. In the time it takes him
to tighten his girth, Osha and I will have disappeared into its
rugged depths on foot.

"Fenris," a voice shouts up ahead. Brim, calling to his
second-in-command. "Take your unit and scout the perimeter.
Then face-out as usual." The guards begin to form a wide ring
around the pools looking towards the forest to give the Mor
their privacy and to scan for threats. It's their usual defensive
formation. I've seen it often enough from inside that circle, but
from this perspective it's far more intimidating.

Osha must be trying to spot me because instead of shedding
her travelling furs like the other Mor, she's loitering at the edge
of the pools, scanning the trees. The other women are already
undressed and stepping into the water, their guards edgy in
their boots, hands on hilts as they squint through the falling
snow. The conditions are far from ideal, the visibility appalling
for a protection detail. I'm surprised Brim let the expedition go
ahead, but grateful nonetheless: it works in my favour – Osha
and I will be harder to see when we run.

"What is it?" I hear Brim ask. "Are you tired, O?" I flinch at
the nickname, *my* nickname for my sister, the intimacy of it in
Brim's mouth!

"I'm fine," she answers. "I think I lost a glove." And

while he scans their route for it, I inch out from my hiding place between the hoary trunks, briefly revealing myself, reassuring Osha I'm here. I know she sees me, for she calls out to Brim loud and clear, "I've found it. Don't worry. It was with me all along." He returns to her side and his smile, the touch he gives her arm, the way he spins around with such self-conscious respect to allow her to undress – every detail punctures my lungs. Jealousy feels like the first stab of the knife but the long aching pain left behind is self-doubt. Am I being selfish, am I doing the right thing, putting her at such risk with this plan? Snatching her from the comforts of Isfalk, away from someone good who can keep her safe, well fed and protected? But as Brim's attention returns to his men, my sister glances through the trees again. The look she offers me is one of such encouragement, such determination and love, it stops my thoughts dead. *I'm your sister, too*, that look says. *Of course I want to stay together.* And I know she's telling me that the risks and hardships ahead, whatever they may be, are absolutely worth it.

Snow slides in a sudden dump from the weighted canopy. I hear the flutter of wings, the tinkle of a tiny bell. Iness's ghosthawk swoops to the branch above me, a volmus wriggling in its mouth. Something warm and wet falls and hits my cheek. A droplet of blood. I squint up at the bird. Is the damn thing following me? I edge away, just as an arrow sings through the trees, lodging in the trunk beside me with a twang, so close the fletches quiver before my nose. I dive to the snow. Another arrow whistles, and another. Screams rise from the pools and a Warder yells out pointlessly, "Ambush!"

I can't see Osha in this position. I want to dart out and grab her, but the arrow-fire is too thick and fast, and seems to come from every direction. All I can hear is Brim's voice barking commands, the groan of injured men. Then I spot them: pale silhouettes appearing and disappearing like spectres among the tree trunks.

They must have been waiting stationed all around the ridge since the early hours, camouflaged by the patchwork of their furs and the obscuring snow. The archers pick off their marks one-by-one, while others go in for the kill, finishing the Warder guard with swords and axes, even rocks and fists.

Only barbarians kill like that. Only Wastelanders.

The hail of arrows subsides, and I venture a look towards the pools. They're hauling the Mor, dripping and naked from the water, tossing clothes at them as they go. Frantically, I scan for Osha, but she's nowhere to be seen. Was she hit in the ambush? Did she run?

Shit, shit, shit. I can't stay here cowering between the drifts. Slowly, silently, I push to my feet, pressing into the hoary trunk of a greenock. I'm about to risk darting to the cover of the next tree when a voice ahead makes me stop.

"Run, Nara! Run!"

Through a billow of mist, I make out Osha, hands tied, hair wound about the fist of a Waster. His dagger rests on her stretched throat. I've nocked an arrow before he even locks eyes on me. I'm good enough to take the shot. I know it, even though his jugular is only one slip away from Osha's. Instinct makes me narrow my eyes, not to see my target but to hear it better – the soft lub-dub of his pulse in my ear. It grows louder the more I listen, just as it does when I'm tracking game, and soon my other senses are recruited too: I can *taste* his determination steely as a blade on my tongue, *feel* his desire to prove himself sharp as salt in a wound. But in between, I pick up the oily scent of his fear, a self-doubt and hesitancy that coats my own palms with sweat. I latch onto it, spreading his uncertainty until I can feel his hand tremble and his grip on Osha loosen.

"You sure you want to risk that, Little Scourge?"

Instantly the connection is broken. I whirl around to see the wrangler, holding up his hands, asking the Wastelanders hold their fire. No. Not asking. *Commanding* them. My resolve fractures like thin ice, watery and uncertain underneath.

"Wrangler? You're with *them*?" I didn't trust his motives, but I never imagined he'd stoop so low as to sell me out to Wasters. He looks directly at me, the deep cut of a frown between his eyebrows, and I turn my aim on him, my bow string poised. But there's a cracking sound behind me, and I don't even have time to flinch before my vision tunnels and the daylight gutters out.

PART TWO:
ACROSS THE WASTELANDS

Cargo

I can't seem to get my bearings. It's dark and I'm on the move in some kind of wagon sleigh, wind whistling through the gaps in the panelling. I smell horses on the frozen air. "Nara? Nara, can you hear me?"

Osha's voice, thank the Mother. At first, I can only see her outline, one pale cheek and her lips where daylight cuts though the slit of a window. Then I feel her hands helping me to sit up. "You won't be able to move much," she says. Immediately, I feel the ropes binding my wrists and ankles, and scrabble at the hobbles in a fit of panic until Osha holds my arms to still me. Being bound, constricted in a small space – she knows what it does to me. "Nara. Nara, look at me. Only at me." My sister's voice is calm but her eyes tell a different story. "It's alright. I'm here. You and me, sis, remember?" The words and her touch ground me a little. My breath slows. We're together now. I have that at least.

Something hurts behind my head. I wince through my teeth, discovering a lump there, round as an egg. "Fecs alive."

"A Wastelander gave you that," Osha says, "when you trained your arrow on that dog wrangler from the Warder mess."

I remember the wrangler's voice behind me, the look on his face as I'd turned. Backstabbing bastard.

"I told you to run, Nara. Why didn't you run?"

"And leave you?"

"You could have been killled." Osha bites her lips, swallowing down a sob or nausea. She never cries and she's the opposite of squeamish, but the shock has made her skin pale. Her fingers are trembling. "Heyda was hit in the crossfire. I... I couldn't stop her bleeding." She can't hold my eye, blinking fast as she mentions our classmate. "Nara, I couldn't save her."

I steady her hands in mine. It's the first time since we ran from the burning cottage in the Fornwood that I've seen my sister even close to losing mastery of herself. I pull her to me. Her herby scent, like wild rumarin after summer rain, is childhood, is home to me. But after a moment she straightens, turns her head, and I'm suddenly aware we're not alone. In the low light, I can see two other women sitting in the straw, leaning against the rumbling wood on the other side of the wagon. One of them, Osha says, is Sigrun Adumssen. She was two years below us at the Mor school. I vaguely recall her face but not her name. The second girl needs no introduction. I know her all too well: Dalla Thorval. The Thorval family are one of the Founding Four, and her lineage made Dalla a favourite match for Brim in redeeming the Oskarsson name in the citadel. I found it especially hard to bear since Dalla used to take every opportunity to taunt me about my outlander heritage in front of our whole year. On more than one occasion, Osha had to stop me feeding her my fist across the refectory tables. I'm sure she'll have a whole new arsenal of insults now I've been revealed as a Brand.

"This keeps getting better," I tell Osha under my breath. "Kidnapped, hobbled like a horse, and now crated inside a tiny wooden box with *her*?"

Osha ignores me. "They had snipers hidden in the trees. "Most of our Warder guards were hit while they were still drawing their weapons."

"Where's Brim?" I ask, suddenly panicked.

"He fell," Dalla answers, looking down distastefully at the blood staining her furs. "They were slitting Warder throats right in front of–"

"Not Brim's," Osha interrupts. "He's alive. They still have him, see?" She helps me struggle to my feet, and I lurch for the window vent, barely more than a hand's width, cut in the panelling of the wagon. A rush of blood pounds behind my eyes as I stand, forcing me to clutch at the opening as I blink away stars. But then I make out a posse of riders surrounding the sleigh, keeping a steady pace as we navigate the open snows along the frozen cut of the Heitval River. I must have been out cold the whole time we threaded down from the Ridge through the thick of the forest.

Up close, the Wasters seem even more grim than I'd ever imagined from a distance. Their coats are a dull patchwork of skins and pelts, their hairstyles motley – some shaved in an undercut, crude tattoos inked above their ears; others braided and threaded with carved bones and trinkets, most likely the trophies of hunts and raids. Even their horses are a rugged mix of piebald and dun, saddles hung with pelts, weapons and all manner of curios – evidence of their existence as scavengers of the Wastelands. Our Mor teachers called them *trogs* – the rats of the plains. They taught us that when the central Continent was ravaged by the Great Malady, the Brands who survived spiralled into barbarism, trawling the dead towns and settlements for food, abandoning their weak and sick to die, sharing women – especially rare Mor – and trading weapons, livestock, even human cargo. "Praise Mother you're on the civilised side of the Walls," Father Uluf would remind us. "And pray to Her you stay here."

I scan the mounted men in search of Brim, but my eyes light on someone else. The wrangler rides a sturdy roan mare, his seat easy in the saddle, reins loose in his hands. In rough black travelling furs, his face set into a squint against the snow, he looks for all the world like he grew up scavenging the open plains. A pack pony is tied to his horse and across it, instead of supplies, I see the body of a man, hands and feet bound, smears of blood staining the beast's flank. Brim.

"Bastard son of a trull!" I shout through the window, but the wrangler doesn't hear, the wind buffeting my voice back into the wagon. How could I have been so gullible, so stupid as to believe we had a deal? *Be careful of him. He's a good soul, born of bad.* I can't believe I was so dense. The Blood-wife meant the wrangler, not Brim.

"You should know, he saved Brim's life," Osha says. "They had a knife at his throat. It was the wrangler who stopped them."

I mull on this, focus switching between Brim and the Reis. "Brim's valuable," I tell her. "He's the only male heir of a Founding Four family. The wrangler knows he can be traded back to the citadel at a price."

"I'm worried he won't be worth anything if he loses much more blood," she says. "They won't let him travel in the wagon. I tried to get them to stop but–" She touches her arm and when I lift her sleeve there's a livid red welt curling around her wrist.

"Did the wrangler do this to you?" I ask, bile rising in my throat.

Osha shakes her head. "No. It was the raider with the bullwhip. But see that one over there?" She points out one of the men through the narrow gap. "He got angry and stopped him. I think he's their leader."

The Waster is taller and broader than the others, his size accentuated by a white bear pelt draped over his shoulders. His brown hair is thick and wavy, tied away from his face with only a strip of leather – none of the paraphernalia of other raiders in his convoy. He rides out of sight briefly, but as he reappears again in the window, closer now, the sunlight catches his face and I'm surprised to see he's younger than I first thought. High cheekbones show the scars of combat but his skin still has the vigour of early manhood and his eyelashes are thick and long, almost too feminine for the cleft in his chin, the line of his jaw, where the faint blue thread of a branding runs under blond stubble, and comes to rest under his ear. When he turns, perhaps sensing he's being watched, I realise he's not much older than Brim – too young, surely, to be in control of such a crew? I think of Brim captaining his unit. One or two of his men are closer to his uncle's age than his own, it's true, but Isfalki Warders rise on their merit and are governed by strict oaths of office that obey the hierarchy of command – something I doubt a band of lawless barbarians could comprehend, let alone honour. If these trogs are willing to follow a leader not past his twenty-fifth year, there must be something special about him, brutal even.

One of his retinue calls out and he falls back to answer, bringing the wrangler into view again. Behind him on the pack horse, I notice Brim stir. Osha's right, his wound should be tended before he loses any more blood or infection sets in.

I push my face as far out of the narrow window as I can. "Hey! Wrangler!"

"Don't, Nara," Osha warns.

"Yeah, I'm talking to you!"

The wrangler draws his horse closer. I half expect that sardonic grin, but he only frowns. "Haven't got as much to say to me now, huh?"

"How's the head?" He's serious, unsmiling and I vow to myself I'll take out his eyes with my bare fingernails if I ever get close enough again.

"You expecting us all to piss in this wagon?"

He nods towards the Wasters up ahead. "They probably won't mind."

"What and soil the merchandise?" I clutch at the window, my knuckles white. It's taking everything I've got to control my anger, the latent panic I feel at being crated in this box on skis like we're goods for trade, and the wrangler can see it.

"Don't try anything, Little Scourge. These men aren't Warders playing games with blunted swords at the Moon Pools." He's distracted by the sound of a nuggety-looking raider hocking into the wind behind him. "That fine specimen right there hunts white bears for their skins and sups the brains in a soup. He won't think twice about cracking yours open on the ice."

The wagon lurches and Osha nudges me to come away from the window. I ignore her. "Maybe you should tell your trog friends that women freighted in their own piss don't make for a great bartering price," I shout.

He scoffs, the mist of his breath curling behind him. "You think I was born yesterday? You want to stop so you can fuss over Pretty Boy." He raises an eyebrow at me, and I grind my jaw in frustration. "Relax. The arrow head's out and I cleaned the wound. He'll live. But I'll convey your toileting concerns to Haus."

I watch him heel his horse to ride alongside the chief, and once again he surprises me: the Waster dialect rolls from his lips as if he'd been born to it, the words full of rhotic trills, strangely musical as they talk. Nothing about him is what it seemed. The wrangler has traded, quite literally, on the fact I've underestimated him.

"Where do you think they're taking us?" Sigrun asks.

As long as we're following the Heitval River, I figure we're heading south, but beyond that I've no idea.

"My guess is Orlathston," Dalla answers with conviction.

I peer at her through the shadows of the wagon. "Where now?"

"Orlathston. It's a port in the south-west. The biggest trading post in the Continent, actually. Didn't you know?"

I didn't. I've never even heard the name before. But that's hardly surprising. Lessons in geography were almost non-existent in our studies at the Mor school. The citadel always led us to believe Wastelander clans were nomadic, moving from one Old World ghost town to the next to scavenge and prey on survivors. They never spoke of any organised cities or trading settlements.

"And you know this how?" I ask Dalla.

"Cyrus told me. He's one of my family's kitchen servants," she says. "An outlander. Shocking brandings, but my father took him in because he was the most divine cook. You only had to taste his pies to immediately overlook his skin." She glances pointedly at my scalp and I tug on the wool of my hat, hoping the dim light hides the angry heat in my cheeks. "Cyrus had been a slave in Orlathston. He said it's the biggest colony in the Wastelands. Everything gets traded there – grain, livestock, weapons... women. Well, women like us anyway." She runs her eyes over Osha and Sigrun, making a point of my exclusion.

"And why would *you* give an outlander brandservant the time of day?" I ask her, thinking of all the cold-shouldering and barbs she's given Osha and I over the years.

"Brands have their place. Just not taking lessons in the Mor school." The highborn girl hitches her lip, waiting for my reaction, but Osha is already digging her nails into my hand. I take a breath and my sister smooths over my skin with her thumb. "Sometimes in the school holidays I'd go down to our kitchens for snacks when I was bored and Cyrus would tell me all these stories about the Outlands." Dalla continues, enjoying the fact she has everyone's attention, even mine. "Apparently, it's called Orlathston after Orlath. He's this crazy overlord who runs the entire colony. Orlath's forces control the port and trade routes, and his chiefs from all around have to tithe to him to use them. They compete with each other to gain his favour – and his favourite gifts are Mor. Cyrus told me Orlath has hundreds all lined up in his harems in the Orlathston stronghold." Her voice is edged with grisly fascination now but I feel a kind of validation imagining her, eyes alight and hanging off the words of an outland Brand. "He collects women from every corner of the Continent," she continues. "Even girls from far beyond the Storm Sands, tall and dark as a moonless night. They say he has varied tastes." The words come out as a breathy revelation, as if over some masculine foible to be indulged, like a weakness for sloefire or bone dice.

"And how did your cook happen to know so much about this Waster overlord, princess?"

"Because he worked in his kitchens, fec."

Osha's fingers tighten around mine again. "Thanks for sharing, Dalla," she interrupts, eyeing Sigrun with concern. The younger Mor is hanging on Dalla's every word, her face pale and bloodless with fear. "Most comforting, as usual."

"Well, we might as well know what we're facing," Dalla replies.

"You almost sound like you're looking forward to it," I toss at her.

"At least it's better than what happens to *fecs*."

"And what's that?" I ask. "Did Cyrus get you off on bedtime stories of Branded misery too?"

"He didn't have to. Everyone knows how Brand girls with no family put bread in their mouths." She lets her knees fall wide apart, her provocative meaning clear, despite her hobbled ankles. There are no Mor teachers here to castigate her crudeness, no highborn manners or family reputation to uphold in this wooden box crossing the Waster plains.

I force a smile. "Well, at least if *I* need to spread my legs, I'll get some say in who for. And I'll be earning my own keep. You Mor can hardly say the same, can you?"

Dalla's face drops, silenced for a moment. In fact, none of them speak. I slump against the wall of the wagon, feeling no satisfaction from it. That girl has a way of bringing out the worst in me. Osha rises to the window, turning her back to us... to me. Dalla might be briefly stung, then think nothing more of it, but Osha will lose sleep over my insult. She'll feign thick skin while underneath she'll whittle over my brandings, the differences between us, feeling even more guilty about what segregates us than she did before. Why can't I keep my thoughtless trap shut?

Even in the dimness, I can sense Dalla running her eyes over my stained hunting leathers, my worn boots that have probably been passed around the Sink more often than a winter cold. She's not going to let it drop. "Of course, you're assuming anyone would want to actually buy your wares." I might as well be a steaming turd she just stepped in, for the look she gives me. My palm itches to slap her, but I consider Osha and keep my mouth closed. "Rumour in the citadel has it you can fight with fists and knives, like any common tavern brawler," Dalla goes on. "And that you hunt like an animal. They say Brim Oskarsson taught you."

Mother's tits! "Brim did *not* teach me to hunt. *I* taught *him*."

But Dalla couldn't care less about the details. "My guess is they'll take one look at you and sell you to a fighting pit." I'm not sure what she's talking about, but I won't give her the satisfaction of asking. "Apparently, the only thing Wasters like more than fucking is fighting." A smug satisfaction plays in her voice as she offers me payback for my earlier snipe. "And Cyrus said Orlath's Cooler is the most infamous pit in the whole of the Wastelands. Thieves, outcasts, fire-Brands... fecs like you – they all end up there as fodder for his stable of fighters."

Osha turns from the window and I recognise the crush of worry on her face all too well. All these weeks she must have been agonising about my fate in the Branded village, cataloguing the fevers and poxes I might catch. And now, Dalla's suggesting I could meet my end in some kind of barbarian blood show?

Forced to choose, I'd prefer to go out fighting.

I drag off my hat, running bound fists over my shorn scalp – my best effort at nonchalance. "Good job this Cooler place is for women like me, then, not you," I tell Dalla, letting her get a good look at my branding. "Wouldn't want you mussing your hair or breaking a nail now, would we, princess?"

"Is everything a fecking joke to you, Nara?" Osha rounds on me.

I flinch suddenly shocked and sobered. My sister never uses that word, least of all as a curse. Her cheeks burn with shame, but most of all I know it's from fear: fear for me, fear for herself. Fear for us all.

I spend the next few hours pressed to the narrow window of the wagon trying to block out Dalla's endless taunting chatter with the sound of the icy wind, the bracing air helping to freeze my panic at being bound and confined. As the light begins to fade, an arm nudges my waist. Osha props her chin on my shoulder, peering through the small gap alongside me.

"Dalla's finally dozed off," she says.

"Elixion's cock, but that girl pulls my strings!"

"You allow her to." My sister turns me from the window so I face her. "We have more important things to talk about than Dalla."

Thoughts of Brim, my jealousy, her silence all that time we were parted rear up in my mind. I can't meet her eyes. I'm frightened if I do, all my hurt will spew out as accusations.

"You have to believe me, Nara, I never wanted Brim for myself. But I was so worried about you falling sick without me there to take care of you... maybe even dying before I could see you again. I was desperate and Brim convinced me it was our best chance of returning you to the citadel."

"Why didn't you send word? I waited every day, O."

"I tried to bribe the dorm maids, but you don't understand what it was like after you got expelled. I was being watched, night and day. They put a guard outside my door, and Mother Iness even came to the School to see me."

"Mother Iness?" The mention of the crone makes everything else seem petty. "What did she want?"

"She was asking about our life in the Fornwood, before Isfalk. I guess she was trying to understand who our parents could have been, how you came to be..." She falters, as if still trying to accept my new status. "How you came to be a Brand and I'm not."

"What did you tell her?"

Osha shakes her head. "I told her the truth – mostly. I said we never knew our parents and were brought up by our grandmother. That Amma had told us to head for the Isfalk fortifications if we ever needed protection. And when she died, that's what we did."

"Did you tell her about Amma being a healer, and teaching you to be one too?"

"No, of course not. I simply said she was a Fornwood Solitary. I wasn't about to make things worse than they already were."

"Did she try to force you in any way? Did she touch you?"

Osha frowns at the vehemence of my questions. "No, she didn't touch me. But it was a little odd. I've never been that close to Mother Iness before. When she reached for my hand, I had the strangest sensation, like–"

"Like what?"

"Like she wanted to know everything about me. To see inside my very soul."

"And did she?" I ask, panicked. "Did she touch you?" It seems suddenly crucial that Iness didn't get inside Osha's head the way she had mine on the stage of the Roundhouse.

"No. I already said she didn't touch me." My sister draws away a little at my reaction. "A guard came in and interrupted. He said Lars Oskarsson was asking for her in the Council."

"Good." I release a breath. "That's good."

"Why? What is it, Nara?"

I rub my forehead, thinking of Lars Oskarsson's coin in my pocket, trying to find the words to begin telling her everything that has happened. But when I fumble at the neck of my skins to draw out my pendant, I can't find the leather thong. I feel around my clothes as best I can with bound hands, but Osha stops the search. "The wrangler took it when you were unconscious." I snatch in a curse, locating him again through the window and wishing my stomach didn't dive at this final betrayal.

"What about yours?" I ask Osha.

"I'd hidden it in my boot for the Moon Pool rite, as we always do, but somehow he already knew about it. After he'd swiped yours, he asked for mine. I had no choice but to give it to him. *For safe keeping*, he said."

"Yeah, right."

"He was strangely discreet about it."

"I bet he was, the sly fec. The trogs would have asked for a cut if they'd seen those pendants. He'll sell them later and keep the profit for himself, no doubt."

"But how come he even knew we had them?"

I'm about to tell her when the wagon jolts to a sudden halt. The light is fading fast now but through the small window I can see the dark outline of trees. The Waster chief barks orders to his men and they separate, most of the convoy disappearing into the black forest, while he, the wrangler and a handful of others gather at the wagon. I move to the door, eager to be released first, impatient to get to Brim.

"Nara." Osha's hand is on my arm. "You should stay inside."

She can't help her gaze flitting to my scalp and I know what she's thinking.

"I've been surviving in the Isfalki slums all this time, O, and I haven't caught anything yet."

"But the Brand village is isolated. You've spent most of your life in the Mor school, sheltered from contagions and now... well, you saw them. They're scavengers. They travel the plains. They could be carrying all sorts of diseases that Isfalki have never been exposed to."

I know her worry springs from love, her wish to protect me, as I've always wanted to protect her, but her words cut almost as bad as seeing her on the stage with Brim. I pull down the wool of my hat. It's almost a habit now, a tic to hide the blue-black markings.

"I'm a Brand, Osha. It doesn't mean I'm permanently on my deathbed. I've never felt weak or vulnerable before, so don't make me start feeling that way now." Her cheeks flush and she nods reluctantly, before releasing my arm.

It turns out, I don't have a choice to stay in the wagon. The door is flung open and Wasters drag us all out into the snow. My grand speech to Osha feels like a lie now. I do feel suddenly weak and vulnerable because I'm weaponless, legs hobbled like a horse, and barely fit to stand after the blow to my head. The wrangler stares at my blood-soaked furs and spattered leathers.

"Admiring your handywork, mutt?"

He turns away to shoulder Brim's body from the pack horse, laying him down on the snow. Osha and I shuffle to kneel beside him. "He needs water," my sister says. She motions to a flask hanging from one of the raider's belts. "Water," she says again. "Please." Her voice is calm, gentle as she touches the trog's hand, but I'm still surprised when he gives it to her. Then again, that's Osha. All my life I've seen people respond to her in this way, falling under her spell, trusting her. I always thought it was simply charm, but now I'm doubtful. Could it be the higher skill the Blood-wife spoke of, that ability to sway emotions as well as heal? Perhaps she doesn't even know she's doing it, just like I was unaware of the way I hunted. I watch her lifting Brim's head, wetting his lips, as he rouses. It would explain a lot about my sister.

My thoughts are broken by the wrangler squatting over Brim to check the dressings at his ribs. I knock away his hands. "Don't you touch him! You've done enough already."

He doesn't answer, his face unreadable.

"Nara," Osha says in a low voice, "he saved Brim's life. I told you."

"And it wouldn't have needed saving if it wasn't for him." Brim coughs and as his awareness begins to return, he launches upright, railing against his bonds with such force a Waster clouts him hard about the ear. His head snaps back and he falls limp in the wrangler's arms, unconscious again. I spring to my feet as fast my hobbled ankles will allow. In a single motion I've seized the hilt of the wrangler's sword in my two fists and swung it to the closest neck I can find. It takes me a second to register that neck belongs to the young Waster chief, the man the wrangler called Haus. Cock's poxes! Osha always complains I never do anything by halves. No turning back now. I press the blade further into the pale stubble under his chin and grit my teeth, hoping he'll see only ruthless intent, instead of some crazy bitch with a head injury struggling to steady the blade. "On your fecking knees, trog scum," I spit. The chief doesn't move. "I said get on your—"

My legs buckle under me, kicked from behind – the very trick I use on Brim all the time. Someone yanks my ropes, prizing the sword from my grasp and I'm shoved down in the snow. Haus's cheeks shine with rage. There's the draw of metal, the flash of steel at his side, and I squeeze my eyes shut waiting for the blow to come.

Nothing happens.

When I look again, the wrangler is standing between us, talking in the Waster tongue, his tone with Haus familiar, almost jovial. But the young chief isn't about to let my insult be so easily forgotten. Arms folded and frowning, he thrusts his chin at the wrangler, his reply firm, expectant.

The wrangler turns as if he's about to walk away. His shoulders rise as he draws a long breath, fists working at his sides. And then my vision blurs, my ear feels like it's on fire, and all I can hear is a high-pitched ringing. He's belted me with his open hand. "That make you feel good? You fecking coward," I yell at his back as he studies the dark horizon.

Haus leads his horse to the tree line, apparently satisfied, and once Brim is slung over the pack pony, the convoy follow his tracks.

The wrangler hauls me to my feet by the scruff of my collar and leans in close. "I'm sorry for that," he says, "but I did warn you not to try anything. You need to trust me. Please."

I jerk away from him in disgust. I have no words. Instead, I
hock up a mouth of bloody spit, my only satisfaction seeing it
land squarely on his cheek.

A Song in the Night

The wrangler tugs me after him through the trees. Lights flicker a little way into the forest and, as we get closer, I can make out the Waster convoy at the burned-out ruins of a Solitary dwelling. Memories of our cabin in the Fornwood make my chest tighten. Two walls of the home and part of its roof still stand, offering some shelter from the snow that blows off the canopy of surrounding trees. In the lee of this cabin, a large fire is already burning, tended by a small group of Wasters who've clearly been awaiting our arrival.

Brim is propped against the remains of an animal stall, where the supply packs and saddles are stacked out of the snow. He's still unconscious, his eye swollen shut and his lip split, and my first instinct is to shuffle over to him, but the wrangler tugs me back. "Go sit with them." He motions to Osha and the other women, waiting till I've begrudgingly done his bidding before joining the rest of the convoy setting up camp for the night.

The smell of cooking meat makes saliva pool in my mouth and when the men settle down to eat, Osha turns her head away. Dalla and Sigrun squirm in torment, too. I cast around for the wrangler. He's watering and blanketing his horse, not far off, earning catcalls and laughter from the other men, whose own unkempt mounts nicker and bite each other over feed scattered on the snow.

"Hey, Wrangler!" I shout. "Are we getting fed any time soon? Or do trogs only feed women after their horses?"

He concentrates on his mare, but I know he's heard because he calls to one of the Wasters and a few minutes later something hits my shoulder. Peering at it by the light of the fire, I make out the mostly eaten haunch of a snowjack. Seconds later, a hunk of fat and skin lands in Sigrun's lap, and a thigh bone at Dalla's feet. The girls' mouths are tight with pride, but their eyes are alive with hunger. Sigrun waits, watching me, as if for a cue. Starving ourselves isn't going to serve any purpose other than making us more miserable and weak than we already are, so I brush off the haunch and begin to share what's left of the meat with my sister. The others fall on the leftovers like dogs on a carcass. Mother, but it tastes good. Dalla gives me a look sharp enough to draw blood, but she bolts down the food anyway. She probably hates herself for enjoying it, but survival is our priority now. Even she knows that.

I barely pay attention to the figure who's crossed from the other side of the fire until she holds out a water skin. We've had nothing to drink since before the ambush and Dalla grabs the canteen without thanks, gulping at the contents. It comes back up in a noisy splutter. The raiders whoop into the night.

"It's dramur vit," Osha says, without needing to sniff the contents. She takes the skin from Dalla, marvelling at its weight. "I've never seen so much before... and offered around so freely." In Isfalk, she'd have risked a good deal to get her hands on such a quantity for her medicines. Two cups can make a grown man sleep for a day and a night, or a suffering child slip peacefully into the arms of Holy Mother. But the distillation of vit is known only to Wastelanders and few but the most connected in the citadel have the ways and means of procuring it from beyond the Walls.

We pass the liquor around, sipping cautiously, wheezing and breathing in its herby aftertaste, like the smell of nettles after summer rain. I feel the fire catch instantly in my belly, the night's brittle chill chased from my bones, and my aches and pains gradually retreating. I understand now that it's probably the very reason these trogs can survive night after night in the merciless cold without shelter.

"Here." The woman who gave Dalla the vit hands me another skin. "This one's water. You looked like you needed the grog first." As she draws to the light of the fire, I notice her face for the first time. The sudden shock of recognition steals my breath more than the liquor.

"Annek?" I catch her arm so she turns to me. "Annek Mikkelson?" I remember her voice, the flash of fury in her eyes as she looked at her Elix husband from the stage that fateful Morday Mass.

She lifts her chin in affirmation. "You're from the Mor school." It's a statement, not a question.

"Yeah… well, they are," I say, pointing to the other girls.

"Annek? What are you doing here?" Osha asks. "You were supposed to be sent to the Torvag colony. What happened?"

"Torvag," Annek scoffs, glancing around the fire at the Wasters busy eating. "Don't you get it? *They* are Torvag."

I'm struck dumb, trying to work out what she means. "There is no Torvag," she says, seeing our floundering faces. "It doesn't exist."

"But I saw you that night from the dorm window," Osha says. "I watched Warder guards load you and Estrid into a wagon and take you west across The Fold."

"Yeah, well, maybe if you'd kept watching you'd have seen the sleds that returned with sacks of grain and chests of weapons in the early hours." She folds her arms, watching us as we take in her words. "Did you think the Isfalki citadel could survive all these years on what a village of starving Brands can provide?"

A wave of realisation, terrible and sickening begins to wash through me. After everything I've seen on both sides of the citadel walls, what she's suggesting makes sense.

"I don't understand," Osha persists. She hasn't seen what I have, but she's smart – smarter than me – and I think she does understand; she'd simply prefer not to.

"I'm saying Iness and Fjäll have been trading with Wastelanders all along. Mor breeders in exchange for supplies." Annek can't spell it out much more bluntly.

"But you mean *sentenced* Mor, surely?" Dalla qualifies.

"Sentenced, my arse!" Annek bursts out. "You can't seriously believe those crimes? They're fabricated. All of them."

"But the Council can't possibly have agreed to–"

"The Council turn a blind eye. They don't want to dig too deeply into how the Elixion and that crone manage to keep them fed and pampered. Iness, Fjäll, my *beloved* ex – they're Mikkelson blood and Mikkelsons do whatever it takes to maintain their control of the Founding Four, the Council… the whole fecking Settlement!"

Dalla reacts first, and her words shock the breath from me. "I've heard talk of it before," she says. "Rumours. Among Cyrus and our brandservants in the Thorval kitchens." It's a revelation I wasn't expecting from her, of all people. Her eyes work busily, trying to sort through the evidence in her memory. "I asked Papa about it once, but he only got angry and said to never mention that kind of gossip again. But afterwards he must have felt guilty because he told me nothing bad would ever happen to anyone from a Founding Four family. The Thorval name was too powerful, he said."

Annek barks a scathing laugh. "Don't be a little fool! Thorval, Oskarsson, Friskar, Mikkelson – the Founding Four names are only that – names! They don't protect you if you're not doing what Iness wants. Fec's sake, I paired with a *Mikkelson*, her own great-grandson, and the bitch got rid of me!" She takes a breath, sitting down beside us and snatching the vit skin. "A Mor is only as powerful as the children she can bear. If they can't farm you like a brood sow, you're nothing but a useless mouth to feed." She takes a good swig, wincing on the hit of liquor. "You schoolgirls have no idea of the worst of it. You're not even Paired yet." She turns on Dalla with snide curiosity, "What got a Thorval Mor here anyway? Don't tell me Daddy's Little Girl got too friendly with one of the dormitory maids at school?"

Dalla jerks her chin disdainfully. "We were ambushed during the cleansing rite at the Moon Pools, if you must know."

"Oh, I see. So much classier," Annek says. "And yet here we all are, utterly shafted by the citadel."

Osha turns to me. "Do you think it's true?" she whispers.

I have no doubt at all that it's true. She must see it in my face because she falls quiet, busy with her thoughts. I stare into the fire, ruminating on my own. If all this time Iness was trading Mor to feed the citadel, it only makes sense she'd offer the troublesome Mor first – Paired women like Annek whose husbands claimed they couldn't give them children or those whom Iness found problematic. I think of the night of my own exile and something occurs to me.

"Annek, what happened to Estrid... Estrid Halvar?"

She stills, biting her lips together.

"Annek?" I ask again and she hugs her belly as if the thought makes her physically uncomfortable.

Osha reaches her hands to Annek's brow, brushing gently over a cut above her eye that I hadn't even noticed. It's only half-healed. "Tell us," Osha says softly. The tightness falls from Annek's face and her shoulders drop in exhaustion, as if finally able to set down a burden she's been carrying alone for weeks.

"Warders put us in a sled wagon... after the Mass. They ordered two wranglers from the barracks to take us across The Fold. When we reached the Fornwood, they stopped, but only Estrid was dragged out. I went for the fec who grabbed her. Got this for my pains –" She waves a hand towards the cut. "They locked me in the wagon and took her into the trees."

"Mother's love," Osha says.

"I thought... you know... Estrid was beautiful and a Mor.

Something they could brag about in the village taverns. But it was worse than that." Annek swallows hard. "They came back without her. And I watched them cleaning the blood and dirt from their hands in the snow."

"They *killed* her?" I ask.

She gives a tight nod. "I've no idea why. At first, I thought they'd forced themselves on her and she'd put up a fight and it had all got out of hand. But it happened too fast for that. They'd known what they were about... like they were acting on someone else's orders."

"Whose? Who in the citadel would give such an order? She was already exiled, so why..." Osha presses Annek with more questions but I'm barely listening, too busy staring into the fire and turning over my own thoughts. I think about the way Estrid touched me that time I cut myself on the ice, how I'd trusted her, the sense I'd had of her energy when she was near me, similar to the way I felt around my sister. Estrid was citadel-born, so no one could have taught her to heal as Amma had Osha. And yet she knew instinctively what to do with the wound, and afterwards I'd felt no pain. She had to be a Sway, a healer like the Blood-wife described. Is it possible Iness could have felt the skill in her, as she had in me, and decided to make her exile more final? I think of the ghosthawk, that uncanny bird attacking me on the ice plains and then appearing again on my tail at the Moon Pools, as if the crone was there, tracking me through its hard, glassy eye. I shiver and search the dark canopy, imagining the mocking tinkle of its talon bell. But it's the soft thrum of strings that breaks my thoughts, a sound I never expected to hear at this moment, in a trog convoy in the middle of the forest.

Music.

Across the fire, Haus has drawn a small five-stringed lute from his saddlebag. He tunes the pegs. working the frets with surprisingly practised hands. Slow and lazy at first, as if warming both the strings and his fingers, he gradually slides into a tune of

multiple picking and complex harmonies – a melody in a minor
key that sounds familiar. I can't help but stare, noticing the way
the music changes the atmosphere around the camp, the mood
among the men. Haus's eyes glaze, and his hand strokes the
fretboard with a skill that seems to belong at a citadel banquet
rather than this makeshift camp of raiders.

What *is* that song? It takes me back to the cabin in the
Fornwood, grinding herbs with my sister at Amma's stained
table. Osha must feel the pull of it too, because after a while
she closes her eyes. And that's when it comes to me – the
lullaby our grandmother used to sing to us as children. I
turn to Osha, see her lashes glistening wet in the firelight.
Memories of the past mingle with news of Estrid's fate and our
fraught circumstances, only serving to heighten the pathos of
the music. Haus stops playing suddenly and stares at my sister
across the fire. His voice when he speaks is not a barked order
but a question, surprise and pleasure obvious in his tone.

"The chief asks if you know this song?" the wrangler
translates, directing the question at Osha. And I realise my
sister has been softly humming the melody. She nods slowly.
"Haus invites you to sing it."

"Tell the chief he can go to–" But Osha gives me the hard
stare and clears her throat. Her tongue clicks dryly as she opens
her mouth but then her thin voice sounds in the lonely night.
It's a murmur at first, almost as if she's singing for her own
distraction, just as she used to as a child searching for herbs
along the medicine trails in the Fornwood. I'd forgotten the
words of the ballad – the story of the girl waiting alone on the
plains for a lover who never comes. But as the anguish of the
song grows, so does my sister's voice, limpid and plaintive as
the stars on a clear night above the Fold, Haus's lute weaving
harmonies about it so perfectly they make my heart stutter.

Everyone about the camp is silent, bewitched. In the firelight,
the men's faces glaze as if each is remembering some secret
yearning that burns inside them, more potent even than the

dramur vit in their bellies. And when the song ends – the heart of the forsaken heroine ground into a million pieces against the evening sky – an absence hangs in the air that hollows my chest with some unexplored want.

The young chief studies Osha across the fire. His expression makes me want to place myself between them, but my sister looks straight at him, that self-possession, that quiet determination in her face I know so well from childhood – her own brand of bravery.

When Haus rises and comes to loom over us, I scuttle to shield Osha from him, but he only reaches around me to lift a lock of her hair, as if he's examining the suppleness of a new whip or bridle from a looted settlement. The brandings on his hands are fine but extensive, like skeins of blue spider silk and I marvel at how a Brand could get to his size and strength, just as I did when I first saw the wrangler.

The young chief leaves us, only to return moments later with another skin of dramur vit and a plate of freshly cooked meat. He sets them at Osha's feet, and behind him I sense a change come over the camp. His men shift and exchange glances. Haus ignores them, returning to his furs to bed down for the night.

The rest of the camp follow suit soon after.

The hiss of embers and the soft nickering of a horse wakes me. It's still dark and the rest of the camp snores, save for the three Wasters on watch, whose movements I sense pacing the clearing. Beside me at the fire, I recognise the outline of the wrangler, shoving another log on the embers.

"Haus honoured your sister tonight," he says in a low voice. I don't know how he can tell I'm awake as he's staring into the flames. "Hrossi chiefs are not in the habit of serving women food. It was the song – a smart move on your sister's part." The way he says it is more a criticism of me than praise of Osha.

"Really? That trog scum fed us because of a ditty?"

He angles towards me, one side of his face lit by the warm glow. "It was no *ditty*. That *trog scum* was singing the song of his ancestors. It's part of his Hrossi heritage, his identity."

"Whatever... I hardly care." I roll awkwardly onto my back, fuming at my restraints and staring at the waning moon through the branches overhead. My mind is tripping over itself with questions, but I refuse to give him the satisfaction of asking.

"You should care. The Hrossi believe the heroine of that song, Effa, was a Mor healer of great skill – a Sway in all likelihood. That ballad tells how she was betrayed by a Pure prince."

"Fascinating."

He ignores my deadpan tone. "Other songs sing of her rescue by Ska, the Great Rider of the Plains, and how she became the First Mother of the Hrossi clans. One day, they believe she'll send a daughter of her blood to heal the Continent and return health and prosperity to her people."

"Well, they may sing that song, but it doesn't belong only to them. It's a lullaby my grandmother sang to us when we were children, and she was a Fornwood Solitary, not some scavenging plains rat."

I catch the wrangler's raised eyebrow, the glitter of scepticism in his eye as he looks at me. "Is that so?"

I open my mouth to retort but find the words falling away. When I come to think about it, the lyrics and melody of that ballad were nothing like any other song of the Solitaries we'd sing, or even those of the Isfalki I've heard since. Could it have been a Waster ballad all along? And if so, how did Amma come by it? Did she have some connection to the Wastelands?

"The Hrossi believe Effa was flame-haired – lucky for you and your sister," he continues.

"Lucky?" I push onto an elbow and sit up. "How exactly is that lucky, Wrangler?"

"Because it has saved you for better things."

"Oh, so it gets better than this?" I lift my bound fists.

"Look, Isfalki Mor are the pinnacle of strong breeding stock and highly valued by the Hrossi. Your sister, red-haired as Effa, is especially prized – a good-luck charm for the whole convoy. They're superstitious like that." I grunt my distaste, but he ignores me. "Haus has debts of allegiance to pay. He owes dues to Orlath, his overlord in the south, and even *trog scum* don't offer gifts that have already been... sampled, shall we say?"

"Is that supposed to show some semblance of manners?" I draw away from him in revulsion. "These barbarian scavengers have us hobbled like cattle ready for trade! And you ask me to trust you, knowing you're in on it? You sicken me, Wrangler."

He rubs his jaw silently as if I've punched him there. "Go ahead and hate me." He nods towards Brim, still unconscious by the animal stall. "Being alive and hating me is better than loving him and dead."

"How can you even say that when it was your backstabbing that landed us here in the first place?"

"*My* backstabbing?" He squares up to me now. "Alright, Little Scourge, try to keep up," he says, as if he can't hold his tongue any longer. "Firstly, the crone had it in for you the moment she read your skill on the Roundhouse altar. I saw it in Iness, even from the rear of the crowd – the realisation, the shock of sensing the skill in you. And she felt threatened enough by it to want you dead... to want *both* of you dead." He flicks his eyes to the sleeping Osha, Sigrun huddled against her for warmth.

"How can you know that?"

He stares at my neck pointedly, the scratch left behind by the ghosthawk. And it all begins to slide into place: Estrid, the wranglers who took her to the Fornwood and killed her, Iness's interest in me and my sister. "You followed her tiercel to find me that day on the ice. *You* were supposed to be the one to kill me." He doesn't answer, and I know I'm right. "Except, you didn't. You disobeyed her orders and then beat the bird off when it came for me." I stare at him wide-eyed. "Why?"

He breaks a twig, tosses it into the flames, watching it burn. Eventually he says, "I told Iness you'd swayed me and the bird, and then escaped. She gave me another chance to do it at the Moon Pools, as long as I took out your sister as well."

"So, all this time, you've been spying for Mother Iness? Working for her?"

"Well, obviously not, otherwise you and Osha would be buried under snow by now... so would Pretty Boy."

"She wanted Brim dead, too? Why? It doesn't make sense."

"Doesn't it? The heir to one of her key detractors on the Council just Paired with a Mor she senses is a Sway. That's a threat to her power Iness won't entertain."

I mull it over. Osha said Iness hadn't touched her when she'd visited the Mor school, so how did the crone come to suspect she had the skill? Then I remember. The Pairing rite at Morday Mass – the old woman took my sister's hand to join it with Brim's. Was that why Osha's face looked pained? I thought it was guilt because of Brim, but was she flinching at the old woman's touch, the shock of her energy? And yet, neither of them reacted like Iness and I had when she'd grabbed my wrist. Perhaps the crone was expecting it, was prepared for it this time. Perhaps Osha fell under her Sway without the fight I'd given Iness.

"So why didn't you do it?" I ask the wrangler again. "Why didn't you kill us like she wanted?" He gets onto his haunches as if about to leave, closing down the conversation. "Answer me, Wrangler!"

"Because I don't work for Mother Iness."

"Haus offered you a better deal for us, then? That's what this is all about – your own gain?"

"No," he says quietly, his body seeming to shift under the weight of things unsaid. He stands and nudges a log with his boot, making embers lift into the night like star flies. "This is so much bigger than that," he murmurs at last, and his voice sounds so pensive, his expression so burdened that I almost believe him. Almost.

"Who *are* you, Wrangler?" I whisper. He blinks at me as if he's genuinely considering an answer. But when he steps away from the fire I know I'll get no more from him this night.

"You know, you should have done it. You should have let that bird tear me apart on the ice or stuck your knife in me at the Moon Pools."

"Why?"

"Because the first chance I get at a weapon, I'm going to bury it hilt-deep in your guts."

His lifts his head to look at me, his teeth flashing white in the firelight. He hasn't worn that grin since he told me of my antics at Helgah's. "That's the spirit, Little Scourge!" he says, utterly entertained.

"Go to hell."

"I meant what I said before, though." His voice drops a register. "Don't try anything with these men. I'm not sure how many times I can save your sorry skin."

"I don't need it saving by a Reis mutt."

"I'm serious. It won't hurt to keep them at arm's length. You're not a Mor, after all."

"I'm quite capable of defending my own honour, if that's what you're worried about."

"Oh, they won't bother you in *that* way."

"Why not?" I say, suddenly indignant. "Aren't I good enough for trog scum?"

He clears his throat and I see that mole jumping in this cheek. "I told them you'd worked your way round half the Isfalki taverns – the slummy half. They think you've got a chronic case of groin clap." He's fighting hard not to laugh out loud now. "The only reason they didn't leave you at the pools was because I said you were the dirtiest fighter I'd seen outside of Orlath's Cooler. They're keeping you to sell to his lanista." He looks me up and down, fully enjoying my fury, and I make a note to carve out that poxy mole first if I ever get my hands back on my skinning knife. "You'd be quite the novelty, you know. They don't see female fighters from the north much. Even I'd risk a wager on you, Little Scourge."

"And you'll probably use our pendants to do it, I suppose?"

"Probably."

I lie down again and close my eyes, but all I can hear is the sound of his chuckling. I'd rather toss and turn in the fevered sheets of hell than let him have the last word. "I'm getting those pendants back, Wrangler. Best sleep with your hand on your sword."

Lies and Influencing

We continue our journey before true day. Annek is put in our wagon sled, which becomes even more cramped with another person taking up space and air. My breathing grows shallow and panicked as soon as the door is locked, and it takes everything I've got not to scratch and claw against the wood like some wild thing. Osha knows to keep me near the window slit, and instead of listening to my thundering heart, I try to concentrate on the voices of Haus and the wrangler riding alongside us, the burr of Hrossi words in the Reis's mouth, wondering how he came to learn them.

It's a fair distraction – channeling my terror of confinement into rage at him, and it keeps me vaguely sane.

Around midday, Brim regains consciousness. I peer through the vent as he's mounted on the pack pony, his hands still bound, the reins now led by a Waster who appears to be assigned his personal watch. The man has an array of weapons slung from his saddle that the Isfalki armoury would be hard-pressed to match, and he wears an unusually mechanised bow across his shoulders that in different circumstances I'd have begged to try. But for the most part he stays well away from our window. Even when we make camp that night, he keeps Brim separated from us.

Snowstorms buffet the next few days into endless white and

I lose track of our direction. We spend one merciless night in the derelict hovel of an abandoned settlement, and the rest of them shivering around campfires that flounder in the lee of the wagon sleigh, the lulls in the perishing winds filled only by another kind of howling – wolves and plains dogs scrapping over our leavings. I mark off the days on a panel of the wagon, drawing numerals on the wood with a charred stick from the campfire. It's the only thing I can do to stop myself scratching endlessly at the stubble growing back on my scalp, or gnawing my nails or cracking my joints til they ache. Anything to keep my mind off being trapped in this box, this moving crate too small for us all to lie down straight. Many a time, Osha talks me from the precipice as I suck at the air through the window slit. The icy stab of it in my lungs braces me a little, and Osha's hushed voice in my ear reminds me of Amma's, leading me beyond the panic of my own body and into the wider world beyond. *Breathe. What do you smell? Listen. What do you hear?* The heartbeat of the horses, steady, focused, almost unified; the way their instincts are nothing but dogged pace, their only focus the route through the snow ahead. It reins me in, keeps me one step away from the dread of being trapped, the terrible urge I have to hurl myself against the walls of the wagon until I'm bruised and bloody.

Osha is careful to stay between me and Dalla in the cramped space. But the highborn girl no longer studies my bloody leathers and shaved scalp with leery disdain like I'm something wild just caught from the Fornwood. The truth is, after seven days in the Waster convoy, even she is turning a little feral, losing her Isfalki airs and sensitivities. At night, she scrambles with the rest of us to the fire, scoffing the meat we're fed and grateful for the extra furs tossed our way, however mangy. And she sips the dramur vit as eagerly as we all do – a ritual to keep the cold and our thoughts at bay. It numbs the fear of what lies ahead, but also the hurt of what's behind. I see it in Dalla's eyes when she passes me the skin one evening – the first tentative sign that even she is starting to understand that we're all outcasts now.

Haus continues to favour my sister whenever we make camp, troubling himself to see she's given fresh meat from the spit and a vit skin, even sending over a roll of pelts from his own pack one bitterly cold night. Sometimes he requests she sing again when he brings out his lute, and she obliges. But the music makes me almost as uneasy as the sound of the wagon door closing each morning, the turn of the key locking us inside.

My sister is courteous, constantly diplomatic in a way I never could be, even going so far as to ask the wrangler to teach her words in the Hrossi dialect. In the evenings, she takes out the copybook she carried with her from Isfalk in the pocket of her cloak and reads until Haus finishes giving orders around the camp, whereupon he unbinds her hands and watches fascinated as, lacking ink and quill, she clumsily makes notes of the Hrossi phrases with charcoal from the fire.

His men, however, seem nowhere near as captivated as Haus is watching my sister read and write. Instead, they observe her warily from the corners of their eyes as if she might be casting a spell on their young chief with her scrawled ciphers. I don't confront Osha about it. I know my sister. She'd only ask me what harm there was in learning how to communicate with the enemy. And perhaps she'd be right, perhaps day after day spent packed into a cell on skis with four other girls is making me imagine things. I have no studies of apotheka and physik to distract me from our predicament as Osha does, no bow to restring or arrows to fletch. Maybe I'm spending too much time watching, over-analysing everything.

The night Haus orders all of our bindings removed, I realise I'm not. We all rub at our chafed skin in relief, enjoying the freedom to stretch our legs, even if we know there's nowhere to run for miles around. Afterwards, I notice the way the men turn their faces from Haus, brooding silently over their vit skins as he exchanges words and signs with Osha by the campfire.

The ropes aren't replaced the next morning either and, as if we've rounded a symbolic bend in our route, the blizzards blow themselves out and the sky starts to lift. It comes as a small release to my claustrophobic thoughts.

Over the next couple of days, the temperature rises a little and I see grasses tufting through the snow here and there. Then, one morning, finally blessed by sunshine and free of the constant howl of the wind, the convoy slows unexpectedly. The other girls crowd behind me at the window, eager to find out what's happening. I can hear Haus barking orders, the whinny of horses and bridles jangling, and, in between, the glorious sound of something I haven't heard in a long time: running water. When the wagon finally jolts to a halt, there's a river cutting through the snow, bright sunlight dancing on the surface of a rockpool up ahead. Some of the men have already stripped and are attempting to bathe in the icy flow. Others are discarding their furs and undershirts on the banks, enjoying the luxury of warm sun on bare skin.

The wrangler approaches Brim at the river's edge, motioning for the guard to untie his prisoner's hands. The Waster refuses. Undeterred, the wrangler shucks Brim's furs and undershirt down as far as his roped wrists, baring his pale torso. He removes the dressings from Brim's wound and washes it with river water he's drawn in a cooking pot. The two men exchange words. I can't make them out but I can tell from their body language they're terse, hostile. Both sets of eyes turn to the wagon – to me, peering through the vent. Whatever the wrangler says must goad Brim for, despite being hampered by his bindings, he aims a two-fisted swipe at the Reis's head. The wrangler ducks clear easily, but then there's a splash, a gutteral cry of shock. Brim stands stunned and gasping, drenched in the freezing water the wrangler has tossed at his face.

Kicking off his boots and reefing his undershirt over his head, the wrangler wades into the river. Before I know it, I'm staring at his shoulders, skin smooth and brown as buckwheat honey, the torque of muscles around his ribs, the swell of his naked buttocks. His branding is a blue-black line wandering down his neck all the way across his shoulder and under his sword arm. It stops my breath. I've never seen markings spread beyond the head, neck or hands before. They seem far too pronounced and extensive for his height and build. *The worse the branding, the weaker the Brand*, the citadel saying claims. Definitely not true in the wrangler's case.

He dives under the water, and I follow the ripples until he surfaces again, panting at the cold, his messy locks dripping, sunlight catching the burnished metal rings that bind them. Brim watches him too, his bare back to me, and I study the two men: their similar heights, their physiques honed to a life outdoors, the hefting of weapons and the scars to prove it. And yet how far apart they are in birth and status. the aura each one gives off as different as a lone wolf from a purebred hunting hound. Comparing them gives me an uneasy feeling. I don't know why.

When the wrangler calls out to Brim, his only response is a volley of spit in the Reis's direction. I've reacted to the wrangler in exactly the same way myself, but I get a strange prickle of shame under my skin watching Brim do it. Despite everything I've accused the wrangler of, Osha is right: he saved Brim's life when the Hrossi threatened to kill him; he's tended his wounds and seen he was properly fed at night. I might heap insults on the wrangler, but it suddenly seems poor entertainment to watch Brim do it.

"Admiring the view?" Osha says, nudging my shoulder at the window. I startle, frowning at the heat I feel creeping up my neck.

"I'm… getting our bearings. It's the first time we've stopped in the middle of the day."

Osha nods slowly, giving me a wry look that says she knows better. She joins me, gazing out beyond the river at a line of distant hills, their skirts a crimping of purple-edged forest. In the middle distance, a herd of scrawny goats bleat over patches of yellowed grass that have broken clear of the snow. They're the first domestic animals I've seen out in the open since last summer in The Fold. It already seems like years ago.

"I think we're heading west now," Osha says. "Did you notice?"

I nod. "They're not going to get us much further in this." I kick the side of the wagon with my boot and as if I've conjured it, the door is suddenly unbolted. Wasters motion us out, and I'm the first to oblige. It's the only time we've ever been released in full daylight, and I squint and stretch, taking in lungfuls of the crisp, bright air. The guards toss our furs on the snow, emptying the sled, and when I see the hateful box being driven away to the east, I let out a deep breath of relief.

A guard shoves me towards the rest of the convoy at the river and Osha catches my arm, still fearful of my vulnerability to the outside world, the sicknesses I might contract. But I can see on her face she's conflicted – hungry for fresh air, for daylight and a taste of freedom. We all are. "Relax, O. If I haven't caught anything from these trogs by now, I'm hardly likely to, am I?" She's quiet as we reach the bank, so I bend down and flick her with the freezing water, until she can't take it anymore and splashes me back. Sigrun, Dalla and Annek follow suit and before we know it, we're all squealing like children. The shock of the water, the sunlight and air feel like a rush of life after the sleigh's confinement. When we're soaked through, we find a spot to unbutton our wet clothes and wash. Haus calls out to our guards and they keep their distance, giving us a little privacy.

Osha climbs up onto a smooth boulder where the snow has melted and sits cross-legged, face tilted to the sun. I follow suit, basking in the brightness, the lulling gush of water, relishing the open space and freedom for a while. Not far along the bank, the wrangler braves the depths again and I watch as his dark shape moves under the surface.

"I know you don't trust him," Osha says. "You think he betrayed us."

"Who?"

"Don't be dense," she says impatiently. "I see the way the wrangler looks at you when he thinks no one else is watching."

"What, with blind greed? He's probably imagining his cut when they trade me to some fighting pit."

"Narkat, come on... there's something between you. I can see it." I turn away, making it clear I'm not about to honour that comment with an answer. "Why did you screw up your face?" she says. "Is it at my suggestion, or at the thought of him submerged in that freezing water? I can't tell."

"Both." I pick up a pebble and begin scratching at the surface of the boulder, trying to avoid her questioning.

"You know, we'd still be hobbled if it wasn't for him. Haus had our ropes removed, but the wrangler put the idea there, and you know it."

"Big deal! It's not like we've got anywhere to run. We're hundreds of miles from Isfalk, Wasters all around us, with no supplies, no–"

"I have this sense that he's looking out for us. You said he didn't kill you like Mother Iness ordered. I think we're more than simply a trade to him."

"Is that so? Well, I have this sense that he's a lying traitor who got us into this shit in the first place." I slash an angry line through the marks I've scratched, then toss the pebble into the current. "We could have been living in the Fornwood by now if I hadn't trusted him. And if he makes me spend another day locked in a wagon, I swear, give me a knife and I'll open his guts without a second thought."

"No, you wouldn't."

"Wouldn't I?"

She fixes me with that frank look – the one that says I'm being simplistic and naïve, the one that always makes me want to wriggle away so I don't have to confront the messy truth.

"If he's only motivated by greed, why didn't he get Haus to pay his cut up-front and save himself this wretched journey?"

"He took our pendants. I'd say he's motivated by greed."

"Maybe, but then why is he still here? He spared your life, but he didn't have to spare your virtue, did he? If he's just a *lying traitor*, why would he be so interested? It doesn't make sense." Osha nudges my thigh with her knee to get an answer. I move my leg away, narked by her logic. "He watches you, Nara. I've seen it. You have more sway over him than you imagine."

I flinch at the word. *Sway*. It's taken on new meaning ever since the Blood-wife. I've told Osha about the wrangler saving me from the ghosthawk and disobeying Mother Iness's orders, but I haven't spoken of our visit to the witch, the visions I had and what the Blood-wife told me about Sways. I let my sister assume Iness wanted me dead for stirring up Brands in the village, because that was partly true. But I've failed to tell her the whole story because we're never alone, we've never had a moment's peace without the other girls overhearing. Until now. I've never kept things from her before, but there's so much to tell I struggle to find the words to begin.

"Forget the wrangler for a minute, Osha, okay?"

"Alright." She shrugs.

"When Mother Iness touched your hands at the Pairing ceremony, what did you feel?"

She frowns, puzzled at the turn in the conversation. "I'm not sure what you mean."

"You said when she came to see you at the Mor school, it felt like she wanted to look inside your soul. And when she finally touched you at the Pairing ceremony, you flinched like you were shocked or scared. I saw it."

"She'd just slashed my palm with an altar knife. Of course I flinched." She laughs a little, but flippancy is my trick, not hers and my expression must tell her so because she says, "I probably looked scared because I'd realised Pairing with Brim was a terrible mistake. That's all."

"Really?"

She nods.

"So you didn't feel anything when Iness touched you?"

"No. I've said so, haven't I?" She's tense, her answer curt.

I stare at her, not expecting it. "What about when you heal? Do you feel something then?"

"What do you mean? Like what?"

"Like you can understand the sick person... like you can sense what's wrong with them when you touch them."

"Nara, what is this about? Is it because Amma treated us differently? Because she taught you to hunt and me to heal? Are you harping on that again?"

I lick my lips. "Maybe."

She sighs. "You've always been so hung up on the differences between us. I know it must be even harder now because I'm... you're a..." She doesn't finish, as if she can't put words to the condition that draws a hard and fast line between us.

"I'm a *Brand*, Osha. You can say it."

"Look, I know you've always felt different, like you never quite belonged in the citadel. And I know you always thought going back to the Fornwood and trying to find out more about our parents would be the answer." She looks at me with a sadness and a guilt that cuts sharper than any knife. "It must make everything seem all the more confusing because I'm still Pure... but, Nara, this is who we are, and I don't see how we're ever going to be able to explain it. Everyone who knows about our past is dead. We'd do better to focus on the here and now."

"You're wrong," I tell her. "It's not about that. Just listen."

I run my fingers over the stubble of my scalp and down my neck, trying to find a place to begin, but words have never been my strong suit. And with the passage of time and the reality of our situation here among the Waster convoy, everything the Blood-wife told me suddenly sounds so far-fetched. How can I explain it to my rational, practical sister?

"When I hunt, I get this feeling," I tell her. "It's... well, it's as if I know the innermost workings of my quarry. Like I can almost hear the pulse of the creatures I track, smell what they smell, understand their desires and fears. It's like all my senses come together to make a whole new perception that allows me to understand their behaviour, to influence it even. I hardly know I'm doing it, and I'm not very good at switching it on and off at will. But I know other people don't hunt like that."

I check her reaction. Her face is unreadable. "I've seen you heal, O, the way you lay your hands on the sick sometimes, the concentration on your face, and I thought... I mean, do you ever experience healing like that... the way I hunt?"

She lets out a breathy laugh. "What, like I know the innermost minds of the sick? Are you serious?" Reaching over to palm my forehead she says, "Maybe you haven't eaten enough today? Are you feeling light-headed?"

I push her hands away. "Stop it, O. I'm not joking for once." She sits up straight, looking down over the river instead of at me. I notice her cheeks are flushed. "Just tell me. Do you ever feel that way when you heal?"

For a split second, she hesitates. Her mouth opens and her lip quivers, as if searching for an answer. And then she fixes me with those shrewd eyes, eyes that only ever believe what they can see. "No," she answers.

"You're sure?"

"Yes."

We've told fibs before, mainly to protect each other's feelings, but this is the first time I've felt like she's openly lied to my face. "If I heal someone, it's because of a combination of everything I've studied in the archives and everything Amma taught me about herbal properties and genuine treatments. It's the result of observation, the empirical evidence of scholars and skilled practitioners." Her voice changes, becoming hard-edged and stubborn. "Hard work and dedication are how real apotheks heal – that's what interests me, Nara, not some mystical experience that sounds like the puffery of spae-wives and shamen."

Her words silence all the others I'd planned. I might have

guessed Osha would react this way, but her close-mindedness still shocks me. She's rational above all things, even when she takes risks. She'll pore through forbidden texts to discover medical truths, she'll break the rules to heal a priest with the very herb-lore he denounces, and she'll Pair with a man she doesn't love to keep me safe. But she won't believe in something she can't logically explain. What I'm asking her to entertain isn't something she can read about in the dusty *Anathomia and Physik,* or a symptom she can easily observe or account for with her own eyes. What I'm asking her to believe is instinctive, intuitive, a sixth sense... and my sister doesn't do well with that.

"You're right," I say quietly. "I don't know why I brought it up. It's nonsense."

She exhales, almost in relief, but the way she straightens her smock and scratches at a stain in the fabric with her fingernail, the way she blinks too fast tells me she's lying. And not only to me. She's lying to herself.

We sit in an uneasy truce, both of us breathing a little too heavily. Perhaps she's doing it to protect me. Perhaps I'm protecting her, not telling her the full story of my visions. And now I don't feel inclined to tell her about Lars Oskarsson's coin and the symbol that matches our pendants. Not when she's as good as said I'm blindly obsessed with knowing who our parents were. I feel like a tiny fissure has opened between us, like a crack in the ice – too much pressure and it's only going to widen.

"Narkat?" Osha says, trying to bridge the silence. "Is it really worth fighting over this, with everything we have in front of us right now?

"It's alright, O. Let's forget it."

To show her I have, I look over at the wrangler, standing waist-deep in the pools. He's talking to Haus who sits bare-chested on the rocks nearby. Unlike his crew who are mostly short and rangy under their furs, Haus is as tall as any Isfalki

Warder. When I search his skin to assess his brandings, what I see aren't simply the marks of the Brume, but a latticework of pale scars scored on his torso and shoulders, standing in clear relief in the sunlight. He slips his shirt on when he catches me staring, but his attention soon moves to Osha. She has her copybook in her lap and is fiddling with the dog-eared pages. "I'm not the only one who gets watched, you know," I tell her, and it's a test of sorts. Will she continue to keep things from me on this subject too? "You've had a far bigger influence on the chief than I've had on the wrangler, I think."

She glances at Haus. "Hardly likely. I don't even speak his tongue." Haus lowers his chin at her in acknowledgment.

"You seem to understand each other well enough when he brings out his lute at night."

Osha turns a page in her copybook. I think she's going to deny it and my heart drops. Then, to my relief, her eyebrow arches and her lips tilt in a reluctant smile.

"Osha Fornwood! Have you been deliberately flirting with him?"

"Well, you pacing around the fire with a face like thunder didn't get us extra meat and furs, did it? Not to mention the vit skin – that was certainly worth a song or two, don't you think?"

"So, all those studious little poses with your book by the fire and asking the wrangler to teach you Hrossi phrases – it's all because you've been playing Haus?"

She can't help grinning now and I take in the full beauty of it, her green eyes bright, her hair glowing like resin on sunlit bark. Perhaps my sister isn't so unaware of her charm as I thought; perhaps she's learning it can be a weapon as effective as any sword. Or is there something more to it? Does she have the higher skill the Blood-wife described? Is she influencing Haus, swaying him as I do my prey, without even knowing she's doing it?

"Of course, I'm playing him," Osha says. "He's a barbarian. What did you think?" But as Haus beckons us over, I can't help noticing the flush on my sister's cheeks, the pulse flickering in her throat as she rises. Has she lied to me again? Has she lied to herself?

The wrangler watches us from the water as we approach. He gives a shudder and I find it amusing to see how long he'll stand there covering his modesty under the waterline at the expense of his blood turning to ice.

I cross my arms, making a point of studying him. "We camping here all day, or what?"

Haus laces his tunic and nods at the wrangler to answer me. I'm beginning to suspect the young chief understands more Isfalki than he lets on.

"Some of the men have gone to trade the sleigh for supplies and more horses," the wrangler says. "We're all in the saddle from here." Haus looks expectant, as if waiting for something more and the wrangler clears his throat "Mor Osha," he asks, a little awkward with the formality, but clearly translating the chief's words, "Haus wants me to tell you there are medicine trails near here. He understands you make remedies, given the correct roots and barks?"

"Yes," Osha says, eyes on the chief.

"He'll show you where they are if you wish to collect them."

"For his headaches?" she asks.

Haus nods and I glare at my sister. "Don't even speak each other's tongue, huh? There must have been an awful lot of sign language between the two of you at the fire."

"He saw the botanical sketches in my notebook. He knows I make medicines," Osha makes a point of explaining. Haus is already walking away, smiling at her over his shoulder. And she begins to follow him as meekly as if she's walking to class under the cloisters of the Mor school.

"Osha, wait!" I call after her. But she shakes her head to stop me.

"You do your influencing and trust me to do mine."

The Gildensfir

"She'd better be safe alone with him," I round on the wrangler.

"You might ask the same about Haus," he says, still standing in the water, his skin like plucked gooseflesh. "He's so smitten I think he'd roll over and sit up and beg if she clicked her fingers. And I'm pretty sure she knows it." I grunt my disapproval, watching Osha and the young chief disappear into the tree line. "Can you throw me my shirt?" the wrangler asks.

I ignore him. "She doesn't know how to defend herself like I do. What if he—"

"You assume, like most Isfalki, that all Wasters are barbarians."

"You expect me to believe they've got soft ears and like to be petted? How do I know he won't take what he wants from her by force?"

"You don't know Haus. He has far too much self-respect to do anything like that. And you also underestimate your sister. Can you throw me—"

"Don't tell me what I do and don't know about Osha. I've only known her all my life."

"Then you'll realise her power isn't physical. Haus's men think she's bewitched him. They may not be so far from the truth."

"You're suggesting she might have the higher skill? That she's swaying him?"

"Maybe. I don't know. A seer would need to read her to be sure."

"A seer? You mean like the Blood-wife?" He nods but he's starting to look impatient. "But you told the Blood-wife you could sense the skill yourself – in me."

He shifts, as if uncomfortable with the questions as much as the glacial water. "I grew up knowing how a powerful Sway feel when you're around them – the crackle of their influence, like static before a storm."

"And you feel that around Osha?"

He gives a sigh. Or perhaps it's a shiver. "It's complicated. I can't seem to read her as I can you," he says tersely. "How does it feel with me?"

"Oh, it feels like lightning, Little Scourge. A bolt from the heavens. Now, enough with the questions." He clearly needs to get out of the water but knows I'll get an eyeful. "Can you throw down my clothes?"

I settle on the rock Haus has vacated. "So, what's with all the scars on the big chief's chest?"

He jams his hands under his armpits as he stares back at me, then wades a little closer to the bank. The line of the river laps low at his hips. I catch myself looking and when I master my sights again, he cocks his eyebrow. I reach for his undershirt strewn beside me on the rocks, but I've got no intention of tossing it to him. It's a different kind of bluff we're playing now.

"You could call them souvenirs. From the Cooler," he says.

"The Cooler? Was Haus a fighter, then?"

"His father was Orlath's best lanista. He trained Haus to f-fight in the Cooler as a b-boy." The wrangler clamps his mouth shut, trying to stop his teeth from chattering.

"He got those scars as a *boy*?" His nod is a whole body shiver. "Hell's poxes. And you want me to believe these Wasters aren't all barbaric?"

"They're n-not." His bones must be clattering together

beneath his skin, his lungs so seized he can barely catch breath.

"And you, Wrangler? You have no qualms trading innocent Mor to some crazy Waster overlord? Dumping me in one of his fighting pits, at the mercy of charmers like Haus's father?" I hold his pants over the water and let the legs drag in the icy current. "That's cold-hearted of you. Very *cold*." He sends an arm out for his clothes, but I keep them beyond his reach. "My sister doesn't buy it, you know. She thinks we should trust you."

He looks further up the bank where the guards are starting to pay attention to us. And before I can blink, he's hauled himself out, jumping on the rock in front me, water gushing from him. I reel at the splash, glancing down, only to realise my mistake and snatch my eyes up again.

"I am bit cold now," the wrangler says, taking his clothes from me. And as he does, I see the inside of his bicep – the tendrils of the branding on his neck and shoulder coming together in a whorl of blue. Except the vortex, I realise, converges in a recognisable shape, a pattern. It's the symbol of my pendant and Oskarsson's coin, mirrored on the underside of his arm. I drop his shirt and grab his bicep, turning the tattoo towards me. He gives himself up to the examination and I begin to suspect he's intended me to see it, meant it as an answer of sorts.

My questions trip over each other. "What the... how come... what does it mean?"

"It means your sister's smarter than you." He starts to dress, and I'm so stunned I don't even turn away. There's a link between us, one I don't understand, but a definite connection forged long before we'd ever met. His voice drops. "Osha's right. Of course I'm not going to leave you with them." He flicks a glance at the Waster guards along the bank.

"And you didn't think to share that with me before now?" My anger almost chokes the words in my throat.

"No. There's still so much that could go wrong – unexpected

behaviour or letting something slip." The expression on my face is probably enough to turn his blood back to ice, for he says, "Not just you. *Them*." He looks towards the other girls, Sigrun watching Dalla and Annek squabbling over something as they dry themselves. "It was too risky. You all needed to believe I'd sold you out or else Haus and his men wouldn't believe it."

"I still believe you sold us out. Wrangler... until you tell me what in Hell's poxes is going on." I run my thumb over the tattoo on his inner arm, checking I'm not mistaken. And he lets me. His brandings run naturally into the blue-black symbol, as if they were designed that way, and the delicate spiral of glyphs matches my pendant perfectly.

"You've never heard of the Gildensfir?" he asks softly. "The circle without end?" I shake my head. "It's an Old World emblem. It represents the cycle of light and dark, death and new life – the balance of the universe, if you like. But my people – the Reis – call it the Halqa, and they believe it relates to a prophecy." He looks at me warily. It's the first time he's openly admitted his Reis heritage and I think he suspects I have more than the usual Isfalki prejudice about it. But I'm not about to stop him now.

"Go on."

He knuckles his jaw, as if he finds the words awkward. "Reis histories tell that a few years after the Brume virus first spread, when Sways were just starting to discover their skills, a handful of the most powerful began to have visions. They predicted the coming of a great healer, a Sway who would redress the balance caused by the disease. I told you the Erossi call her Effa. In Isfalk, you know her as Elna, the holy daughter of First Mother. But in Reis, she's called the Elita and the Halqa symbol is synonymous with her coming." I think of Oskarsson's Reis coin still snug in the lacings of my leathers. I want to get it out and look at the spiral again but then the wrangler will know of its existence and probably take that from me too. Thanks to my imaginary groin clap, the Wasters haven't searched me that thoroughly and I don't exactly look like I'm carrying anything of value.

"The Reis sing stories of the Elita and offer up prayers to her, but not as the Isfalki do Elna, in some vague religious hope for the Branded to eventually be saved in the next life. They truly believe in the prophecy of her coming – that she will be born on earth as a Sway who, at the height of her powers, will cleanse the blood of the tainted by eradicating the legacy of the Brume, and influence leaders to bring peace and prosperity back to the Continent."

He pauses, giving me time for his words to sink in. It feels odd to hear him speak so formally, and I draw in my chin at his stony face, wondering if he's setting me up. "Are you serious?" I scoff. "You don't expect me to believe this shit, do you?"

He sniffs, then sits down, hanging his hands between his knees and studying the rock beneath his boots, waiting. I drop to sit beside him, a signal that I'll hear him out, even if I don't believe him. "For more than a century now, the Reis have trained a handful of seekers in each generation, young men and women who travel the Continent, or live in other settlements, searching for the appearance of the Elita. People like me."

I cast him a dubious look. "And how are you supposed to know if you've found her – this *almighty* Elita?"

He sighs, as if mustering his patience. He knew I'd scoff at him.

"This is why I didn't tell you before. The prediction is archaic. It uses the language of our seers, which is… open to interpretation, to say the least."

"Well, do your best interpreting then, Wrangler, because this is highly entertaining."

The tattooed symbol flexes as he leans back on his arms. "It's not easy to be clear. We're dealing with a long-lost text that has only been kept alive orally."

"Weren't you bragging about your oral talents at Helgah's?"

He presses back a grin. "Alright. You asked for it." He clears his throat, and begins to translate words he might have recited by rote as a child in Reis:

"The Elita, she of... flame-hair and steel-will,
Shall rise a... a warrior of light in the dark."

He struggles for the right words in Isfalki, watching my reaction all the time.

"The Elita, commander of the Halqa,
Will sway her armies to her purpose like a hammer... no, wait...
a smith at the forge,
Sending them forth to... scorch the earth
With the fire of regeneration.
The strength and purity of her blood
Will cleanse the Branded,
Healing the sick, making the weak strong,
The poor, rich, servants their own masters..."

He breaks off awkwardly, more self-conscious than I ever thought possible. "Yeah, well, it rhymes in the original Reis, and sounds slightly more poetic. But it's still not that helpful when you're checking out Mor girls in alleyways behind the Roundhouse."

I give him a hard stare, barely knowing whether he's serious. "So, let me get this straight, you believe there's a Sway out there so powerful she'll be able to reverse the effects of the Brume?"

He hesitates. "Some Reis believe so, yes. Ever since the Great Malady, the prophecy and the hunt for the Elita has become part of the Reis faith. But, religion aside, you can imagine how such a higher order Sway might be politically important... how she could end the social divisions that have grown between the Branded and the Pure, and bring back the prosperity of the Old World."

"You mean, how powerful she'd be to the ruler who controlled her?"

"There is that," he concedes. "And it's part of the reason why the Reis search for her."

"Why, because you think you have the moral high ground?"

He frowns, as if the question has plagued him before now. "My people take the old predictions more literally than others in the Continent. We don't relegate the Elita to a cultural identity myth or the realms of spiritual solace for the Branded. We actively search for her here among us because we understand Sways and we know she needs training and nurturing. But at the height of her powers, no one could *control* her, as you put it."

I draw in a long, slow breath, studying his face. "You truly believe this horse shit, don't you?"

The wrangler crosses his arms loosely, and I can't tell whether he's angry with me and pretending not to be, or genuinely non-committal. "It's been my training since I was a boy." He circles the tattoo absently with his thumb, the symbol of his calling inked among the brandings of his fate. I see that now. "There've been plenty of times when I've doubted, believe me. But recently–" He glances towards the trees, down the track Osha and Haus have taken.

"No," I say, shaking my head. "You said Osha *might* have the skill. That you're not even sure she is a Sway until she's read by a seer. You can't possibly think this – this Elita – might be my sister?"

"Honestly? No. I was convinced it was you at first." I turn to get a better look at his face, trying to work out whether he's joking, baiting me as usual, but he continues in all seriousness. "I saw your hair, your pendant, sensed the fight in you that night I took you to Morday Mass in my sled. And then..." He runs a hand behind his neck, his eyes flicking to my scalp.

"Then I became a Brand," I say bluntly, finishing for him.

"The prophecy is specific about it – the Elita will be unmarked... Pure. A Mor."

A stupid flush of rejection prickles over my skin. I'm reminded of the pain of discovering I was branded, that I was ordinary, flawed, weak, even more different from my sister than I'd been before. Then I think about my life in the Sink afterwards – hard, yes, but liberating in a way I'd never known since leaving the Fornwood. And a strange relief washes through me.

"So, what now? You want to get my sister read by one of your Reis seers?" I ask the wrangler.

He stands now, as if going into detail about his plans unnerves him. "It's the only way the skill will be primed in her, if she has it. She'll become more aware of it, so it can grow, just as the Blood-wife primed it in you."

"Yeah. Fat load of good that did me."

"Why do you say that?"

"Because I'm still here, aren't I?" I flick a glance at the Wasters watching over Annek, Dalla and Sigrun. "Haven't exactly managed to sway you or any of these brutes to free us yet."

"Did you not listen to Frenka? Only a handful of the most powerful Sways develop that kind of skill and it has to be trained in them, honed over years of practise. You've got quite the sense of entitlement, haven't you?"

"Why not aim high?" I say, jumping to my feet and grabbing his throat in my fist.

"The higher you aim," he throws off my hand with a block and hooks his leg around my knee, "The harder you fall." And fall I would, if it wasn't for the fact he's grabbed my collar and stops me hitting the rocks. His face spreads into that mole-twitching grin as he leans over, our noses almost touching. "You have a lot to learn about yourself, Little Scourge."

"You have a lot to learn about me too, mutt."

His eyes glitter with amusement and he's about to answer when his attention snags on something behind me. The wrangler stands me upright and I twist around to see a Waster studying us – the one with the bullwhip who'd lashed Osha's wrist.

"Wait," I say, as the wrangler makes to leave. "What are your plans?"

Keeping his voice low, he says simply, "I'm taking you and your sister to Reis, of course."

And there it is. Our choice: Orlath's harems and fighting pits; or the wrangler and Reis, hearthlands of Amma's murderers. I don't like the prospect of either option. But as Osha says, *Better the pox you know than the one you don't.* Do I really know the wrangler any better than these trogs? Can I bring myself to go along with him again?

"Wait," I say. "Question."

"Of course there is." He rolls his eyes.

"Unless you're planning to starve us all crossing the Storm Sands, don't we need a ship to get to Reis?"

"Why do you think I've been courting Haus all this time? Without the chief as an escort these past weeks we'd have been seized by any number of Waster clans attempting to cross the plains. I'll get us our ship – in Orlathston."

"And how do you plan to do that?"

"Let me worry about the plan, alright?"

My temper flares, but as I study his face, I realise his response is pure evasion. "You haven't actually got a plan, have you?"

"Three days' riding until we reach Orlathston. Plenty of time to think." He grins but that mole soon stills as the Waster with the bullwhip walks towards us. "Poxes, that Ordin's a suspicious one," the wrangler says. "Probably thinks there's been too much whispering and not enough arguing between us."

"What?"

"They think I sold you out. Us whispering together like this isn't exactly giving off the right vibes. You're supposed to hate me."

"I *do* hate you!"

"Make a show of it, then." He nods towards the approaching trog. "Get angry. Take a swipe at me or something." He braces as if I'm about to hit him. "Go on." When I hesitate, he groans in exasperation. "Oh, sweet mercy!" And before I can respond, he's pulled me to him and pressed his mouth to mine. I stiffen from the shock of it, fists clenched on his chest, about to shove him off. But his lips are soft and full... and his tongue is warm and decadent, utterly distracting. I feel like he's unravelling me, as if the rest of my body is is being controlled by all the sensations in my mouth. Is that my palm along his jaw? My hips pressing into him? Wait.

"What the fec!" I jerk away, forcing myself to regain some self-control.

"Well, well, Na'quat," he says, but his voice is low in his throat, and he stares at me with eyes that could melt tavern maids to puddles. "You were supposed to give me a left hook for that, not kiss me back." When that grin starts to spread across his face, I wipe it from him it with an almighty uppercut that makes sure he gets a taste of blood.

"Trull's tits!"

"You should have been clearer about what you wanted, Wrangler."

He rolls his jaw. "I could say the same of you."

Seeing the punch I've thrown, the guard, Ordin, begins to laugh and catcall, his suspicions allayed. The rest of the convoy down the riverbank must have also seen the tussle because one of them shouts out in Hrossi, making a show of scratching his balls.

"What did he say?" I demand.

The wrangler shakes his head, chuckling. "Just some stupid joke about you rejecting me."

"*Tell me*," I take him by the scruff of his shirt and draw my fist again, "what he said."

"Alright, alright!" The wrangler holds up his hands. "He said he had the groin clap once and I'd be better off with the five-knuckle shuffle." My mouth falls open, and then I'm snapping it shut and grinding my teeth in silent fury. "You did insist, Little Scourge." He's barely able to keep a straight face.

"I... I... detest you, Wrangler!" I spit out, ashamed I can think of no better retort.

"Well, that's good to know. I was starting to think you'd got the wrong idea. The way you kissed me was a little confusing."

When I storm up the riverbank, I see that someone else has been party to the whole performance. And he certainly has got the wrong idea. Brim can barely hold my eye, his shoulders heaving as if he's been running.

"It's not what you think, Brim," I say. His guard shoves me away when I try to get close. "For fec's sake. I only want to talk to him!" But even if the Waster had let me speak, Brim has already turned his back on me.

Accusations and Ultimatums

I get my chance with Brim the next day.

Haus's riders have returned with supplies and horses, and while Osha and the other Mor ride two to a saddle, it's my misfortune to be slung behind Ordin.

Ordin seems to be tasked with much of the dirty work in the convoy and he makes it clear he's unimpressed to have me – a poxy brandwhore – riding pillion. He jabs me with the butt of his lash and hocks over his shoulder whenever our bodies jostle in the saddle. I'm not too impressed myself with our riding arrangements: up close, Ordin's stench is overwhelming – wet dog laced with stale vit. His branding looks uncannily like his own whip lassoed about his neck, and it's not long before I'm wishing it was. I'd take great delight in pulling it tight.

The terrain doesn't make for easy riding either. Heavy rain turns to drizzle and slows our progress, the heath we're navigating already waterlogged from the melting snows. The Wasters ride stolidly on, hunkering down in their furs and setting their hoods against the brunt of it, but I'm soaked and cold to the bone within the first hour of the journey. Ordin must feel the same, for he takes up his vit skin and treats himself to a good slug. The guard who has Brim's pack pony on a lead rope draws up to our flank, eager for a hit. I've heard the other men call him Mekke, the Hrossi word for cock, according to the wrangler, and now I see it's because of the brand on his cheek – shaped like a bantam's crest. *Damn the wrangler*.

Ordin hands the skin over to Mekke. I sense Brim staring at my back.

"Enjoying the fresh air?" he calls ahead, as casually as if we're training again in the Fornwood. I don't turn around, cutting my eyes to Mekke instead. He's busy drinking, deeply involved in a low-voiced exchange with Ordin. "Your trog's a real charmer," Brim says, and as if on cue, Ordin spits over his shoulder. Wet flecks hit my cheeks and I'm thankful for the drizzle. "Then again, it seems your tastes run to outlander scum these days." When I glance back, Brim is squinting at the wrangler on his roan mare, eyes hard as river stones.

"They haven't let me near you to explain–"

"Can't say I've seen you trying very hard," Brim says. "You were never such a pushover in the citadel."

"I tried, Brim. I got a sword to the chief's neck when you were out cold." I struggle not to raise my voice, but it's difficult, especially when I feel like I'm a mess of emotions around Brim. "They almost killed me for it. If it wasn't for the wrangler–"

"Thought you'd have better luck siding with a fec – one of your own kind, is that it?"

The lash of his insensitivity makes me smart. "No, that's not it!" Ordin turns an ear towards me, but Mekke passes across the grog and they continue their talk. "You don't understand," I whisper.

"What's to understand, Nara?" Brim says boldly. "We need to get our hands on weapons, take out these vermin and get our Mor back to the Settlement."

"Brim, do you not see Annek Mikkelson with your own eyes?" I nod towards the girl up ahead. "They had Estrid Halvar, too. Mor who were supposed to have been *exiled*." I turn as much as I can to look at him. "Don't you understand what Iness and Fjäll have been doing to feed the citadel?"

I fall quiet when Mekke grunts loudly, as if loosing a curse.

But it's not for us. Ordin answers him, apparently in sour agreement over a topic that has them both distracted.

"There's nothing to understand," Brim says. "They were obviously ambushed on the way to Torvag, just as we were at the Moon Pools."

"There was no ambush, Brim. Annek said she was traded in return for food and supplies."

"Well, she's lying." He sniffs, and when I turn to look, he rubs his wet face on his shoulder, avoiding my gaze. "They dishonoured their duty and were punished for it. Of course they'd concoct lies about the Council."

"*Dishonoured their duty*? Brim, take off your Isfalki blinkers for one minute and think about it." I suck in a breath, trying to stay calm and rational, to present it the way Osha did as we sorted through the evidence before us the night we met Annek. "Why is it those who are exiled to Torvag are nearly always Mor? How come men in the citadel are more likely to get the lash or execution? Can't you see a pattern? And every Mass over the past year seems to have had at least two, sometimes three Mor exiled – too many to be likely offenders. Their crimes are being fabricated."

He shakes his head stubbornly. "There's no way the Council would trade Pure women to Waster trogs. It's barbaric. And it's the equivalent of putting our most valuable weapons in the hands of the enemy."

Weapons? I know he means because of the breeding potential: a Mor's sons are bigger, growing into healthier men with the potential to be trained into the strongest soldiers. But I can't believe he actually sees Mor as *weapons*. "Is that all these women are to you – breeders for the Warder armed forces?" He doesn't answer, his seat upright in the saddle, his foot flexed elegantly in the stirrup – ever the Elix heir, even though his arms are still roped behind him and his clothes and hair have become as wild and unkempt as any Waster's. *Holy Mother may lead the man from the citadel but the citadel never leaves the man*, Father Uluf used to preach in his sermons, waxing lyrical about the moral fibre of Isfalki Pures carrying the torch of civilisation from the Old World. I never thought it would be Brim making me see how deeply indoctrinated citadel lies really are.

"The women don't want to go back," I say, desperate to show him the truth. "None of them, not even Dalla Thorval and she's of Founding Four blood." I haven't actually asked the girls but it isn't a blatant lie. Whenever we've talked about the possibility of escaping the convoy, none of them has brought up returning to the citadel. In fact, any talk of fleeing seems to peter out among them for that very reason. "We could run," I'd heard Annek say when Haus had removed our bindings, "but where would we go?" Even Dalla seems ever more resigned to the fact that no Warder rescue party is coming for her. If she was caught up in Iness's plot by accident, then no one in the citadel believes her valuable enough to risk her retrieval. Elix Thorval isn't short of daughters or granddaughters, and Dalla knows it.

Brim's eyes are busy looking anywhere but at me, fighting something in himself. It's as if I can see the Warder captain – the proud, unquestioning defender of the civilised world – at war with the Brim I knew as a child – truanting to the Moon Pools, teaching me to hone a sword, making me helpless with laughter at his impersonations of the Elixion. His frown turns from anger to confusion, his jaw softens, and I think he might be coming around to me. But then the wrangler calls out to Haus up ahead, some shared jest passing between them, and Brim's face hardens again. "We need weapons," he says, ignoring everything I've told him, his moment of doubt gone. "See there?" His eyes go to the saddlebag under Ordin's right leg. "Your trog escort has something belonging to you. Get it back," he says quickly. "Cut me free after dark. We'll take our Mor and the horses and ride north."

And for the Warder captain, it's as simple as that.

"Brim, these men were born in the saddle and grew up scouring this terrain. They'll hunt us down before daybreak."

"Not if there's no one left to come hunting."

"Wait, I–" But the words stick in my throat, turned into a winded grunt by Ordin's elbow in my gut. Mekke draws the pack horse level with his and deals Brim such a cuff to the jaw it nearly unsaddles him. Blood pumps from his nose, keeping time with the pulse pounding in my stomach.

"I'll be waiting," Brim mutters wetly through a mouthful of blood. I can't draw enough breath to reply. Even if I could, I don't know what answer I'd give.

The Lesser of Two Evils

Our Mor. That's what Brim called them. His words preoccupy me, more souring than Ordin's breath the further we journey into the dusk. *We need to get our Mor back to the Settlement.* Like my sister and the girls are citadel property, livestock to round up and herd to The Fold. He's no better than the Wasters and their convoys of human cargo. Of course Brim would fight the truth. The very idea that the Council has been trading Mor with its enemies to feed the citadel undermines everything he is and believes in. Even as a child he dreamed of being a Warder, to rise through the ranks as his uncle had done, protecting Isfalk and upholding its founding values through a life of action over politics. But now to be told those values are a lie, that Iness has stooped so low as to traffic Pure women with our primary enemy to keep the citadel fed – of course it's unthinkable to him. And yet there was a moment of doubt. I saw it in him. If I could only find a chance to talk to him again, to tell him how Iness planned to kill us, I might make him see how things have changed. But what then? There's no way Brim would trust the wrangler or go along with any plan to flee to Reis. Do *I* even trust the wrangler?

And this isn't just about me. I need to ask Osha and the other girls what they want.

The Wasters make camp on a blustering plain. It's dotted

with stunted scrub buffeted into outlandish shapes by a near-constant westerly. The rain has stopped now and the coarse tufting grass distracts the horses from their skittishness. While the food stores and bed rolls are unpacked for the night, Sigrun and Dalla huddle together around the fire, as Osha and I coax the windblown flame. Annek passes around a vit skin and I watch the girls sip. "You'll want a good slug of that tonight," I tell them. "It's the only ease we'll get against this gale." And against the hard decisions to come.

Osha looks at me with wind-stung cheeks and lips, sensing something's afoot, but I wait until the flush of alcohol spreads through them, until their shoulders have dropped and their frowns have eased a little. After that, there's no point mincing my words, so I launch right in. "If any of you had the chance to return to Isfalk right now, would you?" No one answers, so I elaborate, telling them about Brim's plan and then the wrangler's. I wish either proposal sounded more like a proper strategy, and a little less like I was giving them a choice between two poisons, but I don't have a more palatable plan to put on the menu. I can't pull off an escape without Brim or the wrangler's help; with so many Wasters I need someone backing me up who knows how to fight. And even if I could do it alone, where would I take them? Amma's burnt-out cabin in Fornwood? I might survive the return journey north, but are the others stubborn enough? Without the shelter of the wagon sled, without supplies and weapons, the idea of leading them, trying to keep all of us alive single-handedly, seems the most certain path to death

To my surprise, it's Sigrun who speaks first. "My sister was exiled to Torvag," she says, out of nowhere. We all lift our heads to look at her. Sigrun doesn't speak up much but, Mother's tits, everyone's paying attention now.

"When?" I ask.

"Eight years ago. I'd only started at the Mor school. Freya was a lot older than me and already Paired." Her eyes flick to Dalla. "She became part of the Thorval family."

"*Freya Adumssen*? The Freya who was matched with my brother Asger?" Dalla says, realisation suddenly dawning. "I had no idea she was your sister." She studies Sigrun's face, as if seeing her in a new light.

"That's hardly surprising," Annek scoffs. "You highborn rarely pay attention to anyone who doesn't have a Founding Four name. In fact, I'm amazed Papa Thorval even approved such a humbling match." Dalla stares moodily into the fire, eyes busy at her thoughts. "But then, I hear your older brother had something of a reputation to manage," Annek prods. I'm expecting an all-out argument at that. The bickering between the older woman and the highborn girl has become as unrelenting as Ordin's ripe aroma. But, for once, Dalla is silent.

"I don't remember that exile," Osha says.

"Well, none of you are old enough to have gone to Mass back then," Annek points out. "They said Freya slept with her brandservants and First Mother punished her with some kind of infection."

"It was a lie!" Sigrun cries. "It wasn't true. Freya would never have done such a thing!"

"Hey… hey," Annek soothes her, "you don't have to convince me. I've been there myself, remember? You're the only person who needs to believe it." She cups Sigrun's chin and lifts it from the shame that has clearly kept her quiet about her sister's story all this time. "You know, I remember Freya. She was a couple of years above me at school," Annek says. "So kind and gentle… softly spoken."

Sigrun blinks as if fighting tears, and Dalla suddenly looks away.

"Asger Thorval slept with every trull in the Sink – the entire citadel knew it," Annek tosses at Dalla, angling for a fight. "He probably came up with that infection story because his own cock was itching at the time."

But Dalla isn't fighting back. "They got rid of her," she says in a low voice, almost to herself. "I understand it now. They got rid of her." She wraps her arms about her waist and searches the dark empty plain, as if to order her thoughts against it. When she's aware of us again, she says, "I remember Asger and Papa talking to Father Uluf and Mother Iness about it one night. They said Freya dishonoured the Thorval name in the eyes of First Mother and was a blight on the family. Uluf claimed it was because of her wantonness, her corruption. But in the kitchens, one of the brandservants told me Freya had lost three babies." Dalla shakes her head sorrowfully. "The maid was always complaining about the blood on the sheets, how Freya might be a Mor but if she couldn't ripen a baby, she'd be in trouble."

A tear falls, rosy in the firelight. "I was young. I didn't understand. But I know now... they got rid of her. And it could have been any of us, couldn't it? Any one of us, Paired off and struggling like that, getting more and more desperate with each lost pregnancy." Her breath fogs in rapid puffs. "I'm so sorry, Sigrun. I didn't realise... I didn't want to see..."

"None of us wanted to see, Dalla," Annek answers, her voice softer than usual. "They've been lying to us for years."

And that's when I realise it. This trading of Mor began long before Isfalk's poor harvests and the overhunting of The Fold. It isn't only about food and supplies. Iness has been playing the game for decades, like a drawn-out round of eschak, advancing and defending the more strategic pieces on her board by sacrificing Mor like pawns. Some, like Freya and Annek, who don't serve the purpose of her allies in the Council are traded; while those she suspects might grow to threaten her power on a personal level – budding Sways like Estrid and Osha – are simply removed from the squares. How many years, how many innocent lives has it taken for Iness to cement her control of Isfalk? And how much does the rest of the Council turn a blind eye? How much does Lars Oskarsson know?

Annek stabs the edge of the fire with a stick until it snaps. "I've suspected for a long time. I think others have too. But none of us dared stand up and say anything. And now I'm beyond the citadel walls, it all seems clearer." Beyond the sway of Mother Iness, I think to myself. A vein pulses in Annek's temple and her cheeks shine in the firelight. While Dalla and Sigrun stare wet-eyed into the fire, Annek's grief is pure anger, something I recognise. Her strong hands and square shoulders under her furs are tense, itching to act. Properly trained, she'd be someone I'd want on my side, not against me. "I wish I'd spoken up in the citadel, done something sooner," she says, jabbing at the fire with the stub of the stick. Osha gently removes it from her hand and we're quiet for a while, the wind flattening and flaring the fire, and making us hunker down into our own thoughts.

"Journeying to Reis doesn't exactly feel like an escape," Annek says eventually.

Dalla sniffs, slowly returning to herself. "I heard Reis tribes only survive in the desert by heathen magic and ritual. And Father Uluf said they share their women, Branded and Pure alike." We all look up at her. "Not that I trust Uluf anymore," she says quickly, flushing red in the firelight and biting her lips together. "That puffed-up pulpit-basher can preach the moon is round and I wouldn't believe him now."

Annek's lips twitch in amusement. Then she turns to me. "And the wrangler, do you trust him?" she asks.

"Nope," I tell her. "Wouldn't trust him with the guts from my quarry." And Osha raises an eyebrow. I think of the wrangler beating the hawk off me on the ice plains. "That said…" It's difficult to come out and say it, especially when I'm not convinced it's the truth, but they look so hopeful. "Maybe the wrangler's the lesser of two evils right now."

Annek nods, relieved to have something to cling to, and Sigrun follows her lead.

"Do we agree, then?" I look by turns at each of the girls. "We give up on Isfalk, even if we don't know what lies ahead?" I expect to see doubt and uncertainty written on their faces, but it's more like a growing resolve passing between them over the guttering flames, a solidarity knitted from betrayal, the multiple treacheries of a home we'd thought was a refuge. Osha nods at me in encouragement, but still no one speaks, as if fearful of saying the words.

It's Dalla who finally breaks the silence. "Well, there's no way I'm going back to the citadel." She glances at Annek, eyes glittering – a look I can't quite fathom. "The Council and its Elix heirs can go fuck themselves!"

I never believed it possible, but for once she seems to speak for all of us.

A Test of Loyalty

There's no music in the camp tonight. The wind is noisy and unsettling, making the whole convoy sullen and tetchy. When the men do speak, it's to squabble over cuts of meat, their share of vit or their places by the fire, like over-tired children. Haus appears jaded and ignores them for the most part, but their resentment seems to seethe beneath the surface every time he stares at Osha across the fire. He's fashioned a small pillow for my sister from coney skins and as she lays down her head and settles for the night, she returns the young chief's smile. If my sister is still playing Haus, her attentions are certainly going beyond the call of duty and I wonder again if she's being entirely honest with me, with herself, about what she's doing. I plan to question her about it again in the morning, but right now my mind is more preoccupied with Brim, who watches me with stealthy concentration from between the saddles and tack where he's been tied. The wrangler looks between us, as if sensing something afoot, but eventually he, too, settles to sleep, a little removed from the group.

It seems an age before I finally hear the snores of the men, the mutterings of their dreams. The Waster on first watch paces a steady, unvaried circle about the slumbering camp, then around the supplies and gear, before checking the horses and starting again. Brim's guard, Mekke, seems dozy and hungover

214

from his little drinking spree on the road with Ordin, while the latter snores loud enough to shame the gale that howls around us. I suspect I could cross the camp with bells on my ankles and no one would hear.

"Did you get it?" Brim asks as soon as I crawl up behind him. His fists clench and unclench impatiently, straining against the ropes that bind his wrists at his back. "Wait until the guard reaches the horses again." He assumes I've reclaimed my skinning knife from Ordin's saddle bag and am going to set him free.

I lie on my side, hidden between the supply packs. "Brim, listen to me," I whisper. "The others don't want to return to the Settlement."

"What are you talking about, Nara? Quick, now! Cut the ropes."

"Brim, you have to understand. Iness tried to have us killed."

"What? Have you been drinking? You're not talking any sense."

"Mother's sake, Brim, would you just listen!"

"You listen! Why in Mother's name would Iness want *you* dead? She wouldn't give you a second thought. You're a fec." I pull up short. Not because I don't know what I am, but because he already thinks so little of me.

"She sent the wrangler to kill me because she thinks I'm a fire-Brand." I can't bring myself to tell him about the vision I shared with Iness on the Roundhouse stage or the Swaying skill I supposedly have – it seems too far-fetched and, besides, there isn't time. "Iness doesn't like what Osha and I represent," I say instead.

"Is this about my Pairing with Osha? You're still torn up about it?"

"Poxes, Brim! Not everything is about you!"

"But can't you hear how ridiculous all this sounds?" he hisses. "My uncle and I are Founding Four. Iness would never risk–"

"She wanted you dealt with too. A stray arrow through your chest would mean one of her greatest opponents on the Council had no heir. In fact, the wrangler saved your life."

"That's how it is between you now, is it? Him putting mutinous ideas in your head." His voice gets louder as he struggles to contain his rage. "You're really going to trust him more than me, after all these years?"

The night watch comes into view again and I flatten myself to the ground among the packs. "Keep your voice down," I whisper, "or it won't matter what either of us believe."

"Cut me free. We'll talk later."

"Brim, I–"

"He's a Reis, Nara! They murdered your grandmother and kept my uncle a prisoner for years. You think they aren't every bit as barbaric as these trogs? There's no way I'm letting you listen to an outlander and risk losing our Mor because of it."

"*Our Mor* again. You talk of Osha and the others as if they're livestock to be counted. You're no better than them." I glance across at the sleeping Wasters. "We're not going back with you, Brim."

His breath stutters in the dark. "So, you'll try your luck with these scum in the pox-ridden outlands?"

"Not with them, no."

There's a beat before he understands. "Seriously? Some Reis stable boy makes eyes at you and now you trust him with your life?" He scoffs. "Do you even know how the Reis treat their Pure women, Nara? They let the Branded Pair freely with them, all bloodlines overlooked, women passed around like kornbru. They take no responsibility for weakness and disease, letting it spread freely, thinking their pagan magic and superstitions will be the answer. Has he told you that, your wrangler? Has he told you what kind of people he's from?"

He thrusts his hands towards me violently now. "Cut these bastard ropes!" His voice is so loud I'm certain the guard will come running. I have no knife to use: I didn't get a chance to steal mine from Ordin as Brim suggested But I take hold of his hands now and lean in closer, catching the familiar smell of him – twine and leather and always something polished, like honed steel.

"Brim... I..."

His fingers squeeze mine and his tone softens. "Nara, we've known each other most of our lives. Haven't we always looked out for one another? If you ever cared anything for me, you wouldn't need to think about this."

"You heard the man." A whisper in the night, a shadow crawling alongside me in the dirt.

"Fec's sake, Wrangler!"

"Cut him free," he says. Metal glints in the moonlight. He's offering me a knife.

"But... I..." At my confusion, the wrangler takes the blade to Brim's ropes himself. "Stop. Wait."

"For what?" He pauses to peer at me in the darkness. When I don't answer he continues to saw at the bindings anyway. Before I can stop him, Brim has his arms free. He turns on us, agitated, lungs working hard. If it wasn't for his bound ankles, I think he might have launched himself at the wrangler and wrestled him down already. "Calm yourself, Pretty Boy," the wrangler says, brandishing the knife. "You want me to cut you free or not?" And he sets to work on Brim's hobbled feet.

"What are you doing, Wrangler? Stop!" This could all go to pot in a matter of minutes and disrupt any plans he had of getting us to Reis. Given more time, I might have brought Brim round to the truth about Iness and Fjäll, but now I don't have it. Brim's free, pulling off the ropes and drawing his feet under him. The wrangler, expressionless, gives me the hilt of the knife, putting the situation firmly in my hands. I flounder, unnerved.

"Give it to me, Nara," Brim says, reaching for the blade.

It's an order now, from a Warder officer.

I jerk it out of his reach.

"Hand me the knife!" And that's the command of an Elix lord.

I clutch the hilt tightly. "What are you going to do with it?"

"I already told you." Brim looks at the wrangler as he continues. "You can trust me, Nara. I've always been who I said I am. I've never let you down." The wind lulls. All I can hear are our mingled breaths coming hard and fast. Then Brim lunges, the wrangler flattened beneath him, gasping for air as Brim squeezes his throat in both hands. But I'm just as quick. I throw myself onto Brim's back, fist yanking his hair and baring his neck to my blade.

"Let him go," I grit out. But Brim doesn't heed me, his knuckles white, his whole body straining with the effort of choking the wrangler. "None of the women want to return to Isfalk. If you're asking me to choose between you and them," I press the blade further into his throat until it nicks his skin, "This is my answer."

Brim winces. The knife bobs as he swallows. Slowly he releases his hands and the wrangler gulps at the night air, trying to muffle his gasps and splutters. I feel the brush of Brim's hair against my cheek, the familiar smell of sword practice in the Fornwood and unlacing leathers at the Moon Pools. But then the metallic tang of blood is on my tongue, as if I've pressed it to the nick in his throat, and his pulse grows deafening in my ear, keeping pace with mine. And that's when I hear it, hollow and echoing in my chest – the doubt, the uncertainty in him, growing stronger the more I listen. By the time I speak, my voice is certain, strangely emotionless; I barely recognise it as my own.

"You're confused, Brim," I say, low but steady. "Deep inside, you doubt yourself." Fist in his hair, I angle his head towards the horses, their black shapes shifting as one in the dark. "So when I take this knife from your neck, best to run for a horse, yes? And ride as far from this camp as you can without looking back. It'd be better for everyone, don't you think?"

He lifts his head, trying to nod, and I remove the knife. "Tell me."

"Yes," he says. The edge is gone from his voice and his mouth is slack as a boy's spellbound by a tale of adventure. I feel the breath of relief in him, the eagerness of his acquiescence.

"If you speak to me, or make a sound, the wrangler might wake your guard and tell him you were trying to escape." I tug at his hair again even though I've already lowered the knife. "All good, Brim?"

He nods and I crawl off him, feeling oddly queasy. Something trickles over my upper lip, and I lean against the saddles and packs, a wave of fatigue washing over me. The realisation, the shock of what I've done to Brim begins to settle, making me feel mean and dirty, like I've betrayed him. I suddenly want to take it all back, want to get up and stop him leaving, but my nose gushes and I'm overcome with exhaustion. My whole body feels tender, like it used to when Brim first started training me to spar at the Moon Pools and I'd wake the next morning with every muscle screaming, so desperate was I to land a hit on him. I catch the nicker of horses in the darkness and then the vague drumming of hooves across the plain. But the sounds are soon scooped up and carried away on the wind. I have the overwhelming urge to sleep, right here among the packs and saddles but the wrangler pulls me upright and drags me to the fire. "Get under your furs and sleep."

"Stop telling me what to do."

"Someone's got to – you seemed pretty confused back there."

"I needed more time with him. I could have brought him round to the truth," I say, fighting the weight of my eyelids that seem intent on closing, despite my anger with the wrangler. "Why the fec did you set him free? You knew he'd go for you... Were you angling for a fight with him... was that it? Or did you want... to test his loyalty to me?" My breath feels patchy, my thoughts scattered. All I really want is to burrow under my furs and sleep until spring. The last thing I'm aware of is a hand at my cheek, the wrangler's thumb wiping blood from under my nose.

"It wasn't his loyalty I was testing, Little Scourge," he murmurs.

Holding the Reins

My sleep is fitful and overwrought. Strange and vivid dreams vie with waking moments of intense cold, my arms and legs so numb they feel bloodless, heavy as stone. I shiver so badly my teeth hammer in my mouth, and the wrangler taunts me, standing waist deep in the warm water of the Moon Pools, holding out my necklace. He threatens to drop it below the surface, but the pendant spins in the mist, its spiral glyphs merging to reveal the outline of a woman's face. For some reason the sight of her makes happiness flood through me as if I've joined the wrangler in the thermal depths, thawing my frozen limbs. "You should smile more, Little Scourge," he says. "You've got your mother's smile, see?" But when I strain to trace the woman's face, it's only Iness's withered features I make out.

I shrink away, crying out for Osha and she materialises. "I'm here. I'm here," she says, palming my forehead, my neck. "Shhh, Narkat." I feel as if someone has lit a fire in my chest, but my skin still shivers with cold. She pulls back the furs and unlaces me to my underclothes, baring my chest and torso to the cool wind. But hands next to hers cover me again.

"She's burning up inside," my sister says. "We should keep her body cool."

"No." The face beside her becomes the young chief's. He

221

heaps more furs upon me. When he lifts a cup to my lips, I taste vit, scorching like I've swallowed an ember, stoking my stomach like a furnace.

"She needs water."

"Later," Haus says.

"Trust him. He knows what he's doing." Voices merge and overlap all around me, a jumble of Hrossi and Isfalki words scattered like ashes in the wind... funeral ashes... *my* ashes. I'm cold as death, but the life inside is trapped, burning to get out. It kicks for the surface, crying out for space, for air, for freedom.

Is that the best you've got, Little Scourge? The wrangler's voice. Only he would goad me like that.

Drink it. It'll hurt like a bitch.

"Wrangler?"

I think you're probably one constant pain.

And we're back in the Roundhouse, spying on the Pairing Rite through the high window. Except, at the altar Osha clasps her bloody palm not with Brim but with Haus. The vows make no sense to me because for some reason they're speaking Hrossi. "Don't, Osha," I call out. She can't hear me, but when I quieten and listen carefully, I can hear the sound of their heartbeats. My sister's pulse trips fast and light, a syncopated double time dancing around Haus's loud, heated drumming. Gradually, they come together as one steady beat.

I wake in darkness with no idea how long I've slept. The wind has died and the camp is still and peaceful, the fire a hot mound of glowing embers. Dawn isn't far off. The furs are tangled around me, my collar open, the weight of a hand resting on my chest. Turning, I see Osha asleep under the covers next to me, and at her side, Haus, deep in thought, gazing into the coals. When he sees me stir, he touches my sister's hand and she startles awake, snapping upright. Her face is pale, her eyes swollen, and she clutches at Haus's fingers as she looks at me. She's terrified, I realise, and he's been the one reassuring her.

"Mother's mercy, thank you... thank you..." Osha's eyes begin to fill as she fusses over me, palming my brow, checking the glands in my throat. "Narkat." Her breath catches and she tries to blink back tears, but when they spill anyway, she turns on me. "Don't you ever do that to me again, do you hear?"

I try to speak but my mouth is dry as the gritty scrub we're camped on. Haus passes my sister a skin and she helps me drink. The clean cool water feels heavenly against my raw throat and I tip up the flask, trying to gulp down more, but both Osha and Haus stop me. "Slow," he says in Isfalki, then continues in Hrossi.

She nods. "Yes, slow down. He says it'll make you sick." I wonder how many other Hrossi words my sister has learned.

"What happened?" I croak.

"It was a fever," Osha tells me. "You got sick in a matter of hours and I... I think I panicked. I've never seen a calenture like it before. I kept trying to cool you down. I didn't read the signs properly." Her eyes work busily, attempting to see where she went wrong, that same deep cut forming between her eyebrows as when she's puzzling over contradictory notes from her tomes in the archives. "Haus recognised it straight away, though. The Hrossi call it the frost fever." She lays her palm on the skin of my chest. "Inside the organs burn, but the skin is frozen to the touch and develops a blue-black hue, just like ice bite. You kept throwing off the furs and pulling at your clothes and I could feel you like a furnace inside. Haus said we had to keep you warm or there'd be lasting damage to the nerves in your hands and feet. He wanted you to sweat so the fever could burn itself out. I think if it wasn't for him, you might have–" She shakes her head quickly, throwing off the thought, but the admiration in her eyes when she glances at Haus is there for any fool to see. "He's seen cases like yours before. You've come through it uncommonly fast. He expected you'd be fighting it for days yet."

"Back in the land of the living, Little Scourge?" The wrangler grins as he squats down beside us, but his voice lacks its usual shiny sarcasm, and I can see he hasn't slept. He says something to Haus in Hrossi, and the chief reaches for me.

I flinch, but Osha says, "Let him, Nara."

"Since when did the chief become a healer?"

"Since he saved half this crew from the frost fever last winter," the wrangler says. I shut my mouth and give myself over to the chief's examination. He pulls down my eyelids to examine the whites of my eyes and presses his thumb to my chin so my lips part.

"Stick out your tongue," Osha says for him, and they both peer down my throat. Haus seems fascinated but perplexed.

The idea of being a helpless patient, doesn't rest easily with me, so I sit up, albeit shakily. "I feel fine now." And I realise I do. The water has revived me, my body only aches a little, and I'm more bothered by the gnawing hunger in the pit of my belly.

"You shouldn't feel fine. That's the thing," the wrangler says. "You were only sick for a day and a night, and even after the fever has burned out, you should feel weak–"

"Wait, we've been camped here for *two* nights?"

He nods. "Haus wouldn't move on until you were well." His eyes dart to Osha as he says it, and I guess at the real motivation behind the chief's kindness. "We expected to be here for a few more days at least."

"Yeah well, maybe I'm stronger than Haus thinks," I say, indignant. But I can still feel the outline of Osha's hand imprinted on my chest when I woke. Haus knew how to diagnose and treat my fever, but was Osha the reason I got better so quickly? Did she sway me as I slept, speeding my recovery? My sister smooths down her skirts as she stands, not holding my eye. If she has the skill, she's still in denial about it.

"Do you feel strong enough to ride?" the wrangler asks.

"Give her a chance. She needs food first," my sister says firmly. Touching Haus's arm, she uses a Hrossi word, struggling over the pronunciation. The chief's lip hitches in amusement, but he calls to one of his men, who starts stoking the embers to prepare breakfast. Haus moves to the other side of the fire, where he takes herbs and roots from his saddlebags and offers them up for Osha's inspection. She crushes them between her fingers, sniffing so she can commit their smell to her uncanny memory, as I've seen her do so often before. The two of them begin to measure and grind the simples on a rock, their low intimate exchange a mixture of Isfalki, a little Hrossi and some sign language.

"So, that's an interesting development," the wrangler comments.

"What is?" I feign ignorance, even though I know he sees right through me.

"I'm as surprised as you are. Turns out your sister's not the precious Mor I thought she'd be. She doesn't have the usual Isfalki prejudices." He watches as I roll my shoulders and crack my neck, testing my body. "Why can't you just admit it? Haus isn't the ignorant trog you first assumed either, is he?"

I'm not admitting any such thing to the wrangler. "He knows more Isfalki than he lets on."

"Your sister's not doing so badly with the Hrossi either."

"She's always been a fast learner."

"So it seems." He casts his eyes around the men in the convoy who are watching the pair working together over the herbs.

"What you said before about Haus saving half his crew, was that true?"

"Would I lie to you?"

I pin him with a cynical look. "You've lied plenty so far."

"Being reticent about the facts isn't lying, Little Scourge."

"Stop calling me that."

"What do you want me to call you? How about Na'quat?"

"What? No! And it's *Narkat*. Your Isfalki pronunciation is shit."

"There's nothing wrong with my pronunciation." He pokes a stick at the fire, smiling to himself. The mole twitches in his cheek. I turn away and watch Haus with my sister.

"How come he leads this crew anyway? These trogs are rough-as-guts and he can't be much older than you."

The wrangler hesitates, as if he hadn't expected that question. "In the outlands, people can live entire lives in the time it takes the Isfalki to finish their Mass prayers. Haus was born with a weight on his shoulders. He's calm when things turn messy and the men trust his judgement... for the most part." He's serious now, and I can tell his respect for the young chief is genuine, whatever his own agenda might be in using him to cross the Wastelands. "Haus knows himself. And there's a goodness there. You might only see a Waster, but your sister sees more. She brings out the humanity in him."

"Humanity, my arse!" I burst out. "In a trog?" I shake my head. "Osha may prize humanity, but she's been locked up behind walls with her nose stuck in a book for most of her life. She doesn't know the world."

"And you do?" I can barely disagree with that. Hunting in the Fornwood and being able to swing a sword doesn't mean I understand anything of life beyond the northern forests.

"Osha's curious, isn't she?" the wrangler continues. "She's compassionate, idealistic... am I right?" He's got the measure of my sister, but I shrug him off. "You may not want to hear it, but that appeals to someone like Haus. He admires her for it. He might have even been like her – fascinated with herb lore, wanting to heal instead of harm... if it hadn't been beaten out of him."

"His past is nothing to do with me."

The wrangler sucks a breath through his teeth. "Sweet mercy, woman, talk about hard-nosed! Your sister certainly got all the empathy and trust when your mother was handing it out."

"Funny." I throw him a caustic look. "You expect me to believe that kidnapping Mor to pay his debts shows Haus's compassion and humanity? I might still be wet behind the ears, Wrangler, but I'm not suckling on that."

He scratches at that mole, runs a knuckle across his jaw, watching Osha. She pinches a measure of ground simples into her palm and sniffs, holding it out to Haus to do the same. When she brushes the powder into a cup of steaming liquid, he takes her palm afterwards and smooths it clean with his thumb. "It makes no difference what you think of the chief," the wrangler says. "Your sister's already made up her mind."

And when I look again, I see there's not a shred of guile or artifice in Osha's expression, no game being played as she lets her hand linger in Haus's. It's a small gesture, innocent and sweet, and it makes me queasy with fear.

"What is that horse piss they're mixing, anyway?" I ask, trying to distract myself. "I can smell it from here."

"No idea. But gird yourself, Little Scourge. You're going to be the one drinking it."

The wrangler's right, even if I wouldn't admit it to his face: Haus isn't what I'd thought a Waster chief would be. I'm expecting him to send men to chase Brim down, but the only response to the loss of their prisoner is a quarrel among the convoy that nearly comes to blows and ends with his guard, Mekke, becoming the butt of much ridicule. "Apparently, Mekke *handles his vit like a hairless boy*," the wrangler tells me, taking great delight in translating their gibes. "They say he deserves a job in the Isfalki taverns because he *bends over so easily* and *enjoys getting shafted by bloodless Ice- eyes*. And you thought my teasing was bad, Little Scourge."

Haus says nothing. He seems concerned only with lingering

by the fire near my sister. Eventually, I'm forced to drink the restorative they've mixed, holding my nose and gagging as I swallow, another source of great amusement to the wrangler. But within an hour or two I feel so revived, I itch for a bow in my hands, to be busy with a sword or skinning knife... anything but this waiting around. I don't know which I hate more – being man-handled as a prisoner or fussed over as a patient... and now it seems I'm both.

Haus can see how improved I am, but he's in no hurry to move on the following day, even though staying camped for another night is not a popular decision with his men. They spend the time whetting blades, fletching arrows, or inspecting their horses, but I can sense they're restless and resentful. Their scowls deepen at every conversation between Haus and my sister, and I can tell they've noticed the softened voices, the brushing of hands, and flushed complexions, just as I have.

In the evening, when Osha draws out her copybook, Haus retrieves something from his saddlebags that I never expected to see in the hands of a Waster: a quill and ink. Where he got them, I've no idea. I doubt they're his; even the wrangler suggested the Hrossi aren't literate, that their wisdom is shared orally and their history through story. Perhaps he obtained them especially for Osha when the wagon was traded. It hardly matters, for as a delighted Osha begins to sketch the roots and herbs she's seen on our journey, watched by an enthralled Haus, she might as well be dipping the nib into the chief's own blood and infecting him with all the poxes of hell, for the stares his men give her. Ordin hocks bitterly into the flames, muttering to Mekke over a vit skin, and I don't need to understand the words. His tone is clear: there's rancour and dissent in the convoy. And when I look at my sister's face – more alive than I've seen it since we left the Fornwood as children – there's a deep unrest in my heart.

The next morning complicates matters even further. The camp is packed and Wasters begin to help the girls to mount.

My sister tries to split Annek and Dalla up – no doubt an attempt to save us all from their bickering – but the two Mor invariably end up riding together. Mekke is about to boost Osha behind Sigrun when Haus, already mounted, intercepts. Leaning down, he offers his arm to her and my stomach sinks as she accepts it. With considerable grace and skill, Haus catches her about the waist and settles her before him on his horse's withers. The men seem to freeze as one. All eyes track the chief in a loaded silence, broken only by the arrogant snort of Haus's stallion.

Osha colours a deep red but recovers herself quickly. Hiking up her skirts, she turns and straddles the horse, taking the reins from his hands. I catch the flash of a grin from Haus – the first glimmer of true joy I've seen break his solemn face, like the glint of a melting river through winter snows. And suddenly, he's no longer the Hrossi chief, the Wasteland raider, the scarred pit-fighter. In that moment, all I see is the blinkered gaze of a man in love. My sister looks over her shoulder, checking I'm alright, but as Haus heels the stallion, she sets her mouth into a determined line. They lunge across the plain, leaving the stares of the men behind, and me with grit in my mouth.

Is this the same Osha who scolded me for truanting school, for skipping the citadel walls and taking too many risks? I don't have time to work out whether I like this change in my sister, for within minutes, I'm surrounded by plumes of dust, the entire convoy chasing after their chief. And when the air clears, I realise I'm alone on the endless steppe.

"Hey!" I yell after them. "Wait!" I watch their trail heading for the horizon – flat, dry and wind-battered as far as the eye can see. I'm without a horse, supplies, even a skin of water. "Bastard sons-of-trulls!" Did I miss something? One minute everyone's trying to save my life and the next I'm completely abandoned? If the trogs didn't think an Isfalki heir and the horse he stole worth recovering, it's not likely they'll bother returning for a near worthless Brand. How long will it be before Osha takes her eyes off Haus and realises I'm gone?

A horse nickers behind me. I spin to find the wrangler leaning down from his saddle to fasten a stirrup.

"Cock's poxes," I breathe, unable to disguise my relief. "I thought…" But he's already gathering his reins, his mare restless to pursue the convoy. "Hold up! You can't leave me here."

He pulls the horse short and turns. "Sorry, Scourge, my mare isn't a pack pony. She's too fine to haul a load. But I'll send Ordin back to collect you." The thought of waiting alone on the plains for the return of that expectorating, fetid drunk is enough to make me look past the insult and, frankly, beg. The wrangler knows it. He's having so much fun with this, I can tell from that fecking mole twitching on his cheek. But I'm also learning that my anger is exactly what he wants, his warped way of entertaining himself on this endless journey. So, I force myself to stay calm, reaching a hand to the pommel of his saddle.

"Come on now, make a little room up there for me… just until we catch up with the others." I'm ashamed at the wheedling in my voice, but when his horse side-steps and my arm ends up on his leg, his surprise is gratifying. I run my palm along his thigh and the amusement slides from his face, an odd vulnerability replacing it. The warm muscle of his leg flexes under his leathers. I try to ignore the flutter it causes low in my belly and reach again for the pommel, clenching it hard in my fist until it hurts.

"On second thoughts, scrap that," I say. "*I'll* tell Ordin to come back for *you*." And in one fluid move, I've launched myself upwards, driving a knee into his side. The kick barrels him right off the horse, slamming me straight into the saddle. He lies in the dust, winded and blinking. I'm as shocked as he is that I pulled off the move, although a good deal more satisfied and not quite as dusty. He wheezes something in Reis – probably an expletive ripe enough to make my eyes water if I could understand it.

"Really, Wrangler? The hand on the knee – that was all it took?" I can't pass up the opportunity to gloat. He wouldn't. "And here was me thinking you prized wits above tits." I laugh long and loud, making the horse skitter and nearly catch him under hoof.

"Treacherous mare," he says, scuttling away.

"Don't blame your horse."

"I wasn't."

I lean down and offer him a hand, making a show of the courtesy he refused me. He ignores it, brushes himself off, then grabs the pommel and swings up behind me. *"Thank you. You're welcome,"* I say, returning his own brand of sarcasm with childish satisfaction. But as I give the mare her reins, I now have to deal with the close fit of him, his warmth at my back. Maybe this was a mistake.

The horse springs forward, eager to be off. Refusing to hold onto me, the wrangler bumps along, squeezing his thighs to stay mounted. Given our speed, he does an impressive job of it, I have to admit, but the feel of his chest leaning into me is far more intimate than if he'd taken my waist and hung on. It makes me think of Brim, how we'd ride together across The Fold as children, how some of my happiest memories of the Settlement were breaking rules with him. Guilt flushes through me – guilt for betraying him when he was only trying to protect us, guilt for the way every cell in my body seems to ring like a struck bell at the press of the wrangler against me. He must notice my discomfort for he lets out a breath of amusement that warms the bare skin of my neck and makes me flinch.

"Is something funny?" I ask, slowing the mare to a trot.

"For someone who managed to unsaddle me with a single kick, your horsemanship is as stiff as a toy Warder."

"I'm not used to having someone cramping me when I ride."

"I thought you grew up used to it. Wasn't Pretty Boy the one who taught you?"

"How do you know that?"

"You forget. I worked in the Isfalki stables."

I had forgotten. How many times in the last few years might he have watched me sneaking out with Brim? How many times did we pass him mucking out stalls, with not so much as a glance his way? He was only a Brand, after all. Just as I am now.

"At least Brim knew how to hold on properly. He didn't have me in a thigh lock." I fidget in the saddle, illustrating my point.

"If it's hands you want, Scourge, I'm happy to oblige. Although, we Reis usually prefer an invitation first." And with that his arms circle my waist so slowly my breath feels like its been stoppered in my lungs. When he has hold of me, he gives a sharp squeeze that makes me jump. "Better?"

I heel the horse again, refusing to give him the satisfaction of an answer, uncertain of the steadiness of my voice if I did.

We canter in silence until the tail of the convoy comes into view ahead. Rather than catch up, I slow the mare to a walk. There are questions I need to ask the wrangler in private, and now is a good time. I open my mouth to speak, but he starts first. "He's asking for trouble, you know."

"Who is?"

"Haus. Putting your sister on his horse like that, giving her the reins."

"He didn't give her the reins. She took them."

"Either way, Wastelanders aren't in the habit of riding behind women."

"Like the way you're riding now?"

"I'm not Hrossi," he says, shifting his palm against my hip. "They won't ride behind a woman unless they're braid-promised."

"And what's *braid-promised*?"

"Hrossi weave a lock of their lover's hair into their own as a sign of commitment. It's a kind of Pairing, if you like."

"Do these people even understand the concept of Pairing? Father Uluf told us they join with women however they wish, until they tire of them. That's why they're trogs."

"And everything the Settlement teaches is true, right?"

I don't answer, realising how Isfalki I sound. I started witnessing the citadel's lies in the Sink, long before the ambush, and yet the Settlement's prejudices are so ingrained in me. Am I no better than Brim?

"The Hrossi only weave braids if they intend to be lyfhort – exclusive to each other," the wrangler continues. "It's not so common among them anymore, but I guess that makes the promise all the more serious when it's made these days. Pledging to be someone's life-heart is a sign of the deepest commitment, harking back to the customs of the Old World. But when the woman is Mor... well, among the Hrossi, that's a recipe for trouble."

It takes a moment for me to understand. "Do you mean because a Mor will be coveted by other men, even if she's promised?"

His agreement is a low hum in his chest that makes me uneasy. "The Hrossi have a saying: *A man might lose his horse, his blade, even his brotherband, but he should never lose his bloodline.* They believe strong sons and daughters are Effa's gift to the blessed, the same as the Isfalki do. Any Hrossi man who becomes braid-promised to a Mor must be prepared to fight off plenty of other interested parties. Your sister and those girls were already intended for Orlath, and the convoy respect that. They have a debt to their overlord only Mor will discharge. And a Mor like Osha... well, she stands out from an already exclusive crowd. Haus's actions are tantamount to betraying his–"

"Hold up. You're telling me Haus just staked his claim on Osha? Like one of your alpha dogs pissing on his territory?"

The wrangler barks an incredulous laugh. "You really don't have a romantic bone in your body, do you, Little Scourge?"

"What's romance got to do with it? I'm not about to let

my sister become the chattel of some trog barbarian simply because he wants strong sons."

"But it was okay for her to become the chattel of an Elix heir behind walls?" I close my mouth. "Anyway, for the Hrossi, becoming braid-promised isn't about owning a woman," he explains. "A promised man places *himself* in his lover's thrall, not the other way around: he gives *her* the reins. It allows her an incredible power over him, one that he's prepared to honour with his life, if necessary."

"He didn't give her the reins. I told you, she took them." He stays silent, letting me worry the leather straps between my own fingers, as I think over the possible implications of that. For some reason my mind returns to Amma, to the Old World tales she used to tell us sometimes about fabled warriors wielding swords with women's names. And I wonder now if these were Hrossi stories.

"Plenty of Wasters see a braid-promise as a weakness," he continues. "Old World monogamy that leads to ruin in a Continent already struggling to recover a healthy population. Orlath knew Haus was scouting for Mor to pay off his debt, so if he finds out about his infatuation with your sister, it's not going to be pretty. The men only see him tampering with the goods and believe it's a death wish."

"Haus better not be tampering with her."

"Maybe she likes his tampering."

"Osha wouldn't–"

He makes a nonchalant sound into my neck. "Keep telling yourself that if it makes you feel better."

"Don't try to teach me about my own sister!" I twist in the saddle, indignant, only to find his face in mine, his lips a hair's breadth from my own. "She's playing him... if you must know, she's... faking it..." I trail off, distracted by the way he's studying my mouth.

"She's doing a good job of pretending." His voice is a low murmur in his throat, and I can almost taste each word. My mind floods with the memory of the kiss by the river, the way it felt like sinking into the thermal warmth of the Moon Pools. And I know he's remembering it too, wanting to make this one so much better, intentional, real. I can see it in his face, the way he tips my jaw, but lets me close the gap between us; the way his tongue waits for mine, slow and beckoning as a summer's eve.

When Brim and I almost kissed, it was never like this – this balance between us, like I had the right to reach out to him, like I deserved to feel his skin against mine. The wrangler's a Brand, an outlander, an outcast – same as me. He might get under my skin like nettle rash, and I might plague him worse than a pulled quick, but neither one of us could draw away now, even if we wanted to.

He tugs my hips and I forget the reins, turning until I'm sitting sideways across the saddle, fisting his collar to stay on the horse, but more importantly to bring him closer. His tongue runs under my ear, his hands over my waist and thigh, and I can't tell whether the sigh I hear comes from me or him.

"Nara?" It's a moan more than a question.

"Mmm?" And it's a shiver more than an answer.

He straightens, draws away and I could whimper at the loss of him. Swallowing, he takes a slow breath, as if about to speak, but I press my fingers to his mouth.

"Enough talking."

I kiss the corner of his lips, his jaw, his larynx, liking the way it bobs when he swallows. And when I get to the warm hollow of his throat and see the twin leather thongs at his neck, I slip a finger under them and draw out the pendants – mine and Osha's. "I told you I'd get these back. Who knew I wouldn't have to use a sword?"

And when I tug both necklaces over his head and slip them about my own, he lets me. "You're making this too easy," I say.

"Not everything has to be a fight." And I think he means it, but then he says, "Do me a favour, though? Keep them out

of sight. Maybe even from Osha too, for now. The Wasters
will leave you alone but I don't trust them around her." And
because he's so serious, for once, and because his thumb is
tracing lazy circles along my inner thigh – the only mysterious
spiral shape I care about right now – I nod, and he drops
the pendants inside my clothes. He feels for the shape of
them between my breasts with his fingertips and his smile is
languorous, that mole winking at me from his cheek as if it
was in some heated conspiracy with my core, as if that was
another girl who wanted to gouge it out with a knife mere
days ago. Who was she anyway? The hitch of his mouth, the
softly glazed ring of brown eyes, is enough to make *this* girl
turn full circle in the saddle, unthread her shirt and invite his
cool hands to the warmest parts of her. *This* girl is about to do
just that when, without warning, the horse whinnies wildly
and rears up so violently we're almost thrown.

The wrangler grabs the pommel, his arms keeping me from
falling. "Easy," he calls out to his mare. "Easy now." And then he's
on the ground before her, standing in her line of vision, hands
out, uttering a soft stream of Hrossi words. She quietens, settles.
He scans the dry grasses, fixing his gaze on a point up ahead.

I hear the creature before I spot it – a long hiss broken
by rhythmic clicks, tight and neat, like a needle puncturing
leather. There's a flash of amber in the dusty scrub, followed by
a moving pattern of golden diamonds. The snake comes into
view, its size monstrous – as thick as my thigh and ten times as
long. Its slitted eyes are tinged with a blue haze that reminds
me of the glacial ice at Tindur Hof.

"What is that?" I ask the Wrangler, but my mind feels vague
and isn't truly on the snake anymore. It's wandering back to
Amma's cottage in the Fornwood, remembering the shape of
my grandmother's silhouette in the moonlight, the flash of the
curved blade, her blood splattered across a shiny black boot.
The acrid smoke of the blaze fills my nose and I can feel the
heat of the cabin walls pressing in, hear Osha's coughing as I

drag her after me. My breath turns ragged as if I'm once again fleeing through the woods, fear deep in my bones as we hide in the hollow of the greenock tree, numb and shivering from cold and shock.

"Turn away!" the wrangler shouts from somewhere distant. "Don't look at it, Nara!" I feel myself being dragged from the horse, the wrangler catching me, spinning me round so I can't see the serpent. And then there's the swish of drawn steel, a dance of footsteps in the dirt, a thud. In the stillness that follows, the dam of my heart gives, blood rushing through my veins and warmth flooding my limbs once more. I hadn't even realised I was icy cold.

My legs feel boneless and I sink to my knees.

"You alright?" The wrangler kneels beside me, but it's only the outline of him. "Hey... Nara." I can't seem to answer; I feel far away, disembodied. His palm slips under my jaw, and he moves my head a little. "Come on. Back to me, Nara." I like the sound of my name in his mouth. A noisy breath comes whistling through me, as if I've surfaced from deep water. I blink at the bright daylight.

"Holy Mother's holes! What the fec was that?"

Relief softens the wrangler's face. "And she's back... cursing like an overworked trull on Midsummer's Eve."

"Cheap, Wrangler, even by your standards." But I let him pull me to my feet.

"*That* was a sand siren," he says. "The Hrossi call them kraits." Behind him, the snake is a twitching coil of amber and gold, its colours somehow dulled, impotent now as the lopped curl of a seductress. Its head lays in the grit at his feet, jaw open, a droplet of black venom dripping from one fang.

"What did that thing do to me?"

"Sirens use sound and the draw of their gaze as a hypnotic trigger. Responsive prey can end up revisiting their worst fears or memories. It literally paralyses them with fright – ready for an easy kill."

I toe the head of the serpent, scanning its milky eyes, thinking of Amma's cabin and the night of the blaze. "I went back to the Fornwood," I tell him, "back to when I was a child. Except it didn't feel like a memory – everything was so real again. I saw details I hadn't noticed before." I remember the feeling of being trapped in the cabin's scorching walls, that terrible clawing suffocation, like a cat trying to get out of my chest. I think of Amma's blood marring the shine of a polished boot.

"I guess we lock away the memories associated with our worst fears... especially from when we were children." He squats to his haunches, rolling the severed head of the snake to expose a vulnerable under-cheek of milky white. "A side-effect of the siren's paralysis can be revisiting those memories. Their venom is even more powerful and highly prized... but then, you've already experienced its properties." I frown at him, and he clarifies: "In the tea the Blood-wife gave you."

And with that, he begins to mutter over the serpent, the same Reis words he recited over the white melrakki I'd felled on the ice plains. I guess it's some kind of prayer to the Elita, for this time I recognise the invocation of her name as he runs the tip of his dagger down the length of the snake's cheek. The skin cleaves and very carefully he retrieves a thumb-sized gland, which he holds up for me to see, pinching the severed duct to prevent the venom from spilling.

"How potent is it?" I ask.

"Reis seers dry it to a powder and burn it with incense to enhance the clarity of their visions. Some even take the poison orally," he says. "It's more intense that way but far more dangerous. Anything more than a drop and you risk not seeing anything... ever again."

"So, potent, then."

He draws a tiny pewter phial from his saddlebag and drains the gland into it, refitting the cap afterwards. "Best stay quiet about it," he says, holding up the poison. "Mesmer has a good market value in the right hands and one or two of the men wouldn't think twice about slitting my throat if they knew I had this."

"I'll keep that in mind for next time you plan to leave me behind," I say, returning to the horse.

He grins, thumbnail rubbing his bottom lip, as if remembering the kiss. He steps towards me and my stomach flips at the same time as the faint tinkle of a bell sounds. Shading my eyes I catch a shadow overhead, the all-too-familiar diamond of the ghosthawk hovering so still against the blue you'd think it was Mother Iness's seal stamped upon the sky. I shiver, feeling her presence as strongly as if she was standing across from me, gnarled fingers clenching my wrist on the Roundhouse stage. The hawk dips, banks, then climbs a steady spiral until I lose sight of it.

"She's watching us, isn't she? Through that bird."

The wrangler squints into the sun. "Iness has a higher skill more powerful than anyone I've ever met – even stronger than Frenka's. She holds Sway over animals and people alike. That hawk is her eyes and ears. She can master it over vast distances across the Continent."

"While she hides away in its most remote colony."

"Don't underestimate her because she hides away," he says. "Iness's power extends much further than the Walls of Isfalk, believe me."

"Was it her, behind the krait?"

"Maybe, maybe not. Sand sirens usually keep to the scrub and deserts south of Orlathston, but they're sometimes known to venture north as the weather warms."

I mull on that for a while. "If Iness is such a powerful Sway, why doesn't she help the Branded more? Why does she let villagers suffer all around her when she could use her skill to heal them?"

He shrugs. "Iness believes in the inherent superiority of the Pure – that they're the chosen people of your First Mother, the future of the Continent. The healing part of her skill, if she has it, doesn't serve her political purpose, I guess."

I'm lost in angry thoughts for a while, thinking how Iness might have had the power to heal Brands suffering every day in the Sink, to save orphans like the boy and girl I met in the Fornwood, innocents like little Jarl. Instead, through Church doctrine, she's effectively outlawed healing as witchcraft and ensured the Branded are treated as little more than beasts of burden, expendable working stock, good only for serving the Pure.

"We should get going before Ordin sobers up and comes looking for you," the wrangler says. When I'm settled in the saddle again, he looks up at me, eyeing the reins in my fist. "You can keep hold of those for now. But don't go getting any ideas." The mole hitches.

"Sweet that it crossed your mind, Wrangler, but braids–" I point to my hat "–not really my thing, even when I had hair." And once more we're back to the familiar baiting and needling, as if that kiss was something too fine, too luxurious, too unnerving for the road ahead.

Still, when he swings onto the horse, I make a point of snaking his arms about my hips, and he presses a palm to my belly.

"Wouldn't want you eating dust again," I tell him.

"Your words, my hands," he answers.

"Always the last gibe, huh, Wrangler?" I say as I heel the mare. But my own bid for the last word is shredded by a long, lonely scream tearing up the plain. The tiercel swoops to the west and I begin to suspect it's Iness who'll have the last say.

Orlath

After two days' riding, we rejoin the river that we've been loosely tracking as it turns south-west. Once more, I'm back behind the delightful Ordin in the saddle, but the wrangler stays close by, no doubt to enjoy watching me squirm every time the trog hocks over his shoulder.

Navigating a long bend we reach a point where land falls away and the current gushes suddenly down a ridge. From this vantage, with the river cutting lazy arcs through the plain below, I get my first glimpse of something I only ever dreamed of seeing. The whole convoy stops to admire the glittering line of it on the horizon.

"Your first sight of the sea, I'm guessing?" the wrangler says. When I turn to him, he's looking at me, not the view.

I close my mouth, trying not to appear so awed at its vast, unfettered promise. "Everyone said it was blue. But it's not. It's grey. And it's so… flat."

"From here it is," he says. "But close up you'll find the ocean's about as changeable as your moods, Little Scourge."

Annek, Dalla and Sigrun are silent as they take in the sight of it, the ships outlined along the horizon, smaller boats navigating the river delta. But Osha lifts her nose instead, savouring an aroma on the air that is utterly new to us. The Wasters talk excitedly in Hrossi, and I realise they're not interested in the

241

sea, but the colony that spreads across both banks of the river
and the island in between. At this distance, the settlements
spanning the north and south of the river seem nothing more
than a squat patchwork of cobbled-together hovels – about
as inspiring as Sink laundry hung out to dry on a dull day.
But the island is different, dominated by an impressive tower
that rises, fat and concave in shape, the one key landmark of
Orlathston. It stands in ancient sentinel over an enclave of
buildings, some Old World in their roof lines, the rest a mirror
of the shanties on either bank. Ramparts surrounds the core
of this enclave, not ancient like Isfalk's but substantial enough
that I can trace the ring of them even from so far away. Isfalk
may be grander and more imposing, but that double defence
of ramparts and water, makes for a fortress I imagine would be
near impenetrable.

Over the next few hours, as we descend the ridge and ride
closer, the tower looms before us, grave and regal. A tall sapling
sprouts from its stonework and seabirds wheel about, nesting
on its half-caved rim.

"Is that tower Orlath's keep?" I ask the wrangler. His eyes
are busy scanning the span of the river out to the sea.

"Ah that, my Little Scourge, is the Cooler." He turns in his
saddle so he can fully enjoy my reaction.

"Was that a wink? Did you just fecking wink at me?" I
stiffen with outrage, struggling not to raise my voice behind
Ordin. "We're riding straight into the trog capital, and you still
think it's a joke?"

He darts a look of warning, but before I can spit any more
bile at him, Ordin elbows me in the stomach, and I have no
more breath to speak. The wrangler shakes his head, before
heeling his mare and leaving me fuming behind my handler.
We continue down gently sloping pastures, where horses
graze, and a few outlying pens of livestock thicken the briny
air with the smell of dung. The animals appear far healthier
than the sallow-looking Brands who tend them or silently raise

their heads from field work to watch us pass. By midday we've reached the first streets of Orlathston proper where, among the hobbled houses, a windowless tavern and stables offer dubious welcome to the colony. We dismount, and I notice a barkeep in a stained apron leaning against the doorjamb, watching us. His brand is thick as an eye-patch over one side of his face and he studies the Mor girls with prurient interest as Dalla chatters hopefully to Sigrun of food and drink, her high-born prejudices about branded slums well and truly forgotten. But we're not to stop here. Two of Haus's men lead the horses away for stabling, while the rest of us continue on foot.

Close up, the streets of Orlathston's northern riverside are broader than those in the Sink or even the better parts of Isfalk's village. Evidently, this is to make room for horses, which seem to outnumber people in the raider colony. They're stabled among the dwellings as if sharing equal status with the branded inhabitants, the smell of dung thankfully tempering the less tolerable stench of human shit. Buildings here appear to be made from a motley wattle of reclaimed materials and scrap, scavenged from Mother knows where and daubed with pale, dried mud. It's as if the colony grew from the detritus of an Old World flood, dredged from the river itself. The Isfalki village, even the Sink, seems quite the cultivated metropolis in comparison. And yet, here I am, trusting the wrangler, letting him bring us into the beating heart of the Waster capital without any clear plan as to how we're to get out of it again.

"Wrangler," I hiss, drawing alongside him, intending to stress the urgency of our escape once more. But I'm hampered by a posse of sunken-eyed and snotty-nosed kids, who weave between our party, becoming a noisy escort, and I notice we're attracting attention like players come to town. Brands stop to gape at the pure-skinned faces of Dalla, Annek and Sigrun, and their eyes linger on the beautiful redhead at Haus's side. But they also stare at the Chief himself, whispers going up as he passes, like he's someone the colony knows all too well. Haus strides on with fixed intent, not oblivious to the attention but certainly uncomfortable with it.

Approaching the riverbank, we thread through an alleyway of market stalls, where traders and hawkers are too busy to stare. They haggle over sacks of grain and sides of meat, dried goods and salt, pelts and kegs, caches of weapons and tools, even Old World curios, the purpose of which I can only guess. I've never seen such a wealth of supplies, and I begin to understand why Mother Iness might have sued for trade with these people.

When we reach the water, multiple quays dart short fingers into a harbour, teaming with a flotilla of vessels, large and small. Flatboats and coracles vie for space among bigger merchant craft, loaded with goods for trade. But what fascinates me most lies beyond this floating marketplace and out to the western horizon and the sea. There, the masts of ships I'd seen from the distance of the ridge come into closer view and a strange thrill runs through me. I'm not given the time to wonder at them or the greater world beyond, for we're halted at the quay by a group of Wasters. They appear to be guarding access to a large rope-barge connecting the riverbank to the island.

Haus gains us entry onto the jetty and as we await the barge's arrival, our gaggle of tailing children climbs the railed edge like Fornwood tree-mice, hanging precariously over the river. They circle Osha, mouths slack as they stare at her hair. Fanned by the sea breeze, it picks up the sunlight, bright as wild fire in a colourless scrub. One bold girl reaches out to touch, and when Haus steps between them, Osha stays him, offering up a lock. The other children lean in, daring each other, holding fingers to the curl as if it might burn like a torch. My sister can't help smiling, despite our predicament. Doesn't she always find the humanity in every situation? And there is Haus beside her, watching with a pained look on his face.

When we're ushered onto the barge, a ferrymen yells at the

kids and they scatter, running off the jetty and re-forming on the banks to watch our progress as we push away. Clearly the boundary of their world doesn't extend to the island.

"Some of those skelfs didn't show any brands," I say to the wrangler, watching the kids lose interest and disappear down the narrow streets.

"They're probably Pure, that's why," he replies. "Soldiers' brats. Some of Orlath's Mor are..." he clears his throat, "I understand they're passed on to trusted chiefs who have served him well."

"How generous of him."

"Any offspring of those unions are free to roam the streets while they're young, but Purebloods are eventually rounded up – the girls for breeding, the boys to the barracks to be trained for Orlath's guard." His words shock me at first, until I think of the Settlement: Mor daughters in the citadel, Pure sons training for the Council or the Warder army. "These *barbarian trogs* are not so unlike your oh-so-civilised Isfalki when you get down to it," the wrangler says, as if reading my thoughts.

A vessel overtakes us, heading for the island. At first, I think it's another passenger ferry because it's loaded shoulder-to-shoulder with people. But then I realise they are all women, of varying ages and races, some Branded, some Pure and I don't need to see the collars about their necks or the cuffs at their wrists to understand: they're not passengers but cargo, human freight, the Purebloods bound for Orlath's harems, the Branded to his kitchens or trull houses, perhaps even his fighting pits. Just as we are. Haus may have removed our restraints and begun treating us more like guests, but we're no different from those women.

I look to Annek and Dalla debating the origins of strange fruits in the floating market-place, laughing as a hawker tosses Sigrun an apple-like fruit from his curricle, and the cold reality of our situation takes me by the throat. What are we doing crossing this river into yet another stronghold? And how can

I have meekly stood by and let the wrangler lead us right up to the very gates of it and still believe he has a plan of escape? Am I the only one among us who remembers that Haus and his men have a debt to settle, and that we are his payment?

I look to my sister, but she's preoccupied with the chief. I catch the movement of their fingers lacing between the folds of her skirt, his expression tortured as he whispers in her ear. There's such colour in Osha's cheeks, such a stricken look in her eyes now that I know for sure there was never any game of flirting and manipulation, even if she hoped there was. Hell's poxes, how could my calm, level-headed, scholarly sister be so foolish as to lose her heart to a Wasteland chief?

When the wrangler draws Haus aside, I take his place beside Osha. She won't hold my eye, staring out across the churning brown water instead. But her knuckles are white on the barge's edge and I can tell she's afraid.

"When were you going to tell me, O?"

She's doesn't answer, watching as a rat swims among the refuse floating downstream. I sense her shiver.

"Please tell me the two of you have some bigger plan at work here, because we seem to be headed straight into Orlath's stronghold, and the wrangler isn't offering an escape route either."

She won't look at me.

"Poxes. You've really got it bad, haven't you?" I say.

And then the floodgates open. "I didn't mean to, honestly. I thought... I thought I was in control and then..." She gives up explaining and nods her head in miserable acknowledgement.

I take a long breath.

"Don't judge me, Nara. He's not what you think. He's smart and perceptive... he's taught me so much about the Hrossi and their medicine." She lifts her chin, aiming for pride, but I know she's desperate for me to understand. "And you might not want to believe it, but he's gentle and kind."

"He's a trog who kidnapped us to pay off his debts!"

"Nara, you don't understand. It's not as simple as that. He'd do anything for me."

"Does that include presenting you to Orlath on a silver platter?" I pull off my hat and run a palm over my hair, now growing back in short licks. "Mother's tits! If he loves you, why are we even here?"

She shifts her weight awkwardly. Despair mars her smooth skin. "He didn't want to come. At first, he wanted me to run away with him, but I wouldn't leave you or the others. He tried talking to his men, but it caused a rift: they threatened to turn against him if he didn't meet with Orlath. Their livelihoods – their very lives – depend upon paying their dues to him. If they turn away, Orlath will hunt them down – that's how powerful and feared he is. Haus struggles with his conscience, his duty to his men. But he tells me he has some influence with Orlath, some shared history from his days in the Cooler. He hopes to reason with him."

"Reason with him?" I scoff. "Somehow, I don't get the impression that a man whose hobbies include a harem and fighting pits is the reasoning type. But Mother's love, O, I hope I'm wrong because I don't much like our prospects in there." She turns and squints up at the fortress casting its shadow across the water. Its wooden fortification gate is five wagons-wide at the least and ornamented with dented helmets, rusty shields and breastplates, epaulets and grieves of leather. A stench of rot fills the air as we disembark, and as I follow our escorts up the hill I begin to realise that it's not only old armour the gate and its walls sport. The entrance to Orlath's fortress is a gallery of the body parts still inside that armour.

"Fecs-in-hell." My eyes run the gamut of the grisly decor. "The overlord doesn't go easy on his enemies."

"They're not his enemies," the wrangler says. "They're the glorious remains of his legendary fighters – less a warning to visitors than a guard of honour for the pits beyond."

"Dalla said he was a collector, that his tastes were varied, not outright *sick*." I look behind me and find Dalla covering her mouth as she stares, eyes wide at how sugar-coated her cook's stories really were. Just enough to titillate a spoiled Mor unable to sleep, not enough to turn her warm milk sour. Annek slips her hand inside Dalla's.

"Think the worst, Little Scourge," the wrangler says, "then times it by ten." His face is deathly serious.

I grab the wrangler's arm, pulling him short. "What happened to *trust me, please* and *I'm taking you home to Reis*? Your plan to get us shot of these trogs is long overdue, don't you think? Or was that another of the many lies you've spun me?" I flick my chin to the girls. "You want me to wrap a ribbon around them before you present Orlath with his gifts?"

"Have some faith," he says, striding up ahead before I can press him any further.

At the gate, our convoy is stripped of its weapons. "This keeps getting better and better," I mutter as a guard relieves the wrangler of his broadsword and dagger. "Why don't you take a leaf from Mekke's book and bend over for them too?" He gives me a withering look. We're led down narrow streets, no more sophisticated than those we've wound our way through on the northern banks of the river. There's the same patchwork of dwellings, seemingly cobbled together from scavenged junk, the ever-present stables and the stench of shit – both human and animal. Finally, we approach a cluster of buildings, rising above the mushrooming shanty. Old World in construction, their grubby stone is weathered with age, their pointing in need of repair, but the general impression is palatial compared to the slums over which they hold court. Guards patrol the rooftops of the outer structures, and behind them the skyline is dominated by that looming tower, its fat girth appearing to move against the clouds, seabirds wheeling above its half-caved rim.

We're marched into a vast hall, its derelict roof supported by rusted iron girders. The lower windows are long-empty of glass, but the upper ones, taller even than a dozen men, still retain a few broken panes that refract grubby sunlight, catching motes in the cavernous space. The flagstone floor is buckled and uneven, littered with leaves and dung, lanky weeds sprouting here and there through its cracks. A wooden podium forms an altar of sorts at one end and on this is set the only furniture in the entire hall – a throne, fashioned from what looks like the cogs and forged parts of Old World gadgetry.

We wait. The girls huddle close, Haus and his men pacing uneasily. Without the weight of their weapons, they seem more feral, somehow, wary-eyed as animals caught in a trap. The wrangler lurks at the back of their group now. Surely I've been a fool to trust him, to allow him to get so close? How can I criticise Osha when I've been just as guilty of letting myself get pulled into the orbit of someone I barely know? But that kiss, his hands, the way he looks at me, even now. Has it all been an act? Has he been playing me? Fec's sake, have I been that gullible?

My thoughts are broken by the slow clop of hooves. A giant grey stallion nickers as it enters the hall. It must be twenty hands at the least, dwarfing the rider who sits in its saddle, making him seem almost a boy. He weaves the beast lazily through our party, looming down on us, eyes roving. I'd guess that he's only a little older than Haus, although his head, entirely shaved of hair, makes his true age hard to pick. Tattoos swirl up from the furs at his neck and climb the back of his scalp, looping around his ears and under-jaw in strange and complex patterns that I might have found beautiful were it not for the fact that his skin seems utterly bloodless, his eyes as black and hard as river stones with lips tinted to match. When he finally opens his mouth to speak, my breath stops for a moment. His teeth have been filed to points as sharp as any fleet-lynx's.

His voice rumbles through me, a low and unsettling purr. Haus nods once in response and the man I assume is Orlath continues to scrutinize the bounty of Mor. When his eyes fall on Osha, he sees fit to dismount his horse, the tight leather of his pants creaking in the silence. On the ground, Orlath is leaner than I imagined, shorter than Haus, and with a rangy build easily overshadowed by his vassal. His long nails are inked, black as his tattoos, and gold and silver rings sit on various fingers, making delicate hands that would rival any precious Mor's from the citadel.

He pulls Osha out from behind the chief and brings her into a channel of sunlight beaming down from the high windows. My sister's face is entirely drained of colour, and her hands fist against the trembling of her fingers. I try to step in front of her, only to have the wrangler block my path.

The tithe lord hooks a strand of Osha's hair in his finger. Expressionless and unblinking, he brings the lock to his nostrils, but instead of sniffing, he opens his mouth and runs his tongue along it. I think of the sand krait tasting its surroundings and stiffen with repulsion, the wrangler's arm across my hips barring me from Osha. Orlath thumbs apart her lips to examine her teeth and twists her head this way and that.

It's too much for Haus. He lurches forwards, his face darkening, jaw a hard line of muscle. Seeing his reaction, Orlath becomes curious, as if suddenly entertained. He palms my sister's neck, eyes on Haus, as he slides his fingers up into Osha's hair, gentle as a lover. And then he tugs forth a tiny braid that has been wound and pinned at the base of her scalp. The red is woven with brown – the exact match of Haus's.

Orlath turns on him. He grabs a fist of Haus's hair, to reveal a braid also hidden on the underside – the twin of Osha's. I catch that Hrossi word, lyfhort, being whispered among the men, the term the wrangler told me meant braid-promised. Angry murmurs rise from the convoy as they distance themselves from their chief. Ordin spits, the expectoration glistening at Haus's feet.

"Shit, Wrangler! This is not good, is it?"

"Like I said, the chief was asking for trouble paying tribute to your sister when she was intended for Orlath. Now he's gone and bound his fate to hers."

The overlord takes a step back as if to survey the lovers more clearly. And then, to my surprise, he grins and holds his arms out wide, taking in his audience and affording us an unmistakable view of those teeth. On a less confident man, they might have seemed diminutive, tiny as kitten's teeth. But in Orlath's mouth their unnaturalness, the pain involved in their creation, their homage to something wild and savage, has entirely the desired effect. The skin of my neck prickles.

He speaks, the Hrossi words low and emotionless, that rumbling purr. Haus reaches for Osha and before I can blink, two of Orlath's guards have him in their grips.

"What's happening?" I shout, but the wrangler ignores me, listening intently as Orlath speaks. When he's finished, the young chief hesitates, looking sorrowfully at my sister, before giving a reluctant nod. His men seem torn by his reaction, some grunting their gruff approval, others pained, as if he's been spared the noose only to be sent to the axeman's block. "Fec's sake, Wrangler, tell me what's going on?"

"It's better than I thought," he says at last. "He's been given a chance. Orlath says Haus can win his approval of the braid-promise he presumed to make with Osha."

"Win how?"

"In the Cooler. Haus won his freedom from the pits years ago. Now he's unlocked the arena doors and walked back in of his own accord. He must best Orlath's champions again if he's to earn the right to your sister."

"But why would Haus agree to that? He may never survive it."

"Well, the alternative was having his balls made into bunting for Orlath's walls. Haus took the offer." The wrangler shakes his head at the young chief and Haus only frowns in return.

"And what of Osha in the meantime?" As if in answer,

Orlath's guards catch hold of both my sister and Sigrun. Dalla tries to dodge two Wasters who come for her and fails, but Annek lands a decent right hook on one of them, getting as far as the entrance before they catch her up. "Where are they taking them, Wrangler?" I shout, trying to get past the barrier of his arm.

"To Orlath's harems with the other Mor, subject to the outcome of this agreement."

"What? No, you can't let this happen!" I shove past him and lunge for my sister. "Take your fecking hands off her!" The guards aren't sure what to do with me as I cling to Osha's waist, eyes casting about for any kind of lifeline I might use to get us out of this... and landing only on the wrangler. "Do something!" I yell at him, but he can't even meet my eye anymore. "You said you had a plan! Wrangler?" He won't answer, so I turn to Osha. "It's going to be alright, O. I'm going to get us out of this, okay?"

The commotion draws Orlath's attention to me. I feel his fist clench my forearm, spinning me to face him. He fingers the short red hair of my scalp, evidently making the connection to Osha, but frowning when he unearths my brand among the roots. Ordin tosses a comment into the ring and the men hoot with laughter, one scratching his balls to underscore the joke.

The wrangler steps forward and I think he's going to intervene, but his face is stony as he speaks, the glottal stops and burrs of the Hrossi words making him seem suddenly harsh and foreign to me. Dread begins to creep over my skin like melting ice through clothes. I've trusted him, this wrangler, even when I knew I shouldn't. I chose a Reis outlander, whose history and motives I know nothing of, over the only friend I've had since childhood, who's always been there for me, who's always had my back. *Be careful of the boy. He's a good soul, born of bad.* The Blood-wife's words return to haunt me.

Orlath squeezes the muscles of my biceps and shoulders, runs his fingers over the calluses on my palms, my nicks and scars. When he lifts his chin, one of his men throws the wrangler a leather pouch, the coin inside jangling as he catches it. My heart stops at the sound and I can barely draw breath.

"Wrangler?" I snatch, unable to keep the hurt from my voice. He looks at me, eyes heavy, wiping beads of sweat from his mouth on the crook of his elbow, as if struggling with himself. *Know that if he betrays you, he will break his own heart doing it.* Please let the Blood-wife be wrong. "Don't do this."

But he turns, pocketing the payment.

"Where's he going?" I hear Dalla ask.

"Probably to fill his gut and empty his balls in the nearest tavern," Annek says, giving the Waster holding her a look that makes him shift his feet nervously.

Fine! Let the Blood-wife be right! Let the mutt's heart smash into a thousand pieces. Anger scorches through me, burning my voice raw. "You heartless son-of-a-trull!" I yell as the wrangler walks away and disappears into the daylight outside. "If I ever see you again, you're dead, do you hear me? You. Are. Dead."

Orlath's amused look is given voice by the men around him who crow with laughter. The overlord cuffs me across the head, almost affectionately. "Good!" he says in Isfalki, and he takes his thumb and wipes the spittle that's landed on my chin, bringing it to his tongue to taste. "Good!" he repeats. Perhaps it's the only word he knows in my language. Either way, the approving roar of his men ricochets through the cavernous hall.

Osha, Sigrun and Dalla are dragged away, Annek refusing to walk so she has to be carried, still hurling obscenities at Orlath as she disappears from sight. I wrench against the guards's arms, but the shake of Haus's head is a warning to me, the very real fear in his eyes schooling my fury. It only confirms my suspicions: if this sick fec, Orlath, calls the shots, his Cooler promises to make everything I've been through till now seem like a dip in the Moon Pools at sunset.

The Cooler

I lie on a pallet in the grey light of my cell. Dawn is breaking above me and the birds nesting on the rim of the great tower have begun their morning ritual: wheeling on the sea breezes, screeching and loosing their droppings. Some falls hundreds of feet to the bloodied sand of the arena below; some splats over the cells of my fellow fighters, set into the caged iron supporting structure that runs around the inside of the tower's concave walls.

Ten nights I've been in the Cooler and already I've got used to waking every sunrise to a baptism of shit, and a body that aches like a crone's. My knuckles are cut, one eyebrow and a lip split, and I'm blue in places I didn't know could bruise. Haus has taken it upon himself to give me training drills in preparation for my debut bout, and from the first moment I faced the Waster chief in the training yard, I knew Brim's lessons were little more than child's play. Haus spares me nothing, barely speaking, barely resting, and when I beg for recovery time, his face, set somewhere between glower and grimace, tells me I can rest when I'm dead – and that might be sometime very soon.

In truth, I'm lucky not to have been eaten alive already – tossed into the ring as fresh meat for Orlath's gladiatorial wolves as soon as I arrived. But Haus has more influence in the Cooler than I imagined and he haggled a delay with the lanista, an acolyte of his late father's. Haus argued I might be trained as a proper Ringer, offering at least the semblance of a real fight to one of the Cooler's female champions, and making odds that could be profitable to Orlath's wager-men. The lanista agreed and the reprieve seemed like a relief at first. But now I understand that despite intending to keep me alive, Haus might actually kill me with his training before I even see a match. And if his drills don't finish me off, I could just as easily manage it myself walking between my cage and the practice yard. For one thing, the steps from the cells all the way down the outer façade of the tower are little more than a foot's width, have no rails, and are so weathered and shit-corroded I've already had one crumble to dust underfoot, only saved from breaking my neck by the quick reflexes of the guard who unlocks our cages every morning. For another, the Cooler has more rules and codes of conduct than the Mor school. No talking during meals; no looking a Ringer in the eye before a fight; no drinking before Ringer champions at the water bucket; no taking Effa's name in vain – or Ska's, or any of the other gods the plains people revere; no cursing the birds above; no private gambling on fights; and, most importantly, no asking about anyone's past.

Some of these unwritten dictums I'm taught by Haus, as best he can manage between his broken Isfalki and taciturn moods. Others I'm learning the hard way, pinned by fighters in the grit of the training yard or shoved against the wall of the latrine. One time, a brawny little Ringer called Teta San came to the water barrel between drills, bird droppings spattered on her forehead and crusted in her long black braid. I made the mistake of offering her a wet cloth to wash it off and her hands were round my throat before I could even blink, curses raining down as she kneed me to the dirt. Afterwards, Haus explained that in the Cooler, *gifts from the skies* are a sign of Effa's favour in the bouts to come – the equivalent of a blessing from First Mother herself. Any suggestion of removing said shit is tantamount to a death wish upon the bearer.

I only begin to understand Haus's past reputation in the Cooler when he's given a cell high up in the tower, almost nested with the terns and gulls. It's only a row below Orlath's current champion, a fighter known as the Maw. A colossus with a height and shoulder span straight out of Old World myth, the fighter makes Brim, the wrangler, even Haus himself, seem like children in comparison. Every time he paces his cell high above, his shadow is a cloud eclipsing the sun and I imagine his size originates from some famed Pureblood lineage. But when he finally descends to the training yard, lingering at the weapons racks, I can't help staring. Not only are his eyes bright as summer skies against the rich black sable of his skin, but he has brandings on his face and neck, blue as midnight shadows across the forest floor. And once again I'm forced to swallow my Isfalki assumptions that all Brands are smaller and weaker than Pures.

When I press Haus about it, he only grunts, disinterested. I draw a map in the sand asking him to show me the Maw's origins, and finally he takes a finger and outlines islands far beyond the Storm Sands, further even than Reis country – lands I never knew existed.

Without the softening of my sister's presence, Haus is a changed man in the Cooler. He has bound Osha's fate to his and he seems to carry the weight of it in every muscle of his body, constantly tense, barely allowing himself room for talk or rest or recovery. But now and again as he watches the Ringers spar, eyes on each lunge and thrust, I sense his focus drifting, his mind elsewhere, until some crack of practice sword or groan of injured fighter makes him flinch and return to the moment. I suspect memories of his Cooler past interweave with worries about Osha and the future, and if that weren't enough, he's taken on responsibility for me as well. But with the silence at mealtimes and being returned to our cells whenever we're not training, my only chance to ask Haus questions is during drills. It's slow going, not only because he's almost given up talking, but because Haus is such a taskmaster. I need all my wits about me to defend myself and I'm breathless most of the time. In almost two weeks of training, I haven't been able to land so much as a hit on him.

"Foots," he grunts every time I swing my practice sword and he deflects, "too big!" *Too wide a stance* is what he means. It was the wrangler's criticism too, and I almost want to spread my feet further apart just to spite that two-tongued snake. Any flicker of hope I'd had that he might return to break us out of here has long been doused by the sand of the arena. I lick at the split in my lip, vowing to myself that one day it will be *his* blood I taste. And, as always when I conjure the wrangler, my thoughts turn to Brim. What a fool I'd been to let him go so easily, to throw away my trust after so many years. Why didn't I try harder to make him see what was going on in the citadel? And if I did exert any kind of *sway* to make him flee, why in Hell's poxes didn't I use it to bring him around, to make him understand why we couldn't return to the Settlement? As much as I blame the wrangler, I should have had more faith in Brim. I should have had more faith in myself. Regret settles heavy in my bones.

Haus senses my mood and leads me to the water barrel for a rare break. He scoops a ladle and offers it to me, but I nudge it back for him to drink first. "You learn fast," he says, vaguely amused that I'm respecting the code of the Cooler, but he shakes his head, pressing a thumb to his chest. "I am champion no more. Drink."

I take the ladle and study him from under my eyelashes, wondering what he must have done on these sands, what he must have seen to become a champion so young. He toys absently with the braid at his neck – brown shot with my sister's auburn, curling it around and around his fingers; his habit when he's thinking. Seeing me staring, he lays his palm on top of my head for a moment, then suddenly yanks the

wool of my nabhat down over my eyes, just like a brother
with an annoying little sister, just as Brim would have done
when we were kids. "Drink," he says again. I straighten the hat
and do as he says, marvelling at how the man whose convoy
ambushed us, whose throat I tried to cut not so long ago, is
now my only comfort in this Mother-forsaken hole.

There's a lot I've learned about Haus since we've been thrown
together in the Cooler. I've seen him fight twice now, peering
down from my cage above the arena, the tower crammed
with what seemed like the whole of Orlathston carousing in
the viewing stands or hanging off the lowest cages, some even
swinging their legs from the crumbling rim for a bird's eye view
of the ring far below. *Lynstum! Lynstum! Lyn-stuuum!* they called
in unison, and I watched Haus stalk into the pit like a different
man, as if the flickering campfire, the harmonies of his lute, the
way he looked at Osha, were all another lifetime away.

He'd toyed with his opponent like a wolf with a cub, letting
him land a few scratches, making sure to baptise the sands
with his own blood a little, to tease the crowd into a frenzy of
gambling, his eye ever on Orlath's approving grin. But when
the time was right, the death blow he'd dealt had come as if
from nowhere, mercifully sudden and accurate – a grunt, the
sigh of metal on flesh, life in the balance for the briefest second
before that final thud.

Afterwards, when the rabble was gone, I'd heard the guards
marching Haus back up the outer steps to his cell, seen him
clutch at the wall as he passed my door, steadying himself as
he hurled his guts into the night below. He won't tell me what
Lynstum means, but it's plain to see it causes him anguish.
Never ask about anyone's past. Haus makes it clear that rule
applies to him also.

But one day, I notice the Cooler's ancient cook watching
me as I prod the chief for more about his fights. Standing in
line for our midday feed, his shrivelled face follows me with
curiosity and when Haus walks away to eat, he holds on to my

bowl. "I can tell you what Lynstum means, if you want," he says in perfect Isfalki.

I nearly drop my stew. "You're from Isfalk?" I notice now his watery grey eyes, that strange translucence about his skin that northerners get with age. "You're from the village?"

"I said I'd tell you about him, not me."

Perhaps he was outcast to the tundra for thieving, or worse, and ended up here on the back of a Waster slaving convoy. Who knows? He's a Brand, the blue-black spots blossoming thickly among the age marks on the skin of his hands, his left cheek. But Brands in the Settlement rarely live to his age. He isn't about to tell me his story, though. His face shuts down when I mention Isfalk. Yet when he looks over at Haus sitting in a patch of sun in the training yard, his pale eyes glimmer with admiration.

"Lightning strike. That's what Lynstum means," he says. "The Ringers gave him the name when he was still a boy." I lean against the wall, spooning the stew as I listen to his tale. "His father was the lanista then... made him train with his champions. Barely old enough to make a fist, he was. But they taught him everything – swords, staves, war hammer, whip. It was a sight to behold: a lad barely fifteen besting Ringers almost twice his age." The cook hums to himself, wiping at the crusted corner of his lips as he sorts the memories. "But his father's punishments... well, they were part of the way he made such ferocious champions. If they lost a spar, he stopped their rations for a day – not that they were hungry much after they'd had the Score of Shame." He makes a slash at his sunken chest with a thumb and I think of the latticework of scars I'd seen on Haus by the river – not fighting injuries, I realise now, but deliberately marked. "Liked to keep a neat tally, Lynstum's father. Literally scored it in their skin." The cook indicates Haus with his chin. "Being a boy, he notched up his share of losses... But I used to watch him, then. He should have won many of his training spars, but he started losing – deliberately, like. So, his father takes to beating him, cutting deeper, almost starving the boy to snap him out of it. But Haus would only stare back, not making a sound, all mulish. I reckon he was messing up just to spare his Ringer friends and piss off his pa. Teenage boys can be like that, you know." He shakes his head as if I understand what he means. And perhaps I would if I'd grown up in the Sink, had been allowed more contact with teenage boys. "There was a champion – Urso was his name. Kept to himself mostly, except where the boy was concerned. He must have seen something being crushed in Haus's spirit because he took him under his wing, taught him how to nurse his anger, brew all his resentment in private, then unleash it in the arena – quick and fatal. You should have seen his bouts after that. All grace and focus and bloody determination." He taps his pocket. "Poxes but I made a pretty penny off the boy." I scowl at him, and he clears his throat. "Anyway, that's how Lynstum earned his name and his freedom."

"His freedom?" In answer, the cook's gaze runs the rusted and weathered armour atop the training yard's walls, the human body parts blackened and shrivelled inside.

"Urso's hanging outside somewhere. Which helmet, I can never remember. A lot go up, a lot rot away in fifteen years of feeding fighters. But it was Lynstum who put it there. And after the fight, Orlath let him walk out of the Cooler with his freedom."

I hand the cook my bowl, my hunger shrunk to nothing as I scan what I can see of the gruesome décor, glad it doesn't daub the inside of the yard as well. It had already occurred to me that Haus could have been responsible for some of it in his time, but I hadn't considered his opponents might also have been his friends, his brothers-in-arms, his mentors growing up. "Lynstum. Lightning Strike. It's a good Ringer name, as honourable as they come," the cook says. And I think about it. A death blow that is quick and sudden is as close to mercy as you can get in a place like the Cooler. I understand that now.

And perhaps I understand Haus a little more – what he sees in my sister. The healing, the compassion, the saving lives – who wouldn't be drawn to that after a childhood meting out bloodshed and death? Perhaps Osha isn't simply a Mor to him. Perhaps she is atonement.

After the cook's story, I train like every day is my last, not because it easily could be, but because of a new-found respect for Haus. I can't imagine how you might live with yourself after having to end the lives of men who've become your friends, your family. But I won't judge him for it. I've clung to my own life, too, when it's come down to it. Didn't I run from the burning cabin straight into the forest, leaving behind Amma's bleeding body, leaving behind everything we knew? The will to survive can't easily be denied, even if the heart is already broken.

My first public fight comes the same night that Haus bests one of Orlath's champions, a thief called Five Hands. Haus is given lead-in bouts to re-establish his reputation, matches he easily wins but which send the crowd into a fever-pitch of anticipation for his battle against the Maw, excitement that ensures the wager-men are kept busy. Still, the sight of Five Hand's lifeblood splattered across Haus's cheek and pooling at his feet sickens me with fear. His clash with the Maw is inevitable now, but the giant has reigned supreme in the Cooler for more than a year. He's almost twice the chief's size, making Haus's only possible advantage his speed and agility. But if he fails, I lose my only friend in the Cooler. And I lose Osha.

Meanwhile, I've lost hope of my own promise to my sister that I'll come for her. Lost it almost as soon as I felt Teta San's fists close around my throat that second day in the training yard. Besting Brim in the Settlement is one thing, but these Ringers have a life of fighting for survival behind them, learned on shanty streets and slaving docks. Desperation has been their wet nurse, hunger and disease their swaddling, the lash their tutor. My life seems little more than a summer stroll through the Fornwood compared to the misfortunes that must have brought these fighters to the Cooler. I might brawl and grapple and cling to life with every last claw but, deep down, I'm starting to think all I can hope for now is my own lightning strike – an opponent as merciful as Haus to dispatch me, clean and quick.

The sound of the crowd keeps time with my pounding heart as the guard leads me to the Cooler's arena. *Lyn-stum! Lyn-stum!* they call from the stands, still celebrating Haus's victory. I'm grateful for the noise: it distracts me from thoughts of who my own opponent might be. I haven't been told – apparently a deliberate trick on bout nights to test the mettle of new fighters, preventing them from planning and strategising. I'm guessing it will be a much-loved Ringer veteran, judging by the fact our fight is billed after Haus's.

Slowly, amid the smell of piss and spilled dramur vit, the blood and acrid sweat of the ring, a new chant begins to rise: *Te-ta! Te-ta! Te-ta!*

Teta San.

My heart seizes as if she's already thrust a dagger in it. Holy fec, I don't stand a chance. Teta San is about my size but she's skilled and quick and has a sword arm as unflinching as a Fornwood logger. I've seen it in the training yard, along with a feral determination I've only ever witnessed in trapped animals ready to gnaw off a limb in a bid for freedom. My best hope lies in the weapons draw: if fate deals her short daggers or a longer bowie, I might outreach her if I'm lucky enough to draw a spear or pike. But if chance hands her a broadsword... well, I pray I've found Teta San on a merciful day.

I take shallow breaths, fighting the urge to hurl what little stew I've eaten into the sand. The heat of the crowd and the blazing torches around the arena hit me like an open oven. Shouting over the thunder of the rabble, the ringmaster grabs my fist and thrusts it into a barrel of wooden tokens. I pull one out and he holds it up to show the crowd the crude picture of a sheath knife. When he flips the token, the line of a whip is scored on the other side. Holy Mother's holes, I'm done. Haus has barely taught me to crack that thing, let alone get it round an opponent's neck or limbs. Maybe I can strangle myself with it before we start and save Teta San the energy.

As the weapons are shoved in my hands, a half-hearted chant is tossed here and there between the crowd: *Kulflamma! Kulflamma!* Others respond with jeers and laughter, scratching at their crotches. I don't need Haus to translate that one. I rain curses on the wrangler, rage burning through my nerves. It isn't enough he's left me here to die; now I must take my last ignominious breath in the guise of a trull with groin itch.

"Caestus!" the ringmaster calls as Teta San takes the weapons draw. I drop my shoulders in relief. The spiked knuckle leathers will only be dangerous if she can get near me, and I have speed on my side. But when her second weapon is announced, I'm teetering on the precipice again. "Pike!" I've seen Teta San training with the long double-bladed shaft in the yard, using it both as a sword, then as a lance, spearing a dummy through the heart at twenty paces.

Turning side-on so she can't see the horror on my face, I glance towards the walkway, searching for the reassurance of Haus. He's at the water barrel, being stitched up along the eyebrow by a cutman. He nudges the youth's hand away to look at me. With a lift of his chin towards my opponent, he draws back his arm, mimicking a spear toss, clenching the fist of his other hand exaggeratedly before he releases it. It's Teta San's tell, the tension in her balance arm right before she thrusts or lunges. He's pointed the tic out to me before in the training ring. I nod in return, but my heart feels entirely drained of blood.

Teta San makes a low growl in her throat like a war cry, and the rabble picks it up. The bout is on. Coin flashes, dramur vit skins forgotten, as fists pound and faces leer all around me with grisly fascination. It's like some nightmare hell-scape. I reel back to the edge of the arena and there's a cacophony of boos and hisses. Sweat slicks the grips of my weapons and stings my eyes. I blink and in that second Teta San runs at me, pike horizontal at her hip, cheeks aflame and dual braids swinging like some warring goddess from Old World myth. I let her come; she's likely to thrust the pike like a sword first, reluctant to take the risk of throwing it and losing her best weapon so soon in the game – tactics Haus has taught me. She raises it level with her jaw as she closes on me. I watch for the clench of her other fist and the moment it comes, I jump clear of the assault, slashing a deep notch with my dagger in her bicep as she passes me. Teta San's breath hitches, I see the whites of her teeth as she spins, the pain turning to fury in an instant.

Retreating, my heel catches the brick rim of the ring, and I stumble. Birds wheel black against the circle of twilight high above as I stagger backwards into the crowd. Jeers and then a howl of delight goes up through the tower as arms catch me, a hand kneads my breast, another a buttock and, before I know it, a wet tongue swipes my lips. I squirm away, to see it belongs to a goatish little Waster with a blackened grin and a fragrance like a trull-house piss pot. I lift the butt of my sheath knife to give him a kiss of my own but find a fist has beaten me to it. An arm tugs at my waist from behind, pulling me to my feet. Spinning round, I catch the black locks and galling grin of the wrangler.

I draw my whip. "You mother-fecking–"

He catches the stock mid-swing. "No time for sweet nothings now, Little Scourge. Your fight's with her." And he spins me round to face Teta San in the ring. "Focus," he says in my ear. "You can do this, Nara. Hone your mind. Find her fear, her doubt, and sway her, just like you did with Pretty Boy."

Before I can answer, he's pushed me back into the pit. Teta San is winding a rag about her arm, my little excursion into the crowd buying her time to staunch the bleeding. *Sway her*.

How can I sway her when I barely know how I do it? I try to remember that night on the plains with Brim, the way I'd listened for his pulse, blocking out all other noise; the way I'd imagined I could hear his thoughts. But the crowd is so loud now. I have difficulty hearing anything else. Teta San pounds across the arena at full tilt and I can see every flex of her thigh muscles, feel each flicker her lashes make, taste the dry fear in my mouth as she swallows. Her steps keep time with the adrenalin throb of my fear. *Lub-dub, lub-dub, lub-dub-dub.* Except... that isn't my pulse. That stutter on every third beat isn't me. It's her.

I draw a steadying breath and with it comes a voice. At first it's only a mutter on my exhale, but then it grows louder. *I'm a Ringer champion. I can do this.*

But, damn, this cut is bleeding like a bitch. How did she swerve in time?

I jump on those last thoughts and swell them in my own mind until Teta San's doubts turns to panic – *Lynstum has taught her my tells. She knows my weaknesses. She's small but she's faster than me. I might not win this.*

Fear crackles through her like static, making her movements brittle. Her throw is stiff and cramped when it comes, riddled with nerves, the pike's point quivering uncertainly in the air. With a crack, the lash of my whip yanks it down into the crowd. They're almost as stunned as I am, a moment of silent awe hanging over them, until they break into an uproar – anger or delight, I can't tell which. Before Teta San can find her next move, I'm on her, spring-boarding against her thigh, the sheath knife poised. She turns and deflects me at the last moment, and we tumble entwined, sand in my mouth and eyes, my nabhat knocked from my head. But I end on top and I'm quicker. I pin her caestus arm with my knee and press my blade to her throat. She flails with her free hand, ripping my shirt at the neck, the two pendants swinging loose from my tunic as I bend over her. Twin Gildensfir symbols glint gold between us in the light of the torches, her focus suddenly caught by them. She scans my bare head, the stubble now regrown to short red kinks that cover my branding once more.

Slar! Slar! Slar! the crowd yells. It's the first Hrossi word I learned in the Cooler. *Kill.* My grandmother taught me killing was my strength. But this isn't quarry and I'm not hunting the Fornwood for food. I look down at Teta San's face, the whites of her eyes, the grimace of her broad teeth, breath sucking like a bellows and... I can't do it. I think of Amma and Osha, my mother too, the hours they dedicated to studying medicines and herbs to save the lives of others, and here I am about to end one merely for sport. The knife hilt slips in my sweating palm. *Kill! Kill!* the crowd chants. Panicked, I cast a look around the stands and my vision stalls on the face of the wrangler. His expression is not one I've ever seen him wear before – lined and tired, almost sad, and I realise there's no answer for me written there. Teta San's hand covers mine on the hilt of the knife, a stream of words tapping from her tongue like prayer. I don't understand them but they're strangely familiar, an incantation I've heard before. "No! Stop!" I yell, suddenly realising what she's about to do, but her hands are a vice around mine, her arms unyielding. I try to tune into her thoughts again, but all I hear is the conviction of her orison – no doubt, no fear, no panic anymore. Only acceptance. And I'm too weak to break it. "Don't!" I cry again, but the woman jams down on my fist, driving the blade into her jugular with a single unflinching thrust. She coughs wetly and her blood surges around the hilt, bubbling and frothing over our hands, mapping pathways to the sand below.

The roar of the rabble bursts into my consciousness like a blow. Everything is too noisy, too fast, too brutally alive: coin and drink exchanging hands, the flippant chatter of cut-boys dragging the body from the sand, the heckle of grog vendors and trulls plying their trade among the crowd. I feel light-headed, a rush of warmth at my nose, my tongue metallic as the smell of rusted swords. I long for Osha, for someone to ground me, someone who might ease the turmoil in my head. But the wrangler turns his back on me, elbowing through the crowd into the night beyond. I'm overwhelmed by a great surge of exhaustion. All the colour and din of the Cooler reduces to a pinprick. All the pain and regret and guilt sloughs away, until there's nothing but the bliss of feeling nothing at all.

The Writing on the Wall

I wake in the night to the snores and sleep talk of Ringers in their cages. Above me the birds are quiet, roosting under a near-full moon. The rim of the tower seems closer, my pallet more elevated, and I remember they brought me to Teta San's cell after the bout, raised like a champion to be closer to the stars. Unable to sleep, I get up, but dizziness sends me to one knee. I reach for the brick wall as my head swims. Images from the arena rush my mind with the clarity of recent waking: Teta San's braids splayed before me in the sand, the bob of my knife against her glossy skin as she swallowed, the branding that arced from throat to earlobe like the path of some dark comet. She was stronger than me; she could have thrown me with a single buck of her hips, but she barely even struggled. It doesn't make sense.

It's not only her submission that plagues my sleep: it's the wrangler's reaction to it. I remember the look on his face just before he turned his back on me and quit the arena. There was no surprise written there as Teta San yielded, only tiredness and a sad inevitability. And I realise something, now, with the clarity that only the dead hours can bring: he hadn't been surprised because he suspected Teta San would sacrifice herself. For that's what she did, didn't she? She could have beaten me ten times over. But she let me live. And the words that left her mouth as she thrust the blade into her own throat were familiar because they were the same Reis words the wrangler had muttered when I'd skinned the melrakki on the tundra, and when he'd sliced the head from the sand siren on the plains. They were a death prayer. Teta San was a Reis, and the wrangler knew it.

I pace the cell, trying to find connections, answers, but all I have are more questions. From the moment I met him, my life has unravelled like knitted yarn in the wrangler's fingers. And while I try desperately to see its old pattern, I sense that the thread of my small existence is being pulled loose, to be caught up in a bigger design that I can't make out and don't understand. I rest my forehead against the wall of the cell and try to cool my throbbing skull. Hell's poxes on the wrangler. Why did he bother returning anyway? Why didn't he take his money from Orlath and quit this forsaken fec-hole weeks ago? Poxes on him for turning his back on me yet again, trapping me first in a wooden crate and now a damn cage halfway up a crumbling tower of human meat and bird shit.

I yank at the grille in the cell door. I have to get out. I have to find Osha and the other girls. I could have escaped the Waster convoy and taken them to live in the Fornwood. I could have taught them to hunt and fight. We'd have survived fine; Osha and I did all those years ago with Amma.

Why didn't I trust myself? Why did I listen to the wrangler? Perhaps I can still get out of here. Perhaps I can find them and steal horses and supplies, take us north again. I just need to get out of the Cooler, out of this damn cell.

My hands work almost as frantically as my thoughts, scrabbling in a frenzy over the rough wood of the door, trying to feel some chink in the darkness, some weakness in its construction. But all I get are splinters. I do the same along the wall, feverishly shredding my nails and the pads of my fingers against the brickwork. When I finally give up, my hands are bleeding and I'm seized by full-blown panic, whimpering and sucking at the dank air, my skin flashing hot and cold, my heart flipping like a fish trying to jump my chest.

"Hal shu frig, Kulflamma!" My neighbour strikes the bars of his cage with a dull thwang. *Shut the fec up, Groin Itch!* My Hrossi's good enough to understand that. Swearing is in no short supply in the Cooler and I've a good memory for profanities. The din reverberates through the tower, rousing other Ringers until the Cooler is a cacophony of curses raining down and rising up on all sides of me. At least it provides a distraction from the clamour of my own thoughts.

It's a while before the prison settles again and relative quiet falls, but I can't lie still, let alone sleep. Moonlight casts through my cage onto the back wall of the cell, picking out the blood from my fingers smeared against the brickwork. I notice other markings there, too – faint strokes in the silvery glow. I sit up to trace the graffiti, angling my head away so the full light of the moon falls upon it. And what I see sends a shock of recognition through me.

The Gildensfir. The symbol of our pendants marked crudely on the stone.

The lines are inked in dark russet and I look at my broken nails, the new cuts bright and fresh, but the nicks and wounds from the training ring now dried brown as rust. Blood is the only paint the Cooler boasts, the varied palette of gore. I think of Teta San's words as she drove the dagger home. I've no idea what her whispers meant, but they clearly invoked the name "Elita" in the same way the wrangler had after the melrakki and the krait were killed. I think Teta San had believed in this *Chosen One* too. And I think she'd had enough faith in the prophecy to ink its symbol on the wall of her cell; enough zeal to colour it with her own blood. That isn't simply faith. That's fervour.

My fingers shake as I run them over the pattern of the symbol, over the cold metal of the twin pendants. I can't deny it feels like a cog locking into a mechanism, some small part of the puzzle clicking into its proper place, although, truth told, I've no more understanding of what I'm looking at than if I'd been presented with an entire scripture written in Reis.

I count out the steps from one side of my cage to the other, the close cross-hatching of bars grinding beneath my feet, moaning a little at their anchor points in the vast brickwork of the tower. I wonder vaguely what Old World purpose the Cooler served. Here I am, suspended in a cage connected to a greater maze of cagework inside this great monolith, utterly in the dark. The pendants feels the same: a small part of something far bigger that I can't comprehend... something that Amma perhaps meant for Osha and I to confront when we were old enough to understand it. If the wrangler is the only person who might explain that to me, I need to swallow my fury and find him again.

But how the fec do I survive this bloody purgatory long enough to do that? I continue to pace, panic rising once more, the low grind of the cell bars setting my teeth on edge, until I catch another sound echoing along the walls.

"Shhh." Not a yell this time but a whisper.

"Haus?"

"Sleep." His voice echoes softly down the walls.

"I can't... I don't know what to do to... I don't know how I'm ever going to get out of here... I–"

"Shhh... Breathe." And the sound of him takes the edge off, knowing he's there, listening in the dark above me. Knowing I'm not alone.

The next morning after training, Haus pushes at the slops of his breakfast with a spoon, disinterested. Dark circles ring his eyes and I think he's had even less sleep than me. I nudge his arm with mine, but the chief remains somewhere far away. I can't blame him for being preoccupied: he's to fight the Maw this night. They tell me I'm to be the warm-up act, although against whom remains to be seen. The Cooler is a hive of preparation for the spectacle: carpenters build extra stands in the arena, hawkers set up stalls along the outer perimeter, and wagermen debate the odds, counting out their purses. The Isfalki cook told me that gossip about Haus and the reason behind his return to the Cooler is apparently all over Orlathston, the night's fight wildly anticipated.

"Haus," I say gently, trying to draw him from his thoughts. "Hey, chief?" He glances up at me, distracted, eyelashes still too long and pretty for the hard line of his jaw. "I said, let me clean that up, okay?" I nod to the short gash still weeping in his shoulder from the bout with Five Hands. Fetching water and bandages from the cut-boy, I begin to bathe the wound. I want to speak to him, to return the small comfort, the reassurance he gave me last night, but I struggle to find something he might understand. Words are Osha's strong suit, not mine. In the end, I settle for companionable silence.

A while later, it's he who speaks, making me startle. "You fight good – with Teta San."

I hang my head, concentrating on his wound, and I sense him studying me. I can't hide the shame that burns across my face. "She let me win, Haus. She gave up."

He nods as if he already knew, and for a brief moment I think he knows about the symbol I keep hidden, the prophecy, about Teta San's faith in the Gildensfir. But he only says, "It was her will." His eyes scan the brickwork of the arena looming before us in the sun. "Teta San chooses death. It is the last..." he struggles, searching for the Isfalki word, "peace?"

"Dignity?" I suggest. He nods, seeing in my face that I perceive his meaning.

I wring out the cloth in the water. Perhaps he's right. Perhaps choosing your own death *is* the last dignity in a place like the Cooler. Maybe it was as simple as that for Teta San? Maybe it had nothing to do with my symbol or the Reis and their prophecies? His explanation is a small comfort.

"Nixim," Haus says, "he sees you."

"When I fought? Yeah, I noticed," I answer, peevishly pitching the bloody rag into the bucket, and dousing my leathers in the process. "Fecs alive!" I stand to pat myself down. When I look at Haus, there's a wry curl to his lip. "What?"

"You and he…" he begins, crossing his fingers, as if suggesting some kind of connection. It knocks me utterly off track.

"There is no me and him," I bark. "I have no idea why he's still hanging around. He sold me out to Orlath and got his money. I supposed the two-faced bastard thinks nothing of staying to gamble it away on us, as well." I fish out the washer and squeeze it as I vent. "Never trust a snake-tongue. That's what they call the Reis in the Settlement. I should have listened. I wish it was him in the ring tonight. I wouldn't think twice about jamming my knife in his throat."

Haus only rubs his knuckles along his jaw and makes an amused grunt towards my fist.

"What?" I say, before realising I've throttled the washcloth, wringing water all over my boots. "I hate his poxy guts."

"Too many words for hate," Haus says with a grin. It's the first I've seen on him since we entered Orlathston. "I know now," he says.

"What?"

"Your name." He blinks slowly, sizing me up. "She calls you Narkat – most wild and fierce of the Fornwood."

I don't answer him, remembering the image of Teta San's lifeblood bubbling through my fingers. I'm not sure I have the stomach to be wild and fierce anymore. He must see it in my face, for he takes my shoulders in his broad hands. "Still you fight, Narkat," he says. "*We* fight."

"Lynstum," I murmur the name, trying it for size in my mouth. "How do you bear it?"

He's quiet for a while and I think I won't get anything more from him. But then he says, "Think your best happy time."

I smile. "You mean my happiest memory?" I lean against

the stonework, closing my eyes for a moment. "I guess, playing with Osha in the first snows of winter. Or my grandmother gifting me a bow when I was six... Maybe even Brim teaching me to ride."

He nods. "You are lucky. You know many." Perhaps he's right. I suspect most Ringers in the Cooler don't have their pick of happy memories.

"What are yours, Chief?" He looks guarded. "Come on," I press him, intrigued now.

"I have one," he says reluctantly.

"Only one?"

"One to make all others as nothing."

"What is it?"

He pauses again. "You win this fight, I tell you."

When I protest, he only lifts me by the elbow and points me to the training yard. "Come. Body is better weapon now, not tongue."

Trained by the Enemy

I stand in my cell waiting for the guards to bring me to the arena. Below, the crowd is packed in and around the stands, and I can feel the heat of their clamour, their excitement rising up to me. The birds above circle as if on the thermals of anticipation itself. All the shame I felt for Teta San's death, my anger and disappointment in the wrangler, flowed through me and into the practice dummy during my warm-up with Haus, and now my body thrums, taut as a plucked string. The lock turns and two guards stand in the doorway with a cut-boy. "Kulflamma," the boy calls with a snigger. He barely looks fourteen, his beard no weightier than the fluff of a seed clock on his upper lip, the ridge of his voice box just starting to show. I feel it bob under my thumb as I grab his throat.

"The name is *Fornwood*, you little cock-fiddler." The cook's been teaching me some Hrossi endearments over my stew, and to make up for my laughable pronunciation, I pinch the boy's full lips together with my other hand, drawing him so close he must wonder whether I'm about to kiss or bite him. Terrified by either proposition, he lets out a whimper and I hear a stifled laugh from the guards at the door. "My opponent?" I ask. The boy shrugs. "*Who is my opponent*?" I press, digging my nails into his cheeks.

His answer is too fast, too wordy when it comes and I tell

him to slow down and say it again. I pick out a few of the words: *new… fighter… no name.*

He's used the masculine for fighter and I tighten my grip, checking I've understood right. "*Him?*"

One of the guards grunts a yes and tells me to let the boy go.

Sweet mercy, please let it be true! Male and female Ringers spar regularly in training, but on fight nights the men billed as opponents for women champions are usually luckless offenders brought in from the shanty. They may appear strong enough to make the odds tempting for spectators, but they're usually unskilled and clumsy, little more than fodder for trained gorgons such as Teta San. Orlath's wager-men always walk away firmly in pocket. A single win hardly makes me a champion yet, though: I'd need to best more of the Ringers in the cages above mine. And yet I can't stop hope from flaring inside me. If I'm to prove myself against some unpractised trog from the slums, I might stand a chance.

I'm about to ply the guards with more questions about my opponent when I'm stopped by a cold wet splat on my head. Through the bars, the shadow of a gull wheels across the circle of sky above and I squirm as shit slides down my scalp and forehead. Drawing a breath of wonder, the cut-boy yanks free of me and speeds off down the crumbling stairwell, no doubt eager to tell the wager-men to adjust their odds: Kulflamma has been blessed by Effa herself.

I swipe at the guano as the guards march me down to the arena. I'll take whatever passes as a blessing in this hellhole, but I'd give it up in a heartbeat if these sniggering feckers would answer my questions about my rival. Their only reply is a scratch of balls, a mouthful of Hrossi they're lucky I don't understand, and a prod forwards with the hilt of a blade. It makes me edgy, unable to strategise as Haus stressed I should before each fight. The cook told me tonight's fight between the Maw and Haus is the biggest in the history of the Cooler, and I wouldn't put it past Orlath to lace every bout with surprises, giving the punters their thrills, while filling his coffers with rigged bets, especially if he stands to lose a woman as rare as Osha. I still have my doubts that he's going to let that happen. Handing over an Isfalki Mor in the likeness of Effa to one of his vassals? I suspect that's not an option for a man like Orlath. It's a matter of power, not only greed. Anyone who builds a vast trading colony and names it after himself must have a decent god-complex and probably isn't very good at sharing or playing fair. But then, what do I know of Orlath or of Hrossi culture? Haus believes the man will honour his word, so perhaps I shouldn't be such a cynic.

I follow the guard down the walkway behind the stands, taking deep breaths to steady my nerves. The fresh wood and sawdust scattered under the newly added tiers gives the arena a more wholesome smell tonight. It reminds me of the cabin in the forest, the scent of Amma's clothes after chopping firewood. A bout has recently ended and cut-boys drag a dead Ringer out past me, a weighted net still caught about his feet, his breast pierced by a pike. Shame fills me as I watch the body hauled through the sand; shame as I think of Amma and all the healers in my family – Osha, my mother, too – all saving lives, while my only skill seems to be in ending them. How I longed to be allowed to wield a sword, to fight, to kill the Settlement's enemies when I trained with Brim in the Fornwood. Now I'd give anything not to.

I try to smother these thoughts, the knowledge of the bloodshed ahead of me. What choice do I have? If I don't steel myself against weakness and misgiving, the blood spraying the sand will be my own. I have to survive this. I have to find a way out of here, for Osha's sake, for the promise I made her... for the promise I made Amma.

Kul-flamma! Kul-flamma! The crowd stomps their impatience, feet thundering the stands. *Kul... flamma...* Slowly, the cries peter out, but not because of my appearance in the ring. Up in the boxed podium, the Waster lord is taking his seat, the first time he's deigned to watch a fight of mine in the weeks I've been here. And beside him in robes of gold sits a woman, her hair russet as the leaves of a kasta tree in autumn, red as the old blood of the Gildensfir etched in the brickwork of Teta San's cell.

My sister looks down on me, her face illuminated by the glow of the torches, something about it changed. I cross the arena, standing right below the podium to get as close to her as I can. "O!" I shout up, and as she turns I see the bruise spread upon her cheek and jaw, blue-grey as storm clouds edged yellow in the evening sun, the scratches upon her neck, still scabbing over. "You scum-blood son-of-a–" I'm too busy elbowing my way through the crowd and scrambling up the stands to finish the curse. The personal guards circling Orlath's box arc up like feral dogs, making to push me back down to the ring, but the overlord raises a hand. Leaning over the balustrade, he gifts me a wide grin, the picks of his teeth yellow in the torchlight as he twists Osha's jaw, displaying her neck for my perusal. The scabs aren't scratches, I realise now – they're bite marks.

"You sick fec!" I launch myself at the box, spitting fury, only to be blocked by two guards, who drag me down the stands and throw me to the sands. Haus is being paraded around the arena opposite the Maw, ramping up bets on the main event. But seeing Osha, his face has drained of colour and set hard as a fist. He thrashes against the arms of the Wasters restraining him, extra guards coming to their aid. Seeing the commotion below, Orlath pulls my sister's face to his and with the gentlest of touches, peppers her bruised skin with small indulgent kisses. Afterwards he rounds on the young chief, eyes glittering with amusement.

Haus's whole body strains with rage and he pants like he's just finished a bout. But when he speaks, his voice is clear and unwavering above the murmurs of the crowd. I don't understand all the Hrossi, but I guess his words must hit their mark, for even the drunken and debauched Cooler rabble falls silent, the weight of anticipation heavy in the arena.

Orlath sucks his tongue over his teeth. There's a tightness in his face that might turn cruel. But, to my surprise, he says nothing, giving only a bored flick of his hand for the games to begin.

I'm shoved into the centre of the sands and the chorus of my name is taken up again, released by the crowd into the circle of night above the Cooler. Slowly the chanting changes, a new name mingling with my own that at first I can't decipher. *Licks*? Is that what they're calling? Or is it Lix? Then with utter dread, I grasp the word: *Elix*. Fear douses me, cold as a bucket of glacier water. *Elix! Elix! Elix!*

I don't want to look, I don't need to, and yet I've never been able to turn away. The man on the sands before me has a split lip and a bloodied nose, likely broken. His bare chest is oiled, and the muscles under his bruised ribs torque in that all-too-familiar way.

Brim.

They must have caught him on the plains. I want to run to him, throw my arms around his neck, apologise for everything I've said and done. But I also want to back away, to somehow escape this living nightmare that has me pitted against the one person, other than my sister, I care most about in the world. All the times Brim prepared me to fight for my life, I never thought it would be against him. I know his every move, his every tic and weakness, and he knows mine. I understand the working of his limbs and muscles, his strengths and talents almost as well as my own. His is a body I've sparred and sweated with, bathed alongside since we were children; Mother's love, a body I've even coveted on sleepless nights.

He doesn't speak, but his eyes as he looks at me are full of sadness, heavy with their own regrets and things unsaid. The ringmaster calls us to the weapons draw. Everything becomes surreal, slow and distant, as if in a dream. Brim draws a long spear and shield. I find a broadsword and dagger thrust into my hands. A yell goes up and the throng roars in response.

Standing at the edge of the arena, I'm petrified with indecision. Brim mirrors me on the other side. Thoughts of casting aside my weapons, sitting down on the sands, and letting come what may cross my mind. But the cook told me what happens to Ringers who refuse to fight. Their hands and feet become food for Orlath's dogs; their bodies hung, still living, on the perimeter of the practice yard to watch the brave in training, until eventually they expire of thirst or blood loss or shock. Call me a coward, but I'll choose Brim to do the final honours any day over that.

He trips towards me, pushed from behind by one of the guards. The crowd is becoming impatient. Orlath grins with his tiny feral teeth, but his eyes are on Osha, not the ring. Her torment is his entertainment as he waits greedily for her to break. *You don't know my sister if you expect tears, you evil mother-fec,* I think, willing Osha to find that inner reserve now more than ever before. My throat is tight with rage and my fists grip the hilts of my weapons so hard my fingers numb. I start to jog a loop around the arena facing the rabble, working them up into a frenzy of jeering and heckling, buying myself precious time to think, to fumble a plan. Brim watches me, wary and confused. *You know me, Brim. See what I'm doing?* I try to tell him with a look, and soon I see a flicker of awareness in his face.

When I finally turn on him, heaving my broadsword, I can only pray that he remembers our training together, remembers the way he criticised my two-handed technique. He always said my left arm was stronger, my swing veering to the right. I've worked hard with Haus to correct it, but now I accentuate the weakness again, hoping Brim is quick enough to recall it and react. He is. But only just.

Side-stepping, he dodges my stroke by a finger's width, grunting with the effort, the shock of my attack. I raise the dagger to his neck and he brings up his shield, catching my arm and throwing me off. But our movements are tempered, lacking the force we each know the other possesses. Hovering now, we face each other, and I take my chance. "Orlath," I mouth, eyeing his spear. Brim's grip on the weapon tightens and his focus moves to the overlord, who is busy watching Osha's reactions with the cruel fascination of a boy tearing the wings off starflies. Brim's grimace flickers with doubt. It's a long throw; it'll need the finest accuracy, and if he's off, he could hit Osha. I lunge at him, make another feint with my blade. He parries with his shield. "It's all I can think of," I shout over the noise of the crowd. I'm aware of his spear swiping behind my knees, would have been quick enough to jump it, but I let the stroke knock me to the sand. Brim loses grip of the spear in the fall but manages to straddle me, pressing his shield edge into my throat.

"Too risky," he says above the din. "You have to! Take the shot!"

He frowns down at me, tortured like I've never seen him before. *E-lix! E-lix! E-lix!* The rabble's thirsty for blood.

I belt his shield away, straining towards the spear. But he pins me back again, knee to my chest, drawing his fist.

"Make it look real, at least," I tell him. Brim curses, but a beat later my head snaps to the side, his knuckles like stone against my jaw, a spray of blood from my mouth. The crowd erupts in delight.

At first, I think it's stars in my eyes the punch blurring my vision. But then I realise the mist curling low along the sands is smoke. It drifts out from under the tiered seating, the smell hitting me a second later: the tang of newly caught fire, the wood shavings from the benches catching quick as kindling. I can just make out a figure on the walkway to the sands, clad head to foot in black leathers. He loiters nonchalant as a punter, something jangling at his side.

The chanting of the crowd turns to panicked yells. *Harr! Harr! Snapt!* Fire! Quick! Within seconds the whole arena is a mess of bodies fleeing, screaming, scrambling over each other for the too-narrow exits. The concave walls of the tower draw the air upwards like a vast chimney, fanning even the smallest flame into an inferno and I know the stands will catch in a matter of minutes. But I'll be damned if I lose this chance to get to my sister.

I push Brim off me and seize his spear, taking aim at Orlath myself. "Nara!" he yells, as a guard runs at me, broadsword raised. Brim kicks out at his legs, but I already know he's a beat too late. I brace my arm uselessly against the blade, but the sword falls to the sand mid-swing. The guard collapses on me, mouth and eyes wide with shock, an arrow piercing his throat from behind.

I shove him off and scan the arena. There, amid the turmoil, the bow still thrumming in his hands, is the wrangler.

"Nara!" my sister cries out from Orlath's stand and, unthinking, I grab the guard's sword and begin clambering up the abandoned benches towards her, sensing the wrangler's arrows picking off Wasters in my path. Smoke begins to fill the arena, making my eyes water, my lungs tight. Orlath is already heading for the exit, dragging Osha with him. I won't reach her in time.

Glancing over my shoulder, I see Brim grab the spear, trying to take aim before all visibility is lost. I hear the thwang of wood as the weapon sails past me, watch as it hits the bracket of a torch above Orlath's head, causing sparks to rain down on him. He stops dead, beating at his clothes to snuff out the embers, and Osha seizes the chance to dodge and run, lifting her skirts and jumping the benches towards me. Orlath yells to his men, but the sound turns into a scream of pain. He clutches at his face, blood pumping through his fingers where an arrow has pierced. His guards close rank around him.

I grab Osha's hand and run, yelling out for Brim as I go.

The wrangler appears before us through the smoke. "That should keep Orlath busy."

"He's still alive," I tell him. "You missed."

"So did Pretty Boy," he tosses back. "Follow me. Up here." He begins navigating the benches, climbing as high as he can – the opposite direction to the exits.

"What are you *doing*?" I yell at him. "The stands are going to catch any minute. We need to get *out*!"

"The doors that way will all be blocked," he shouts. He's right: I can see the clamouring crowd bottlenecked at every exit.

"Wait!" Osha says, tugging her hand from my grip. "Where's Haus?"

"Up here," the wrangler calls. "He's waiting for us... trust me."

Trust. That word. It's the last thing I want to do again, but I've little choice – we'd be lucky not to get crushed in the chaos below. "Brim?" I yell.

"I'm here... I'm here." His hand on my shoulder guides me forward, making the decision for me. We climb as high as we can up the stands to a point where the lowest row of Ringer cells can be reached by anyone tall enough to jump and hang onto the bars. Inside one of the cages, I make out the silhouette of Haus and beside him the hulking shape of the Maw. Why in Hell's poxes have these two broken *into* a cell when the whole Cooler is trying to get out? And then I see: the cell door is wide open to the night beyond, and not only this door – all of them. There are no Ringers screaming for release as the smoke streams upwards, no bars being rattled in terror as the inmates find themselves trapped inside this colossal chimney. The fighters are long gone... and there's only one person who might have released them, one person who was free to steal the cell keys while the guards were busy watching the bouts. Only one person who knew the Cooler was going up in flames because he was the one who struck the flint.

"Wrangler?" I yell. "We can't reach up there."

As if in answer a brawny arm shoots down through the caged floor and I hear Haus calling for Osha. Smoke rushes upwards, and I can only just make out the cross-rungs that have been forced loose of the crumbling brickwork, opening a gap wide enough even for the Maw to squeeze through.

Perhaps the cell's former occupant gouged away at the point work, desperate for an escape; perhaps all it took was the Maw's strength to wreck the Old World caging. Either way, I thrust Osha before me, the Maw pulling her up through the gap, as if she weighed nothing.

Wasting no time, Brim jumps and hoists himself up. "Nara," he reaches back down, "come on!" The heat and smoke are blinding now; I'm barely able to see my own hands ahead of me. Doubled over by a fit of coughing, I lose all bearings and when I try to grope above my head again, there are no bars, only emptiness.

"Brim!" I yell. "I can't find you!" But then familiar arms clutch my hips from behind and I feel myself jacked up through the cage. I don't have chance to turn to the wrangler. Once through the hole, Brim drags me to the cell door, where I fall to my knees, sucking greedily on the clean air of the night outside.

"Hurry," he says, pulling me to my feet and following the others, who are navigating the steps down the outside of the Cooler. But I tug from his grasp. *Fecs in hell!* I chide myself as I dart back into the cell. *After everything I've vowed, why am I doing this? I must be the biggest fool in the Continent.*

Hearing the sound of his coughing, I grope across the cage on my knees for the hole in the floor. "Wrangler?" I reach down through the haze. "Wrangler!" My palm slaps hard against skin and I find myself vaguely hoping it's his face. But then his arm grabs mine as he searches blindly through the billowing smoke for the gap in the cell. He latches onto me like a drowning man to a raft, clambering up while I heave with all my might. We topple towards the door and he's on his elbows and knees above me, spluttering and gasping for air.

"Charming as ever," I say.

"Took your time," he wheezes.

"Still came, didn't I?" I push him off and we stagger to our feet, making for the narrow stairway. As we pass the open doors of the empty cells, he bends over, wracked by coughing. I catch the scruff of his collar and pull him closer to the wall. "Fec's sake, take my arm before you fall and break your neck."

"Is that concern I hear in your voice, Little Scourge?" he manages between breaths.

"It's smoke inhalation."

"Mixed with a dash of gratitude, perhaps?"

I wipe the tears from my streaming eyes, surveying the hordes running for the river below us. "Tell me how you're getting us out of this hellhole," I croak, "then I'll think about being grateful."

New Freedoms

We make a run for it, down towards the river, our soot-blackened faces and clothes blending into the chaos of spectators fleeing the tower and the fortifications of Orlath's compound. The Maw certainly isn't a man to go unnoticed for long, though, and well before the jetty, where the crowd gathers to watch the blaze, the wrangler veers us through a maze of dimly lit laneways and back alleys. He navigates the island's outlying shanty like he's an old friend to it, and perhaps he is after so long loitering in Orlathston. I'm guessing we have a tiny window of time on our side while all eyes gather on the burning Cooler, and before Orlath regroups and comes looking for us.

At last, the wrangler beckons us beyond the scattered hovels and into the open night, and we come out on a lonely dirt track running alongside bullrushes. It feels like we've skirted the island.

We follow the track along the water's edge for some time until he wades between the rushes and draws up a sorry-looking skiff, still half-loaded with grain and rotten vegetables from its other life as a floating market stall. Something small and dark scurries across its deck and plops into the water with a distinctly rat-like flick of its tail.

"You can't be serious?" I toss at him in disbelief. "*This* is the boat that's taken you nearly a scorenight to buy?"

He looks sideways at me, sucking his teeth. "Still so doubting."

"Can you blame me? There's a vast difference between the golden menu of promises that comes out of your mouth and the shit I get served up, Wrangler. Even you have to admit it." He fights a grin at that, but his chin juts towards the horizon and I follow his line of vision until I spot the silhouette of a ship cut black against the tarnished silver of the moonlit sea. Its sails are stowed but even from this distance I can see the hull is sizeable, solid-looking and frankly the most hopeful thing I've seen in a long time.

"Does it get your seal of approval?" he asks me.

I rub at my streaming eyes with a wrist. I'm not entirely sure the tears are from smoke now. For the first time, freedom seems suddenly real, attainable, not simply a dream.

"Mother's love, is that silence, I hear?" the wrangler teases, hand at his ear. "Does the Little Scourge have nothing to say?"

"Back off her, Wrangler," Brim cuts in, squaring up to him.

"Or what, brother? You'll see she's returned to the safety of Isfalk? How's that plan working out for you?"

Brim turns away and says no more. There's a change in him, something defeated or broken that I've never sensed before. He doesn't put up a fight about leaving with the wrangler. He hasn't much choice, unless he wants to stay in Orlathston, but I'm surprised he's not pushing some counterplan or opinion of his own.

I take his hand as we get in the skiff and I keep hold of it as I sit down, hoping to capture all the things I can't find the words to say right now. Brim gives me a squeeze in return, briefly drawing my fingers to his lips. I know it's an apology of sorts. From both of us. My heart swells with relief. I have Brim back.

"No wait, Haus. We can't just leave them." Osha pulls away from the chief as he tries to get her into the boat. "I'm not abandoning them here. I said we'd stay together." She wipes the heel of her hand across her brow, smearing it with soot and I can tell she's desperate: while I've been deliberately ignoring thoughts of the other Mor since we left the Cooler, Osha won't be able to live with herself if she leaves Sigrun, Dalla and Annek behind.

Shame flushes through me. But, the fact remains that even if we could break into Orlath's harem, returning now when his men will be hunting us would be a death wish for sure.

"Nara?" she pleads, hoping to recruit me to her cause, but I only press my lips together and shake my head uselessly, the arguments in my head sounding as insubstantial as the night mist curling between the bullrushes.

It's the wrangler who answers, "If we stage a rescue without a proper strategy, we risk getting those girls killed as well as ourselves. Orlath's stronghold will be like a fortress under siege after this, his guards on full alert. It'd take an army to get them out."

"You don't understand. I made a promise," Osha says. "How hard can it be to get three of them out? You got us out of the Cooler!"

A loaded silence descends. The wrangler's voice emerges out of it, gently reasoning. "There aren't only three of them, though, are there."

Brim's mouth tightens as if the words he's about to say are bitter. "He's right. There are dozens of Mor in there. I've seen them."

"When?" I ask.

"After I fled the camp that night, I turned around and started to follow the convoy at a distance," he explains. "I lost track of you in Orlathston, but eventually found my way to Orlath's island. I lived underground, eating rotten leavings from the markets for days, while I spied on his compound and harem, studying the weaknesses in the fortifications, the changeover of guards, trying to work out a plan to get Osha and the others out. And gradually I discovered a spot where I could glimpse the women walking within the walls. That's when I saw them... dozens of ghosts... faces I remembered from the citadel, from

Morday Mass – Isfalki women supposedly sent to Torvag. Our own Mor, Nara." He stops, looking at me but seeing something else entirely, I suspect. When he speaks again, it's a confession, almost as much for himself as for us.

"In Isfalk, my unit was sometimes ordered to unload sacks of grain and supplies in the Settlement stores. I turned a blind eye to where it came from, never once questioned how the Council got its hands on such provisions in the middle of winter." He looks up into my sister's face. "I made a promise too, Osha. I took the Warder vow to protect you all But that protection turned out to be the worst kind of control, didn't it? Women traded like… livestock." The word I've used to him so often before now. He hangs his head, studying his boots, and I realise what that broken thing about him is: it's his boyhood dream of being a Warder. The Waster ambush might have tossed it to the dirt, but it's the citadel that has truly ground it underfoot – the colony he upheld as the last bastion of civilisation.

His voice when he speaks again is quiet but adamant. "We can't return for three and leave behind three dozen more. And, by my count, that's only the Isfalki women. Orlath is holding hundreds of Pure girls from across the Continent." He runs a hand over his sooty hair and glances at the wrangler still in the water steadying the skiff. "Maybe you're right." Brim nods, surprising me. "It isn't a rescue unit we need. It's an army."

The wrangler holds Brim's gaze, and it's the first time I've seen any kind of agreement pass between them. Water laps the sides of the boat, gentle but insistent. I reach out for Osha, but Haus, standing among the reeds beside her, leans in close, lips brushing her ear. Whatever he promises her, I'm grateful to him, for my sister lets him lift her into the boat.

The wrangler shoves us out past the rushes, then jumps aboard with a gush of silty water. I inhale sharply, loosing Brim's fingers as the cold washes over us.

"Apologies, lovebirds," the wrangler says, splashing us again as he reaches for the oars. He thrusts one at Brim. "Alright, Pretty Boy, let's put those hands to better use."

Brim rises. "Watch your mouth, Wrangler!" he snaps, rocking the boat with the sudden movement.

"Sit down, hotshot, before you give us all a dousing," the wrangler says lazily.

"I'm your Warder command–" Brim stops, realising his mistake too late.

"Alright, then. Sit down, *Sir*," the wrangler scoffs. Outside of Isfalk, Brim is nobody's commander, and especially not now.

Brim sits, begins to row, his gaze fixed on the departing banks of rushes, but his mind clearly elsewhere. I gnaw on a thumbnail, sandwiched awkwardly between the two men, watching Osha and Haus whisper frantically to each other in the stern. The Maw sits up ahead, silent as a masthead looking out to sea. Everything has changed. The world as we know it has shifted around us. We're not prisoners of Orlath anymore, nor are we bound by the rules and expectations of the Settlement. All kinds of chains have fallen away, and this is new territory, not just for Brim, but for all of us.

A shout goes up from the banks we've left behind. I hear the drumming of hooves, and above it all, a long plaintive cry. Instinctively, I look to the sky. The ghosthawk is a black kite against the night. It circles us, leaving a trail of pretty tinkling in its wake that makes me sick to my stomach. Without warning, it folds into itself and dives, swooping the boat so close I catch the flash of a stony yellow eye, and feel the breeze of its beating wings as a shiver along my neck. Before I can even lift my arms in defence, there's a rush of frantic feathers as the wrangler deflects the bird with his oar, sending it winging off towards the north.

I stare at him, breathless. Why is Iness still watching us? Why does she even care anymore, now that Osha and I are long gone from Isfalk? There's so much I still don't understand, so many questions I need answering. And as the wrangler blinks slowly back at me, I know it's Reis that holds the key.

PART THREE:
TO REIS

Another Kind of Sickness

We're spectacularly sick our first days aboard the *Na'quat*. So sick I don't even have the energy to give the wrangler grief for his ironic naming of the ship, or tease him about the spelling mistake. Only he, the Maw and the five crew who man the caravel seem able to hold down their meals. The latter are indentured sailors, wiry and weathered Brands who holler and sing as they shoulder into the hard yards of manning the vessel, alive with the thrill of the open sea and their new-found freedom. By all accounts, the wrangler has promised the ship, and their liberty, will be theirs once we're safely delivered to Reis. His generosity shocks me, and the respect he shows the sailors might have been intriguing if I didn't feel like I was dying. I'm a heaving mess and the wrangler's an easy scapegoat. The security of land, solid and unmoving under my feet, already seems like a distant memory.

In the rare moments I'm not spewing my guts overboard, I'm both in awe and frightened of the noisy mystery of the ocean, its fickle colours and moods, the flashes of strange scales and fins beneath the waves. But mostly I yearn for the stillness and quiet of the tundra, or the Fornwood under the mantle of deep winter. Sometimes, as I retch, I sense a hand at my neck, a cool cloth against my clammy skin, easing my roiling head. If it had been Brim, I might have been grateful, but he's too busy turning his own stomach inside out.

"All I seem to do is puke when you're around," I groan, trying to push the wrangler away. "Don't look at me when I'm like this."

"Like what?"

"Snivelling and weak and wretched."

"You won't be for long. You'll get your sea legs soon enough."

"But in the meantime, I'm dying and it's all your fault." I rest my forehead on the gunwale and take deep breaths of salty air.

"You're not dying, Little Scourge. I won't let you."

The ship breaches a wave and I moan again, reaching for the side to steady myself and gripping his arm instead. "I thought you *were* going to let me die... in the Cooler. You took long enough to come back."

"Well, ships for this kind of journey aren't easy to come by. I'm sorry I kept you waiting."

"Say that again."

"What? It's true. The Hrossi don't give up a caravel and its crew without a good deal of haggling."

"No, the other bit."

He rolls his eyes. "Alright. I'm sorry, Nara."

I nod my acceptance as he raises a damp cloth to my forehead, the rarity of my real name in his mouth distracting me for a moment. "I'm also sorry to do this, but it's been bothering me for a while now."

"What?"

He rubs at something in the short licks of my hair. "You have bird shit just here..."

I bat his hand away. "You're a boorish, unrepentant fec, you know that, Wrangler?"

"A fec who saves your sorry skin time and time again? Who makes an enemy of the most dangerous man in the middle Continent to spring you from his fighting pits? Who, under his very nose, manages to procure a sailing crew, supplies and one of the fastest caravels this side of the Storm Sands? No, don't mention it. You're welcome."

He enjoys my silence, running his palms fondly along the ship's gunwale. "You have to admit, she's a beauty," he says.

I grunt. "The *Na'quat*, huh?"

"One of the crew painted the new name for me. I did consider *Scourge of the Seas*, but *Na'quat* seemed more... snappy."

"You might have got the spelling right, at least. It's Narkat, N-a-r-k–"

"I told you: there's nothing wrong with my spelling." And that mole hitches, making me all sorts of confused.

"You know, Wrangler, I vowed if I ever saw you again, it would be your end. But why is it always me nearly dying whenever I'm around you?" I lean over the side of the boat, stomach churning once more.

"You'll be your ever-charming self in a few days," he says. "You can give me the ending I deserve then."

I cock an eyebrow at him. "Really?"

"What? No, I didn't mean *that* kind of ending."

"Oh Mother, you make it too easy!" I chuckle and he curses at me under his breath. His teeth when he grins are white against the brown of his skin, and the reflection of the sun and sea makes that ring of bronze in his eyes so much brighter than it was on land. He looks in rude health and it's utterly unfair.

He stares across the sparkling swell for a moment, his smile fading. "Pretty Boy seems to have accepted the truth about the Settlement," he says, surprising me with the turn in the conversation. "Things could be different between the two of you now you're free of Isfalk's rules and restrictions."

I straighten, taken aback at his frankness. The seasickness that's crippled me since we've been on board has barely left me with the energy to think about Brim, about what his awakening to the corruption of the citadel might mean for us.

I haven't had time to pull out those old longings, like stolen gems, or to consider that they might be something I could admit to owning one day. But then I remember the facts.

"You've forgotten," I tell the wrangler, "Brim's a Pure and I still have this." I finger the branding under my hair.

"If that's all he thinks of when he looks at you, then he's a fool."

Cheeks heating, I look away, watching the ocean changing colour under scudding clouds. I feel uncomfortable when he talks about Brim, as I do when Brim speaks of him. The two feel poles apart in my mind; it feels odd knowing they're even on this same ship together.

I change the subject. "Why was Iness's bird still tailing us in Orlathston?" I've more pressing concerns right now than my relationship with Brim.

"I don't know," he answers. "It's been bothering me too. Perhaps it's Pretty Boy she's tracking now. He's a Founding Four heir, with a seat on the Council, after all."

I hadn't thought of that. And yet somehow I know that isn't right. "Brim wasn't there when the sand siren attacked us, but the ghosthawk was still on our tail."

He shrugs. "No harm keeping tabs on you and your sister, I guess. If Iness can't get rid of a threat entirely, she'd make it her business to know where it ends up."

"And where *are* we going to end up? What should I expect in Reis? You've told me next to nothing."

He looks at me through heavy lashes, a frown settling between his brow as if there's some confusion or pain involved in the telling.

"Wrangler?" I say, suspicions rising. "What are you hiding from me?" I turn to face him. "Listen, Osha's escaped one barbarian lunatic. I can't risk losing her to any more crazies, just because your people think she's some kind of prophet saviour–"

"Woah," he says on a long exhale. "Wait a minute. No one said for sure that Osha was the Elita."

"But you suggested she could be to the Blood-wife." He rubs the back of his head awkwardly, and I can tell he wants to dodge my questions. "Don't try to fob me off this time. I've put two and two together. Teta San was Reis, wasn't she? When we fought in the Cooler, my hat came off and she saw my red hair, and the pendants, and then she... she grabbed my hand and I couldn't stop her. She *cut her own throat, Wrangler*." He looks back across the deck, not holding my eye. "I recognised the words she spoke. They were similar to the ones you said when you killed the sand krait. Words about the Elita."

"The Har Athan," he says eventually. "It's a Reis prayer, used to offer up a life, human or animal, to send the dying into the next realm."

"So, did you know her – Teta San?"

"No. But I suspected she was a follower of the prophecy and then when I saw what she did..."

I wait for him to go on, but he doesn't. "There was a Gildensfir – a Halqa – carved on the wall of her cell and it was painted in blood," I tell him. "She wasn't simply a follower, Wrangler. She was a fanatic." I shiver at the memory of the Ringer's calloused fingers closing around mine on the hilt of the dagger. "She sacrificed herself so I could live. Why would anyone do that?" He won't look at me, knuckles clenched on the gunwale. "Did she think *I* was the Elita?"

I hear him swallow. "Perhaps."

"But you said... my branding, the fact that I'm not a Pure–"

"She wouldn't have seen your branding now your hair's growing back. Maybe she mistook you... I don't know." He straightens, trying to shrug it off. "Perhaps she was a zealot. A year or two in the fighting pits of the Wastelands and you'd probably be a few arrows short of the full quiver, too."

"Hey," I seize his arm, making him look at me. "This Elita business, it isn't only a prophecy. It's a whole religion, isn't it? And you think Osha might be – what? Its head priestess? A prophet? Its fecking *saviour*?" When he doesn't answer, I let out an incredulous laugh. But underneath I'm scared, wanting him to discount it, to tell me I'm blowing this out of all proportion.

He doesn't.

I pace the deck, feeling dizzy, but not from seasickness this time. "I won't let my sister be swallowed up in some sort of cult, Wrangler."

At last, he answers me. "Look, whether you believe the prophecy or not, you should understand that for the hungry, the enslaved, those trapped by the circumstance of their blood, yes, the idea of the Elita has become the promise of salvation. Eradicating the Brume, bringing back the health and prosperity of the Old World means a return to choice, to freedom – for everyone, not only the Pure." His voice has changed its timbre and he speaks now as if he's recounting something he learned by heart as a child. "The Elita is food for the hungry, liberation for the enslaved, a babe in the arms of the childless, crops thriving again in abandoned lands..." He runs a hand over his head, confused, frustrated, I can't tell which. "So the prophecy says, anyway."

"No shit! This Elita's going to be a busy woman." I fold my arms, and try to stem my cynicism.

The wrangler studies the deck uncomfortably, "I know it's a lot to swallow."

"It is," I say. "And what you need to swallow is this: some Reis outlander has kidnapped us, spun some fantastic tale of magic powers and salvation, and now expects me to bring the only person I love more than myself to the home of the very people who–" I stop, not sure I want to add my personal history with the Reis into the mix right now.

"People who what?" he presses.

I shake my head, regretting that I brought it up. His eyes seem to deaden with disappointment.

"People who leave their babies on the edge of the Storm Sands so only the strongest survive?" he says. "People who share their women in drug-fuelled orgies, not caring if they're Branded or Pure? Is that what you heard about the Reis?" He grunts in disdain. "You know, Nara, the Settlement isn't the best place to learn tolerance of other cultures. I've heard some crazy shit about the Hrossi and the Reis spouting from the mouths of gossiping Warders and drunken brandservants alike, all thanks to Iness's isolationism. She wants everyone in the Settlement to think they live in the last seat of civilisation because her precious bloodlines keep her armies strong and the Branded slaving in return for their protection. But you Isfalki hole yourselves away behind the Walls and none of you know any different."

"Don't presume to tell me what I do and don't know. What I've learned of the Reis I've seen with my own eyes, not from listening to drunken Ifalki in the taverns."

"And what could you have seen of the Reis with that sheltered and privileged upbringing of yours?" he says.

"I've seen them behead innocent old women when they're unarmed. I've seen them burn down a home without any provocation... They're no better than the worst Wasters."

"What?"

I palm away angry tears, feeling in that moment as if he'd wielded the sword and the torch himself that night in the Fornwood. "My grandmother was killed by Reis raiders. Didn't you find that out when you went snooping about us? Our home was torched by your people. That's why Osha and I ended up in the Settlement in the first place."

He's silent, roving my face with wide eyes. "How do you know it was the Reis?"

"Because I wasn't born sucking on a citadel teat. I'm a Fornwood Solitary and I've seen more than the inside of a Mor dorm." I sigh, impatient now. "They had their heads and faces covered with cloth. The reis-chafi – isn't that what you people call it? And the blades they carried were curved."

"That doesn't make sense. The Reis don't venture so far north."

"Well, you did."

He shakes his head. "Killing old women, attacking children, the unarmed – it isn't our way… I mean, it's not unheard of for rogue clans to enter the Wastelands, maybe even plunder and loot sometimes, but they'd never burn. It's not the Reis way to waste resources like that. Your story doesn't make sense."

"It's not a story! I watched my grandmother cut down before my own eyes. That was very real, Wrangler. I know what I saw!" My mouth is dry as I turn away from him. How have I let myself forget that I'm sailing to the hearthlands of Amma's murderers? I blink back the threat of more tears.

"Nara, wait." He catches my arm. "Don't go." I try to push him off, but he must sense it's half-hearted, for he draws me closer. I feel overwhelmingly tired from deep within my bones. When I stop struggling, he cups my jaw and studies my face with such concern it makes me ache to let everything go. I don't know whether to be angry or ashamed or simply bury my head in his chest and weep.

His breath stutters and it's like something breaks in him, something he can't hold in any longer. "I don't care about the prophecy," he says. "Maybe you're right. Maybe it *is* all superstitious chaff, I don't know. But I care what *you* think about my people. I care what you think about me. Nara, trust me on this: killing the vulnerable, the unarmed – it isn't the Reis way."

I want so badly to believe him. I'm worn out with running and fighting, with being angry and uncertain. He's seen me at my most vulnerable and lost, and he's been there for me, however much I complain that he hasn't. And then there's the physical pull of him, the warmth of his body against me, solid and reassuring, his eyes that won't let go. I want him to make me forget everything – all my rage at the world, all my worry over Osha, all the unanswered questions about my parents and who I am. At this moment, I want only to feel his hands on my skin, strong and calloused and tender.

"Is everything alright here, Nara?"

I startle, jerking away from the wrangler. Brim rakes his eyes over the two of us, his face stony.

"Of course," I snap, even though my stomach flips and my jaw still burns from the wrangler's touch.

"Am I interrupting something?"

"No." I shake my head, straightening the shoulder of my jacket. "Nothing. Nothing at all."

The wrangler lets out a soft grunt like someone just elbowed him in the gut.

"Wrangler?" Brim says.

"You heard the Little Scourge," he says, running the back of his hand over his mouth as he looks at me. And he's so obviously disappointed I die a little inside. "Like she said, it's nothing. Nothing at all." His tone reverts to its usual sarcasm, but he can't disguise the manner of his walk as he leaves – spurned, dismissed.

"What was *that* that all about?" Brim asks me.

"Nothing," I lie again.

I sit with Osha on the deck of the *Na'quat*, our backs to the gunwale, hunkered down against the wind. The sun cutting through the bite of it might feel comforting if it didn't illuminate the bruise that's yellowing on Osha's cheek, the constellation of small scabs still visible on her neck. She's hardly spoken since we left Orlathston and now our seasickness has settled, it can no longer act as an excuse. Even Haus has managed to draw little from her, his ministrations ignored until he distracts himself helping the crew.

Worried about her, I lift a hand to my sister's cheek, gently tracing the edges of the lingering bruise. She flinches, turns her head from me. "I don't want to talk about it," she says with a firmness that makes me falter, and I stopper the long list of questions lined up in my mind.

Instead, we watch the Maw at the helm, the vast wheel dwarfed in his hands, as relaxed as if he was born on the open sea. Perhaps he was for all we know. I've never heard him speak a word, either inside the Cooler or out of it.

"He makes quite the captain, doesn't he?" I say, after a while. Sunlight glints off the five gold rings he wears in one ear. A pelisse trimmed with sleek black fur ripples luxuriously about his neck and shoulders. He must have found it in the hold, along with the red silk jerkin he wears beneath. His size prevents him from tying it, so he leaves the laces loose at the torso, his ebony skin ridged with muscle underneath. He looks more pirate prince than escapee of Orlath's fighting pits.

"I wonder what his story is?" I muse to Osha. The last thing I want to talk about right now is the Maw's past, but if I want my sister's confidences again, I know I must go slowly. The sun turns Osha's lashes to bronze as she squints at the champion fighter.

"I envy him."

"The Maw?" I ask, surprised. "Why's that?"

"His muteness." Her voice is flat, deadened as I've never heard it before. "There's a freedom in silence. Never having to explain yourself. It's a kind of anonymity."

"It'd be difficult for the Maw to stay anonymous for very long. Look at him. Have you ever seen a Brand so huge?"

Osha turns away again, her disinterest making my stomach knot with worry. There's a weary glaze about her eyes that I know is more complicated than seasickness. When Haus begins to climb the shrouds following the lead of one of the crew, she watches his energy and athleticism, but her attention is listless.

"I know what you're waiting to ask," she says, at last. "You want to know what Orlath did to me. You're just like Haus. You need the details." I stay silent, giving her space to talk, fearing that she won't. I've never seen her like this – so numb, so far away. Not even the night we fled the flames of our cabin as children. I wish I could draw her out. find her again. "Why is it so important to you what Orlath did? I can't go back and change anything, can I?" she says. "And crying about it only lets him hold a power over me that I want to forget."

She has a point, I guess, but Osha's strong and for her to be speaking this way must mean whatever the sick fec did to her was probably worse than I can imagine. I want to make him hurt for it. I want to take my skinning knife and open him up from leather pants to tattooed throat. But all I can do is hold her hand and be here next to her.

Osha scrambles to her feet suddenly. Knuckles white on the gunwale, she leans over and vomits. I hold her hair, try to soothe her. In the rigging, Haus stops what he's doing to watch us. Osha's lingering sickness surprises me. Everyone else has found their sea legs, but my sister's nausea persists with uncanny regularity – always before breakfast. Dread realisation ripples through me. This isn't seasickness. This is another kind of sickness entirely.

I fold my sister in my arms until they turn numb. "Everything will be alright, O," I say. *You and me sis*, I want to tell her, as I always do. But I can't because it would be a lie now. It isn't just the two of us anymore.

"I wanted to forget, Nara," Osha moans into my shoulder. "I wanted to put it past me and move on. But there's to be no forgetting now," she says. "No forgetting, and no knowing for sure either," she adds, fixing her sights on Haus with a look of hopeless longing.

"Oh, Osha." I can't help the sigh that breaks out of me. "So you and Haus…"

She nods. The wrangler read my sister better than I did. She's always known her own mind, and clearly she made it up about Haus long before I acknowledged it.

"Don't judge me, Nara. I'm not ashamed that I wanted him."

"But, poxes, O, you're a herbalist! I thought Amma showed you the remedies she gave women to stop a babe from catching."

"I didn't have those herbs to hand! They don't spring up along the Waster plains just because you have need of them. And I wasn't going to get hold of any in Orlath's harems. He'd have killed anyone providing preventatives to his breeders."

"I'm sorry. I wasn't thinking." Her face is so anguished; I cup her cheeks and rest my forehead against hers. "It's so ironic," I tell her. "In the Cooler, the female Ringers were given the monthly remedy, free as water. I took it even though I didn't need to. You never know what the guards or other fighters might try in a place like that. And all this time, you were the one who needed it."

"Nara, I'm not ashamed to have this child. I'm not ashamed it might be branded, if that's what you think. I'm only ashamed that I can't be sure of…" She trails off as she watches the chief in the rigging "…I can't be sure of the father." Her lip quivers but she traps it between her teeth, blinking furiously as if letting one tear drop will open the floodgates that might drown her.

"Osha, you need to tell him. He deserves to know the truth."

"No!" she snaps. "And you won't tell him either. Bloodlines are as important to the Hrossi as they are to the Isfalki. I won't have him raise a child of Orlath's out of obligation or some guilty sense of duty to me. I won't ask that of him." She straightens, closes her eyes. When she looks at me again, she's calm, but her face has hardened. "I can't live with his pity, do you understand? And I won't live with yours either. I'd rather do this alone."

I study the jut of her chin, the way she holds on tight to her turmoil, reining in her demons in a way I've never been able to. *You're the strong one. Look after her.* I'm beginning to think Amma was wrong about that. I might track the ice plains at dawn, spar with grown men twice my size, even survive the carnage of Orlath's fighting pits, but in this moment I understand that my sister is far tougher than me, braver than any Ringer with a broadsword. Where did she get it from, this resilience, this mettle? Was it from our mother?

I take the pendants out of my shirt and slip the leather over my head, dangling the necklaces between us. Her smile doesn't quite materialise, but her eyes light up a little and it's enough for now.

"I knew he'd give them back," she says.

"Don't be so smug about him. I was the one who took them back." I think of all the places I kissed the wrangler to get them, feel the ghost of his thumb tracing circles inside my thigh. I know she sees me blushing, but she says nothing, only touches her pendant to mine as we've always done.

Sweet mercy, but I wish our parents were here. I wish Amma were still alive. Why is it now, when I most need to be an adult for Osha, I feel like a child again? All the things we've endured over the past months, and now I'm like a skelf, out of my depth, trying to swim in a current way beyond my strength and flailing for a hand to catch me. But there's never been a grown-up who came running when we called, not since Amma's murder. From the moment we fled the fire in the Fornwood, it's only been Osha and me. And as much as I itch to know our mother, to find out who our father was, who *we* are, maybe all I'll ever have of them is a sentimental piece of old jewellery.

Still, I touch my neckace to Osha's, hoping the childish habit gives her some small comfort.

"You're not doing this alone, O," I tell her. "You've never been alone. And you never will be. It's still you and me, sis. Except now we'll be three."

The Settlement at Heart

The night is still, the wind has died away to a soft breeze that rings the rigging, and for the first time since I've been aboard the *Na'quat*, my seasickness has gone. I lean over the bow, watching as the caravel ploughs through a sea of stars, breaking their reflections into watery ribbons of silver. But the beauty of it and the wonder I feel at sailing the ocean for the first time isn't distraction enough from my worry about Osha. I'm taking my pregnant sister into the hearthlands of the very tribes who murdered our grandmother and destroyed our lives, people who also happen to think she's their long-awaited prophet-healer with a mystical ability to set the Continent to rights. Overall, I don't think our lives could get more complicated. How in all Hell's poxes did I get us into this? I'd feel more confident delivering Osha's baby surrounded by hungry wolves on the ice plains of Tindur Hof than on the shores of Reis right now.

I close my eyes and see again the curved blades and the reis-chafi of the riders surrounding our cabin in the Fornwood, tossing the torches that set it alight. There's something about the memory that's been grating on me ever since the road to Orlathston, ever since the sand siren crossed my path. It's a tiny detail playing constantly at the edges of my thoughts, there in the half-dreams at waking and behind my eyelids when I fall asleep: a polished leather boot in the moonlight, blood spattered across the toe, marring the shine. Perhaps over the years I'd forgotten the image, but it's been revisiting me with a strange urgency ever since I felt the hypnotic effects of the krait's mesmer. A leather boot in the moonlight. Why that, of all things? And why does the memory slip through my fingers the more I try to hold it, like trying to catch a snowflake?

"Nara?"

I jump, gripping the rail to steady my nerves. The pallor of seasickness has left Brim's cheeks and he has a good deal of colour in them right now. "Can we talk?" he asks.

"Now that we've finally stopped puking, you mean?" I smile at him, even though something inside me shrinks from the conversation to come.

"I want to say I'm sorry," he offers quickly, as if worried the moment might be lost to jokes and small talk. "Sorry for a lot of things – for that last Morday Mass and not telling you about the Pairing. For not listening at the Waster camp, and not believing you about Mother Iness."

I shake my head, not needing the apology, but he carries on. "I never felt that way about Osha, you know... not the way I feel about you. We only decided to Pair so that we might eventually have you living with us in the citadel, living together under the same roof. But I realise now what a mistake it was, how impossible that would have been for you. And, you should know, Osha and I never consummated the Pairing, you understand–"

"Mother's mercy, alright, Brim. Forget it." I don't want to hear this right now. His actions in the Settlement seem so trivial set against the bigger picture we're all finding ourselves in, but I appreciate his efforts to make amends. "I'm sorry too," I say. "At the Waster camp, I should have given you more time, worked harder to convince you to stay." How can I even explain to Brim what I did to him – that feeling of the skill rising in me, swaying him – when I barely understand it myself?

"I still can't believe I took a horse and abandoned you there with all those trogs and that damn Reis." I can see him puzzling over it, disappointed with himself. "It was like..." he shakes his head, "like seeing you with him brought out the worst version of me."

"Stop," I snap. I don't want him to talk about the wrangler that way. He's taken aback at my tone, and I try to laugh it off. "He brings out the worst in me too, mostly." But it feels like a lie the moment it's left my lips.

Brim calls me on it. "You don't believe that. Or if you do, I don't think you care."

"What's *that* supposed to mean?"

"Come on, Nara. It's obvious." He grips the railing, lowers his head between his arms. "He's in love with you, and..." he struggles visibly with the admission, "I think you might be in love with him."

My face catches fire. "Don't be ridiculous. He's a Reis from Mother-knows-where... and he's sold me out more times than I care to count. I'm in full control of my heart and my decisions, thank you."

"And yet, here you are, on *his* boat, sailing to *his* homeland, trusting *him* again."

I stiffen, trying to find something to disprove it, but all I can manage is, "We didn't have a lot of choice with the Cooler burning down around us and Orlath's guards not far behind." His eyes scan mine, but he doesn't speak. "It's complicated, Brim." I inhale a deep lungful of salty air, trying to navigate a path between the words and my emotions. "He... he knows things about me. He's told me more about my past and who I might be than anyone I've ever known before–" I break off, suddenly hearing the insult and wishing I could take it back, rephrase it somehow. But it's too late.

"So, he knows you better than anyone, does he?"

"That's not what I meant. It's just that he's told me things, incredible things about Osha and myself, things that seem to make sense, too."

"Well, I've heard they're good at that, the Reis – spinning stories and fantasies, sucking in the gullible with their dark arts and superstitions."

"It isn't like that."

"Isn't it? It seems you prefer deceptions to the truth. I've always been honest with you, Nara. Perhaps too honest for your pride sometimes. I'm sorry I've always been so candid with you about the difficulties of our relationship. I'm sorry I can't simply turn a blind eye to the challenges of loving someone like you."

"Someone like me?" I say, blinking at him, incredulous that he could seriously intend this as an apology.

"You know what I mean. Don't play dumb, Nara."

"No, enlighten me, Brim. How is loving me so impossible?"

"Stop."

"Say it. How is it impossible? Because I'm a pain in the arse? Because I never do as I'm told? Because I shaved my head? Why?"

"Because you're a fec!"

And even though I've baited him, I flinch at the word in his mouth. "Shit! Nara, wait," he says, obviously regretting it and stepping towards me. But I'm already distancing myself. Only Brim could declare his love and make me feel unworthy of it at the same time.

"You've said enough." The heat burning under my skin isn't from shame now but anger. Anger at myself for ever idolising him, for ever believing he was anything more than what the Settlement had made him. We might be far from Isfalk, but I'm still a Brand to him: inferior, marred, weak. I always will be. "Why did you even bother coming with us?" I ask him. "You should have gone back to the Settlement."

"What? Why?"

"Because you'll never be free of it, you know."

He pulls in his chin, looking confused.

"You might flee the citadel, but you'll never get beyond it.

It's in the way you think, the way you speak, the way you carry yourself. Your blood is Founding Four and the citadel is in your very bones."

I let go of the gunwale, heading for the hatch to the galley. "Nara, wait," he calls, but I continue walking, running my hand under my nabhat, scratching at the curls growing over my branding.

I'm done with apologies.

A Choice of Poisons

"Have a drink with us," the wrangler slurs when I make my way below decks. "Come on, Scourge. Just one drink. With me and the Maw." He's holding a jug of kornbru and swaying like a punch-drunk Ringer, his eyes hazy as a summer's eve. Seeing him in his cups might have been vastly amusing in other circumstances, but all I want right now is to get to my bunk and be alone with my thoughts.

Unfortunately, my small cabin in the forecastle is only accessible through the confusion of hammocks that form the mates' quarters. Navigating them now means getting past the wrangler and the Maw, both of whom appear to be on a kornbru bender. The Ringer champion was the first to discover the barrel of bru in the stores, and the sight of him diligently working his way to the bottom of it has become a nightly spectacle on the journey to my bunk. What is less familiar is seeing the wrangler perched on a keg, keeping him company.

I try to skirt round him but he tilts to his feet, balancing a jug in one hand and catching the Maw's hammock in the other in an attempt to right himself. The two men swing together briefly, the wrangler letting loose a snicker worthy of any schoolboy. The Maw nudges a dangling foot towards a tankard – an invitation for me to join them – and the wrangler fills it from his jug. Half the liquid reaches the cup, while the rest slops over my leathers as he hands it to me.

"Cock's poxes," I curse, trying to dodge, but soon realise scolding him is pointless: he can barely stand, his jerkin unlaced, his shirt sopping.

I press a hand to his shoulder, as much to prevent him from falling on me as to refuse the drink. "Tempting as you've made the invitation, I'm turning in for the night," I say, setting the tankard down. "Maybe you should too, Wrangler?"

"Oh, we're only just getting warmed up, aren't we Maw? Plenty more sorrows to drown. But your concern is touching, especially considering I'm nothing... a mere nobody." He chuckles but I feel the barb, squirming as I look longingly towards my cabin door. "Have a drink with us," the wrangler wheedles with a pout. "C'mon, Scourge." He takes the tankard I've set on the crate and thrusts it towards me. "I'll make sure you don't get into trouble – no bar dancing this time!" The bru splashes over me once more.

"Wrangler!" I curse.

He grimaces and presses a finger to his lips, in a ridiculous mime of confidentiality. "No dancing. I won't menshun the dancing."

I brush off my leathers. The last thing I want to do is cloud my head with grog when it's only now become clear enough to think beyond the seasickness, but I take the cup to silence him. "Alright. One toast," I say impatiently. "To you, Maw."

The Ringer grins, the first time I think I've seen him smile. I notice a wide gap between his front teeth that's oddly boyish and mischievous.

"Wait. Why are we toasting *him*?" the wrangler complains.

"Well, he did force the bars of that cell so we could get out of the Cooler. Plus, he's a champion fighter, handy in a crisis, oh, and gloriously silent. My kind of man."

The wrangler watches me, eyes swimming, shifting his feet to stay upright as if we're in rough seas. I can't help but smirk.

It's a novelty to see him so out of control. He pulls his head back a little to refocus. "Sweet mercy!" he says to the Maw, closing one eye and squinting with the other. "I thought one of her was bad enough, but now there are two." I catch him under the arm with my shoulder just as he loses his footing. I should have let him crack his damn head on the boards, but I can't quite bring myself to. I owe him one. He didn't abandon me when I'd been in the same state that time in Isfalk.

"Bedtime, don't you think, Captain?" I tell him.

"A little forward of you, Scourge, but if you insist!" He gives me a lewd grin.

"Alternatively, I could leave you here to sleep in a pool of your own vomit."

"So charming, isn't she, Maw?"

But the Ringer champion is already snoring, the canvas creaking under his prodigious weight. I watch him for a moment as he sails on the lulling sea of his dreams. I hope they're happy ones, far from the Cooler, where I know both Haus and I return in our sleep, calling out and waking in cold sweats before dawn.

"Come on," I tell the wrangler, "let's get you to your cabin." I try to shuffle him towards the Captain's quarters in the stern. "And if you're going to hurl, give me fair warning, okay?"

"Warning!" he says immediately. I jerk away, only to find him giggling at his own prank.

"Let's be clear," I say, jamming my shoulder under his arm as painfully as I can, "this is payback for that time at Helgah's, alright?"

"The dancing time," he grins suggestively.

"After this we're quits. You can sleep on the boards under the Maw's drool for all I care."

He sighs. "Why bother?" His voice has suddenly turned to self-pity. "You said it yourself, I'm *absolutely nothing* to you." When I don't answer, he leans against the panelling of the narrow bulkhead, facing me. "Don't worry. Pretty Boy may be in love with you but you're safe with me." He frowns. "I know how to stay focused on my mission. That's what you and your sister are."

"A mission? Right. Let's hope you can stay focused enough to remain upright, then."

He staggers across the ship until he's resting his head against the hatch of his cabin, where he stops for a moment, before sliding slowly to the floor. It's a fight to get him up again, but eventually I open the door and angle him towards the cot. His shirt is still sopping and reeks of bru. "You shouldn't go to sleep wearing that," I tell him, only to find he's already horizontal and unconscious on the bed. Guilt gets the better of me. That's what I tell myself anyway. I wrestle off his jerkin and unlace the sopping undershirt. He flops against the pillow, his arms above his head, his skin smooth and dark against the linens. Up close, his brandings curl around his neck and shoulder like the tendrils of a climbing cylla and I can see the lines are formed from tiny freckles, like scatterings of pollen. The tattoo of the Halqa sits on the underside of his bicep, the glyphs cryptic, mesmerising. It's the first time I've ever thought of the symbol I've been wearing around my neck all these years as something truly beautiful. But the Blood-wife's words return to me. *A pretty piece of nothing*, she'd called it. Perhaps she's right.

There's so much I don't understand about the prophecy, so many layers to what little the wrangler has told me. I want to scream in frustration, to push it all away, pretend it has nothing to do with me or Osha. But how can I pretend I don't feel the skill growing within me the further I get from Isfalk? When I'd influenced Brim and Teta San, I'd felt it as an instinctive, organic part of me – like all my other senses combined to make this sixth sense, and I knew its purpose inherently, as I did when I hunted. What scares me more are the visions I've had with Mother Iness and the Blood-wife. I've told no one about them, not even Osha, flicking what I saw to a corner of my mind as if I might simply relegate it to the realm of weird dreams. Except it wasn't a dream. It was something important, something Iness and the Blood-wife were both shocked by. I saw it written on their faces. I might try to ignore the visions, but somehow I sense they won't ignore me. And this journey to Reis feels like I'm running headlong into more of them.

The wrangler stirs, rolls on his side, almost trapping my hand, and I realise I've been stroking my thumb over the symbol on his skin. His lips twitch in sleep and I have to steel my fingers against the sudden urge to touch his mouth, to feel its warmth against my own again.

Hell's poxes, Nara, get a grip. He just admitted, with the frankness of the truly drunk, that he's simply following the orders of his calling, scouting for the Elita and bringing potential candidates to Reis. My sister is his mission and I'm tangled up in that – an afterthought, at most an entertaining diversion, nothing more.

I stand abruptly and his wet jerkin falls to the deck with a crack. Reaching down, I squeeze the leather to find a hard object lodged in its pocket. Extracting it, I recognise the pewter phial the wrangler used to store the krait's venom, the vessel no bigger than my thumb. I remember the sand siren's call, the way it had latched onto my fears, transporting me to Amma's cabin, to that night in the Fornwood. And the image of the leather boot catching the moonlight taunts me again, the splattered blood marring its shine. *Our seers take the poison orally to increase the intensity of their visions*, the wrangler had told me when he was extracting it from the krait. If the siren's song alone had made me remember things I thought I'd forgotten, what would its venom induce? Might I return to that night and see Amma again, even for the briefest of moments? Might I find out for certain who my grandmother's killers were? *Anything more than a drop and you won't see a thing... ever again.*

Before I have time to think through the stupidity of the decision, I've seized the wrangler's dagger, dipped the blade into the canted phial and withdrawn its tip. It glistens with black poison, heavy and viscous, the venom bearing down towards the ship's boards as if eager to join the vast expanse of liquid matter heaving below. *A drop.*

I hesitate, holding the knife high to examine the tear of liquid quivering in the lamplight. It grows heavy and falls. But not before I've intercepted it, darting out my tongue in the same way Osha and I used to as children, catching snowflakes in the Fornwood, another lifetime ago.

The Memory of Moonlight

It's the smell that hits me first. Like freshly turned earth and nettles flattened by a summer storm. Osha is grinding Breath's Ease in the mortar and the scent of it is a blow to my senses, distilled as it is by the clarity of the scene – the autumn kitchen, strung with drying herbs and roots, the fire crackling with that particular intensity of dry wood, not yet mouldered or swollen with damp from the winter snows. Osha rubs her nose with the inside of her wrist, breaking briefly from a song she's singing, the chorus of which bubbles up in my own chest. It's the one Amma taught us, the ballad about Effa that Haus asked Osha to sing by the campfire. All this time, I'd buried the lyrics, the melody, the memory. But I used to sing it too, didn't I, albeit poorly, only murmuring the words in deference to Osha's clear and haunting voice.

There's something in my hands, silky and brittle at the same time. Feathers. I'm fletching arrows. The quills are good and strong, white with black tips. I remember the snow goose I felled, the way it spiralled from the sky, thudding into the brush at the edge of the clearing. Through the window, there's the dull scrape of a hoe: Amma putting the vegetable beds to rest. Soon the ground will be too hard to work and I'll need my arrows more than ever for hunting, while Osha and Amma scavenge the forest for late berries, nuts and mushrooms.

Outside, the daylight is fading fast and the moon is rising full above the clearing, pale and lonely as an old bone. I call through the window for Amma to come inside before she catches a chill. The sentiment is adult, but the voice – high and piping – surprises me; a child's voice, keen, trusting, unmarred by the disappointments and fears of everything that came afterwards.

"In a minute, Narkat," my grandmother answers. "You eat without me. I want to finish up here."

The meal is leftovers – the last of the goose flesh, stewed in a stock of beets and potatoes. We do as we're told, filling our stomachs and settling by the fire afterwards to finish our chores and wait for Amma. Osha ties herbs and I inspect my arrows. The fresh logs hiss in the grate and the warmth they throw off dulls the biting night with its smell of snow. Food in my belly and heat on my skin, I begin to grow drowsy. By the fire, Osha is already dreaming, and I curl up beside her and cover us with Amma's quilt.

In my dream, my grandmother speaks, a panic in her voice that I rarely heard in life. *Don't make me do it,* she says. *Don't make me give them up.* And I know she isn't talking to us because there's a low rumbling answer, like logs rolled against the hearth.

It's no longer safe here. You know that. I stir at the man's voice and, squinting through sleep, I see him in the doorway: a big dark shadow, broad and imposing in furs, the streak in his hair glowing white as the moonlight. I didn't recognise him then. But now I know the man is Brim's uncle, Lars Oskarsson.

Listen to me, I can protect them behind the Walls.

You must be mad! The vehemence in my grandmother's voice shocks me, but I don't dare move. *I've spent these eight years keeping them away from Iness and the Isfalk Council.*

And now you need to let them go, Oskarsson says firmly. *You forget who I am, Cura. I kept their mother safe on that journey with those girls in her belly. And she'd have wanted me to keep them safe now.*

By taking them into the mouth of the wolf? Are you sure about that?

Oskarsson draws closer to the hearth and I close my eyes tight, but I know the hand that cups my head is his. *You're sitting ducks here, Cura. Those burnt-out Solitary cabins, the raids, the attacks – you don't really believe that was the work of the Reis? You know whose hand is behind it.*

My grandmother releases a scathing breath. *I know what that Mor bitch is capable of,* she says stiffly. *She likes to shoot two birds with one arrow – hunting down Sways and stirring up a pot of tribal hatred at the same time. That's Iness's style.* Through my eyelashes I see her shake her head anxiously before the Elix. *But now you want to take them to live under her very shadow? It's madness.*

But that's exactly why it's the safest option. They'll be hidden in plain sight. Oskarsson's voice is patient but determined. *If they enter the Settlement under my banner, no one will suspect they're anything but the product of an Elix lord's indiscretions. It won't be the first time a Councillor has sired bastards out of Pairing. The citadel will look down upon them, sideline them, ignore them, for the most part. But they'll both be seen as Pure, cared for as such. And if there is any trouble with Iness, I'll be there in the background to protect them.* He says it with confidence, a certain arrogance – his Founding Four blood, I understand now.

And when they're older? Amma asks. *What about their Pairings?*

I'll face that when the time comes, the Elix says.

I crack my eyelids and see my grandmother pressing her fingers to her mouth. *You're sure it's the only way?* Her voice breaks in a sob.

One more week, Cura. Say your goodbyes. I'll come for them then.

I'm surprised when Oskarsson stands and clutches her shoulder, my grandmother squeezing his arm in return – an unspoken solidarity passing between them. They're unified, this Elix lord and my Solitary grandmother, joined in the task of keeping us alive. Oskarsson bends once more to run his palm over our hair as we sleep. And then I hear the click of the door as he slips into the night.

Amma weeps as she slumps in the chair by the fire. I've

never heard her cry before. My adult brain wants to shake the child me, tell that little girl to wake up and ply her grandmother with questions. But I'm rigid with fear, the childish fear that if I open my eyes, it won't be a nightmare anymore and I'll have to face the truth: my Amma is going to send us away, give us to a stranger who is going to lock us up in a place she told us never to go. So I keep my eyelids shut tight, telling myself it's nothing but a dream. And soon, surrendering to the undeniable sleep of childhood, that is what it becomes.

It's the chill that wakes me. The fire still burns in the hearth but the door to the cabin has been left ajar. A man's voice calls over the whinny of a horse. At first, I think Elix Oskarsson has returned, but then there's the jangle of bridles, the drum of hooves.

I rub my eyes at the window, peering through the frosted pane. Amma stands in her night shift, barefooted in the new snow. The riders – four of them – circle her, their curved swords almost pretty in the light of the moon, as if their purpose is purely decorative. The heads and faces of the men are covered with scrolls of loose cloth, in a style I've only seen once before – on a trader at the Solstice markets. Amma had told me he was Reis, from the southern reaches of the Continent across the Storm Sands and I'd marvelled at his black eyes, the planes of his cheekbones, brown and hard as polished halderwood, peeking from his scarves. One of the riders growls a command, but I don't hear the words. I'm too busy watching Amma shaking her head again and again, until she sinks to her knees.

The stroke of the sword is so clean and swift and quiet that at first I can't understand the red that suddenly slaps across the snow. Two of the horses rear backwards, spooked as she falls. But the rider who felled her has already moved on, a lit torch in his hand. His mount skitters outside my window, the light of the flame catching one glossy boot. A splatter of blood mars its shine and spoils the stitched cuffs.

Red cuffs stitched with yarn died red as bearberries. *The citadel seems to like the colour.* Warder red. Warder boots.

Smoke begins to stream through the burning thatch into the cottage. I want to fling open the door and run to Amma. I want to lift her face from the snow, clear her hair from the pool of blood that stains its silver strands. But the riders are waiting. So I wake Osha and we lift the floorboards, crawling under the cabin and running straight for the trees. *Don't look, O. Don't look back,* I tell her, remembering Amma's words. But she trained me as a hunter and hunters look death in the face. When we're deep in the thickets, clear of the smoke, I turn to glance over my shoulder. A rider rings the clearing, the hoof of his horse clipping my grandmother's body, sending her arm out disjointedly across the snow. It's like she's showing me again the route to take, the right direction.

And it's a straight line to the Settlement.

The Shores of Reis

I'm freezing cold and wracked with shivers when I come to. The truth of Amma's death smarts like an old wound reopened and rubbed with salt: I'm not only grieving her murder all over again, I must bear the fact that we lived with her killers all that time – inside the very citadel that should have protected us. The realisation makes me breathless with angry tears. I try to lift a hand to fist them away, but find my fingers caught in something. Looking down, I realise it's the wrangler's hair. He's propped on a crate beside the bunk in the Captain's cabin, his head slumped against my hip, fast asleep. His drunken night with the Maw is well past, for his bru-soaked shirt has been replaced by a fresh one and he smells of soap. His twisted locks are loose now of the rings that bound them, the dark hair shaggy and dishevelled but soft in my fingers, almost at odds with the rest of him. The small surge of comfort it gives me only seems to underscore the aching hollow I feel inside.

He stirs at my movement, lifting his head suddenly. "Nara," he says, and it's a long sigh of relief. He palms my forehead, probes the glands under my throat, feels my wrist. "You were cold as the grave... we couldn't wake you... shit, I thought..." Satisfied I'm truly breathing and have a pulse, he swallows his concern and launches in a different vein entirely. "Fec's sake, what were you thinking! Krait's venom isn't something you can *dabble* with. It's a poison. You could have–" But he stops short. The fat tear that tracks down my cheek must be answer enough, for his expression softens, and he pulls me to him. I give in, burying my face in his neck, shivering against his warmth like it's the only thing that might fill the terrible emptiness in my chest. He lets me sob over the memories, his arms wrapped around me. And when I'm ready to speak them aloud, he listens, saying nothing while I recount the mesmer vision.

"You were right: it wasn't the Eeis who killed my grandmother. I know that now." And the relief of telling him, the relief I see on his face makes something shift in me. I thread my fingers in his and hold on, as if for dear life, while all the new questions the krait's vision has left behind seethe like a nest of hungry snakes in my mind. How did Lars Oskarsson know my grandmother? Why did he never tell us? And what journey did he protect my mother on when she was pregnant? Why did he keep us alive when citadel Warders were sent to burn down our cabin? None of it makes any sense, most of all why both Amma and Lars Oskarsson kept the truth from us all these years.

"There could be answers in Reis," the wrangler says, and I realise I must have spoken half these questions aloud. "You said Brim's uncle was a prisoner there, right? So maybe someone in Reis remembers him? When we get there, I can ask." His thumb brushes my hand, gentle, reassuring. "I'll help find out whatever I can. And Reis is going be alright. I promise."

"Thank you."

He nods, but I can't help feeling the words I spoke hanging over us. *It's nothing. Nothing at all.*

The ship rocks gently, boards creaking, and water laps at the hull. Neither of us speaks, but we don't make a move to draw apart either. There's a delicate truce in our clasped hands, our almost-embrace. Even the slightest movement might break it.

"How long was I unconscious?" I ask.

"Three days."

"Three *days*!" I pull away with the shock of it. "Osha—"

"She's fine. Relax. I sent her to get some sleep. She's barely left your side this whole time."

Now there's a little space between us, I notice there's a cut in his eyebrow, cleaned and salved with a dark paste – my sister's work. "What happened here?" I trace my fingers over the bruise blossoming around it.

"Brim. Managed to land one on me." He laughs softly. "He found out about the venom and... well, how you got your hands on it."

"Oh... I see." I flush, remembering how I'd undressed him. I feel guilty for more reasons than I care to examine right now.

As if the mention of Brim has broken the spell between us, he straightens and clears his throat. "We've reached the coast of Reis and anchored for the night. In the morning, we'll go ashore."

The words are bracing, returning me firmly to reality. His hands draw gently from mine and leave a chill in their wake. "I don't want to arrive," I blurt out. "I mean... it's peaceful for once... here with you. I feel like when we leave this cabin everything will be complicated again."

"You admitting you actually like my company?" He grins. "I thought I was nothing to you?"

"Don't start, Wrangler. You know very well you mean more to me than that." Embarrassed by the confession, I rise carefully, testing my legs. He offers his hand but I ignore it, moving to the porthole to look out at the silvered sea. He follows and after a moment I feel his arms snake around me from behind. I lean into him, my head falling back against his chest, and he exhales long and deep. "I don't want to arrive either, Na'quat," he whispers into my neck.

I turn around to study his face, just to be sure I understand. But it's all he needs to say; his expression tells me the rest.

We're gentle, uncertain with each other at first, tender as

the moonlight that falls in a channel across the cabin deck. But soon, everything that has gone before – all the baiting and teasing and pretending – makes us hungry, impatient.

I pull him against me, my kisses turning desperate, and I know he feels the same because he lifts me up, wrapping my legs around him and holding me against the cabin wall.

Who was I trying to fool all this time? his hand confesses as it slips under my shirt and skims my belly.

I want you and I always have, my thighs answer as I feel him hardening against me.

"Say it again," he pants between kisses.

"What?" I ask.

"My name."

Perhaps I breathed it while my mind was busy with the feel of his lips, his teeth at my neck, the smell of him up close, like autumn in the Fornwood.

"Wrangler," I say and try to kiss him again, but he turns his cheek, pivoting to the bunk and dropping us on it, still caught inside my arms and legs. He pins my hands to the pillow and begins to trace the lobes of my ears, the line of my collar bone, my breasts with only the tip of his nose until I can barely think for wanting him.

"Say it again. My real name."

Has it bothered him all this time that I've only ever called him Wrangler? I guess that's precisely why I did it.

I breathe out a laugh but when his kisses travel downwards, the teasing turns to sighs.

He stops, hovering stubbornly, waiting. I free a hand and press my thumb to his mouth, wanting to kiss the hesitation from him, to kiss that mole in his cheek that manages to infuriate me and still make my core flip.

"Are you certain, Nara?" he whispers.

I nod, but still he wavers, frowning. "Mother's love, Wrangler!" I turn us, straddling his hips and reefing off my shirt. "Is this certain enough?" I draw his hand to my breast, and he bites his lip, a look of such boyish awe on his face it makes me want him all the more. I lay my palms along his jaw, bringing him close. "Nixim," I say, and I swear his pupils dilate at the sound of it, "Don't you dare stop."

The rumble in his throat is desire and relief rolled into one, as if he's been holding off, uncertain all this time. "That punch you gave me," he murmurs between kisses, "by the river?" I find the spot where I hit him and press my mouth to it. "I've never recovered," he says. "You floored me."

"It wasn't my kiss, then?" I laugh, feeling the fit of his body against mine, as if we're shaped only for that purpose. His tongue sends curls of warmth through me, reaching places that felt cold and empty long before I took the krait's poison. Long before I'd even left the Settlement. And I think I might never recover either.

The planes of his chest, the relief of his abs are a sight to behold, but their warmth under my lips is something else and I think I might die of need. Reaching to unlace his leathers, he stops my hands. "Wait, Nara," he says gently, eyes heavy with more than desire now. "There's something I need to tell you."

"There's a hundred things you need to tell me, but not right now." I pull him back to me.

"It's important."

I seal his mouth with mine and he groans, half frustration, half need, falling under my spell again before he recovers himself. "Listen, you're going to learn things in Reis," he says, stopping my hands again, "things about me… that I think I should tell you… before we–"

"Are you serious? You finally decide to volunteer inform-ation about yourself, and you want to do it right at this moment?"

I loosen his leathers, my hand resting lightly on the hardness beneath, and he sighs in blissful agony. I kiss the mole on his cheek, moving down his neck and chest again, tracing that wondrous curve of muscle above the jut of his hip that guides me downwards. His words turn to gasps as I release him. "Nara," he pants, "if you touch me... I won't be able... to stop..."

"I told you," I answer, "I don't want you to stop." And suddenly he rolls me over, settles between my legs and promptly forgets whatever he planned to say. We both snatch our breath at the same time as I draw him into me, moaning at the fullness, the completeness of us. "Holy Mother."

"Nothing to do with her," he says. "This is all you and me, Na'quat."

We find our rhythm as if we've always known the song, his moans and whispers hot in my ear, bringing me on.

"Nixim?" And it's a plea of sorts, a prayer that he won't stop. "Nix—"

His breath is just as urgent against my neck. "Say my name like that once more... and I swear I'll..."

I lock eyes with his. "Nixim?" I'm begging him not to leave me on the edge. And he doesn't. He nudges me over the precipice, the freezing void of the mesmer vision chased away by wave after wave of warmth, more luxurious than sinking into the Moon Pools at dawn. He cries out as he watches me, shuddering till I feel it in my bones like a fever.

Afterwards, I doze in his arms, limbs tangled in his, drugged by the delicate circles he traces along my hip, the complicity of the lulling boat.

He nuzzles my neck. "That was... impulsive. I shouldn't have..." he murmurs.

I twist to look at him, stomach dropping. "Shouldn't have what?"

He's frowning.

"Are you saying you regret it? Already?" I push away from him. "What the fec, Wrangler, you could up your game on the pillow talk."

He grabs my arms, drags me back. "Put your claws away, Scourge," he says, kissing my fingertips. "Who said I regret it? Far from it. I meant I was pretty reckless with you."

I lick my lips and settle into him once more, thinking I understand the issue. "In the Cooler, female Ringers were given the monthly herbs. I took them too… in case, you know, any of the Wasters decided to overlook my *groin-itch*." I pinch his nipple, hard, and when he's finished squirming, I kiss it better.

"That wasn't quite what I meant, but I'll admit I deserved that and more for leaving you and Haus in that hellhole for so long. I never did apologise properly. So I am now." He strokes my cheek. "The idea of anyone touching you in that way makes me want to… I mean, did anyone try?"

I lay a fist under his chin, knee dangerously high between his legs. "What do you think?"

"Um, no?" He hoists my knee away from his jewels and drapes my leg over his hip. "Na'quat," he says, starting to kiss me again along my jaw, my ear, and up over my branding.

"It's still Narkat. Repeat after me, N-A-R-K–"

"You know, you're the most infuriating pain in my arse? You always think you're right. You never believe a thing I tell you. And you attract trouble like flies to shit… So, tell me, how is it I could die a happy man in this bunk, with you wrapped around me?" He touches his lips to my eyelids and I feel every inch of my skin flush with pleasure. When it feels like we've kissed all the barbs and bickering away for good, I break to breathe and he says in a low, serious voice, "How am I going to keep my hands off you?"

"That's funny because, before I became so irresistible, you seemed to want to tell me something very urgent." He closes his eyes and I feel him grow tense. I inch away a fraction, so I can study him. "So, what was it?" He props his head on an elbow, staring towards the porthole, jaw muscles twitching. "Tell me, Nixim." He looks at me when I say his name, drawing a breath to speak but a rap on the cabin door makes us both jump apart. I pull the sheet around me.

We might have imagined ourselves as castaways drifting

alone on an endless ocean, but suddenly the rest of the world comes achingly into focus with each knock on the wood. I reach for the wrangler, pressing my palm to his cheek, pinning his gaze to mine. I don't want him to answer the door; if he does, this fragile thing between us will shatter like spring ice, I can sense it. I have no idea what Reis holds in store for me, who Nixim will become in his own hearthlands, who Osha and I will be in this new country... and for once I don't want to know. I want to stay ignorant, to freeze this moment that teeters on the cusp of change, where only he and I exist, a rogue wrangler and a rough-cut runaway, with no one else to spoil the fantasy.

But the knock sounds again, more urgent this time. Nixim rests his forehead on mine, loosing a long sigh.

I can hear feet shuffling beyond the door. "What?" the wrangler snaps in Hrossi, his face full of apology as he looks at me.

One of the crew answers. I understand some of the words. *Women. Two. Aboard the ship.*

"Who are they?" he asks through the door, but I suspect he already knows the answer because he's rising, hurriedly shrugging into his clothes. I'm left with only the rapidly cooling shape of him in the bunk.

The sailor answers. I pick out *Reis women* and *sister*. The wrangler won't hold my eye. Outside, the Hrossi clears his throat. And then I recognise another word, one I remember all too well from that first exchange between Orlath and Haus, a word the wrangler taught me as we crossed the Waster plains: *lyfhort*.

I don't need the wrangler to explain. It's written all over his guilty face.

"So your sister's aboard the *Na'quat*?"

He nods. "Reis scouts saw the ship from the lookouts. Azza rode ahead to welcome us."

"And the woman with her?"

He seems surprised that I understood so much, but then he shakes his head. "I wanted to tell you... I tried, but–"

"Who the hell is she, Wrangler?" When he doesn't answer, I begin to dress.

"Nara, wait. You don't understand."

"I understand that word well enough. You were the one who explained it to me, remember?" Lyfhort... *braid- promised.*

"It's not what you think. The sailor just used that word because he's Hrossi. We don't promise with braids in Reis."

"Just tell me the truth, Wrangler! Tell me who she is!"

"Alright, alright!" And looking me straight in the eye, he says, "she's my betrothed."

I stare into the small, cracked mirror on the wall of my cabin, listening to the sounds of the caravel. Water laps the hull, there's the soft creak of the foremast, a breeze in the rigging. The same music that lulled me last night, except now there's no moonlight, no magic, no Reis spell, only brash morning sun streaming through the porthole, the ocean green as tarnished copper. There are new sounds carried through the boards, too: the thud of a skiff moored starboard, the rumble of foreign voices, a woman's laugh, deep and confident.

Be careful of the boy. If he betrays you, he will break his own heart doing it.

I shut the Blood-wife's words from my mind, fighting the memory of the wrangler's touch, how right it had all felt... how wrong I was to trust him again. I wouldn't listen to his explanations, not even when he sent the messenger away and tried to hold me by the shoulders, eyes desperate, pleading with me to listen. I only closed his cabin door behind me as I left. I want to nurse my anger alone. I want to coddle the flame of it till it scorches though me like an inferno, leaving nothing behind. Anger is something familiar, my constant companion since Amma's death, since becoming a Brand, since Orlath's fighting pits. I know anger. It keeps me vital and strong. But I can't handle the way my heart gnaws inside my chest, my mind melting useless as Settlement slush when I think of his hands on my skin, his voice settling deep in my bones, how I gave him the whole truth of myself as we lay together... how he only gave me lies. Those feelings leave me hollow and weak, sicker than a starving Sink-born sucking her last breaths. And that isn't who I am. That isn't Nara Fornwood. I won't let it be.

So I wait for my old friend anger to catch up with me, keeping the door of my cabin locked, even turning Osha away. I wash and put on a clean undershirt, rolling the cuffs over my forearms. It's too hot here for my hunting leathers, so I take my jacket and cut off the sleeves with a knife, making a rough gilet. Someone set shiny new boots by my bedside when I was in the throes of the mesmer dream – Osha or Brim possibly, no doubt found among the clothes the Maw discovered onboard. But I can't bring myself to try them on. Instead, I sink into the comfort of my old boots, the worn leather like a reliable friend. They've served me well, taken me further than I could ever have imagined. Scuffed and beaten as they are, I won't give them up so easily. Mother's love, I feel the need for true and steadfast things around me now.

How do you bear it? I'd asked Haus in the Cooler.

We fight.

I scrub a hand around my hair, then pull out the short curls in the mirror. They've grown thick and cover my branding again, but I take the knife and lop them off. Dipping my hands into the water bowl before me, I catch the soap and lather it along the left side of my scalp. My hand is steady as I guide the blade, carefully shaving the licks of red hair in a single band above my ear. The skin is pale as death underneath, except for the smattering of tiny seeds blown randomly across it as if on a summer breeze. Seeds that can't be brushed away, seeds that aren't random at all, for they're who I am, who my parents were. And on the shores of this new land, I'm determined to get the answers to that. Wrangler or no wrangler, there's no turning back.

Osha's worried voice begs me to let her in. When I finally open the door, I'm ready to step outside and brave the decks. She studies me, fingertips running over the bared branding along my scalp, then down to the pendant swinging freely at my chest. But she says nothing. She doesn't need to. I take her hand. Our hearts might be broken but our futures are not.

Acknowledgements

The act of writing might be a lonely business, but publishing a novel certainly isn't. A whole convoy of people deserve my thanks in making *The Branded* what it is today.

Catherine Drayton, thank you for explaining the world of agenting to a newbie and for prompting ideas about super-warriors and viruses long before COVID-19 ever hit – your powers of prescience might be up there with the Blood- wife's. Thanks for staying the course with this novel even after lockdowns, when the last thing you probably wanted to flog was a virus book.

Thank you Claire Friedman for seeing a spark in this story and for your perceptive feedback on the earliest version of it.

To Ali and the crew at Pantera, I've sat around many a boardroom table in my time, but never with a team of professionals talking about something I've put together with anything close to your enthusiasm. You were so warm, welcoming and excited by the book, I was too thrilled to manage French patisserie with any semblance of sophistication.

Lex Hirst, thank you for being so gracious at Writing NSW's YA and Spec Fic Festival way back in 2017 when I threw self-respect to the wind and basically elevator-pitched my story under the guise of a panel question. Holy fec, how rude! I still feel unworthy to have you as my publisher.

Anna Blackie, I knew you'd sensed the pulse of this novel the moment I met you. Your structural edits were the work of an OG Sway and I'm sorry you didn't get to see this through to launch.

Vanessa Pellatt, you can be my wrangler of words any day. Just when edits and deadlines were making me feel like a punch-drunk Ringer, a little margin comment from you would cheer me on. Kirsty van der Veer, you have the patience of Osha. Thanks for being so calm and collected under pressure.

Thank you Debra Bilson for the stunning cover design: your vision of the ghosthawk had me starry-eyed from the get-go.

To my warriors from across the waters, Gemma Creffield, Caroline Lambe and Amy Portsmouth, thank you for welcoming me to the Angry Robot clan. And special thanks to Stacey McEwan for championing my words: who knew throwing my book across your office while performing an impressive array of karate kicks on TikTok was in fact a love language? Love you too, Stace.

Thank First Mother for the amazing women in my writing group! Suzanne Brown, Sam Milton, and Barbara Hatten (Lucy Lever), you've been holding my hand for many years now; without your support I might have given up writing when that Difficult Second Novel got the pox and died. Thank you for convincing me it was OK to write the book I'd want to read… and then going on to critique it so many times. If I was kidnapped by Wasteland raiders, you're definitely the Mor I'd want to drink vit with by the campfire.

Thank you to Michelle Barraclough for the website, walks and writerly discussions – your friendship is pure Reis gold.

Chloe Green, my very first beta reader, you can't imagine how your positive feedback kept me going through submissions – even if no one else liked it, you did. (Also, hair inspo! Please never get drunk and shave it off.)

To Nina Cockerill, creator of bullet points to warm the heart, thanks for reading and giving feedback faster than a speeding arrow.

To Lydia, thanks for the meal calls when your obsessive mother wouldn't come out of the shed. You inspire me every single day with your ideas and art and music – thanks for keeping me company across the garden path, baby.

To Henry, thanks for teaching me the true meaning of the grind, reminding me not to take myself too seriously, for the impromptu ab workouts and *The Office* re-runs when I'd hit a wall. I feel lucky both of you found your own passions early on. Stay true to them, always disrespect the Walls, work smart and budget for physiotherapy.

To GJ, thanks for making me smell the coffee and pat the dog. None of it is possible without your love and support behind the scenes. Would definitely Pair with you again.

And finally, to my big sisters and first heroes – this one's for you. Thank you for making sure my back is never bare.

**Enjoyed The Branded?
Check out the sequel The Rising
available February 2025**

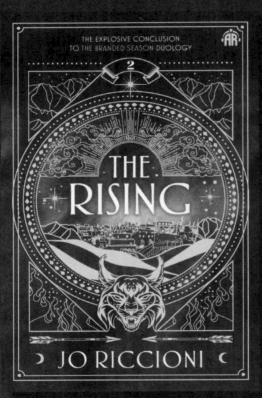

Read the first chapter here...

The Fool and the Storm

Be careful of the boy. He's a good soul born of bad. Know that if he betrays you, he will break his own heart doing it.

The buck at the water's edge is no bigger than a fleet fox. His thin antlers curve like the ribs of a slum kid back in Isfalk. He raises a wet nose, one delicate foreleg ready to run, as if he can sense me in the dense foliage downstream. I close my eyes, reach again for the sound of his tripping pulse. But I can't seem to latch on – can't subdue its beat to my own as I usually can when I hunt. Sweat beads on my lip, and my mark on the beast falters. I could blame this bastard bow, the riser far larger than my weapon in Isfalk, its draw-length longer. I could blame this suffocating heat, the humidity of the Reis jungle that hangs so close it feels like even my eyeballs are sweating in their sockets, blurring my vision. But there's only one honest reason I can't channel my skill this morning.

He will break his own heart.

His own heart.

His own.

I crack my neck and feel the release roll down my spine. *Fec's sake, Nara, get a grip.* Lifting my chin, I line up again. The bow strains, string creaking, but even as my fingers release, I know my aim is wide. The buck rears as the arrow nicks its rump, but almost simultaneously there's the soft pock of another shot. The deer topples into the shallows, heart-shot quivering long after its body is still.

I spin around, searching for the archer. Boots crush the sultry tick of the undergrowth, and the jungle shivers and parts. The wrangler wears a sleeveless gilet of soft leather, bronze arms dewy with sweat. Loose linen pants match the sand scarves draped around his neck, and rings of gold clamp his black curls, picking out the gilded tooling on his leather boots, the scabbard of his curved sword. He couldn't appear any more different from the stable hand I met mere months ago, bundled in patchy furs as he exercised his sled dogs across the Isfalki tundra. Now, he might be a prince of Reis stepped from his hunting lodge.

He cocks an eyebrow at me. "Bow arm a bit off this morning, Little Scourge?" He knows I never miss a shot. And he'd never miss an opportunity to bait me about it.

"Still following me like a lost puppy, Wrangler?" I tighten the strap on my quiver so I don't have to look at him, trying to ignore the angry race of my heart.

"Not such a good idea to be out here alone," he says, tone changing.

"That's one I haven't heard before. Tell me something new, why don't you?"

"I'm serious. All manner of hunters stalk the Kyder – human and animal. But if you must go exploring, at least don't do it alone." He inspects his boots, sheepish. "I thought Brim might–"

"Brim might what?" He has the audacity to look jealous. "You thought he'd be keeping guard over me as usual?" I shake my head in contempt. "Here's some news for you, Wrangler: Brim might once have been my Warder, but we're not in Isfalk anymore. I don't need permission for my movements, from him or anyone else. And I'm not about to go jumping into his arms simply because yours are taken." I shoulder my bow. "Not that it's any of your business if I do."

"Straight for the jugular. Just as I'd expect. But your assumptions are as off-mark as your aim this morning, Scourge." He smirks and I want to slap him right across that mole winking in his cheek. "What I was going to say is that I thought Brim, as a military man, would have wanted someone at your back, especially in unknown territory." He takes a breath, voice softening a little. "I knew you'd head out here at the first opportunity. It was written all over your face as soon as you caught sight of the jungle yesterday – that longing for the wilds... the need to be hunting again." He says it like he's talking of himself as much as me.

I turn my back on him, casting my gaze about the clearing like I'm scouting for game. Brim might have eventually guessed where to come looking for me when I didn't join Osha and the others for breakfast, but the wrangler knew before I was even missed. After all his lies and secrecy, it galls that he knows me so well. I don't want him to see my anger, though. Getting angry shows I care: indifference will pain him more. I know him well, too.

"Look, Nara," he says. "About yesterday..." But he trails off, like he can't find the words to describe the events that changed everything between us.

"Yesterday?" I ask. "You mean when your girlfriend stepped aboard the *Na'quat* while I was still naked in your bed? The betrothed you forgot to tell me about?"

He sighs. "Nara, let's talk."

"No, *you're* the one who should have talked... weeks ago when we were riding through the Wasteland Plains and you kissed me."

"*I* kissed *you*? Are you sure about that, Scourge?"

I snatch a breath. After everything he's done, he dares suggest I was the one who made the first move. "Go to hell, Wrangler."

"Tempting, but keeping an eye on you is a far worse fate, I think."

"I don't need anyone keeping an eye on me, least of all you! Fecs alive, if I'm to be a prisoner here, too, I might as well have saved myself the journey from Orlathston. Or from Isfalk, for that matter."

"You're not a prisoner here." He frowns like he's offended. "You can go where you like."

"Really? Is that the truth, Wrangler?" It takes all the willpower I possess to gentle my voice and quiet my rattled breathing. "So, I'm free to do what I want?"

"Have you ever done otherwise?" He folds his arms and scans the clearing as if my being here is a case in point.

"Can I ask a favour, then?" My change in tone takes him by surprise and his expression slips from suspicion to hope.

Perhaps he can't quite believe I'd give him the chance to earn my forgiveness, and yet he seems to long for it anyway. I draw close, so close that his lips almost brush my own. "There's something I want, Nixim." I trace the neck of his gilet with a finger, and his pupils dilate when I say his name. "Will you do it for me?"

Voice a low rumble, he answers, "Your will, my hands, remember?"

"I remember." I bite my lip and his breath hitches. "So, what I want," I say, stabbing a finger in his chest, "is for you to skip on back to your lyfhort and leave me the fec alone!"

His shoulders drop and he lifts his face to the blue sky peeping between the jungle's canopy. "I guess I deserved that."

"You deserve a whole lot more than that."

We freeze at the sound of the undergrowth being trampled nearby. A husky voice calls out, but its owner is no man. The slender woman who emerges from the trees has thick black curls escaping her sand scarves. The thin sleeves of a fitted chemise boast athletic arms. When she shoulders her weapon, I realise the heart-shot that felled the deer was hers. The wrangler isn't even carrying a bow. If I was in any doubt as to who this woman is, the little mole to the side of her mouth settles it for me. She's the wrangler's sister; one of the two women I rode behind in sullen silence for hours on the journey inland yesterday.

She makes a quick exchange in Reis with her brother, before running kohled eyes over me from boots to crown. Her face had been shrouded during our ride across the desert, and now, up close, I notice her skin is a shade darker than the wrangler's, her stare even shrewder. The colour of her irises is complicated, like his – an inner ring of pale brown, changeable as the evening dunes we'd crossed on the long ride from the coast. When she adjusts her quiver, the underside of her wrist shows a delicate branding peeking from beneath her cuff.

"Hra kim, sha Azza Ni Azzadur," she says boldly, a note of challenge in her tone. I flounder at the Reis words, determined not to look at the wrangler for help. "Azza Ni Azzadur," she repeats.

"Sorry, I..."

The mole dances at her lip. "It is my *name*. I am not interrogating you."

"You know Isfalki," I reply. "You barely opened your mouth yesterday, so I assumed–"

"Perhaps I had nothing to say." She shrugs, but it's clear she's the type of woman who has plenty of opinions, even if they don't reach her tongue. Her Isfalki is accented but good, and I'm wondering where she could have learned it this far south when she asks, "So, do you have one too?"

"One what?"

"A name." She draws it out as if I might be simple, glancing at the wrangler.

"Oh... yeah... I mean, I'm Nara," I say, feeling all kinds of stupid.

"Rest easy, Nara Fornwood. I know who you are. My brother has told me all about you." Under her scrutiny, the wrangler busies himself with his water flask, taking a long drink and squinting off through the trees. But when I stare a beat too long, he meets my eye, emotions scudding across his face as quickly as clouds across the taiga – regret, guilt, frustration. I don't care to know which.

I sip from my own water skin, trying to be as casual as I can with resentment pulsing on my tongue and anger burning up my cheeks.

His sister hums softly at our silent exchange. "My brother," she muses. "Still trying to tame the storm, I see."

"My sister," the wrangler retorts, "still spouting ridiculous proverbs, I see." And with that, he hacks peevishly through the foliage and is swallowed by the jungle.

Azza's chuckle at his departure has a smoky hoarseness to it that belies her neat frame. "It is a Reis saying: *The fool who tries to tame the storm eats only sand.*" Her eyes glitter.

"You think *I'm* the storm... the trouble that needs to be tamed? Bit of an assumption when you've known me, what, one whole day?"

She lowers her chin with a look that warns not to take her for a fool. "Nixim has never been very good at staying clear of trouble, and you, Nara Fornwood, are trouble. Anyone with eyes can see it." She frowns. "But there is more resting on your arrival in Reis than my brother's heart."

Her words hit the pit of my stomach – not the put-down, but the threat of the unknown. The weight of what it means to be here kept me awake for most of the night, tossing with worry for Osha. She's my main concern; she always has been. And yet, on the wrangler's advice, I've brought her to a land we know nothing of, looking for answers to an ability she won't even admit to possessing, both of us ignorant of what getting those answers might cost.

"I couldn't care less about the heart of your trouble-loving brother," I tell Azza. "But I do care about my sister, and he's told me fec-all about what the Reis intend to do with her.

So, any light you want to shed on that would be gratefully received." Not the most diplomatic request for information, I'll admit, but at least I asked without putting my arrow to her throat.

We lock eyes for a moment, and I can feel her appraising me. "You Isfalki," she says, heading off in the direction of the felled deer, "you talk too much when you hunt."

As if the wrangler wasn't enough, now I have his poxy sister to deal with too.

For more great title recommendations, check out the Angry Robot website and social channels

www.angryrobotbooks.com
@angryrobotbooks

About the Author

JO RICCIONI graduated with a Masters in Medieval Literature from Leeds University, where her studies included Icelandic saga and the Arthurian and Robin Hood legends. Her short stories have won awards in the UK and Australia and have been anthologised in Best Australian Stories. Jo's first novel, *The Italians at Cleat's Corner Store*, won the International Rubery Award for fiction and was long-listed for the New Angle Prize in the UK.

ANGRY
ROBOT

We are Angry Robot

angryrobotbooks.com

Science Fiction, Fantasy and WTF?!

@angryrobotbooks

Science Fiction, Fantasy and WTF?!

@angryrobotbooks 📷 🐦 f ♪

Science Fiction, Fantasy and WTF?!

@angryrobotbooks 📷 🐦 📘 🎵

Science Fiction, Fantasy and WTF?!

@angryrobotbooks